# WOW!

## CLAUDIA PATTISON

PAN BOOKS

First published 2001 by Pan Books
an imprint of Pan Macmillan Ltd
Pan Macmillan, 20 New Wharf Road, London N1 9RR
Basingstoke and Oxford
Associated companies throughout the world
www.panmacmillan.com

ISBN 0 330 48794 9

7 9 8

A CIP catalogue record for this book is available from
the British Library.

Typeset by SetSystems Ltd, Saffron Walden, Essex
Printed and bound in Great Britain by
Mackays of Chatham plc, Chatham, Kent

*For Colin*

Thank you to: my sister Rachel for her unfailing enthusiasm; Chris for her technical support; Luigi for his literary expertise; Mari and everyone at Pan Macmillan for pulling out all the stops; and last – but definitely not least – Colin, who always makes my day.

'Interview: A confession where vulgar impudence bends an ear to the follies of vanity and ambition'

Ambrose Bierce, *The Devil's Dictionary*

# ONE: AT HOME

Listening to them talk makes me want to puke. But being a pro, I ignore my heaving stomach, smile my brightest smile and nod in what I hope is an encouraging manner. As senior staff writer for *Wow!* magazine, *Britain's best-selling celebrity weekly*, I have become an expert in the art of masking my true feelings. Sitting opposite me on a zebra-print couch the size of a swimming pool is Lee Jackson, star striker for Arsenal FC and England. A combination of footballing prowess and a questionable fashion sense have earned him a place at the very apex of the celebrity B-list. And now that he's newly engaged to sometime bra model CoCo Fernandez – the woman whose long, honey-coloured limbs are currently coiled around his – Lee's cool quotient is set to rise even further.

'Have you set a wedding date?' I ask, having barely digested the nauseatingly detailed account of Lee's proposal. Just in case you give a shit, it was midnight, in the rose garden at Babcross Hall, the B-list stars' country retreat of choice.

'Nah,' says Lee in his Essex footballer's drawl. 'We'll probably leave it till next summer and then have a really massive do up at Babcross with a big fuck-off Bentley and a dress code, red and white for Arsenal ... you know, the works.' He looks across at CoCo and pats her leg. 'It'll be great, won't it, angel face?'

Judging by the look of horror that flits across CoCo's perfect Anglo-Mexican features, matrimony Spice Girls style would be anything but great. But seeing my feelers start to twitch at this whiff of disharmony, she quickly summons up an appropriate expression of delight. For added emphasis, she stretches out her left hand and admires the rock of an Asprey & Garrard diamond that glitters on her ring finger, tilting her hand so it catches the light just so.

While Lee continues his monologue about the Big Day, I let my mind drift, trusting my dictaphone to capture each and every stomach-churning anecdote. Despite their declarations of undying lust, I doubt this pair's relationship will last the end of the football season. They've only been dating six months, after meeting over a cosmopolitan in the Met Bar, and already they've milked *Wow!* for the dating exclusive *and* the Spanish holiday. Now they're set to collect a cool twenty grand for this *at home*, a mere five hours' work. My brain does the arithmetic: that's four grand an hour, money for old rope if you ask me.

In many respects, I have the dream job. At the age of

28, I enjoy twice-weekly tête-à-têtes with stars in the comfort of their very own homes, dozens of invites to swanky society soirées, regular Caribbean travel and entrées into the weddings of the rich and famous. But after three years on the job, I'm beginning to feel a mite worn down by the endless air kissing, arse licking and weekend working (most weddings are on a Saturday, after all).

My name's Ruby, Ruby Lake, and believe me, this wasn't what I had in mind when I set my heart on a career in journalism. As a student on City University's prestigious postgraduate journalism course, I fantasized about writing impeccably researched investigative pieces for the *Sunday Times*. Still, I mustn't be sniffy. This job more than pays the rent and always guarantees me centre stage at friends' dinner parties.

'Who's the rudest celebrity you've ever interviewed?'

'How many boyband members have you seen in their underpants . . . and which one's got the biggest bulge?'

My mates, like most people, have a seemingly insatiable hunger for celebrity gossip. But I don't mind their endless cross-examination; in fact, I rather enjoy it. When you spend your working life listening to other people talk, it makes a nice change to bask in the limelight for once.

A loud crash, followed by an even louder expletive, yanks me out of my daydream. The lounge door opens and in limps Charley, the photographer's assistant. 'I think I may have damaged the elephant,' he says sheepishly, pointing into the hallway where a four-foot-high soapstone elephant with jewelled tusks stands on duty at the foot of the stairs. 'I just sort of tripped over it.'

'No worries man,' says Lee, dismissing Charley's concerns with a wave of his hand. 'We're insured up to our eyeballs and I know Harrods still stocks 'em.'

That's pretty magnanimous of him, I think, and he instantly goes up in my estimation. I once smashed an ugly old vase in the home of a certain TV actress after I snagged my shoulder bag on the corner of a ridiculously positioned occasional table. She screamed blue murder and sent the magazine an invoice for ten thousand quid. She claimed it was a priceless Ming ceramic . . . a likely story. The magazine paid out, of course. We didn't have much choice. She would've been straight on the phone to one of her gossip column cronies otherwise.

'Cool, so long as it's not a family heirloom,' says Charley, covering his embarrassment by pretending to check something on his light meter. 'Uh, I just came to tell you that T.K.'s ready for the bedroom shot.'

Phew, saved from death by drivel. I reach over to the onyx coffee table with its four supporting pillars of solid marble (I bet they leave a nasty dent in the carpet) and click off my dictaphone. 'Nice timing, Charley, we're just about finished here . . . Are you guys ready to roll?' I ask my hosts.

'Yeah, sure,' says Lee. 'I'll just get a lick of Brylcreem and a touch of powder from Lyndsey and then I'm all yours.'

He unwraps himself from his fiancée and bounds up the stairs to where *Wow!*'s hair and make-up artist is waiting to work her magic. Lyndsey's got this amazing gadget I've never seen before. It's like a paint diffuser, only full of liquid foundation, which she uses to smooth out extra-pitted skin. A certain teenaged pop diva never leaves home without one, apparently.

'How about you, CoCo?' I say. 'Are you going to change for this one?' The model jumps to her feet. No wonder she's such an eager beaver: talking isn't her strong point; looking pretty for the camera, on the other hand, definitely is.

'Do you want the butterscotch silk peignoir (she pronounces it *peg-nwah*) or the Donna Karan pyjamas?' she asks excitedly.

'Er, I think we'll have the PJs; after all, we're going for casual rather than over-dressed,' I say (crushingly, I hope).

Obediently, she trots off to change, leaving me in the over-designed living room. Actually, I'm not entirely alone. Hilfiger, CoCo's disgusting Yorkshire terrier, is rubbing his arse on the carpet. With his owner out of sight, I take the opportunity to deliver a cruel, but eminently satisfying kick (well more of a nudge really) to his little tush. He's been worrying my lower leg ever since I stepped through the door. That'll teach him. Then I follow the others upstairs, cringing at the Michelangelo-style ceiling fresco en route – the guy who did that must be laughing all the way to the bank. When I get to the master bedroom, T.K. Stead, *Wow!*'s star lensman, is plumping bolsters on the king-size bed.

'CoCo's doing a quick change and Lyndsey's giving Lee the once over,' I tell him. 'Do you want me and Charley to stand in for a sec?'

'Nice one, Rubes,' he says, and then asks us both to get on the bed and make like we're Lee 'n' CoCo, except Charley hasn't got highlights and I'm about two foot shorter than CoCo. 'Okay, Rubes – lie on your stomach, ankles crossed, chin on one hand . . . like it, like it. Now, Charley lean towards her, heads closer together, come on, really close and . . . hold it . . . lovely!'

Thomas Kyle Stead is one of *Wow!*'s elite band of photographers and an old hand when it comes to *at homes*. He's already done the kitchen (CoCo slicing star fruit, Lee wielding the cafetière, even though he doesn't have a clue how to operate it), the garden (Lee astride his quad bike, CoCo looking on admiringly) and the dining room (the couple clinking Baccarat crystal glasses and gurning like mad over the candelabra). Only the bedroom and lounge to go, plus the classic 'ring' shot – a close-up of the couple's intertwined hands (a must on any engagement shoot) – and a nice cheesy close-up for the cover.

You need a certain type of photographer for a successful *at home*, someone who can strike up an instant rapport with his star subjects, however arrogant or pissy they are, and help them to enjoy the shoot (after all, five hours is a long time to hold a smile). Oh, and it helps if you're good-looking. With his permatan and shaggy Kurt

Russell 'do', T.K. is always a hit with the female celebs, especially the older ones. Many's the time I've seen him stay behind after a shoot for a 'coffee', if you know what I mean.

The bleating of my Nokia sends me scrambling off the pseudo-Elizabethan four-poster. I rummage in my shoulder bag and pull out the mobile, which is displaying the number of *Wow!*'s esteemed editor Eva Halkin. 'Everything's going to schedule, Eva. I've just finished the interview and there are only a couple more shots to do. T.K.'s doing a fantastic job . . .' I gush. 'Okay, I know this is a rush job. I'm only in Chingford, so I'll be back within the hour.

'Sorry T.K., gotta fly. Eva's gagging for the copy, we're going to press in the morning,' I explain. 'You'll be okay finishing up on your own, won't you?'

'No problem, Rubes, this one's going like a dream. Nice working with you, as ever. I'll check you later,' says T.K., emerging from behind his tripod to give me a quick kiss on the cheek.

'Bye Charley – I'll see you next week at Gatwick . . . you're assisting on the Mustique job, right?'

Charley's a sweetheart. I love working with him. He assists a couple of *Wow!*'s regular photographers, so we see a lot of each other. He's the cutest-looking guy you ever saw, with these bright greeny eyes that kind of mesmerize you and a wild shock of blue-black just-got-out-of-bed hair. A while ago, I had the hots for him bigtime. He's been going out with his girlfriend Emma for almost a year and despite my best efforts to lead him astray, he never took the bait. So we're just friends, and that's cool.

'Certainly am,' says Charley. 'Can't wait for all that sun, sand and shampoola . . . is it true we're staying in an $800-a-night hotel?'

'You bet . . . nothing but the best for Jessie Reynolds,' I say, referring to the impossibly pert soap star who is getting an all-expenses-paid trip to paradise in exchange for ten glorious, bikini-filled pages in *Wow!* And guess who's going to be writing her holiday diary – yours truly of course.

'Right, I'm outta here. Bye Lee, bye CoCo, thanks for a great interview,' I call into the dressing area, where the couple are fighting for possession of the full-length mirror. 'The mag's out on Saturday, I'll send you some copies.'

'Thanks sugar,' comes Lee's muffled reply. 'Any chance of a set of prints too?'

'I'll see what I can do,' I reply – and then, under my breath, 'Not.'

Three-quarters of an hour later and I'm parking my four-year-old silver VW Golf outside *Wow!*'s HQ, which lies in the stalag known as Canary Wharf. It's five p.m., but the office is still buzzing. I nod a greeting to Eva, who is hunched over her desk, barking into the phone.

'If it's not an exclusive we're not interested. And we'll need two photographers – one covering arrivals, one inside the venue. It's a 5k flat fee, going up to 8k if we get Robbie and 15k if David and Victoria show,' she says, referring to the sliding scale we use for showbiz parties. Every celebrity has a price on his or her head that fluctuates according to their current market value.

Eva is one tough cookie, take it from me. She's something of a celebrity herself, having scooped a handful of flashy journo awards during her twenty-five years in publishing. She cut her teeth on women's mags before switching to newspapers and rising to become features editor of the *Daily Mail*. She's been top dog at *Wow!* for sixteen months now and everyone agrees she's hot shit. Only trouble is, she can be a bit of a bitch to work for. I've always managed to stay on her good side, but most people on the magazine have incurred her wrath at one time or another. And yet, to look at her, you'd think butter wouldn't melt. She's pretty-ish in a toothy Geena Davis sort of way, with long chestnutty hair, flecked with red lowlights. She always wears designer gear: Amanda Wakeley or Ghost for spring/summer, Armani or Nicole Farhi for autumn/winter, with accessories from Prada and LK Bennett. She's newly divorced from husband number two and lives alone in a mansion flat off the Brompton Road. I guess she'd have a hard time finding a new man because she works such long hours. Editorship of *Wow!* is more of a vocation than a job.

I arrive at my desk, switch on my iMac and set my dictaphone to rewind. Writing this is going to be a piece of piss – *at homes* follow a precise formula and after this long on the job, I have it down to a fine art. My feature will begin with an excruciatingly detailed portrait of the house: location (must be suitably vague in order to deter would-be burglars), approximate age, number of bedrooms, general ambience and finally, but most importantly, a description of the decor and furnishings. Like a highly practised estate agent I have developed an alternative lexicon to ensure my copy is always positive, never critical, so *hideous* translates to *unusual*, *cramped* becomes *intimate*, OTT is *lavish* . . . you get the picture. Stage two consists of an account of the couple's appearance – it's *youthful* if they're 40-plus, *radiant* if they're in love, *healthy* if they're anything other than *svelte*. Then comes stage three: this is the easy part when I let rip with the interview itself, which more often than not follows a rambling question-and-answer format. I'll write around fifteen hundred words for a C-list celeb (four to six pages), two thousand for a B-list (six to ten pages) and up to five thousand words for your bonafide, 24-carat A-lister (can run to as many as twenty-two pages). Quantity rather than quality is the name of the game – no detail is too small, no anecdote too dull for *Wow!*'s half a million loyal readers.

By nine-thirty p.m. my two-thousand-word piece is complete, and I print off a copy for Eva. I'm her star writer, she knows I always deliver the goods, so as usual the changes are minimal. I also fax a copy to the home of Lee Jackson's agent for his approval, *in loco parentis* as it were. I include a covering letter, which specifies the six-hour turnaround required, as agreed in the contract. We run a tight ship here at *Wow!* The magazine is competing with not only our arch rival *Yeah!*, Britain's *longest-running celebrity weekly*, but also the entire tabloid press, especially the Sundays. News-sensitive pieces – namely engagements, weddings and new babies – will appear in the magazine within days of the interview and photo shoot, before the opposition can catch a whiff of the story and ruin our exclusive. If news of Lee and CoCo's engagement breaks before *Wow!* hits the news-stands, rival reporters will be staking out the couple's home, as well as Arsenal's Highbury ground, hoping for a quote or two and a glimpse of that diamond knuckle-duster. Failing that, they'll go sniffing round the couple's friends and acquaintances, many of whom would be only too glad to provide information for a 'spoiler' feature in return for a few quid.

'Are the pictures in yet?' I yell across the office to Angela Kennedy, our permanently harassed art director. Angela has a tough job and when it comes to the overall look of the magazine and the quality of the photos on its glossy pages, the buck stops with her. She and I are two of the longest-serving members of the magazine (staff turnover here is pretty high, mainly due to the unsocial working hours) and we've been through a lot together.

'They've just arrived,' says Angela. 'They're on the lightbox if you wanna go through them.'

I mosey over to the art desk where the transparencies from the day's shoot are displayed on the light-filled box.

Swiping an eyeglass from the nearest designer's desk, I scrutinize the shots. 'Not bad. T.K.'s done us proud, as usual.'

'Yeah, he's done a brilliant job and they're a really photogenic couple. Eva couldn't be happier.'

'How many pages will it make?'

'Eva wants eight. She reckons the house is so horrendous, the readers won't be able to get enough of it.'

'Yeah, check out that chandelier,' I say, handing over the eyeglass so she can admire the specially commissioned crystal monstrosity. 'Makes that Man United mid-fielder's joint look positively minimalist by comparison.'

Together we pick out the best shots, marking our favourites with a waxy chinagraph pencil, although Eva will, as always, have the final say. My one remaining task is to scribble down some notes to correspond with each set of shots – information that will help the sub-editors formulate the picture captions. I detail everything I see: the stainless steel oven (Miele), the his-and-hers towels and matching bathrobes (Versace), the photographs displayed in the entrance hall (Lee lining up for his opening game of Euro 2000, CoCo's poster for the Gossard *Glossies* campaign). Now the feature is in the hands of the subs, who will work through the night to meet the five a.m. deadline, when the final proofs must go to the repro department, and then on to the printer's.

Back at my desk, I switch my phone to voicemail, scoop up my bag and my new Joseph mac and bid goodbye to my colleagues. 'Nice work, Ruby,' says Eva who, just occasionally, shows her human side. 'I really like the line about Lee bursting into tears when CoCo said "yes" – we'll use that as a coverline.'

'No doubt his Arsenal team mates will find it highly amusing,' I say . . . Poor bastard will probably never hear the end of it. 'See you in the morning.'

Walking out into the chilly evening air, I thank God, not for the first time, that I live only a fifteen-minute drive away. I own a one-bedroom flat (or 'apartment' as the developer had described it to me) in Rotherhithe, a reasonably up-and-coming suburb of south-east London, nestling by the Thames. It has been a long day and I'm looking forward to a chilled glass of Chardonnay and a long soak in a Molton Brown bath. The only downer is that, being a single girl, I have no one to share these small luxuries with.

# TWO: SECRET ADMIRER

Outside number two, Galleon Place, the Secret Admirer is waiting. Dressed in indigo Levi's, black polar fleece and navy Kangol beanie, he walks slowly along the river path, but not so slowly he'll draw attention to himself. This route extends for half a mile, and runs behind the rows of smart apartment blocks that have come to dominate the landscape over the past three years. At this time of night, the path is almost deserted – it's not a shortcut, it doesn't lead anywhere – save for the occasional dog walker or snogging couple.

The Secret Admirer has already been here for over an hour. At first he'd waited in his car, which is parked discreetly in a visitor's bay outside Clipper Court. Then, when he grew restless, he decided to stroll along the river path, making sure that Galleon Place was never out of sight.

Surely she'll be home soon. He'll give it another half an hour, then leave his gift and go. Still, he hates to forfeit a glimpse of his prize – and what a goddess she is, with that cascading hair, voluptuous figure and porcelain skin. What he wouldn't give to run his fingers through that Titian mane, to feel those full breasts graze the dark hair on his chest. Rooobee . . . he loves the way that word tastes in his mouth, full and creamy. Thank God she's single. He can't bear the thought of another man touching her, pleasuring her. She's had lovers, he knows that much, but he can tolerate the occasional lapse, as long as she keeps her soul pure for him.

As he is teasing himself with these erotic thoughts, he catches a flash of headlights on the road that runs parallel to the river path, in front of the apartments. Walking briskly back towards Galleon Place, he feels a frisson of excitement as he spots the silver VW glide into a resident's parking bay. He's jogging now, moving towards the now-familiar spot directly behind the low privet hedge that separates the rear of the apartment blocks and the river path. If he hunkers down on the other side, the hedge will shield him from any late-night strollers. From here, he has a perfect view into the living room with its large sash windows and, more critically, the bedroom beside it.

The Secret Admirer hears the blip of a car alarm being activated, followed by the slam of the heavy communal door that services the apartment block. He squats into position, his knees grazing the damp grass. His dark clothes will help him blend into the shadows, should a resident chance to glance out of a window. He must be careful . . . a man in his position can not afford to be compromised.

Any thoughts of exposure evaporate the moment he sees the soft wall lights of the living room flicker into life. Each window is draped with panels of sheer white voile which, when illuminated from within, afford a perfect view of the room to anyone looking in. Feeling his pulse quicken, he watches as she shrugs off her coat and then bends over to unzip her knee-high leather boots. He loves leather . . . gloves, handbags, boots, what a turn on. His breath comes in ragged spurts as she eases off her foot-gear. Dirty minx. She knows exactly how to push his buttons.

Now she's padding over to the kitchen area, which is separated from the living area by a granite-topped breakfast bar. She opens the fridge door and pulls out an already-opened bottle of wine. She reaches into a high cupboard – he sees a tantalizing band of flesh as her black sweater rides up – and brings out a huge chalice of a wineglass. She pours herself a full glass, right up to the brim, then walks towards the door and stretches her arm towards the switch, which will kill the lights.

The Secret Admirer looks expectantly at the bedroom window. His mouth is open; sweet Jesus, he's practically drooling – see what she does to him. He's waiting for the muted glow from the bedside lamp. This isn't the first time he's been here. He knows the layout of the apartment, her little routines – the way she sometimes cranks the stereo up and does a mad, dervish dance, the way she favours soft lighting at night-time. She'd put on quite a show for his last visit. Stripping down to sheer white bra and matching G-string (a little plain for his taste, he'd sooner see her in something from Agent Provocateur), she had walked up to the bedroom window and enjoyed a long, leisurely stretch, standing right up on her tippytoes – almost as if she knew he was there, watching, waiting, hoping somehow to inhale her scent through the glass barrier.

He waits one minute, and then another minute goes by. The room remains resolutely black. He lets out a long hiss of air through clenched teeth. Come on, he urges silently. Now he's starting to get pins and needles in his left foot. Maybe she's running a bath. Pity the bathroom has no windows – that's the trouble with these modern flats. He'd give anything to see her curvy body slide into the warm water.

At last! A flicker of light from the bedroom and suddenly there she is, still holding her glass of wine, only now it's nearly empty. She must have had a bad day. They work her too hard at that place. She is picking up a hairbrush and running it through her hair with long firm strokes. Maybe she'll let him do that for her one day soon. He'd love to own some strands of her beautiful hair . . . he'll have to work on that one. The brush goes back on top of the chest of drawers and she walks over to the window. That's right, come to me, my little butterfly. But what's this? She's grabbing a curtain in each hand and . . . fuckfuckfuck, she's pulled them tightly shut. How can she do it to him? He feels cheated and empty, the way he feels after a night of meaningless sex with a faceless woman.

The Secret Admirer knows there's no point hanging around. The show's over. He's going to have to call it a night. He still has to perform the evening's main objective and this thought comforts him. After peering through the privet's dense branches to check no one is in sight, he emerges from his hiding place. 'Goodnight, precious Ruby,' he whispers as he walks down the side road which separates Galleon Place and Clipper Court (God, these developers were unimaginative). Reaching into the pocket of his fleece with one gloved hand, he pulls out a thick cream envelope and touches it lightly to his lips. Still unobserved, he walks up to the communal door and the horizontal row of white metal mailboxes mounted on the wall beside it. Flicking up the lid of the box marked '2', he pushes the envelope into the slot, closes the lid sound-lessly and walks briskly back to his car. Like Ruby, he will spend the night alone.

# THREE: VENUS

I wake at eight-fifteen, feeling slightly muzzy headed . . . my punishment for that half-bottle of Chardonnay on an empty stomach last night. I climb out of bed and shuffle into the kitchen, where I glug down a big glass of Tropicana and a bowl of Frosties. GMTV is my usual morning companion; I like to leave it burbling away in the background while I'm getting ready. It's a useful research tool – you get to hear who has signed a new TV deal/is recovering from a breakdown/has lost five stone because their husband dumped them. I file my dirty pots in the dishwasher, not forgetting to rinse my cereal bowl under the cold tap first (when you live alone, it takes three days to fill a dishwasher, by which time you need a sandblaster to remove hardened breakfast flakes). After a quick power shower, I dry off and go through to the bedroom. Grabbing my favourite paddle brush from the chest of drawers, I work it through my Worzel Gum-midge hair, which is long and wavy and red (or *russet*, as

I'd say if I was describing it for *Wow!*). I open the double doors of my fitted wardrobe . . . now what's a girl to wear? I never know when I might be sent out on a last-minute job, so it's important to look half-presentable, even when I'm feeling crap. I always take a fully stocked make-up bag to work and, although I often wear trainers, I keep a pair of kitten heels stashed in my desk drawer . . . tights I can always pick up at Tesco's in Canary Wharf.

I settle on my black Jigsaw trousers and a baby blue lambswool cardie. It's nine o'clock now, which means I'd better get cracking. I spend five minutes applying basic make-up: foundation, powder, blush, mascara, then grab my bag and my denim jacket. I lock up and let the communal door slam shut behind me. Lifting the lid of my mailbox, I see there's a small mound of stuff waiting for me. Unlocking the little door with my special key, I grab the lot, fast-food flyers and all, and jam it into my bag.

On the drive to work, I think about the meeting I have to attend this afternoon. It's going to be a heavy one. *Wow!* recently pulled off a massive scoop by securing exclusive rights to what is, by anyone's standards, the showbiz wedding of the year.

When veteran American actor, Joe Lucas – youngest son of the famous Lucas acting dynasty – started dating Irish model Niamh Connolly, the gossip rags went into overdrive. According to the official line, the couple met when craggily handsome Joe saw delectable Niamh on the cover of *Vogue*. He engineered a meeting with the Celtic beauty (who, at 28, is some 17 years his junior) and sparks flew. The couple's combined profile is such that they only have to break wind to make page three of the tabloids. So imagine the feeding frenzy when they announced their engagement. A massive bidding war broke out between *Wow!* and *Yeah!* (in financial terms, the tabloids can't compete – they simply can't afford to spend that much money on a single story) and in the end, we won, like we usually do these days.

While the *Wow!* features team negotiates the smaller deals – the minor league soap stars, the TV gameshow hosts, the uglier footballers, the 5–25k brigade – Eva keeps the biggies for herself. And, after guaranteeing the inevitable copy and photo approval, the services of David O'Connor, the hottest photographer this side of the Atlantic, and the small matter of £1.5 million, the highest fee ever paid by a British celebrity publication, the Lucas–Connolly deal was in the bag.

To be honest, I'm not that excited at the thought of covering the nuptials, due to take place in just under three months' time at Kellaway Castle on Ireland's south coast (only that's top secret information). Everyone got their knickers in such a twist about last summer's big shindig – the wedding of soap heartthrob-turned-pop star Christian Cox and film actress/quintessential English beauty Maisie Simpson. I suppose it *was* pretty spectacular, as weddings go, but hardly the most enjoyable project I've ever worked on. There was so much forward

planning – endless meetings about security and copy
deadlines and which of the two reporters was going to be
lucky enough to get a seat at the wedding banquet. In the
event, neither of us did, so I missed out on the butternut
squash soup and the pork medallions in brandy sauce
and the summer berry pavlova. In fact, as I recall, I dined
on three leftover petits fours that night, pinched off the
top table after they'd all hit the dance floor. At that
moment, those three precious sweets tasted so uncom-
monly good that their flavour is etched indelibly in my
memory: white chocolate truffle, marzipan coated in dark
chocolate and hazelnut praline triangle.

I spent the Big Day running round like a headless
chicken, trying to absorb the atmosphere, rally the guests
for the photos, eavesdrop on conversations in the ladies',
grab quotes from the dress designer, the best man, the
sister of the bride, anyone who'd ever had their fifteen
minutes of fame . . . By the end of the night (or should I
say five a.m. the following morning), we had written an
eight-thousand-word, cliché-packed epic. Never again, I
told myself at the time. But now it looks like I'm going to
have to go through the same rigmarole all over again and
this afternoon's meeting between the key players will set
the mighty *Wow!* wedding machine rolling into action.

Soon I'm pulling up outside *Wow!*'s offices. It's pretty
depleted in here this morning as half the staff worked
through the night to put the issue to bed. I select a couple
of tabloids and the copy of *People* magazine from the
post tray, and scan them for news of newly conceived

celebrity babies, impending weddings, recent house moves, etc. There's nothing about Lee and CoCo's engagement, thankfully. Only two more days to go and then we'll be home and dry.

Lydia, *Wow!*'s fashion editor, wafts in – late as usual. 'Hi Ruby,' she trills, shrugging off her Julien Macdonald satin jacket. 'Are you all set for the shoot this afternoon?'

'Uh, Ali's doing it . . . Eva wants me in the office for the Joe 'n' Niamh meeting,' I tell her.

'That's a shame. I think you would've enjoyed it,' she says patronizingly.

Actually, I'm glad I've managed to wriggle out of this one. Spending a day wafting around a stately home with *Generation Game* hostess Kelly Wayne isn't my idea of fun. Those fashion shoots are all the same. Lydia spends hours arsing round with the clothes – does this halter-neck top go with those flat-fronted trousers? Mules or slingbacks . . . what do I think? Frankly, I couldn't give a shit. And to make the job even more difficult, a lot of the more upmarket designers won't lend to us when they know it's only some poxy little gameshow girl, so we usually have to make do with French Connection and Karen Millen. Then there's the agony of the interview itself – usually held over a Marlboro Lights lunch – during which I attempt to extract some vaguely interesting anecdotes from said babe. I have a standard list of questions . . . family background, schooling, dreams and ambitions, 'So Kelly, what's Jim *really* like to work with?' blah blah blah. Half an hour of that and I'm ready to shoot myself. She calls herself a journalist but Lydia can't write to save her life. It's all 'bias-cut this' and 'buttersoft leather that' – which means one of the writers always ends up doing her dirty work.

Good, she's wafted off to lick the foam from her Pret cappuccino and chow down on an almond croissant. I'll just check through my post quickly before I hit the phone. Rooting in my bag, I pull out a postcard from Devon, where my sister and her family are holidaying, a bank statement – I'll save that for later – a clutch of pizza delivery ads and a small but expensive-looking cream envelope. There's no stamp, no address, no name, nothing at all, it's completely blank. Intrigued, I tear it open. Inside is a plain postcard bearing two lines of Letraset:

## www.preciousruby.com
## venus

And that's it. So what am I supposed to do now? Maybe it's some kind of joke. Thing is, none of my friends (north Londoners, each and every one of them) would bother to traipse to darkest south-east London to hand deliver a joke, unless they were really pissed and it was a really funny joke.

Oh well, I'll soon find out if it was worth it. I switch on my iMac and double click on Internet Explorer. After a few seconds, the *Wow!* website springs to life on my screen – a load of old guff, rehashed from the magazine . . . Well you've got to have a website these days or you're considered a Luddite. I highlight the URL and type in 'preciousruby.com'. After a few seconds, the site is down-loaded and I see the word *Ruby* flashing on the screen in massive 60-point letters that are red and fat and kind of sparkling, so that the word looks like a real ruby. The rest of the page is black and empty. I move my mouse and when I hit the *Ruby*, the little pointy hand icon flashes up. I click once and another page flashes up. This one contains a short paragraph, written in lavender-coloured 16 point, in the kind of font that's supposed to look like handwriting:

Welcome Ruby, my precious. Fill in your special password and see what I've done for you. If you're not Ruby, please leave us in peace.

Below this freaky sentence is a blank box, and below that, another box with the word *Enter* written inside. I figure the password can only be *venus*, so I type it in and hit enter. The next page takes longer to download, a good thirty seconds in fact. And when it does, I do a double take; for there on the screen in front of me in full, glorious technicolour is a copy of Botticelli's *The Birth of Venus*, set in a kind of gold curlicue frame. There's the body of the goddess, emerging from her shell, her wind-swept red hair protecting her modesty. But the head on top of that softly rounded milky white naked body isn't Venus's. It's mine.

I recognize the photo. It's been filched from an old

issue of *Wow!*. Last year's National TV Awards at the Albert Hall, if I'm not very much mistaken. I was interviewing Barrymore backstage and our staff snapper took a shot that ended up on the magazine's back inside cover. I know it's that picture because I'm wearing the diamante hair jewels that I borrowed from Lydia's fashion cupboard . . . they make Venus look weird, kind of overdressed. Then I notice a line of text underneath the picture.

Want to see what else I've done for you?

At this point, I'm still thinking it might, just possibly, be a joke, so I download the next page and then I know for sure it's not.

If only you knew how much I long to hold you, stroke you,
kiss you We were made for each other. I know I can
make you happy. I love you with all my heart.
Yours forever,
A Secret Admirer

Underneath this declaration of undying love, there's a list of options, written in the same light blue letters. The background is a midnight blue sky, shot with silver stars that twinkle as I scroll down the page:

our favourite film
our favourite book

# WOW!

*Our favourite restaurant*
*All about me*

Of course the only one I'm interested in is the last one. I click on the *me* and on the left hand side of the screen I see this silhouette, kind of like the dancing girls at the beginning of the James Bond films, only this one's the outline of a man and he's not moving. Well actually, something *is* moving. A fat red heart in the shadowman's chest is pulsating in a faintly grotesque fashion. To his right is a kind of mini CV, written in 14-point Courier:

**Name:** Secret Admirer
**Age:** thirtysomething
**Marital Status:** single but hopeful
**Occupation:** creative artist
**Hobbies & Interests:** Pedro Almodovar films, 15th century art, riverside walks, flame-haired women

Well that's not much to go on ... he's a freak, but at least he's a cultured freak. And he appears to work in advertising – or maybe I shouldn't take that bit too literally. I peer at the shadowman, but he's got no recognizable features to speak of, except for that nasty throbbing organ. Naturally, I can't resist checking out *Our favourite film* (*Flower of My Secret* ... I did think Joaquín Cortés was pretty damn sexy in that, although I changed my mind after seeing him in the flesh), *Our favourite book* (Tony Parsons' *Man and Boy* – this geezer is obviously the sensitive type) and finally, *Our favourite restaurant* (The Ivy – very *meeja*, very *mwah, mwah*, not my kind of place at all).

Each of these last three pages has its own matching wallpaper. The favourite film bit features multiple images of a big orange flower, one of those very graphic, almost sexual close-ups where you can see every grain of pollen. I think it's an arum lily, but I'm no expert. The book bit has a photograph of Kirk and Michael Douglas sharing a bear hug, a special father–son moment. I think I recognize it from the magazine – it was taken at some film premiere or other. Wonder if he knows there's a copyright on that. The final page, the restaurant thing, has a background of ivy creeping over an old stone wall – just looking at it makes me feel kind of smothered and itchy.

At that moment, Ali, one of my favourite people on the magazine, walks past my desk carrying a big armful of page proofs. They somehow catch the newspapers at the end of my desk and the whole lot falls to the floor. 'Oops,' she says, bending over to pick them up. By the time she's up from the floor, I've clicked the little square box on the top left-hand corner of my web page and *preciousruby.com* has disappeared.

'I'm doing Kelly Wayne this afternoon,' she says, shuffling the papers and putting them back on my desk. 'Would you be able to give me some pointers?'

Ali's our junior writer. She came on a work placement

from the London College of Printing, and we liked her so much, we gave her a job when she finished her course. We get loads of workies through our doors – most are rubbish, they either sit there flicking through magazines, too frightened to use the phone, or else they think they're bloody Chrissie Iley and throw a sulk when you tell them that no, they can't do the *at home* with Nicky from Westlife. I might let them shadow me on the christening of some Radio 2 DJ's kid, but that's about it. So when you get somebody good – like Ali – they really stand out.

'Sure. Get some cuttings in and we can go through them together, if you like,' I say. 'Sorry this has been dumped on you at the last minute, but I didn't realize this wedding meeting was happening until yesterday.'

'Oh no, I'm really excited about it. It's just that I don't want to fuck it up. There's no way I'm asking Adrian for help.'

She's referring to Adrian Anderson, our two-faced features editor. He reminds me of the Pillsbury Doughboy with his wobbly gut that hangs over the too-high waistband of his trousers and his beady little eyes staring out of his pasty face like two currants. His role is to inspire and guide the feature writers, but the truth is all he cares about is having an easy life. Soon after she started at the magazine, Ali had a run-in with Adrian after he tried to claim credit for one of her stories. She was chasing an *at home* with Janey Q, lead singer of chart-topping girl group Syrup and, after weeks of chatting up her agent (I'm using that in a journalistic sense, not a sexual one), she managed to clinch the deal for a mere five grand. Rather than marching straight up to Eva and telling her the good news, like I would've done, she tells Adrian first. 'Oh, that'll make a spread. I'll put it on the flatplan,' he says, not even bothering to congratulate her. 'You don't need to tell Eva, I've got a scheduling meeting with her this afternoon so I'll mention it then.'

Ali thinks nothing off it, but when days go by and Eva doesn't say a word, she starts to get suspicious. After all, negotiating a deal like this is pretty good going when it's the first month of your first job in journalism. Not only that, but when the agent comes back to Ali with a date for the interview, Adrian decides to send one of the other staff writers, because he doesn't reckon Ali's experienced enough. This really pisses her off, so in the end she asks Eva outright if she was pleased with the piece, which ran to eight pages in the end – not bad for a 5k deal.

'It worked brilliantly,' says Eva. 'Adrian worked really hard to pull that together.'

Nuff said. Ali confronted Adrian by the water machine later that day, and he tried to tell her he must simply have forgotten to tell Eva that Ali had scored the deal. But none of us was fooled. Being the stupid wanker that he is, Adrian just decided Ali was some precocious kid and he wanted to crush her, instead of encouraging her like he's supposed to. Everyone at the magazine thinks he's a useless piece of shit, except Eva – and at the end of the day she's the only person who counts, so we just have to put up with him. Never mind, he'll get his comeuppance one day.

Anyway, I've got more important things to worry about than Adrian and his clumsy management style. I, Ruby Lake, have my very own stalker. Brooke Shields had a stalker. He sent her dozens of nude pictures of himself and wrote love letters describing her as his 'mail-order' bride. Brad Pitt had a stalker. She was arrested at his home in Hollywood after a caretaker found her holed up in a bedroom wearing a pair of Brad's jogging bottoms. John Lennon had a stalker. John wound up dead.

Get a grip, Ruby, for God's sake! The guy's probably just some deranged *Wow!* reader who happens to have HTML skills. I've had nutters before. There was one man who sent me dozens of letters on ruled blue airmail paper (even though he only lived in Newcastle-under-Lyme). The artist known as 'Leslie' had a thing about Barbra Streisand. He obviously got my name out of the magazine and decided, naturally enough, that being a celebrity writer, I had Babs's ear. When I got the first letter, I thought it was harmless enough. Admittedly, it was written entirely without punctuation and capital letters, but I felt sorry for the guy. He asked if I could help him get in touch with Barbra as he was a really big fan . . . I mean, he'd spelled her name right and everything. I must've been bored that afternoon at work, because I wrote back saying that if he sent me a letter for the diva, I would forward it on to her agent in the States.

Well, that opened the floodgates. Leslie had obviously spent his entire adult life looking for someone with an ounce of compassion. Okay, who am I trying to kid? He was looking for someone stupid enough to enter into a correspondence so that he'd have something to do all day. Three days later, I got another crinkly blue envelope postmarked: Newcastle-under-Lyme: *dear barbra*, his letter began.

*i love you i cant live without you please send someone to bring me to you otherwise i will be so miserable my life is empty and meaningless i have no friends and you are the only thing that brings me joy i hate newcastleunderlyme and everyone here please rescue me i can leave anytime i will be your slave i will do anything you want just say the word . . .*

It continued in this loony stream-of-consciousness fashion for another four pages. Of course I didn't forward it to Barbra's agent, I threw it straight in the bin. Over the next four weeks, I was bombarded with a seemingly endless stream of wafer-thin letters, all asking if I'd forwarded the original letter and why did I think Barbra hadn't replied. Each one was slightly more desperate and threatening than the last.

*dear ruby you have to help me my life has no meaning without barbra if you don't help i may do something silly . . .*

I ignored them all, hoping he'd just take the hint and go away. It's amazing how people can become so fixated on a person they've only ever seen in a magazine or on a movie screen. They honestly believe that if they only had the chance to meet their idol, they would somehow fall in love and live happily ever after.

When *Wow!* published my *at home* interview with a well-known West End stage star, together with photographs of his monogrammed cutlery, collection of antique toby jugs and custom-built Roller, I got dozens of letters from wannabe wives. Some included photographs, some said they were TV actresses, all claimed to feel 'a unique connection' with the ageing millionaire. The guy's fatal mistake in that interview was telling me he longed for that 'special lady' to share his life with . . . only he forgot to add, 'gold-diggers need not apply'.

Anyway, I digress. Where was I? Ah, the lovely Barbra. Well, the next thing was, Leslie started calling me at work. I remember picking up the phone and an icy chill went up my spine as I heard a soft, lisping voice say, 'It's leslie i'm calling from newcastleunderlyme.' He might as well have said, 'Here's Johneeee!' I freaked.

'I'm b-b-busy, I can't talk n-n-now,' I stuttered down the phone. And then I heard the pips go at his end. Even more sinister – he was calling me from a payphone because he obviously didn't want to leave any tracks. I slammed down the phone and went to talk to Eva. She was great and told me to tell her if and when he called again. Of course he did, the very next day in fact. I put him on hold, signalled to Eva and she came striding over to my desk like DCI Jane fucking Tennison. She grabbed the phone and threatened my mate Les with police action if he made any attempt to contact me again. It seemed to do the trick and I never heard from him again.

Did you know that a bed once slept in by Barbra Streisand sold for $33,000 ... mad, isn't it? A San Francisco hotel was closing down and they decided to sell off all the furnishings that had ever been touched, lain on or looked at by a celebrity. Also up for grabs was a piano played by Liberace and a typewriter rumoured to have been used by Jack London to write *Call of the Wild*. The star memorabilia business is worth a fortune, and the internet trade in the stuff is phenomenal. One of the biggest regrets of my life is that I didn't get Christian and Maisie to autograph the Order of Service at their wedding ... I'd have made a fortune at a web auction.

So, I tell myself, the showbiz world is full of nutters and my web nutter is just par for the course. Hang on a minute though ... this particular nutter has my home address. Worse still, he paid a visit to Galleon Place either last night, or early this morning. I *am* listed in the phone book under 'Lake, R.' but there must be more than one R. Lake in the whole of London. Does that mean this sicko could actually be somebody I know? Mentally, I tick off my closest male friends, one by one:

• Jamie – we did share a drunken snog and a bit of a fumble on New Year's Eve because we were the only single people at a party full of couples. We've since agreed it was a hideous mistake and not one we're ever likely to repeat.

• Simon – is getting married in the summer and I refuse to believe he'd pick me over 5ft 8in Katie with her liquid glass hair and Faye Dunaway cheekbones.

• Phil – I can rule him out completely, as he is a total technophobe who doesn't even know what the letters 'www' stand for. Besides which, we haven't communicated for the past year and a half . . . some silly falling out over a sub's job at *Wow!* he was interviewed for but failed to get.

So I'm stumped really. I guess I'll just have to wait for the Secret Admirer's next move.

# FOUR: JEDI

Eva and I are sitting in the fourth-floor boardroom, waiting for the others to arrive. In the middle of the vast oval table is a white china plate loaded with fresh fruit, nice nibbly things – grapes, cherries and tart orange physalis. Beside the plate is a cafètiere of Colombian rich-roast, cans of Coke (diet and regular) and three big bottles of still water. I'm dying to dig in – I haven't had lunch yet – but I'd better hold back till we're all present and correct. The other attendees include Louie Bresler, the American agent who represents the combined interests of Joe Lucas and Niamh Connolly, Keith Reid, *Wow!*'s head of security, and finally, wedding co-ordinator Hugh Willoughby-Smith. The basic wedding contract has already been thrashed out between Louie, Eva and *Wow!*'s lawyer; the purpose of today's get-together is to iron out some of the finer details. As senior staff writer, my role in all this is crucial. Not only will I be covering the event itself, together with a junior writer (Ali, hopefully), but I hope to write a sizeable chunk of the copy in advance, based on information gleaned from the wedding organizer. That's why Eva has requested my presence at this highly sensitive stage of the proceedings.

*Wow!* is fanatical about secrecy when it comes to the big, expensive stories and Eva only ever involves the minimum number of staff until the last possible moment. Those who *are* privy to the planning stages are not supposed to breathe a word to anyone and that includes uninitiated colleagues, family and friends. Like those before it, this project has its own codename, to be invoked in every internal memo, schedule, flatplan and discussion. So from now on, this isn't 'Joe and Niamh's wedding' – it's Operation Jedi (as in Jedi knight, a reference to Joe's surname, the one he shares with *Star Wars* director George Lucas ... don't worry, it's supposed to confuse you).

Through the boardroom's glass door, I see Keith emerging from the lift. Keith (or Special K as I like to call him) is a freelance security consultant and he and his floating team of muscle work most of our big events. A former SAS man (he's got the shrapnel wounds to prove it), Keith is tough, intelligent and utterly trustworthy. He may be nudging fifty, but even the most determined paparazzo wouldn't want to tangle with him.

'Good afternoon, girls,' he says, his broad shoulders practically grazing the sides of the door frame. Keith has an old-fashioned view of women; it doesn't bother me, but it really riles Eva.

'Good afternoon, Keith,' says Eva tartly. 'Do take a seat.'

'How are you doing, K?' I inquire, as he eases his bulk into a leather-covered chair.

'Not bad, Ruby, thanks for asking. I could do with some zeds though. I worked the Versace party last night and we didn't clock off till six this morning.'

'Well you look pretty alert to me . . . must be all that army training. You can take the man out of the SAS, but you can't take the SAS out of the man, huh?'

'Hmmm,' he mutters, getting all cagey like he always does when I bring up his illustrious past . . . it's kind of a running joke between us. 'Mind if I help myself?' he says, reaching for the cafetière as a distraction.

'Be my guest. It's decaff mind you – so it won't help keep you awake,' says Eva, cuttingly.

The door swings open again and Julie, Eva's secretary, pokes her head round the door. 'Mr Bresler and Mr Willoughby-Smith for you,' she says, before ushering them in. This is the first time Keith and I have met the twosome, so Eva does a round of formal introductions.

Louie Bresler, one of the William Morris agency's high-fliers, is usually based at their Los Angeles office, but was seconded to London last month, and will remain here until the dust has settled on the May 18th wedding. He's a small, dapper man, late thirties, with a touch of the Dustin Hoffmans about his prominent features. I check out his clothes, the way I've been programmed to do in the course of my celebrity interviews: an expensive charcoal-grey suit – I'd hazard a guess at Comme des Garçons – teamed with a purply shirt and a perfectly matching tie, looped in one those big fat knots. We shake hands and he gives me a nice smile. Not all agents are weasels you know – most, but not all – and I have a good feeling about Louie, based on a first impression.

Hugh, in contrast, is tall and skinny with a very plummy voice and a weak handshake. Like all good wedding co-ordinators, he has aristocratic connections, being the estranged half-brother of Lord Willoughby-Smith of Norfolk. He's carrying a big ring-binder file that is no doubt filled with hymn sheets and menus and timetables – and I'm going to need every last one of them. Eva and I have never met, or even spoken to, Joe and Niamh themselves, nor are we likely to until we're all holed up inside the ring of steel at Kellaway. Hugh, therefore, is the one who must convey to us their dreams and desires for the Big Day. When everyone has settled in a seat and helped themselves to refreshments, we get down to business.

'Shall we start with Keith's feedback from Kellaway?' says Eva, looking at him expectantly.

'That's fine by me,' says Keith, who spent two days in County Clare last week, recceing the castle and the surrounding area. He produces a rough pencil sketch from the blue cardboard folder in front of him.

'The castle is set in a 260-acre private estate and will be closed to regular guests for a five-day period – three days up to and including the wedding and two days afterwards. The estate has two main points of entry, one to the north and one to the south. As you can see, there are plenty of potential hiding places – the lake, the clubhouse, the walled garden, these areas of under-growth,' he says, pointing to the relevant places on his little diagram. 'Every on-site contractor and each member of the *Wow!* team will be issued with a laminate pass for identification purposes. Anyone not displaying his or her pass will be ejected immediately.'

You'd be surprised at the lengths our rivals go to in order to breach our security and ruin the exclusive nature of our coverage. In the past, Keith's team has found miniature recording devices hidden in the vicar's lectern, reporters in wetsuits submerged in water-filled ditches, photographers in camouflage gear hiding out in trees. And if they can't get their own people in, they'll try and nobble anyone with access to the wedding – marquee-erectors, waiters, florists, even guests themselves, who can easily conceal a pinhole camera in a tie pin or a Dior handbag.

'I suggest twenty men in total: ten placed at strategic points around the estate boundaries, with another ten patrolling the interior for the duration of the wedding. The security team will sweep those areas of the castle being used for the wedding and also the marquees for hidden cameras and listening devices. The first sweep will take place at midnight on the seventeenth and then at four-hourly intervals on the day itself. All guests will be asked to enter the castle grounds from the north entrance

– the south entrance will be sealed off and permanently guarded. Two of the ten-strong team patrolling the grounds will be repositioned at the north entrance from one p.m. through to three p.m. to check guests' invitations – any guest not bringing their invite will be barred from entering. Am I right in thinking that guests have been asked not to bring cameras?'

'Yeah, that's right. It's all there on the invitation,' says Louie.

'I must warn you, Mr Bresler, that if my men see anyone with a camera, it will be confiscated . . . I suppose searching the guests' bags on entry is out of the question?'

'Please Keith, call me Louie. Joe and Niamh certainly won't countenance any searching of personal property – it's far too intrusive and hardly likely to make their guests feel relaxed. However, we *are* happy to authorize the confiscation of any cameras. Now tell me, have you thought about security arrangements for the couple when they fly into Shannon airport on May sixteenth? They will, of course, be accompanied by two of their personal bodyguards, and a 4×4 with blacked-out windows will be waiting to drive them directly to Kellaway. However, you may feel extra cover is required.'

'Most definitely. I would like to post four men at the airport to guard the party through the arrivals hall. If the press get wind they're on that flight, we'll need those guys to get them past the photographers. We'll have two hire cars waiting and once the couple are safely inside the 4×4, we'll escort the vehicle to Kellaway. I've done a dry run and the journey between airport and castle takes approximately twenty minutes – we'll have one car up front, the second bringing up the rear.'

Keith's security precautions may seem a little excessive, given that the press appear to be ignorant of the exact date and location of the wedding. The bride-to-be is three months' pregnant and consequently, the tabloids are speculating that the nuptials will most likely take place in the autumn, after the baby is born. Regarding the venue, southern Ireland, being Niamh's birthplace, is viewed as one of the more likely options, although the couple's home in Beverly Hills and Joe's Moroccan hideaway are still regarded as possibilities. But as the wedding day draws nearer, it's extremely probable that the information will leak out – a guest would get a few thousand quid for the tip-off alone. And once the couple are spotted at the airport, LAX or Shannon, all hell will break loose – so you see, Keith is being necessarily cautious.

We talk a bit more about the security arrangements and Hugh expresses concern about the safety of the ten peacocks he's planning to have roaming the grounds, given that Keith has also requested two sniffer dogs. Keith reassures him that the dogs, which are highly trained, will be on leashes the whole time and will pose no threat to his precious birds.

Eva then asks a worried-looking Hugh to take us through the timetable for the wedding day, which falls on a Friday, a deliberate ploy to keep fans and onlookers to a minimum (a Saturday guarantees open season). He opens his file and unclips four copies of the same document and passes them round the table. 'This is a skeleton schedule for the day. You'll note that all two hundred guests will attend both the wedding service and the evening reception:

2.15 p.m. Guests start to arrive

2.45 p.m. All guests to be seated in the Great Hall

3.00 p.m. Wedding service commences

3.30 p.m. Service ends. Guests make their way to the Gainsborough Room for champagne and canapés reception

5.00 p.m. Guests to take their seats in marquee number one

5.30 p.m. Dining commences

7.00 p.m. Speeches and cutting of the cake

8.00 p.m. Evening reception commences in marquee number two

Midnight Fireworks

12.30 a.m. Ends

'I would suggest that the formal portraits take place during the champagne reception. There's a very elegant, light-filled room next door to the Gainsborough, which would be ideal for this purpose. I have a picture, so you can see for yourselves.'

He unclips a glossy brochure from his file and we all pore over the relevant page. Everyone agrees that the Richmond Gallery, hung with portraits of Irish aristocracy and reasonably furniture-free, will be the perfect spot. From my point of view, the fact that it's so close to the venue for the drinks reception is crucial. I'll be the one in charge of rounding up the guests to have their photo taken, so it's helpful (a) that they are all in one place and (b) the place is nearby.

*Wow!* has commissioned David O'Connor to take the photos on the day – he was Joe and Niamh's personal choice, and a pretty expensive one at that. His fee for the day will be close to £15,000 (and that's on top of the £1.5 million), but we wouldn't have secured the deal without him. He hasn't shot a single wedding before, but Niamh has worked with him on dozens of modelling assignments. All the pictures we use in the magazine will be subject to the couple's approval and because of the time frame involved, we're planning to set up a fully equipped photo lab on site.

'We *will* need a full hour for photography,' says Eva. 'So if the service runs over, we'll just have to delay the sit-down meal.'

Hugh looks aghast at this suggestion and starts to protest that the caterers have been instructed to start serving the three-course meal at five-thirty p.m. and not a minute later. Eva cuts him short.

'As I'm sure you will appreciate, Hugh, *Wow!* is paying a record fee for this exclusive. Consequently, the magazine really cannot compromise when it comes to the posed shots ... We do have fifty-two pages to fill, you know.'

Hugh looks to Louie for backup, but Louie's nodding ... he knows the score. 'I don't think Eva is being unreasonable, Hugh. You'll just have to tell the caterers to be flexible. After all, they're getting a pretty hefty fee too.'

Hugh gulps visibly, but sensibly remains silent. Eva flashes Louie a grateful smile.

'Are you in a position to let us know which celebrities will be attending?' Eva asks Louie.

Up until now, various names have been bandied around, but nothing's set in stone. In fact, you can't rely on a particular star's attendance until you actually clap eyes on him or her on the day itself. Agents know full well that they can increase the cash value of their clients' wedding by throwing out names like Catherine Zeta Jones or Pierce Brosnan, even though they know their attendance is unlikely. Not that I'm suggesting Joe and Niamh's people would play this mercenary game. Frankly, they don't need to – the couple are such megastars that their wedding is sure to be the hottest ticket in town on both sides of the Atlantic.

'Not all the guests have replied yet, so we'd rather not commit ourselves until the headcount is complete. I *can* tell you, however, that Donatella Versace has assured us she *will* be attending. I know you were keen to talk to her about Niamh's gown, so maybe you could arrange to do that on the day itself?'

'That's excellent news,' says Eva. 'The readers will want to know every detail about that dress. Ruby, will you make a note to grab Donatella for ten minutes during the drinks reception? Maybe you should call her American office in advance to check she's amenable.'

'While we're on the subject of interviews, is it possible to fix times for the pre-wedding interviews with the happy couple?' I say, addressing Louie. 'I'll need about an hour and a half with them.'

'Sure. As I think I mentioned, they're flying in to Ireland on the morning of the sixteenth, so how about five p.m. on the seventeenth. Would that suit you?'

'Perfect. And Hugh, can I do a phoner with you at some point before the wedding, just to talk through the menu and the music and get your perspective on the event? After all, you are the creative genius behind it.' This flattery is absolutely essential. I want Hugh on side because, with fifty-two pages to fill, I'm going to be grateful for every little bean he can spill.

'Certainly, call my assistant, Flora, and have her set something up,' he says, sliding a business card across the table.

I've got all the information I need now, so my brain

slips down a gear for the remainder of the meeting. The others thrash out the boring stuff, like whether they should hire a private helicopter to occupy the air space above Kellaway, thus preventing rival craft from taking aerial shots, and if Keith's men should wear lounge suits or DJs.

Finally, the meeting draws to a close and we all get up and pump each other's hands, happy that we've managed to come to agreement on so many points. Eva offers to escort the three men down to reception – judging by the eye tennis that was going on between her and Louie, I'd say she has the hots for him. She's probably going to use the opportunity to suggest a drinks meeting, just the two of them at, say, Teatro or Soho House (Eva's a fully paid-up member of both). I leave them to it and shuffle off back to the office. It's five o'clock now and I'm absolutely ravenous, so I collect a hot chocolate and a shortbread snack-pack from the machine en route. Once at my desk I flick through my email. There's nothing urgent, just my flight details for next week's jaunt to Mustique (I am *so* looking forward to that). I'll read it properly tomorrow – tonight I've arranged to meet some university friends for pizza in Soho.

Before I leave the office, I can't resist another peek at *preciousruby.com*. It's really quite clever the way he's doctored that painting. We use PhotoShop all the time at the magazine, to airbrush out unsightly bruises and pimples. It's also invaluable for repositioning celebrities in a line-up. Say we're designing a wedding cover and we want to show the bride and groom with a couple of their celebrity mates. Trouble is, those celebrities aren't standing right next to Mr & Mrs – there's somebody else in the way. Well, we don't sweat it, we just switch them around so they're where we want them. Easy.

After pushing my way through the rush-hour crowds at Leicester Square tube station, I finally emerge into the relative freedom of Charing Cross Road. I'm looking forward to tonight's get together with three of my journalist friends from City. Amy is my best friend, a real live wire and features editor on one of the big-circulation teen mags. Then there's Simon – oh how we laughed when he started his career at *Railway Modeller*; we stopped laughing though when he became the £40k-a-year news editor of a prestigious advertising trade mag. The third member of our little posse is Jo, a freelance writer, who specializes in consumer affairs. She's trying to branch out into TV and has already got a Richard and Judy appearance under her belt. Our designated meeting place is Kettners, just off Shaftesbury Avenue – at the end of the day, it's just a pizza joint, but you get real linen tablecloths and a man playing the piano, so you feel like you've had a proper night out. When I get there, the others are already sitting at a corner table and they've cracked open a bottle of Shiraz. We do the kissy-kissy thing and I ask Simon how his wedding preparations are going, just to get it out of the way early on. I've already had enough wedding talk for one day. We order our pizzas and a couple of side salads and exchange work gossip. I hear about Amy's day in the studio with the latest, hottest, youngest boy-band ('they make me feel so old,' she groans), and Jo's undercover assignment, which she hopes will expose a rip-off insurance salesman preying on the elderly.

Pretty soon, the talk turns to our love lives. Simon, as I said before, is engaged to the beautiful Katie, Jo and I are both single and Amy's dating Toby, the fashion editor of a so-called style mag, except we all know he's not good enough for her. He's too intense, too pretentious and we all feel hideously and hopelessly unfashionable in the face of his self-conscious Portobello Market trendi-ness. For some reason, Amy hangs on in there, secretly loathing all those Clerkenwell loft parties he drags her to, where they're all sitting around listening to William Orbit and chopping up Charlie with their goldcards. She's the sort of person who always has to be in a relationship, however unsuitable, but hopefully somebody nicer will come along and whisk her off her Miu Miu-clad feet. And please God let it be soon.

'So what about you, Ruby, seen any action recently?' Simon asks with the smug self-assurance of one who has his own romantic affairs so utterly and splendidly sewn up.

'Not as such,' I say, drawing out the words, hoping to provoke further questioning.

'Wait until the wedding . . . I'll have loads of single blokes lined up for you.'

'Cheers. Can't wait, Si – tell me, will they all be as good-looking as you?'

'No need to be like that, I'm only trying to help you out.'

'Well I don't need your help, thank you very much,' I say with mock indignation. 'As a matter of fact, I do have a certain, unsolicited love interest.'

'Ooh, you make it sound all mysterious. Go on, where d'you meet him and what's his name?' says Jo, leaning over the table towards me.

'Er, I haven't actually met him face to face, as it were, and his name . . . well I don't know his name. He just calls himself my Secret Admirer and he's trying to woo me with a custom-built website.' I take a gulp of wine for dramatic effect. 'I suppose you *could* say he's stalking me.'

They all look at me quizzically. Amy breaks the silence. 'You don't mean he's a stalker in the literal sense, do you?'

'Oh yes,' I say breezily. 'He knows my home address and everything.'

I fill them in on the details, sparse as they are. The others are concerned about my safety and Jo thinks I should print out the pages from my website and take them straight to the police.

'Don't you think that's over-reacting, Jo? I mean he hasn't threatened me or anything. He's probably just some *Wow!* acolyte, who's seen my photo in the magazine and has developed a bit of a crush.'

'He's certainly gone to an awful lot of trouble for you, whoever he is,' says Amy. 'He sounds like an intelligent guy – but I still think you should be careful. He knows where you live and maybe he also knows you live alone. Who's to say he won't come knocking on your door one dark night?'

'Shut, up Amy, you're scaring me.'

The others have got me thinking now. I'd almost convinced myself the website was just a bit of harmless fun, but it is pretty weird when you think about it. What if he tries to break in? I can't think of anything worse than waking up to find a man in a balaclava standing at my bedside. Thank God for the window bolts and five-lever mortice lock that come as standard in the new-build home.

'Maybe it's somebody you know,' suggests Simon.

'Well, the thought *had* crossed my mind.' I don't, of course, admit to having fleetingly considered *him* as a suspect.

'Maybe it's Steve,' says Jo. 'He took it really hard when you dumped him.'

Steve is my ex, a charity worker I met through Ali. Our relationship lasted only three months as it became obvious pretty early on that we had nothing in common: he liked real ale, frugal living and the Manics. I, on the other hand, am a materialistic, wine-chugging Andy Williams fan.

'I didn't dump him,' I tell her. 'We parted by mutual agreement – and anyway he's living in Guatemala now, so it's hardly likely to be him.'

'I know,' says Amy excitedly. 'I bet it's Alan Kramer.'

Now it's my turn to snicker. 'Alan Kramer . . . do me a favour.' Kramer is a C-list author, a purveyor of cheap, nasty, boy's own horror stories – the kind where big-breasted women are laid on sacrificial slabs and ravished by sex-starved succubi. I interviewed him for *Wow!* on the occasion of his 35th birthday. As I recall, we covered the party (held at the London Dungeon – where else?) only because he managed to cajole a breathtaking number of B-listers into attending. I'd done the pre-party inter-view at Sticky Fingers – his choice, not mine – and he seemed harmless enough, quite entertaining in fact. We talked about loads of stuff: his books and how he does his research (he directed me to some particularly lurid horror sites on the net), then we moved on to his blissfully happy childhood, and, by logical progression, his regret that he had yet to meet the woman of his dreams and have children of his own. And when the interview was over, we carried on talking and he asked me if I fancied a tequila, so we had one and then a few more. We ended up getting very pissed and sharing a cab home, although I did think that was odd, seeing as he lives north of the river. Nothing happened though, I said goodnight, got out the taxi and off he went.

Five days later, I was covering the party with T.K. Stead. The invitation said: *come as your favourite fic-tional horror character*, so T.K. was Anne Rice's Lestat and I was Morticia Addams (well, she always scared the shit out of *me*). Alan's PR woman helped us collar all the big names for photos, so after about an hour, T.K.

had all the shots in the bag and I had studiously done the captions. We were both quite merry having downed a few Sea Breezes (sorry, 'plasma cocktails') when up came Alan in the shape of Boris Karloff's Wolfman.

'Hi guys, how's it going?' he said, and reached over to kiss me on both cheeks, like we were old friends, grazing my skin with his acrylic whiskers.

'Yeah, it's a great party, Alan. T.K. has got some brilliant shots, so it should make four pages at least.'

'Terrific! And now that the work stuff's out of the way, you two can both enjoy yourselves. Ruby, come and dance with me.'

I figured it would be rude to refuse the Birthday Boy, so I followed him onto the dance floor (situated next to an impressive collection of medieval torture instruments) and we bumped and ground a bit to *The Monster Mash* and a couple of other ghoulish hits. But then Alan got a bit over-enthusiastic and started trying to cop a feel while we were dancing. I didn't notice at first, partly because I was drunk and partly due to the voluminous nature of Morticia's costume. But then I distinctly felt his rubber claws grasp my arse cheek, so I pushed him away, quite hard, and marched off the dance floor. I wasn't particularly angry or upset. I just didn't like the idea of him thinking he could grope me just because he was a bit famous and he'd bought me a few drinks. I sought out T.K., who was chatting up the Bride of Frankenstein, and pretended I needed him to take some more shots. When we were alone, I told him about Alan's behaviour and he sympathized and said the guy was probably drunk and that, anyway, it was time we were leaving. So off we went, and I got a cab home and went to bed and didn't think any more of it.

The next day was a Saturday and by mid-afternoon I'd got over my hangover and was hoovering the crumbs from my Habitat sofa when my entry phone buzzed. I picked up the handset to see who it was, and it turned out to be Interflora. I went trotting out to the communal door, all excited, and when I opened it, there was the biggest bunch of flowers I ever saw, I couldn't even see the delivery guy's face behind them. There were yellow roses and big creamy lilies and gerbera and other stuff I'd never even seen before. 'Oh, thanks,' I told the guy casually like I had been half expecting him. Then I shut the door and raced indoors to rip the little envelope off the Cellophane.

> *Dear Ruby,*
> *Please forgive my brutish behaviour last night. My only excuse is that I find you irresistibly attractive. May I make it up to you with dinner? Give me a call at home.*
> *Alan*

I appreciated his thoughtfulness. He obviously wasn't a complete meathead, and of course I was flattered that a man (okay, a *celebrity*, even though you wouldn't recognize him in the street) was interested in me. He wasn't at all bad-looking, if you like the swarthy Italian waiter type, but unfortunately I didn't fancy him in the slightest. I had his number, from when I'd called him to set up the Sticky Fingers interview, but I didn't use it. What was the point? I wasn't that desperate for a free dinner, and knowing his taste in eateries, he would probably have taken me to the Hard Rock Cafe. The whole episode was a good month ago now, and I hadn't heard from Mr Kramer since. All my friends know the story, I must've told it a dozen times in various states of inebriation.

I must have been silent for an awfully long time, because suddenly Simon pipes up sarcastically with: 'Earth to Ruby. Do we have contact?'

'Sorry guys, I was miles away. You know, Amy, I think you might just be barking up the right tree. I mean, let's review the evidence: (a) he fancies me; (b) he knows where I live; (c) he falls into the category of 'creative artist'; (d) he's a self-confessed net head; (e) there were lilies in that bouquet and photos of lilies in *precious-ruby.com*. I'd say that was a pretty positive ID, wouldn't you?'

# FIVE: FANTASY ISLAND

The voice of Bart Simpson shatters the peace. 'Yo dude, wake up and get out of bed!' I stretch out a leaden arm and cut short Bart's rant. Is it really five-thirty already? I feel like I've only just nodded off. I get out of bed, pull on a pair of fuchsia-pink Totes Toasties and grope around in the quasi-darkness for my fleecy bathrobe. Fuck! I forgot that suitcase was there. I fall back onto the bed and rub my toe till it's stopped throbbing, then I limp to the kitchen. Can't face breakfast at this ungodly hour, but I manage to locate a sachet of instant cappuccino lodged at the back of the cupboard.

Despite the early start, it's impossible to feel too hard-done-by. By the end of today I will, after all, be sipping cocktails on the veranda of one of the most exclusive hotels in the Caribbean. Yippee! I do a little samba on the lino (my Totes Toasties with their little rubber grips stop me falling flat on my face) before carrying my faux cappuccino back to the bedroom. Now, have I forgotten anything?

# WOW!

Passport – check

Bikinis × 3 – check

Trashy novel – check

Mosquito repellent – check

Factor 20 – check

Yep, all the essentials are there. Oops, nearly forgot my dictaphone. I'm going to need that when Jessie Reynolds opens her heart to me – it's the least she can do after *Wow!* has gone to all this trouble to give her and her best mate a fabulous two-week break on the private island paradise of Mustique. The girls flew out to the Caribbean last week and today, photographer Raoul, assistant Charley and lil' ol' me fly out to join them for week two.

One hour later and I'm standing by the British Airways check-in desk at Gatwick, looking around for Raoul and Charley. Peering through the crowds, I spot them a mile off because of all the gear they're carrying – lights and tripods and reflectors. 'Charley!' I shout, as soon as they're within hailing distance. He spots me waving and they push their trolley over to where I'm waiting. Charley and I give each other a big hug and I shake Raoul's hand. This is the first time we've met, and actually he's a bit of a looker, with his lithe footballer's build, olive skin and dark hair cropped really short.

'Sorry we're late. The traffic north of the river was a pig,' says Raoul.

'Well you're here now . . . I've already checked in. No chance of an upgrade, I'm afraid – I've flashed the old business card and everything, but BA aren't budging.'

They offload their six cases of camera stuff and their two travel bags and we regroup in Costa Coffee for tea and Danish. I've got the hotel brochure in my hand luggage, and I get it out so the other two can drool over it, just like I've been doing ever since the PR sent it to me last week. I read out loud: 'Originally an eighteenth-century coral warehouse and sugar mill, the Cotton House offers guests the simple elegance and luxurious charm of a premier luxury resort.' I draw their attention to the Egyptian cotton sheets, the marble bath, the in-room CD player and, best of all, the pillow menu, which offers a choice of five different bolsters to 'make guests feel the Cotton House is their second home'. Of course, if *Wow!* was having to fork out the full whack, a trip like this would be prohibitively expensive, but the magazine gets a massive discount in return for a nice credit at the end of the feature.

The eight-hour flight to Barbados gives me plenty of time to fill Raoul in on our prey. Although he has received a photographic brief from *Wow!*'s art director, Angela, it's down to me to get him up to speed with the real nitty-gritty – the stuff that will help him understand Jessie Reynolds, push her buttons, get her on side. 'Jessie is just about the hottest property in soap right now,' I tell him. 'She's twenty-five, blonde, beautiful, feisty . . . won Best Newcomer at last year's British Soap Awards. As *Hay-*

*ward Square*'s resident babe, Nicole Duvane, she's been involved in some of the juciest story lines in recent months: Louise's drug overdose, the break-in at the corner shop . . .' Raoul's eyes start to glaze over, so I cut to the good stuff. 'Until last month, Jessie was engaged to millionaire nightclub entrepreneur Jake Walsh – he's the man behind Outlaw in Shoreditch and Fever in the Fulham Road. The split was very sudden and nobody seems to know exactly what happened. Jessie's agent released a brief statement to the press, saying the relationship was over, but giving no reason – not even the usual "pressure of work" nonsense. Walsh is keeping uncharacteristically shtoom – in the past, he's positively courted publicity – and Jessie hasn't given any interviews since the break-up. That's why this trip has come at the perfect time as far as *Wow!*'s concerned and Eva is desperate for me to get the story.'

'So who's this friend she's brought with her?' asks Raoul, tearing open the little bag of peanuts that the stewardess delivered with his whisky and ginger.

'Mariah Pryce, a make-up artist – technically off-duty, but I'm sure she'll help out when it comes to the photos. They've known each other since they were school kids and are always being snapped stumbling out of the Great Eastern or Fabric in their matching Manolos, a bit of a double act really. Until a couple of weeks ago, Jake's name was on the Mustique ticket and to be honest, we were looking forward to doing some gorgeous romantic shots of the two of them together. But then the bust-up happened and Jessie asked if she could take Mariah instead. We'll have to tread really carefully if we're to have any chance of getting the story.'

As our flight hits the halfway mark, both of us are beginning to feel a little sleepy, having had such an early start. We recline our seat backs and I plug myself into one of the CD selections, hoping it'll send me off. No such luck – like my hero Alan Whicker, I can never sleep on planes. Raoul, on the other hand, seems to have no trouble at all; twenty minutes later and he's out for the count. I find myself staring at him, well more like squinting really since I don't want Charley to catch me mid-ogle. Raoul has got the longest eyelashes I've ever seen on a man, really thick and curled at the ends. My head's feeling quite swimmy, what with the vodka and the wine and the after-dinner Bailey's, and suddenly I feel an overwhelming urge to reach out and stroke his face, just so I can see how my pale hand looks against his dark skin. I don't, of course, but I have to make myself look away so I'm not tempted.

We push our over-laden luggage trolley across the baking Bajan tarmac towards the six-seater *Islander* plane that will take us on the final leg of our journey. The pilot himself helps us load our gear onto the craft and then we all pile in. There are two other passengers in addition to our little group – a couple of very tall, very tanned, very thin blonde girls in designer sunglasses, who give us patronizing smiles, as though they're wondering how on earth we can afford a holiday in Mustique. They're so up themselves, they must be models.

In less than an hour, the plane is taxi-ing down the runway in Mustique towards a little bamboo-roofed shack which, our pilot explains, serves as a kind of rustic passport control. This place is a real-life *Fantasy Island* and I half expect to see Ricardo Montalban walking towards us with the white-suited dwarf in tow. We climb out and a wave of thick, wet heat hits us although a light breeze blowing off the mountainside helps take the edge off it. A rotund black man in khaki shorts and matching short-sleeved shirt emerges from the shack and introduces himself as Jimmy, an employee of the Cotton House. While we get our passports stamped, he offloads our luggage and carries it over to a glorified milk float – or 'mule' as he calls it. The two beautiful girls, meanwhile, shimmy off to meet some middle-aged Lee Marvin look-alike, who has turned out to meet them.

Although I'm knackered from the flight, I find I'm very excited about being in this magical place and in fact when we arrive at the Cotton House, after ten minutes of bumping over unmade roads in the milk float at 20 mph, it's even more beautiful than I imagined. The hotel con-sists of twenty cottages and suites set in these incredibly lush, beautifully landscaped gardens, dotted with lily ponds and tropical palms.

'This place is unreal,' says Charley, as a maid, having

made a note of our pillow preferences, leads us to our rooms. 'I can't wait to phone Emma and tell her all about it.'

I feel a twinge of jealousy. I'm not jealous of Emma; after all, I got over Charley a long time ago. I'm just jealous of their relationship per se, and of the fact that they've got each other and I'm on my own. Well, not quite on my own, I've got the Secret Admirer, but somehow I don't find that thought terribly comforting, not now that I think I know his real identity.

Our rooms are all located in the same two-storey colonial-style cottage. I'm on the top floor, the two boys are down below. We have agreed to meet in the hotel bar in a couple of hours' time, after we've had a chance to unpack and freshen up in our air-conditioned rooms with their original Oliver Messel furnishings.

I decide to dress up for dinner – it's definitely that sort of place – so I select my pink Whistles dress with spaghetti straps and my little pink cardie with embroidered roses round the neckline, just in case it gets chilly later. A quick spritz of eau de mosquito repellent (how do you think Mustique got its name?) and I'm ready to rendezvous.

When I get to the bar, situated in the main hotel building, the guys are already there, sitting on tall stools and sipping a brown drink from tall glasses. Raoul looks super-horny in white cotton drawstring trousers, white T-shirt and Birkenstocks. His skin and eyes look even darker in contrast to the white, or maybe it's just the effect of this subdued lighting.

'Hi Ruby, you gotta try a rum punch – here, have a sip of mine,' says Charley.

I take a mouthful of the cold, sweet liquid, aware that Raoul's eyes are on me. I'd better not make a slurping noise or leave a big lipstick stain on the glass (I send up a silent prayer in thanks of Lipcote).

'Mmm, that's delicious,' I say, a bit more animatedly that I might do if it was just Charley and me, say.

One of the good things about the Cotton House is that all meals and drinks (including the alcoholic variety) are included in the room tariff, so we don't have to worry about whose round it is. There's no sign of Jessie and Mariah so we bag a table on the veranda, overlooking the sea, and choose from the predictably spectacular menu. The place is starting to fill up and while we're waiting for our food to arrive, I engage in a spot of people watching. Naturally, everyone here is very well heeled, but in a casual sort of way – lots of smart-looking couples, Americans and Germans, in Ralph Lauren and Jil Sander. I wonder what they make of us. I'm glad to have two such good-looking companions, even if Charley has let the side down somewhat with his Diesel jeans and none-too-clean polo shirt.

It's not until we've finished our meal and I'm debating whether or not to go for the chocolate parfait that, out of the corner of my eye, I see a tanned blonde dressed in a gorgeous bias-cut floral dress appear at one of the tables at the far end of the veranda. It's Jessie – and the brunette with her must be Mariah. We wait till they've ordered their food and then go over to introduce ourselves. 'Hi Jessie. I'm Ruby from *Wow!* magazine, I just wanted to introduce myself and then I'll leave you to dine in peace. And I guess you must be Mariah,' I say, stretching out my hand to each of them in turn.

'Oh hi there, we forgot you were coming today. We've had such a relaxing holiday so far, time just seems to stand still,' says Jessie, who looks even prettier and more pert in the flesh than she does on the small screen. 'Did you have a good journey? Our flight to Barbados was just fantastic.'

It would be. They flew business class. 'Oh, you know, plastic food and not enough legroom. But that fantastic flight across to Mustique made up for it. Now, let me introduce our photographer, Raoul Johnson, and his assistant, Charley Lawrence . . .'

They shake each other's hands and I watch as Mariah gives Charley the once-over. He's obviously noticed too, because he gives her this cheeky little grin that he thinks makes him look even cuter. And actually, he's right.

'What do you think of the island so far, have you done much sightseeing?' asks Raoul.

'I'm afraid we haven't been very adventurous, all we seem to have done is lie on the beach or swim in the hotel pool. It's just so nice to really chill out for once,' says Jessie. 'I must say *Wow!* has picked the perfect location here – it's so beautiful, I think you'll be able to get some really fantastic shots.'

'The guys and I will probably do a recce of the island tomorrow to check out the best spots for photography, but we're planning to take things nice and easy,' I say in a reassuring tone. 'We'll leave you to your meal now, maybe we can catch up with you tomorrow night – how about we meet for dinner, around eight-ish?'

'Perfect. I'll look forward to it. Enjoy the rest of your evening.'

In the end, I do go for the parfait – I am on holiday, after all – and the guys have an Irish coffee apiece. The mosquitoes are starting to flutter around us, so we retire to the big cream sofas inside and cane another couple of rum punches each. By midnight, none of us can keep our eyes open, so we call it a night. When we arrive at our cottage, I kiss Raoul and Charley goodnight. We arrange a time to meet up for breakfast and I climb the wooden stairs to my room. The maid has been in to turn down my bed, so all I have to do is peel off my clothes, part the mosquito net and slip between the crisp white sheets. I'm asleep as soon as my head hits the hand-stuffed cotton pillow.

# SIX: FANTASY ISLAND

After a huge late breakfast of Eggs Benedict, granola and banana bread, Raoul, Charley and I set out to explore the island. I've hired a *mule* for the duration of our stay, and we spend an hour or so just driving around and marvelling at the spectacular villas we pass en route, with whimsical names like Stargroves, Jacaranda and Windsong. Mustique has mile upon mile of beautiful sandy beaches and when we see a particularly picturesque spot, we park the *mule* at the side of the road so we can go for a dip. I've got a bikini on under my T-shirt and shorts and all three of us run towards the ocean, stripping off as we go, like three kids. The sand is powdery and golden and when we hit the water it's like walking into a warm bath. Raoul starts swimming right away, long, clean strokes that quickly take him out to sea, while Charley and I stay in the shallows, wallowing in the surf and splashing each other. After a while, I wade back to the beach, conscious of the need to protect my fake tan from the sea's exfoliating effects. We practically have the whole beach to ourselves – the only other occupants being a middle-aged couple and a pair of stunning golden-skinned girls in G-string bikinis, whose arses are completely and miraculously cellulite-free.

I lie back on the sand, letting the sun's rays dry me, and a few minutes later the boys come jogging up the beach. I must admit I find the sight of Raoul, all glistening pecs and clinging shorts, quite arousing.

'That water is beautiful. I could've swum for miles,' he says, shaking the water out of his hair like a dog.

'You certainly looked very confident out there . . . I guess you must do a lot of swimming at home,' I say, trying not to flirt too obviously.

'Yeah, I try and keep in shape. I do free weights as well . . . three times a week.'

'I'm impressed,' I say as I start to rub Factor 20 over my cleavage in what I hope is an alluring fashion. Raoul offers to grease up my back and I do the, 'Well, if you're sure you don't mind . . .' thing and then lie on the sand on my stomach enjoying every goddamn minute of it. He even does the backs of my legs too, and I enjoy the feel of his strong hands as they skim the edge of my bum cheeks. I just hope he can't see any ripples of cellulite.

When the sun gets too hot, we complete our tour of the entire island – it's only three miles by one mile – looking for dramatic backdrops for our shoot, and as this place is so beautiful, we're really spoilt for choice. Over dinner that night, we talk Jessie through the various locations we've found and she's suitably enthusiastic, oohing and aahing when we tell her about the pretty, brightly painted boutiques in the village and the upturned wooden fishing boats on the beach. Mariah, on the other hand, is more interested in Charley and the two of them flirt shamelessly throughout the meal. I doubt she'll get into his pants though. He is utterly and totally devoted to Emma, as I discovered to my cost, and anyway, Emma is miles prettier than her.

By eleven p.m. we've had four bottles of wine, two bottles of champagne and the conversation has loosened up considerably. As a celebrity journalist, I'm so used to having just three-quarters of an hour to probe someone's entire psyche that I've lost my sense of what's acceptable in normal conversation. So if I'm at a party, say, I often find myself asking entirely inappropriate questions of relative strangers: 'So you've just got divorced . . . was your husband unfaithful to you?' or 'Sorry to hear your girlfriend's in hospital . . . is it something life-threatening?' The funny thing is, most people don't seem to mind. I think half of them are so shocked you've asked the question that they come out with the answer spontaneously. The other half have secretly been dying to talk about the subject anyway, so you end up being stuck with them for hours because they see you as some kind of therapist.

Anyway, back to Jessie. One minute we're talking about Marsha Graham's boob job (she's better known as *Hayward Square* landlady Daisy Meadows) – and no, I wouldn't dream of putting this bit of gossip in my article (drunken conversations are strictly off-the-record) – the next thing I'm asking her if she misses Jake, her ex. I regret it as soon as the words are out of my mouth, but she doesn't seem to mind me prying.

'It's hard to miss someone who treated you like a punch bag,' she says – just like that. For a second, I'm not sure that I've heard her right. The others are too busy laughing at some funny story Raoul's telling to pay any attention.

I put my hand on Jessie's arm, which is lying across the table, curled around the kir royale she just ordered. 'Do you mean he used to hit you?'

'Hit me?' She lets out a bitter laugh. 'He beat the shit out of me.'

I can scarcely believe it. Gorgeous, rich, upper-crust public schoolboy Jake Walsh is really a twisted, violent bully? I don't know what to say. The journalist in me is saying, 'Dig, dig, dig,' the human being is telling me to tread carefully and sensitively. Charley takes the decision out of my hands:

'Hey Jessie, we're going to order tequila slammers – gonna join us?'

'Oh yeah, count me in,' says Jessie, looking up from the table.

'Ruby?'

'Yeah, great Charley.'

Mariah, who has been scratching away at her calf all evening, leans over to Jessie to show off a huge, red mosquito bite, and the moment's well and truly lost. I guess that explains the couple's bust-up. I wonder why Jessie hasn't gone public with the story. Jake must be shitting himself. Wouldn't it be great if I got the exclusive? I'll have to work on her.

Around twelve-thirty, Jessie makes her excuses and heads for bed. When she's gone, Mariah and Charley slink off together, saying they want to look at the stars from the beach . . . a likely story – there's only one Big Dipper Charley would recognize and that's the one in his trousers. It's obvious that Raoul and I aren't included in the invitation, so we take a bottle of wine and a couple of glasses and head for the loungers by the poolside.

'So, Ruby, what do you think of it so far?' Raoul asks me.

'I'm having the time of my life,' I tell him honestly. 'Everything's perfect – the island, the weather, the food, the company . . .'

'Yeah, my feelings exactly.'

The truth is, I fancy the pants off Raoul and I think he likes me too. We drink some more wine, a lot more wine actually and talk about Raoul's French mother and his love of rally driving and his ex-girlfriend (they broke up when she asked him to marry her and he said no). Like a lot of men, he's quite happy to talk about himself, but when it comes to asking *me* questions, he needs a bit of prompting.

Eventually, around two a.m. he suggests we turn in – we've got an early start tomorrow as we plan to start shooting before the sun gets too high in the sky. Reluctantly, I agree and we walk slowly back to our cottage. It's still warm, but there must be a slight breeze because I can hear wind chimes singing – they hang from the trees all over the Cotton House gardens. Raoul's arm brushes against mine – I'm not sure if it's accidental or not – and my heart jumps in my chest. Neither of us says a word. Here we are, at the foot of the stairs that lead to my room. I turn towards him and there's a split second when we both look right into each other's eyes and I'm thinking to myself, 'Shall I kiss him on the cheek as usual, or go for the lips?' At the very instant I decide to go for broke (nothing ventured, nothing gained is my motto), we're suddenly and brutally interrupted by the sound of hysterical giggling. We both spin round, and there's Charley and Mariah coming up the little stone path that leads to our rooms. Charley's giving a barefoot Mariah a piggyback and she's clutching a bottle of Bollinger in one French-manicured hand.

'Mariah's lost her shoes,' Charley slurs drunkenly.

'I took 'em off 'cause we went for a paddle and a big wave came and swept 'em out to sea,' she manages to say before dissolving into giggles. It's amazing how things always seem ten times funnier than they actually are when you're drunk. Suddenly, I feel incredibly sober.

'We were just turning in for the night,' says Raoul.

'Yeah, me 'n' Charl had the same idea,' says Mariah, slipping off Charley's back, but leaving one arm trailing round his shoulders.

'Well goodnight all, see you at breakfast. Charley, I need you to be ready by nine a.m. sharp, okay?' says Raoul.

'Sure thing, mate,' says Charley, unconvincingly.

'Night, Ruby,' says Raoul as he walks to the door of his room. As I walk up the stairs to my own room, I twist my head to catch a final glimpse of him, but it's too late, he's already disappeared. What I do see, however, is Charley unlocking his own door and leading Mariah inside by the hand.

Next morning, I drag myself out of bed at eight-thirty. As I get ready I think about last night. I could punch Charley – not just for spoiling the moment between me and Raoul, but also for being a two-timing little git. When I made a play for him, all those months ago, he'd only just started dating Emma, so as far as I was concerned, he was still a free agent. But now they've been seeing each other for a year, I can't believe Charley has spent the night with another woman. I mean, he adores Emma, and he's been phoning her every evening since we got here. It's not as if Mariah is a raving beauty or a fascinating conversationalist. She is persistent, however, I'll give her that.

I'm the first one to arrive at breakfast, so I order an orange juice and a bowl of granola. I'm just tucking in when Raoul arrives, looking his usual gorgeous self in long, biscuit-coloured shorts and a white T.

'How are you feeling this morning, Ruby? We hammered a good few bottles last night.'

'Oh, not bad, considering. I drank a pint of water before I went to bed last night and that usually does the trick.'

'I've taken a couple of aspirin and I'm still feeling a bit rough . . . Nothing compared to the state Charley's going to be in. He and Mariah kept me up half the night.'

'I don't need to ask what they were doing,' I say with a bitter laugh.

'They were really going at it, I thought Charley's head was going to come through the wall at one point. I wish I had his pulling power.'

When Charley eventually joins us, he's wearing a stupid smug grin. 'I can't face breakfast, so I'm gonna start loading the gear onto the *mule*,' he says. 'Mariah's doing Jessie's make-up and they're going to meet us in twenty minutes.'

Raoul goes off to help him with the equipment, and I wait for the girls. When they arrive, Jessie looks absolutely stunning in a floaty white Ghost dress over a turquoise tie-dye bikini. Mariah, who looks like death warmed up, has done a great job with Jessie's make-up – it's very natural, just a dewy foundation, a touch of mascara and some coral-coloured lip-gloss. Her hair is piled loosely on top of her head and there's a couple of small pink blooms, pilfered from the Cotton House flowerbeds, no doubt, pushed behind each ear.

'I've got a couple of changes of outfit in my bag,' she says, patting her backpack. 'I'm glad I had an early one last night. Sounds like you lot had a fun time.'

Mariah gives a self-satisfied little smirk, the stupid cow. We squeeze into the *mule* and make our way to Macaroni Beach, a beautiful stretch of golden sand, fringed by coconut palms. Raoul sets up the first shot here and Jessie takes off her white dress and walks towards the sea. Her skin has a rich golden glow after a week in the Caribbean sun and every inch of her body is smooth and toned. When Raoul is ready, Mariah moves in quickly to dust some loose powder on Jessie's face and Raoul asks her to walk in the surf at the edge of the beach, kicking up spray as she goes. By the time Raoul has photographed the third set-up – Jessie running along the beach, holding a lime green sarong out behind her like a billowing sail – the sun is blindingly high in the sky and he calls a halt to the shoot.

'Thanks Jessie – you put heart and soul into that. Maybe we could do a few more shots back at the hotel this evening, when it's cooler,' he suggests.

Jessie, who is proving to be remarkably compliant for a soap star, happily agrees, and she and I decide to spend the remainder of the afternoon lolling on the beach. Raoul and Charley need to get the camera gear back to the hotel, and Mariah wants to get her head down for a while, so Charley agrees to return for us in a couple of hours' time. Jessie and I make ourselves comfortable on our beach towels underneath a shady outcrop of palms, and take turns to plaster each other with sun-tan lotion while we chat away companionably. I think she feels pretty comfortable around me now, and she's interested to hear about life at *Wow!* and the other celebrities I've worked with. Then she asks whether she'll make the magazine cover.

'Oh definitely. You looked great out there, Jessie. The pictures are going to blow everyone's socks off,' I toady.

'I hope you're right. I really need a morale boost right now,' she says quietly.

'But things are going great for you ... you've just bought that fantastic townhouse in Wandsworth – speaking of which, we'll have to do you *at home* one of these days – and you're one of the hottest women on British TV,' I gush, loathing myself for being so disingenuous.

'But what good are material things if you haven't got someone to share them with? I mean, you're single too, Ruby, you must know what I mean.'

I know exactly what she means. But I can't afford to offer single-girl sympathies ... it's time to go in for the kill. 'But unlike you, I don't know what it's like to suffer abuse at the hands of someone I love,' I say, very gently, but looking her right in the eye.

She looks away and doesn't speak for about a minute, which is a really long time when you're counting every second. I worry that I've blown it, but then she turns back to me and says, 'Yes, and you should count yourself very lucky. It's the worst betrayal you can ever imagine.'

'Have you talked to anyone about it ... friends, a

counsellor even?' I ask, picking up the ball and running with it.

'A few people know . . . Mariah, my sister Tasha and one of the *Hayward Place* make-up artists, the one who had to cover up the bruises on my arms. But that's enough, I couldn't bear the shame of anyone else knowing.'

She's silent for a moment and then says: 'All this is strictly off the record, you do know that, don't you?'

'Of course,' I say – and I mean it. No doubt a tabloid journalist would've been wired for sound, determined to get the story by fair means or foul, but I don't operate like that. If one of my celebrity subjects asks me to keep a confidence, then I do. My job now is to persuade Jessie that her instincts are wrong, that public soul bearing really is the best option – and I'm well versed in all the arguments.

'You know, Jessie, the story's going to come out sooner or later. And it would be better told in your own words. Once the tabloids get a whiff of it – and believe me, they will, sooner or later – they'll come knocking at your door and they won't leave you alone till they've got what they want. And who knows, they may even persuade Jake to tell his side of the story, with a little financial sweetener. Can you imagine how he'll try to twist things so he comes up smelling of roses? I've seen it happen before.'

She's looking at me with big, scared eyes and I can see

she's not convinced. So I go for the second line of attack: 'I know it would take a tremendous amount of courage to speak publicly, and I appreciate how incredibly vulnerable it would make you feel, but think of all the thousands of women who are being abused by their husbands or boyfriends right now. Hearing your story might just give them the strength they need to break free, particularly if you were to give details of a woman's refuge or helpline they could contact.'

Now she looks interested. I don't think she'd considered the fact that someone else could actually benefit from her experience. So I give it one final push: 'I mean, otherwise that brute Jake Walsh is going to get off scott free. Don't you think he deserves to be named and shamed? It'll certainly be a warning to other potential girlfriends to give him a wide berth.'

'But what will people think of me when they know I let my fiancé physically assault me, not just once, but time and time again? I felt so ashamed of myself for putting up with that treatment . . . I still do.'

This is good. We've got a dialogue going, which means she's warming to the idea. 'I'm no psychologist, Jessie, but you mustn't blame yourself. You're the victim in all this. You loved the guy and he took that love and trod it into the ground. This is your chance to tell the story in your own words, to explain to people what it's really like to be in an abusive relationship. You'd have full copy approval and everything. I wouldn't write a single word without your authorization.' I stop short. 'Look, I don't want to rush you into anything . . . just think about it, okay?'

She nods, eyes downcast. I reach out and give her hand a little squeeze, and then I tell her I'm going for a dip in the sea. It'll give her time to collect her thoughts. When I come back, she's lying on her stomach, reading a John Grisham paperback. We don't talk about Jake again and soon Charley arrives to take us back to the Cotton House.

It's our last evening on the island and Jessie has agreed to do the interview before dinner. I deliberately keep things informal and relaxed by suggesting that we grab a bottle of wine from the bar and sit on the veranda outside my room. She, as usual, looks effortlessly stunning in loose-fitting taupe palazzo pants and a matching tunic – Nicole Farhi, she tells me. Her fine blonde hair is loose and perfectly straight and shiny, in contrast to my own tangled mane, which I have scraped into a passable chignon, with the help of about forty hairpins. Next to her, I feel positively frowsy in a two-year-old Jigsaw dress that's already sticking to the back of my legs. We position our padded loungers so they both face out to the ocean and the smell of charcoal comes wafting across from the hotel's little private beach, where they're firing up a barbecue for the guests. I pour us both a generous glass of Chablis and glance at my list of prepared questions. She still hasn't said if she's prepared to talk about Jake, so my game plan is to ask her lots of general questions, about behind-the-scenes life at *Hayward Place* and what skincare range she favours, before building up to the split with Jake. By warming her up first, she might just throw a few juicy crumbs my way.

In the event, I don't even make it to question number one. As soon as I switch on my dictaphone, Jessie starts to talk, and then it all comes spilling out in an unstoppable torrent of emotion with scarcely a prompting word from me.

'I met Jake in the spring of last year, at the Outlaw launch party. We hit it off straight away and by our third date, I knew I'd fallen in love. He seemed so caring, so sensitive, so unlike the other men I'd been out with. I didn't hesitate to say "yes" when he asked me to marry him after just four months and I moved into his flat the following week. Being that much older – he's got nine years on me – he seemed very protective, at least that's the way I interpreted it at first. But he became increasingly possessive, telling me I shouldn't be going clubbing now that I was a "married" woman, as he put it. Then he started on about my clothes, saying I should cover myself up more, not wear so much make-up. A couple of months after we got engaged, he hit me for the first time. It was at the flat and we were arguing about a shoot that I had agreed to do for *FHM*. It was the usual stuff, swimwear and a bit of lingerie, nothing too explicit. He said they'd make me look like a tart and people would think he didn't have any control over me. "Well," I told him, "it's my career and I think this will be good exposure for me . . . Posing for lads' mags didn't do Helen Baxendale's career any harm, did it? And what's with all this *control* stuff. I thought we were equal partners in this relationship." He went absolutely loopy, grabbed my arm and shook me really hard, screaming, "Control, control – I'll show you who's in control!" And, still holding on to me, he brought his hand crashing down on the side of my head. I was, quite literally, stunned . . . my face was stinging, my ears were ringing. He left the house without saying a word to me, and I lay on the bed crying for what seemed like hours. I made up my mind then and there to leave him, but when he came home later that night, he apologized with tears in his eyes and promised it would never happen again. He was having teething problems with one of the new club nights, he said; he couldn't bear the thought of other men ogling me in a magazine; he was frightened he'd lose me – he came up with every excuse under the sun. And I believed him . . . until it happened again.'

As she continued with her horrific tale – a catalogue of physical and verbal abuse that spanned two months, each episode more violent than the last – I could hardly believe what I was hearing. How could one human be so calculatingly cruel to another, let alone to one he professed to love? He threatened to kill himself if she left him, and she really believed him. The worst incident of abuse was also the final one. She'd returned home from a public appearance – the opening of a new feng shui bar in the West End – two hours later than the ETA she'd given him. She'd been having a good time, talking and laughing with a bunch of friends, including her older sister Tasha, and hadn't noticed the time.

'When I arrived home, all the lights were off in the flat, so I thought, "Great! He's given up waiting for me and gone to bed." I got undressed in the lounge, so I wouldn't wake him up, then went to the bathroom to take off my make-up, I *never* go to bed without doing that. I opened the bedroom door as quietly as I could. The room was dark and I was totally naked. I took three steps and suddenly there was this ear-splitting growl, like the kind of noise an angry Rottweiler would make. Jake sprang out of the shadows and knocked me to the ground with an almighty shove. As I fell, I hit my head against the metal bed frame and must've blacked out for a second. When I came to, I was lying on the floor on my back, and Jake was straddling me, pinning my arms down on either side of my body with his knees. He spat on me – I couldn't see him, he was just a shadowy outline above me, but I felt the slimy trail splatter my cheek. "You stupid little bitch. I'm going to teach you a lesson you'll never forget," he shrieked, then he grabbed my head in both his hands and started banging it on the floor. I was pleading with him to stop and struggling to get free, but it was hopeless – Jake's six foot one and fourteen stone. Just as I thought I was going to pass out again, he suddenly let my head go. Seconds later I felt a massive thwack to my jaw, and that's the last thing I remember.

'It was four-thirty a.m. when I came to, stiff and aching on the floor, still naked. My whole head was throbbing and I was terrified that Jake was still in the flat somewhere, but he'd cleared out, leaving me unconscious on the bedroom floor, not caring whether I lived or died. I slid the deadbolt on the front door, so he wouldn't be able to get back in, and went to the bathroom to clean up. I hardly recognized myself when I looked in the mirror. The left side of my face was swollen to double its usual size and my bottom lip was fat and split, and covered in a dark crust of dried blood. I had to hold onto the sink with both hands to stop myself sliding to the floor. I was shaking and crying. I knew I needed help, I couldn't carry on pretending things were okay, that I was this fairytale princess with a perfect lifestyle and the perfect boyfriend.'

Jessie called her sister who urged her to go to casualty, but she was worried someone might see her and blab to the papers. So she called her private doctor instead, who diagnosed concussion and a hairline fracture of the jaw. She spent the next three weeks recuperating in a discreet clinic, after telling *Hayward Place*'s producer she'd been involved in a car accident.

'I stayed with Tasha until I got a place of my own sorted out. For the next month, Jake bombarded me with phone calls and flowers and jewellery, but I haven't spoken to him since that night and I don't plan to speak to him ever again. Tasha tried to persuade me to report him to the police, but I refused. I couldn't bear the thought of being endlessly cross-examined and maybe having to testify in court. I don't think I'm strong enough for that. I'm only speaking out now in the hope that sharing my story will inspire other women in abusive relationships to seek help.'

When I click off my dictaphone, both of us are a little shell-shocked and for a few minutes neither one of us says a word. I ask her if she wants to have some time alone to get her head together, but she insists on going to the barbecue, saying it will help take her mind off Jake. 'I've told the story, and now I want to lay it to rest,' she says simply.

By the time we join the others on the Cotton House's beachfront lawn, Jessie appears to have regained her composure. It is, without a doubt, the most upmarket barbecue I've ever been to – the picnic tables are covered in starched cotton cloths and the whole area is lit up with dozens of flaming torches, pushed into the ground. We fill our faces with red snapper, pork 'n' red pepper kebabs and cold rice salad, all washed down with rum punch and banana daquiris. I keep shooting furtive looks at Jessie, but she seems to be bearing up just fine. She catches me looking at her sympathetically and says, 'Loosen up, Ruby; come on, let's show this stuck-up lot how to party!' The hotel has laid on a sound system, playing reggae and r 'n' b, and before long, we're all on our feet, dancing the strange and uninhibited dance of the drunk. Lorna Bennett's 'Breakfast in Bed' comes on, which is one of my favourite tunes of all time, and I start to sway in time to the bass line.

Raoul comes up behind me and starts to dance with me, and actually, he's not half bad. I couldn't bear it if he was crap. Crap dancing is, in my book, a perfectly reasonable excuse for not sleeping with someone. As we dance, we get closer and closer together, and then he reaches out one arm and curls it round the back of my neck and starts stroking the strands of hair that have escaped from my chignon, twirling them round his fingers, really gently. I move in closer still, till my groin is grazing his and I put both my arms around his waist, quite loosely. It's incredibly erotic, and I could kill the DJ when the tune ends and he puts Desmond Dekker's effing 'Israelites' on, which is far too uptempo to smooch to. Without saying another word, Raoul takes my hand and leads me away from the noise of the beach, towards the hotel gardens. And when we get to a big old cypress tree, with silent wind chimes hanging from it, he stops, takes my face in both his hands and presses his warm lips to mine. My head is swimming, I think it's the alcohol. I feel his tongue in my mouth, which induces me to wrap my arms around his shoulders and press the entire length of my body against his, to ensure maximum surface area contact. I'm delighted when I detect the hard swelling in his crotch – the feeling's obviously mutual then. After a while he pulls away gently and starts nuzzling my neck, planting hot little butterfly kisses around my collarbone and behind my ears. It's all I can do not to scream out 'Yes, yes, yes!' like I'm in some tacky *Thorn Birds*-esque drama.

After about half an hour of tonsil hockey, I suggest we get more comfy in one of the hammocks that are strung up around the Cotton House gardens. We pick one that's not overlooked by any of the accommodation, and I make a rather ill-thought-out attempt to get into it. I hitch my dress up so it just about covers my arse (thank God I'm wearing knickers, it's so hot tonight I must admit I was tempted to forgo them), then place my right knee onto the giant sling and haul myself up. Only instead of landing gracefully in the centre like a girl in a Bounty ad, I end up straddling the whole damn thing, one leg dangling uselessly on either side. Raoul practically pisses himself laughing.

'Well help me then!' I say indignantly and he manages to stop laughing for long enough to pull the hammock down on one side, so that I can dismount. I make a second, more successful, stab at it, then Raoul launches himself on top of me and we resume our snogging.

'You know I want you, don't you?' he whispers in my ear. 'You've got such a fit body. I'd love to fuck you right here in this hammock.'

What the hell, I think. This hammock is reasonably isolated and I am on holiday, after all . . .

It seems mere minutes later that I wake up in the hammock, feeling slightly stiff, with Raoul's arm jammed behind my neck. It's light and I'm just wondering what time it is, when a couple of hotel guests stroll past us, and call out a cheery 'Good morning'. Shit! They must be on their way to breakfast, which means we've spent the whole night in this string bag. I check my watch – it's eight a.m. already.

'Wake up, Raoul, it's morning,' I say, digging him in the ribs.

His long eyelashes flutter and then spring open. 'Oh my God, we're still here,' he says in a croaky voice.

'Yep, and we've got to leave for our flight in two hours' time, so we'd better get cracking.'

He sits up with such a start that the hammock lurches to one side and we both fall spilling out onto the grass below. Shit, that really hurt and I've got a raging hangover. I'm not in the mood to be lovey-dovey, so without another word I head off in the direction of my room. I'm halfway there when I hear Raoul call out my name. The soppy sod probably wants to kiss me. I'll play it cool. I turn around, hands on my hips, and shout back at him: 'Yeah?'

'You've forgotten something,' he says, and the bastard is twirling my mauve G-string around his index finger like some kind of trophy.

# SEVEN: SECRET ADMIRER

The Secret Admirer has a free afternoon and he's going to spend it in his favourite way imaginable. He's so pleased with himself for dreaming this one up; it's going to be major fun. But before the jollity can begin, a few basic precautions are in order. He reaches into his wardrobe and pulls down a cardboard box from the shelf at the top. Carrying it over to his oak dressing table, he opens the lid and removes the short, sandy-coloured wig. He places it over his clenched fist and tilts it this way and that, admiring the way the hair looks so natural – well, you get what you pay for and this baby set him back £75. He puts it down for a second and reaches for a wide-toothed comb which he uses to pull his own hair off his face, then adds a slick of grooming wax to keep it in place. He pulls the wig down over his scalp, checks in the triptych mirror that none of his own hair is poking out, then he ruffles the hairpiece with the flat of his hand so it looks more natural. Not bad at all. Next, he dons a pair of reading glasses, with fashionable rectangular frames, that he picked up from Specsavers. He smiles at his reflection, pleased with the result. A five-day growth of stubble completes his disguise. Why his own mother wouldn't recognize him if she walked past him in the street.

He's going to take the bus to Hampstead, quite a novelty for him. He rarely travels by public transport unless he's going into central London, and even then he usually takes a cab. Seated on the top deck of the number 268, as it traverses north London, he feels strangely aroused by this unfamiliar ritual. Fifteen minutes later and he arrives at his destination. Alighting from the bus, he looks left and right to get his bearings, and then sets off along Hampstead High Street, counting off the shop numbers until he finds the place, nestling in between a deli and an Italian shoe shop, just like the nice lady on the phone told him. He's spent a lot of time and energy finding the right place, one that could deliver a high-quality product that will match his exacting specifications. Just in case there's any room for confusion, he's come armed with a selection of pictures to facilitate the ordering process.

He pushes open the glass shop door and is instantly gratified by the cleanliness and general order of the place. A buxom teenage girl appears behind the counter and offers her assistance . . . how pleasing to see her crisp white overall and neat ponytail. He tells her he has an appointment with the owner and she immediately ushers him into a comfortable, light-filled office at the rear of the shop.

'Mrs Goldberg won't be a moment. May I get you a drink – cappuccino, elderflower cordial, freshly squeezed orange juice?'

'An orange juice would be great,' says the Secret Admirer, giving her a lopsided grin and enjoying her blushes. Even in this get-up, he's still a lady-killer.

After less than a minute, a middle-aged woman with dyed blonde hair and a highly unflattering wrapover dress walks into the room, carrying the orange juice, which she sets on the long low coffee table.

'Mr Domcot, good afternoon,' she says, stooping over the sofa to take his hand in a warm, firm grip. 'My name's Felicity Goldberg. You had no trouble finding us?' She's surprised that he's unaccompanied. It's very unusual to meet a lone male in her line of business . . . the woman practically always takes charge at the sensitive stage of choosing and ordering the product.

'Yes, your directions were spot on, Felicity . . . may I call you Felicity?'

'Of course, we're very informal here. We like to create a relaxed atmosphere for our clients. Now, you said you had something quite specific in mind?'

'That's right.'

He takes a deep breath . . . 'What I would like is three heart-shaped tiers in ascending size from top to bottom – one tier of carrot cake, one of vanilla cream sponge, and one of traditional fruit cake. Each tier is to be covered in pure white rolled fondant and studded with white sugar doves (six on the top tier, eight on the second and ten on the base). The whole cake must be covered in trailing green ivy leaves made of icing. And on the very top I'd like two fondant figurines – a naked, fair-skinned woman with long auburn hair that flows over one shoulder and down over her breasts and stomach, and a naked dark-haired man, with a little ivy leaf over his privates.'

Felicity Goldberg is impressed. Few clients come to her with such a clear brief for their wedding cake, especially when they haven't even had a chance to peruse her own, quite stunning, portfolio of previous triumphs.

'That sounds perfectly delightful, Mr Domcot. You and your fiancée have obviously put a great deal of thought into this . . . well, it is the most important day of your life after all!' she giggles girlishly.

'Oh this is all my own work, Felicity. It will be a complete and utter surprise to my beloved, I can assure you.'

'Well she's going to be absolutely thrilled.'

The Secret Admirer nods, basking in her obvious admiration. He reaches into the pocket of his Barbour and pulls out a handful of magazine clippings displayed in a clear plastic folder. 'I have some photographs here, which will give you an idea of the scale and design of the decorations.'

'My, you have done your homework . . . yes, these will be most useful. Now, I'm not sure when the Big Day is, but we can have the cake ready in six to eight weeks.'

'Oh no, you don't understand.' The Secret Admirer is flooded with unfamiliar panic. 'Our wedding is a very last-minute affair. I mean, I only proposed last week and the thing is . . . my fiancée is very ill . . .' He lets the unfinished sentence hang in the air, waiting for Goldberg to take the bait.

A light flush begins to grow where her dress forms a V against her chest, and spreads up her neck. She tilts her head to one side in a sympathetic gesture. 'I'm so sorry, Mr Domcot . . . I had no idea, you must forgive me.'

'Oh no, Felicity, it's my fault, I should've mentioned it sooner. It's just, it's so very difficult to talk about . . .'

She cuts him off to spare his discomfiture. 'I understand perfectly, Mr Domcot. Now, when is the wedding?'

'We'd need to take delivery no later than four weeks from now. Is there no chance you can help us? I just know you'd do a fantastic job . . . you come very highly recommended. I'd be prepared to pay extra for your trouble and I'd settle the entire bill up front, today in fact.'

'Well, that is extremely short notice – I do have a waiting list of extremely high-profile clients – but I do so want this to be the happiest day of your fiancée's life . . . very well, Mr Domcot, I'm going to pull out all the stops just this once.'

'Oh Felicity, I can't thank you enough. You've no idea how much this will mean to her. Now, if I could just give you the address for delivery . . .'

# EIGHT: GOLDEN GIRL

It's official: I am Golden Girl, the Bee's Knees, the Big Kahuna, the Mack Daddy – or should that be Mommy? Whatever. The Jessie Reynolds issue came off sale one week ago exactly, and conservative estimates by our circulation department put total sales at 650,000.

The morning of our departure from Mustique, I'd called Eva at home. It was nine-thirty on the island, but only four-thirty in London. She was a bit grumpy at first, having had her beauty sleep so rudely interrupted – and on a Saturday morning too – but she quickly forgave me. When I told her I'd got the exclusive on Jessie's break-up with Jake, she was delighted. When I told her the reason they split she was fucking ecstatic. Right there and then she made the decision to drop the following Saturday's cover story – the Las Vegas wedding of a B-list pop star to a C-list kids' TV presenter – in favour of *The Secret Heartache of Jessie Reynolds*.

When we landed at Gatwick, a motorcycle courier was

waiting to collect Raoul's undeveloped film and rush it to the Soho photo lab where it would be processed into transparencies. I said a hasty goodbye to Raoul, Charley and the girls in the arrivals hall and gave Jessie strict instructions to stay by the phone at home, so she could give me instantaneous copy approval. Then my luggage and I caught a black cab directly to the office where Eva, the chief sub and art director were waiting for the goods. I'd already transcribed the copy in longhand on the flight from Barbados – I bitterly regretted my decision not to take the office laptop with me – so all I had to do was type it up in Q & A format, put it in some semblance of order, compose an intro and we were rolling. My body was absolutely knackered after more than twelve hours of travelling, but my brain was running on pure adrenaline, so it took only a couple of hours to hammer out the story on my iMac.

Eva was over the moon when she read all four thousand hard-hitting, tear-jerking words. She actually came over to my desk and put an arm round my shoulders in an uncharacteristic display of affection. 'I knew you were good, Ruby – but not this good,' she said with a massive smile that showed off all her orthodontically bleached teeth. 'This story is going to run and run – mark my words.' There was still the little matter of copy approval to secure. I called Jessie at home to say the story was on the fax, and then it was just a question of waiting. I must admit I was a little apprehensive in case she'd had second thoughts about baring her soul in public, but I needn't have worried – she called me back within the hour. 'It's great, Ruby,' she told me. 'Jake will shit himself when he reads it.'

My words were red hot, but we still needed good photos to sell the story and when the transparencies arrived in the office in the leather-gloved hand of a sweaty courier, we all crowded round the lightbox in nervous anticipation. Angela ripped open the brown hardbacked envelope and the trannies came tumbling out onto the lightbox. Quickly, she spread them out and five heads went down to examine them. I let out an audible gasp as I saw what he'd done . . . there were beautiful beach babe shots, mixed with local island colour and served with a dash of melancholia: the perfect complement to my words.

'This is good stuff,' murmured Eva, almost under her breath. 'We'll use Raoul Johnson again.'

The story ran across sixteen pages and Eva even awarded me a photo by-line, an exceedingly rare honour. Thankfully, Raoul had taken a passable shot of me standing beside the Cotton House pool, when I was standing in for Jessie one time and, cropped to shoulder height, it didn't look half bad – at least my hair was relatively tamed, I must've just washed it. 'Interview by Ruby Lake,' it said under the photo – it was a line I'd earned hundreds of times, but on this occasion it gave me an extra sense of satisfaction.

For the cover, Eva selected a suitably moody shot of an unsmiling Jessie leaning against a coconut palm and

looking into the middle distance. The accompanying coverline read: 'The real reason Jessie dumped Jake: "He
said he loved me – and then he beat me up." ' Not that
these words were ever actually spoken by Jessie, you
understand, but we frequently use a little artistic licence
on the cover in order to enhance a story's dramatic effect.

When I reappeared in the office on the following
Tuesday (Eva had given me the Monday off as a reward),
most of my colleagues had seen the proofs and were full
of congratulations. Ali was especially pleased for me and
after work she took me off to Davy's Wine Bar in Canary
Wharf for a celebratory bottle of Rioja and a shared
bowl of potato skins. Even Adrian slunk over to my desk
to deliver a backhanded compliment – well, even *he*
couldn't ignore my journalistic coup. 'Well done, Ruby,'
he said through gritted teeth. 'I guess you got lucky, huh?'

'Luck had nothing to do with it, Adrian,' I told him
peremptorily. 'It was timing, persuasion and journalistic
skill.' Three qualities he knows nothing about, having
spent his entire career at *Wow!* sitting on his fat backside,
endlessly shuffling flatplans.

Every one of the tabloids picked up the story, not to
mention two of the broadsheets. Jessie got plenty of
sympathy and not one columnist criticized her for not
leaving Jake sooner – he, predictably, got a complete
pasting. In fact Jake went to ground shortly after tangling
with a paparazzo who was staking out his flat. The
shutterbug got a bloody nose for his troubles but it was
more than worth it – his photographs of an enraged Jake

walking towards the camera, shaking his fist, earned him a hefty fee and a page-three lead in the *Sun*.

Second rights on my interview went to the *Daily Mail*'s *Femail* section. Usually, newspapers will rewrite *Wow!*'s copy in their own house style and run it with a staff writer's by-line. But in this instance, Eva made it a condition of sale that they reproduced *Wow!*'s front cover, used the copy verbatim and gave me a credit, which was pretty nice of her. It'll make an impressive addition to my portfolio.

And I wasn't the only beneficiary. The Women's Aid Helpline number was printed at the end of my story and they reported a forty per cent increase in calls during the week the magazine was on sale. Jessie was also invited to launch one of the charity's fundraising appeals, although she has yet to commit herself. She did, however, participate in a Richard and Judy phone-in on the subject of domestic violence – during which agony aunt Denise Robertson praised her for her courage in speaking out. Even *Hayward Place* has reaped the benefits – viewing figures are currently up by half a million and show no sign of dropping.

I doubt if Jessie and I will ever be what you'd call 'friends' – we haven't really got that much in common, but after the Richard and Judy thing she sent me a nice bouquet of flowers at the office, with a note thanking me for 'everything you've done' and urging me to keep in touch. She added that, in the wake of all the publicity, the police had asked if she wanted to press charges – she declined.

There was only one fly in the proverbial ointment, as far as I was concerned. Three days after the magazine went on sale, I received a big, heart-shaped box of champagne truffles at work, together with a *Congratulations!* greeting card. The hand-written message inside read:

Well done precious Ruby! Your Jessie Reynolds story was sublime. Don't forget ... I'm watching you
Yours forever,
A Secret Admirer

I gave the chocolates to Ali, telling her they were from a grateful PR, chucked the card in the bin, and phoned ChocExpress to see what details they could give me. They proved to be singularly unhelpful – the chocolates had been ordered via their website and they weren't at liberty to divulge the sender's name or credit card details. The 'I'm watching you' bit did prey on my mind and I debated going to the police but I didn't think they'd consider sending a box of chocolates as threatening behaviour. You see, I don't even have *preciousruby.com* as evidence any more. When I tried typing in the URL, I got the message: *the specified server could not be found*, which means the site no longer exists. I tried many times over a period of days, but it's gone for good. I resolved to try and put the Secret Admirer out of my mind and now I'm hoping he's over his infatuation.

As for the other man in my life . . . In the two weeks since we got back from Mustique, Raoul and I have been on a handful of dates, which have varied in success from mediocre to absolutely crap. I'm meeting up with Amy tonight – I haven't seen her since Kettners, but I've kept her up to date with my flagging love life via email – so I'll see what she's got to say. Mind you, she goes out with losers too, so she's not particularly well qualified to dispense advice.

When I arrive at Mezzo, Amy is already there, sitting at the bar on a high chrome stool and being chatted up by some dork in a suit. She looks relieved to see me and tells her escort, 'Here's my friend now . . . well thanks for keeping me company. See you later.' The guy slithers off, looking somewhat peeved at being ousted. Amy has that effect on men. She's not what you'd call a classic beauty, but she's certainly striking with her flawless porcelain skin, big dark eyes and glossy black elbow-length curls. And she's looking particularly foxy tonight in her pencil skirt and strappy Jimmy Choo sandals (she's something of a shoe connoisseur, our Amy).

'Hi hon, sorry I'm late. The central line was up the spout as usual,' I say, kissing her on the cheek.

'No worries. Do you want a drink here or shall we go to our table?' she says, draining her vodka-tonic in one mouthful.

'I'm starving. Let's go eat.'

# WOW!

Our chic black-clad waitress leads us to a corner table. The tables in Mezzo are positioned ridiculously close together but thankfully there's no one either side of us, so Amy and I can talk freely. There's nothing worse than other people listening in on your private conversation. We order a bottle of house white and get down to business. Amy, a die-hard *Hayward Place* fan, wants to hear all about Mustique and Jessie Reynolds – did she have cellulite, was her tan real or fake, did she get her boobs out on the beach? I get all that out of the way as quickly as I can, so that I can move on to Raoul.

'So what's he look like, this Row-oool,' she says, with a mouthful of goats' cheese salad.

'Imagine the dark good looks of a young Sacha Distel, combined with George Clooney's sexy smile and the tight arse of Matt Damon.'

'Sounds dee-vine. So what's the problem?'

'You know, Amy, when we were in Mustique he seemed so charming and attentive, but now we're back in the harsh reality of London, he's suddenly metamorphosed into a boring, self-obsessed git. He offered to take me to the launch party for a new exhibition of war photography at the National Portrait Gallery and then spent the whole night talking to his photographer mates, while I wandered around on my own, availing myself of the complimentary kir royales and canapés. He poo-pooed my offer of free tickets for the Café de Paris, saying it was terribly passé, and dragged me off to the Titanic Bar, where he proceeded to chat up the leggy blonde barmaid. I got quite excited when he invited me to a dinner party at the home of his architect friend, which recently earned a spread in the *Guardian*'s *Space* supplement. The night proved to be crushingly boring and all Raoul's poncy friends treated me like something the cat had dragged in. "Oh, you work for *Wow!* magazine . . . I think my cleaning lady reads that," said the host's wife. I could've slapped the snotty bitch.'

'What about the sex? You can overlook a few personality defects if a man's good in bed.'

'I can't criticize his technique, but he's got this thing about doing it in public places. I thought that hammock thing was a crazy, spontaneous, drunken one-off, but no, he'd much rather do it up a dark alley or on a car bonnet or sneak into a Royal Park after hours than do it in a bed like normal people. He even tried to persuade me to shag in a phone booth, but I didn't fancy having my bare arse cheeks pressed up against a cold perspex window.'

'Sounds quite exciting to me,' says Amy with a naughty smile.

'Believe me, the novelty of novelty sex soon wears off. I've given it my best shot and I'm afraid that Raoul just isn't the man for me. There's no point flogging a dead horse – particularly when I'm going to have to work with the man. I've given it serious thought and I think we should just call it quits.'

'Well it looks like you don't need my advice then. You're probably right, no use making do with second best.'

I know she's right, but at 28 I'm tired of playing the field. I want a full-blown, all absorbing, white-hot love affair that will last a lifetime. Is that too much to ask? As our main course arrives – fettuccine for me, herb-crusted cod for her – I quiz Amy about her own love life, vainly hoping her relationship with Toby is on the wane. No such luck.

'Things are going really well. In fact now that Toby's bought his own place, I might even move in with him.' Amy's pseudo-boyfriend has just bought a pseudo-loft in Hackney – it's got the high ceilings, porthole windows and galleried bedroom, according to Amy, but lacks the industrial authenticity of a genuine loft, having only been built last year.

'Oh, so you've discussed it then.'

'Not as such . . . but I'm sure it's just a matter of time before he asks me.'

I remember the first time I met Toby, six months ago. Amy invited us all to check out her latest pull – there was Simon and Katie, Jo, plus a couple of people from Amy's office. I took an almost immediate dislike to Toby. For starters, I didn't like the way he seemed so at home in her flat (they'd been seeing each other for only a matter of days when this soirée took place) – telling us all to make ourselves comfortable on Amy's Conran Shop suede cubes and taking it upon himself to change the CD selection without consulting anyone else. Cooking isn't Amy's strong point and she had prepared her staple dish, bless her: vegetarian lasagne, rocket salad and garlic bread, followed by Wall's Vienetta (I swear I saw Toby recoil in horror when she brought it out – no doubt he was hoping for a more fashionable zabaglione or tarte au citron). During the meal itself Toby bored us all to tears with a painfully detailed account of his recent trip to Iceland for a photo shoot with Bjork – okay, so it wasn't exactly boring, but he didn't have to go on about how he and the elfin princess were now bezzie mates. I was tempted to tell him I had an invitation to Christopher Biggins' 50th burning a hole in my handbag, but I didn't think he'd appreciate the irony. After dinner, he insisted on smoking a cigar (a Havana to be precise – well, it would have to be, wouldn't it?) and tried to impress us by letting his Paul Smith 50% discount card accidentally-on-purpose fall out of his wallet. But I mustn't be negative . . . no doubt he's got some redeeming features or Amy wouldn't give him the time of day. I'm just not sure what they are.

'Any action on the Secret Admirer front?' says Amy, pulling me back to the present.

'He sent me a box of chocolates and a card last week, congratulating me on the Jessie Reynolds story.'

'Why don't you just call up Cranky Kramer and tell him to stop hassling you – or ring his agent and threaten to go to the police?'

'Well actually I don't know that Kramer definitely *is* the Secret Admirer.'

'Come on Ruby, it's gotta be him. It's his *modus operandi*, isn't it? First flowers and now chocolates; he's obviously a very traditional kind of guy.'

'Well, maybe you're right. But I want a normal boy-friend, not a complete weirdo or someone who always wants to take me up against a wall.'

'Listen, why don't you come out with us on Friday night. Toby's having a housewarming this weekend and there'll be loads of single guys there – journalists, PR, fashion types, you'll be able to take your pick.'

'Okay, thanks Amy, that sounds good.' I seriously doubt there will be anyone at Toby's precious party who isn't an A-list tosser, but still, a party is a party. And it sure beats sitting at home, watching after-the-pub TV and polishing off a microwaved sticky toffee pudding (the box says 'serves 4' but what that actually means is four small marsupial portions or two decent-sized adult helpings).

# NINE: SECRET ADMIRER ♥

The Secret Admirer is mightily annoyed. It's the third evening this week he's paid a visit to his beloved, and he's yet to catch a single solitary glimpse of her. Her social life must be in overdrive. *He* can show her a good time, no doubt about that. Once she finally recognizes him as her soulmate, they can spend blissful evenings cosied up, just the two of them, they won't need anyone else, he'll provide all the love, support and entertainment she could ever wish for.

Her car is parked outside, which means she'll be getting the tube home. He's sitting in his own vehicle, which is parked on a side street, so he'll be able to see her as she walks along the main estate road. It's already eleven-fifteen, but he'll give her another half an hour, she's worth waiting for.

Eleven-twenty-two and his heart leaps in his chest. Here she comes, he knew she wouldn't let him down a third time. She's alone and although the road is well lit, it's totally deserted. She really should have thought ahead and got a cab from Rotherhithe underground; anyone could accost her or pull her into a waiting car, no one would hear her muffled screams. He gives it ten minutes, so he's sure she'll be inside the apartment, and then he gets out of his car, making sure he closes the door quietly. He doesn't bother activating the alarm, best to be as inconspicuous as possible. After pulling the brim of his Nike baseball cap well down over his face, he makes his way quickly to his usual spot by the privet hedge. She's switched on the table light in the living room and is squatting on a brown corduroy beanbag, hunched over something on the floor. What is she up to? It must be an intricate task because he can see her hands working away at some unseen object. When she sits back up, he sees that she has been rolling a fat cigarette – it must be a joint because he knows she doesn't usually smoke. She puts it in her mouth and then gets up to retrieve a box of matches from the kitchen counter. He watches as she retakes her place on the beanbag, lights up, inhales deeply and leans back, throwing her head back as she exhales . . . yes, that's definitely a joint. He sometimes partakes himself, and witnessing her enjoyment evokes the taste of the bitter smoke and the way it curls satisfyingly around his mouth.

Suddenly, she's on her feet and walking towards the window. Just in time, the Secret Admirer scrambles round to the other side of the privet hedge on all fours, and luckily, there's no one on the river path to witness his curious behaviour. Ah, she's drawing up the sash window ... she obviously doesn't want to be enveloped in a smoky fug, sensible girl. For ten minutes or so, he is quite content to just study her – the way she runs her fingers through her beautiful hair, raking out the tangles, the careful way she dabs the end of her joint into a huge silver ashtray. Wonder if smoking makes her horny, it certainly has that effect on him. She's back on her feet now and walking towards the door. Then she switches off the side light and seconds later he sees the glow of her bedroom light, muted by the thick curtains. He'd already clocked that they were shut, she must've been running late when she left for work this morning. She'll be flavour of the month in that office right now. He'd felt a warm glow of pride when he saw her Jessie Reynolds cover story ... What a talented writer she is. It must take real skill to tease a painful story like that out of someone. He'd bought two copies of the magazine that week. One copy had been carefully filed alongside the others that displayed any of Ruby's work; as for the second, he'd cut out her photograph that had appeared on the first page of the article. It was only a small picture, no more than two inches square, but how excited he'd been when he spotted it. It has made a splendid addition to his album, which already contains half a dozen carefully clipped pictures of his precious girl at various showbiz parties and awards ceremonies. He always pores over each and every spread in the magazine that boasts her by-line, just in case she's there, smiling shyly on the edge of the frame.

# WOW!

Even though his beloved is now out of sight, the Secret Admirer remains outside until her bedroom light goes off. After that joint she'll doubtless be asleep in minutes. He likes to be close to her, he sees himself as her guardian angel, protecting her from evil forces. It's gone midnight now, so he'd better depart, he has an early start tomorrow. As he gets up and brushes the earth from his knees, he realizes that in her stoned haze, she has forgotten to shut the living room window. Silly girl! An intruder could easily enter in the dark of the night and do her some harm. He must protect his precious Ruby at all costs. He looks left and right to make sure no one is in sight, and then walks over to the apartment, silent in his New Balance trainers. He reaches up and slowly pulls down the window – he can't lock it shut, obviously, but at least he can make sure it *looks* shut. There, she'll be safe enough now. 'Goodnight, precious Ruby,' he whispers as he walks away.

The Secret Admirer has lain awake half the night. Driving home from Rotherhithe, he had the most amazing flash of genius, a wonderful idea that, if it comes off, will bring him even closer to the object of his desire. Now that it's ten a.m. he can at last embark on his daring mission. He checks his rucksack for the fifteenth time to make sure he hasn't forgotten anything . . . mobile phone, cotton gloves, spiral-bound notepad, pens × 2, plastic food bags and wire ties, cardboard folder, a disposable camera with flash – yes, it's all present and correct.

He's nervous as he drives through the Rotherhithe Tunnel, not because of the boldness of the act itself, but because of the possibility that the way might be barred. 'Please, please, please God,' he says out loud as he approaches the highway that serves the waterside estate. He parks in his usual spot outside Clipper Court, then opens the rucksack so he can retrieve the mobile. Scrolling through the list of numbers, he finds Ruby's pre-programmed digits and presses *call* – his phone is automatically set to mask his number, so it can't be tracked via 1471. He hears five rings and then it switches to answer-phone; perfect. Then, as an extra precaution, he calls her work number – it's on voicemail: 'Hi, this is Ruby Lake. I'm in conference all morning, but I'll be back at my desk by one p.m., so please leave a message and I'll get back to you.' Good, she's safely at work and not likely to return imminently. He grabs the rucksack, locks his vehicle and tries to walk as nonchalantly as possible towards the river path. It's weird being here in daylight hours, makes him feel kind of vulnerable. The path is unexpectedly busy and he has to sit patiently on one of the small wooden benches, while three joggers, two businessmen and a woman with a buggy and a toddler in tow go by. He should have bought a news-paper, it would have given him something to do, helped him blend in.

After a full fifteen minutes, the coast is finally clear. The Secret Admirer has rehearsed this moment a thou-sand times in the past ten hours. He stands up, slings the rucksack over a shoulder and slips on the black cotton gloves. Then he walks purposefully towards the rear of Galleon Place, scanning the dozens of windows as he does so ... no sign of a single nosy parker, thank goodness. There's still no one approaching on the path, so he marches confidently past the privet hedge and across the lawn – best to look as if he belongs here. He's right up to the living-room window now – one quick look left and right and then he grasps the central piece of wood that runs vertically through the pane of the sash window and yanks it firmly upwards. It glides open in a beautiful, effortless motion – a moment he will re-live again and again later on, but now he must act quickly. The window ledge is so low, all he has to do is pull aside the voile and step through it, but as he does so, his foot catches the ledge and for one heart-stopping moment he fears he's going to slam noisily against the pane. Somehow he manages to correct his balance just in time and tumbles, rather painfully, through the open window. Quickly, he picks himself up, closes the window and rearranges the flimsy curtain. His heart is racing and his mouth is dry and dusty, but he forces himself to stand pressed against the wall, quite motionless, for a full five minutes, until he's quite sure no one has seen him.

Now he can relax. He turns around to face the kitchen and breathes deeply, inhaling the scent of his sweet girl's home. At last he's reached the inner sanctum, the Shangri-La, the seventh heaven and he couldn't be happier. He's given himself thirty-five minutes max and then he must be out of here. He sets his rucksack down on the wooden laminate floor next to the beanbag – ah, so it's brown leather, not corduroy after all. He can't resist reaching out a hand to stroke the hollowed-out bit, where her bottom has been . . . lucky beanbag, he thinks to himself. He walks slowly around the room, drinking in her unique style. The room is pretty neat and tidy, although last night's ashtray still sits on the reclaimed-wood coffee table, next to a blue colour-washed mug and matching cereal bowl. She was obviously in a rush this morning, no wonder she forgot all about that window, probably forgot she even opened it last night – she would've had a few drinks and there was the joint too. The Secret Admirer walks over to make a closer inspection. A half-inch butt lies in the silver tray and the roach end is branded with a cinnamon-coloured lipstick stain. He picks it up carefully between forefinger and thumb and studies the coloured ring. Now *that* would make a wonderful addition to his collection – his very own lipstick kiss. He debates the pros and cons of removing it and finally decides that if he takes the empty ashtray over to the kitchen counter, which is next to the swing bin, she'll probably think she emptied it herself. He does this and then places his charred prize in one of the plastic sandwich bags, which he seals with a wire tie.

The Secret Admirer is keen to discover Ruby's taste in music, so he goes over to the stereo system, which is all Nad and Pioneer – nice stuff – and her collection of CDs, which are arranged in smart black leather storage boxes.

He's so glad she hasn't got one of those hideous vertical stacking systems that he finds so objectionable. Rifling through the CDs, he finds lots of soul, r 'n' b and reggae as well as early Tom Jones and Andy Williams too, funny thing that she is. He's more of a jazz man himself, but still it will be fun educating Ruby in the delights of his heroes, Coleman and Mingus, then they'll be real soulmates.

He crosses to the other side of the room and spends a few minutes studying the row of black and white industrial photographs that lines one wall – a set of smoke stacks, a huge man-made dam, a pile of railway girders. He finds them very appealing, he knew she was a girl with taste and individuality. Underneath the photos is a long, low bookcase that runs the entire length of the wall. He spends a few minutes browsing and recognizes a few fashionable names . . . Marian Keyes, Jane Green, Adele Parks. On top of the bookcase, next to a set of assorted-size white church candles, are two tickets for a football game. This Sunday's Arsenal v. Chelsea match, kick-off at three p.m. He doesn't have her down for a football fan, a friend must have persuaded her to go, or perhaps they were freebies – he knows that journalists get all sorts of perks.

He moves to the kitchen – he's curious to know what kind of diet she has, to familiarize himself with the foods which nourish that precious body. The fridge looks pretty bare – a small oblong of Emmental, a couple of bio yoghurts, a nearly full carton of skimmed milk, a punnet of cherry tomatoes and half a lemon. The cupboards are similarly spartan – lots of interesting-looking herbs and spices, rice, pasta, a massive 750g box of Frosties and not much else. In her line of work, she probably eats out a lot.

The Secret Admirer feels a shiver of excitement as he spies a packet of photographs on top of the fridge. He takes down the paper envelope, removes a set of glossy prints, and goes through them one by one, careful to keep them in their original order. They look like holiday snaps, somewhere Caribbean judging by the palm trees and the golden sandy beaches, and it looks like a work trip – that must be the photographer because there's a pile of camera gear next to him. And there's Jessie Reynolds, so it must be the Mustique job – she's a looker and no mistake, that dress is virtually see-through. He gets to the next print and his jaw drops: Ruby. In a bikini. Basking in the sun. How vulnerable she looks and how beautiful too. He's never seen her thighs before, or her tummy, and there they are, displayed just for him. He's got to have this one for his collection. If she realizes it's missing, she'll probably think she's mislaid it. He carries it to his rucksack and lays it carefully on the floor while he gets out the cardboard folder. He slips the photo inside, returns the folder to the bag and takes out a couple of the sandwich bags, the notebook and a blue ballpoint, putting them in his jeans pocket for safekeeping.

The bathroom is his next port of call. As he pushes open the door, he is pleased to see that the small windowless room is scrupulously clean. If there's one trait he can't bear in a woman, it's slovenliness. The walls, tiles and suite are white and the floor is covered in a pretty mosaic of Mediterranean blues and greens – that wouldn't have been cheap, he thinks to himself. All the accessories – toothbrush holder, soap dish, towel rail and so on – are a bright polished chrome, and a white wall-mounted cabinet boasts the usual girlie assortment of cleansers, moisturizers and exfoliants, together with a quite staggering array of hair products . . . conditioning treatments and serums and volumizing sprays – no wonder her hair is so lustrous. The Secret Admirer unscrews the lid of a Trevor Sorbie Fizz Control shampoo – mmm, that smells nice. He closes his eyes for a second, imagining holding Ruby in his arms and pressing his face into her abundant hair . . . heaven! It reminds him of a special task he must perform, so reluctantly he returns the shampoo to the cabinet and makes his way to the bedroom.

My oh my, what a pretty boudoir, very feminine. He likes the soft yellow walls and the seagrass matting and the cream appliquéd duvet cover. That bed looks very comfy . . . yes, the mattress is exceedingly firm, almost orthopaedic, exactly what he would have chosen himself; he and Ruby have so much in common. He picks up a pair of discarded pyjama bottoms that are draped over the purple, velvet-covered chair in the corner. They're very sweet with a small pink rosebud design – he checks the label: Knickerbox, size 10–12, 100% cotton. He rubs the soft fabric against his cheek and catches a whiff of washing powder. Then he spies a small silver filing cabinet, doubling as a bedside table. He tries the first drawer but it won't budge, then the second drawer – locked too. Damn, she must have some pretty interesting papers in there – a birth certificate, say, and maybe a passport too – he could have a lot of fun with those.

Now, where is the hairbrush? He looks around until he sees it sitting on top of the white-painted chest of drawers and, joy of joys, it is thick with wavy red hairs. He carefully pulls out about half the long strands and transfers them to one of the plastic bags; it's nice to feel he now owns a piece of her. There's a bottle of Paloma Picasso perfume next to the brush and he sprays a small amount on the underside of his wrist; it smells warm and spicy. He takes out the notebook and writes down the name, he'll have to buy some of that, so he can evoke Ruby's presence even when he's alone.

There are four deep drawers to explore and the Secret Admirer pulls open the top one. It's full of panties – lots of cotton G-strings, half a dozen pairs of big sensible pants (probably the ones she uses for 'that' time of the month) and a couple of pairs of silky camiknickers – these must be her pulling knickers, the ones she'll ease over her peachy bottom when she has a hot date. He doesn't want to think about that, but still he can't resist stroking the delicate material, and while he's at it, he checks the size – 10–12, like the pyjamas. Drawer two houses bras of all kinds, soft cotton flower-sprigged ones, white lacy ones, flesh-coloured sheer ones, a padded Wonderbra (she certainly doesn't need any help in *that* department). He picks out a particularly fetching number in midnight-blue satin and fishes around for the little white label – Oscar de la Renta and 34C. He enters the details in his little notebook.

Checking his Accurist dive watch, the Secret Admirer sees that there are only ten minutes remaining out of his allotted thirty-five, so he pushes the drawers closed, feeling a slight twinge of regret that he hasn't explored the contents of drawers three and four, then returns to the living room. He retrieves the disposable camera from his rucksack and quickly, but methodically, walks around each room taking shots – so he'll have a visual reminder of his precious girl's habitat. In the bedroom, he remembers that he didn't check out the walk-in wardrobe. He opens the right-hand door and a shudder goes through him at the sight of the row of leather shoes and boots lined up neatly on the floor inside. There's no time to inspect them, unfortunately, so he must content himself with a few snapshots, including a close-up of the black knee-high boots.

There, it's all done. He checks to make sure he has all his equipment safely in the rucksack, then ducks back out of the living room window, not forgetting to close it behind him. He just hopes she'll spot it's unlocked and make it secure again – she certainly won't suspect an intruder, he hasn't left a single trace of his presence, he even picked up the dead leaves he'd carried through to the bedroom on the sole of his shoe. What a successful mission! Driving home, he feels quite exhilarated at the thought of the trophies he has collected. It won't be long now, not long at all . . .

# TEN: AT HOME

The day is Friday, the location is super-exclusive Belsize Park, the job is an *at home* with quiz show supremo Stevo Hollis and his actress wife Jasmine Leigh. The couple are introducing *Wow!* readers to their firstborn, three-month-old Kestrel – *Kes* being Stevo's favourite film of all time (at least it wasn't *Terminator*). This will be the first time Raoul and I have seen each other since I phoned him to say that I really didn't think our relationship was going anywhere and why didn't we call it a day. He was in total agreement, which I found rather annoying. I would have preferred it if he'd put up a bit of a fight. Anyway, it's over, and that's the main thing.

When I arrive at the couple's home – a four-storey townhouse with off-road parking in a quiet, leafy street – I rap on the front door using the highly polished brass knocker and am surprised when it is opened by Stevo himself and not some flunkey.

'With *that* head of hair, you've got to be Ruby!' he

exclaims, making an expansive gesture with his arms. 'Come in, come in, the others are in the conservatory.' The conservatory isn't one of those pokey plastic out-houses you see advertised in the back of the Sunday supps, but a splendid light-filled dome with stained-glass windows, a six-foot ornamental fountain and enough tropical foliage to give Kew Gardens a run for its money.

I see a girl with a light meter round her neck who must be Raoul's assistant for the day, Shelley. I know he wanted Charley, but he'd already been booked by T.K. Stead for a *Marie Claire* job in the south of France, the jammy sod. Hovering by the door is a slender, full-lipped twentysomething with a baby in her arms, who intro-duces herself as Consuela, the nanny, and behind her, in the garden, is Raoul. He looks pretty hot in Levi's and a white T-shirt that shows off the remnants of his Mustique tan. We exchange polite hellos and Raoul gets down to business straightaway without bothering with any small talk.

'I thought I'd start here, with a shot of Jasmine and Kestrel – it's nice and bright and the giant yucca will make a good backdrop. What do you think?'

'Yeah, whatever,' I say, rather pleased with my display of indifference.

'Jasmine's just upstairs, getting changed, she'll be down in a minute,' says Stevo. 'Why don't I show you round the house?'

We set off on a guided tour of the luxuriously appointed home and Stevo shows off the six bedrooms, gym, mini cinema, indoor pool and basement granny flat, which is home to Consuela.

'We moved here last year, soon after we got married. We love Belsize Park – Les Dennis is just down the road, you know,' says Stevo, as he shows off a rather nifty little gadget that draws back the shelves of fake books in the master bedroom to reveal an enormous wide-screen TV with Dolby surround-sound.

'Really?' I say, feigning interest. There's only one thing I hate more than a name-dropper and that's a celebrity name-dropper. Equally bad in my book are celebrities who have pictures of themselves with their celebrity mates dotted around the house like trophies. It's funny, but Joan Collins is the face I see most often in those photos, I guess she must know a lot of people. Unfortunately, there's no doubting that Stevo and Jasmine are very well connected. Despite his inane grin and tonic suits, Stevo is more than a pretty-boy TV host – he is also the creator and producer of *Name Your Price*, which has consistently topped the TV ratings in the two years since its inception and is now syndicated in no less than eight countries. After humble beginnings in a Tower Hamlets council estate Stevo is now, to put it bluntly, rolling in it – and the well-bred Jasmine provides the perfect foil for his cheeky East End geezer persona. The porcelain-skinned, raven-haired daughter of a Berkshire property magnate, Jasmine (Jazz to her friends) was a competition-level show-jumper before she won a place at RADA. I must admit she's a bloody good actress, with a couple of solid drama serials and a highly acclaimed Brit-flick, playing Jude Law's love interest, under her belt.

By the time Stevo and I arrive back at the conservatory, Raoul has finished shooting mother and child and Shelley is struggling to move the halogen lights on their six-foot stands through to the kitchen for shot number two, exposing about a foot of bare, toned midriff as she does so. I watch as Raoul comes up behind her – he's got a silly smirk on his face and it looks as if he's staring right at her impossibly small arse, but surely even he wouldn't be that crass – and offers to give her a hand. 'Thanks babe,' she says. 'Babe' . . . don't tell me those two are having a relationship already. It's only a week since I dumped him. But hey, what do I care? She's welcome to him.

Jasmine looks exceedingly pissed off – maybe it's because Baby Kestrel (it's a boy, in case you were wondering) is starting to get grizzly. She hands him over to the pouting Consuela and goes upstairs to sponge milky vomit off her Voyage cardie.

'Everything okay?' I ask Raoul.

'Hard going,' he says, once the others are out of earshot. 'The baby cries every time the flash goes off and Jasmine's nerves are beginning to get a little frayed. I also sense a bit of tension between Mum and Dad – they've barely said a word to each other since I arrived and I've seen her giving him a couple of dark looks. That's why I decided to start with her and the baby . . . give the atmosphere a chance to thaw.'

# WOW!

This shoot was going to be a barrel of laughs then. New baby *at homes* are often the most tricky of all, as the 'proud' parents try in vain to make junior smile for the camera, or even just to make it keep its eyes open. And as Jasmine and Stevo apparently have daggers drawn, things might get a little more fraught than usual, which won't make our job any easier.

Jasmine reappears, minus the cardie, and I see her nostrils flare when she clocks what Stevo's wearing.

'Tell me you're not going to be photographed wearing *that*,' she says, venomously.

'I thought you liked me in this suit. It's the one I wore to the Davro christening, you said it made me look distinguished,' he says, opening his arms and looking down at his wine-coloured crushed velvet threads in a gesture of wounded male pride.

'I was being tactful. You look like a genetically modified aubergine – besides which, it's far too dressy. It's a kitchen shot for chrissakes, we're supposed to look relaxed, informal. Get upstairs and change – the black Armani jeans and a polo shirt – and be quick about it, I don't want to be here all day.'

Stevo opens his mouth and narrows his eyes like he's about to fire a retort, but he looks at me, Raoul and Shelley all watching this scene of matrimonial disharmony being played out, and clearly thinks better of it.

'Right then, my sweet,' he says, in the manner of Basil Fawlty addressing a particularly trying Sybil, adding to

Raoul, 'Won't be a minute, mate,' before disappearing upstairs.

We all stand there, feeling rather uncomfortable, and Jasmine doesn't bother offering any sort of jokey aside to lighten the mood – in fact, she looks rather pleased with herself. In a few minutes, a suitably casual Stevo returns and Raoul begins to orchestrate shot number two.

'Okay Stevo, can you stand with your back to the sink please? That's right, just turn your upper body a little more towards camera . . . great. Now Jasmine, you sit at the kitchen table, that chair on the end please, and can we have Kestrel on your knee?'

Consuela obligingly hands over the sprog, who's wearing a Dalmatian-print babygro, complete with hood and ears, poor little bugger.

'Stevo, cross your legs at the ankle and fold your arms loosely. Now look across at Jasmine and the baby with a big, big smile and Jasmine, turn Kestrel to face me and then you look down at him, but try and keep your chin up. That's it. Bit more of a smile, Stevo, like you're really happy to be a dad . . . lovely, keep that position . . . just a few more seconds . . . and relax.'

Two hours later and we've only got three shots in the bag. Kestrel, sadly, has not inherited any of his parents' star qualities. He's a singularly unattractive baby who has yet to shed the blotchy, frog-like appearance of the newborn and he definitely doesn't like the camera. His little face crumples in protest every time Raoul peers through the lens. Jasmine, meanwhile, is becoming increasingly neurotic. 'I don't know what's the matter with him, he was fine yesterday,' she keeps saying defensively. This is going to be a long old day.

We make a collective decision to break for lunch in the vain hope that a short nap will give Kestrel a slightly sunnier disposition. Jasmine trots off to warm a couple of ciabattas in the oven. The question of lunchtime hospitality is always a delicate one when you're doing an *at home*. Typically, we're pushed for time, so in an ideal world, the interviewee(s) would lay out a few sarnies and a bottle of fizzy water, nothing fancy. I *have* been in houses where the owner claimed to have nothing in at all, which in my opinion demonstrates exceptionally lax housekeeping – are you telling me they couldn't rustle up a couple of slices of Mother's Pride and a hunk of mousetrap? In instances like these, the photographer's assistant generally dashes out to the nearest shop – or, if we're miles from anywhere, we just go without.

In terms of general beverage provision, most celebs (or their domestic staff) will furnish you with cups of tea and coffee throughout the day – although I did spend six hours in the home of an ageing male soap star without being offered so much as a glass of water. But the award for the tightest celebrity goes to a certain uppercrust milliner. During the shoot at his home, *Wow!*'s make-up artist drank her way through a couple of bottles of Perrier, which he had provided for her. At the end of the day, she was packing up to leave when he came up to her, bold as brass, and demanded reimbursement for the cost of the water – she was lucky he didn't ask her to replace the 6.2 squares of bog roll she'd used, or the 4.1 units of electricity. The make-up girl showed her disgust by handing over excessively generous compensation in the shape of a crisp ten-pound note.

Jasmine and Stevo, I have to say, are the perfect hosts and feed us ciabatta with mozzarella and sun-dried tomatoes, followed by yoghurt and fruit and a choice of Volvic or orange juice. Thus fortified, we crack on with the shoot. Kestrel's temperament has improved fractionally, so Raoul takes Stevo off to do some touching dad-with-naked-baby shots in the nursery. I take the opportunity to grab twenty minutes of interview with Jasmine. She proves to be an incredibly distant and prickly interviewee, who seems unmoved by the whole experience of motherhood. She gave birth at the private hospital of St John and St Elizabeth – or John and Lizzies as it's affectionately known – a stone's throw away from her home, and a mecca for pregnant celebrities. I begin the interview by enquiring about Jasmine's labour – *Wow!* readers like to know every detail, however gory.

'It was the most horrendous experience – twelve hours of pure agony. I'd planned to have a natural labour in the birthing pool, but by the second hour of contractions I was begging for an epidural.'

'But having Stevo at your bedside must've been a great support.'

'Not really. He didn't quite know what to do with himself during the labour – spent most of it reading *When*

*Saturday Comes* – and then when I actually gave birth, he practically passed out.'

'Still, I bet he's proud as punch to have a little son,' I say, fishing for something positive in this quagmire of negativity.

'Yes, Stevo desperately wanted the baby to be a boy,' she concedes. 'I expect he'll be taking him to Millwall as soon as he's old enough.'

'Aaah . . . he's obviously going to be the doting dad then.'

Jasmine releases a derisive snort. 'Yeah, right. But he's not too happy about being woken up every hour on the hour through the night.'

Anyone would think she *wanted* to give her husband a bad press. But this won't do at all. *Wow!* readers will be expecting hearts and flowers and cuddly white bunnies from the nation's best-loved quiz master. I'll have to repackage some of my questions later on and hope for a more positive response when Stevo is present to stand up for himself. There's definitely something up with these two – maybe Stevo isn't pulling his weight when it comes to childcare, but then I doubt very much if Jasmine is either, when she has Consuela to do it for her. She started filming a costume drama for the BBC just three weeks after giving birth – still, I'd have dropped everything for the chance to snog the luscious Rufus Sewell.

Shelley appears and requests Jasmine's presence in the gym for a solo shot of the 'busy' mum getting back into shape after giving birth. Jasmine goes upstairs to change and I sidle off to the gym, wondering if I'll catch Raoul and Shelley at it . . . that would be so Raoul's style. But when I get there, she's loading film and he's lying on his back on the bench press, attempting to lift an 80kg weight, the tosser.

'You'll give yourself a hernia, you know,' I say cruelly.

He lets the weight fall with a loud clang and sits up, straddling the bench. 'Ruby . . . I didn't hear you come in. How's it going? What've you been up to since we last spoke?'

'Oh you know, this and that.' Come on girl, you can do better than that. 'I've been pretty busy actually . . . went to a great after-party last week with the girls from work – Melanie Sykes was there, and Elizabeth Jagger – and tonight I'm partying with friends in East London.'

'Sounds like fun.'

'Yeah, it will be – all the fashion crowd'll be there and they're so up for it. What are you doing tonight?'

'Oh, Shelley and I are meeting up with some of the guys from Holborn Studios for a few beers. We'll probably head down to Shoreditch, shoot some pool maybe.'

Oh you are, are you? I'm just struggling to invent another exciting-sounding engagement to outdo Raoul's hot date with Shelley when in walks Jasmine wearing black Lycra micro shorts, a lilac thong-back leotard and Nike cross trainers. She looks amazingly lean and fit for someone who's given birth so recently, but then she probably has a personal trainer to put her through her paces.

'Is it okay if I check out Kestrel's nursery – make a few notes about the decor and so on?' I'll feel like a voyeur watching Jasmine pump and flex.

'Yeah sure. Do what you like. We've got no secrets in this house.'

I walk up two flights of stairs to the nursery – I know I've got the right room by the big silver star on the door with *Kestrel's Room* printed on it. I start taking notes in Teeline (it's good to know that all those compulsory shorthand classes at university weren't a complete waste of time). It's a smallish room with a *charming* (i.e. mawkish) hand-painted Watership Down-style mural painted on the walls. There's a cot in one corner, where a Harrods bear nestles next to a ubiquitous Tellytubby – I'd hazard a guess at Po, but I'd better check with Jasmine because our eagle-eyed readers will write to me in droves if I get it wrong, they can be terribly nit-picking. I open the white-painted wardrobe with its Winnie the Pooh door handles to see what designer gear Kestrel's got. I'm not disappointed – there's Adidas and Clements Ribeiro and a pair of Hermès bootees. I make sure I put everything back where I found it and then wander down the corridor, intending to go back downstairs to the others. On impulse, I decide to take another look in the master bedroom. It's decorated in pinks and peaches, quite girlie really, with a thick mushroom-coloured carpet – I hope I'm not responsible for that smear of mud I've just noticed by the door, I *was* out in the garden earlier. I check the soles of both shoes and thankfully I'm in the clear. The curtains at the big French windows are big and flouncy and come with all the trimmings – a pelmet and wrought-iron finials, and tiebacks in a contrasting colour, far too fussy for my taste. The quilt on the bed is made in a matching fabric and I can't resist peeking under both sets of pillows – just as I thought, a solitary nightie (sugar-pink satin and rather tarty, frankly) and that's it. Which means one of two things: Stevo sleeps in the nuddy, or he sleeps somewhere else (I'd put money on the latter option – the sound of the crying baby has probably driven him out).

I'm just easing open a lacquered walnut drawer on the dressing table (well, she did say 'Do what you like') when suddenly I hear Consuela's distinctive throaty laugh fill the room. I freeze, certain that she's about to catch me red-handed with a tube of Jasmine's facial hair depilatory in my hand. Then I catch sight of the flashing lights on the baby monitor, sitting on the bedside table, and a massive wave of relief washes over me. Phew! She must be in the nursery, where I'd noticed a sister monitor positioned by Kestrel's cot. The monitor crackles into life again, only this time it's Stevo's voice – and it's not a pretty sound.

'Dirty girl! You want it, don't you? You want me to take you here, now, up against the wall, hard and fast.'

'Si, si, I wan' you, touch me baybee,' urges Consuela, sounding like a poorly dubbed porn star.

I am more shocked by Stevo's lack of imagination than the fact that he's carrying on with the hired help. After all, he wouldn't be the first celebrity to *allegedly* succumb to the charms of his nanny. All I can hear now are slurping noises and the occasional muffled moan. I don't particularly want to listen to this, but I daren't make my escape now because those stairs are really creaky. Suddenly, a high-pitched wail rings out. Now I *am* shocked – Stevo's getting it on with the nanny in the nursery while his wife's downstairs *and* the baby's in the room!

'Christ Kestrel! Can't you keep quiet for a second?' I hear him say irritably. 'Come on, Connie, we'd better get back to the others before Jasmine comes running.'

I wait until I hear their footsteps recede down the staircase, then I count to sixty, and follow them down. What a scumbag – having an affair when his wife has just given birth is bad enough, but right under her nose too. Talk about shitting on your own doorstep.

Mercifully, the rest of the shoot passes without incident. I feel sorry for Jasmine now, despite her earlier frostiness. Presumably she doesn't know about her husband's dalliance or she'd have sent Consuela packing – unless she's involved in some bizarre *ménage à trois*, but she seems far too strait-laced for that. Judging by what I've seen and heard, I guess she suspects he's having an affair – she just doesn't know who with.

I don't get a chance to conduct the joint interview until the end of the day when Raoul's finished shooting. My heart's not really in the job, knowing what I do about their tawdry domestic set-up. But I steel myself and reel off the list of standard 'new baby' questions . . .

'Has the new arrival brought you closer together?'
Hardly.

'Who does he/she most resemble?'

I'd say he had his dad's boxer's nose and his mum's moustache.

'Are you planning to have more children?'

I don't think anything could save this doomed marriage.

And, 'Tell me, Stevo, how are you enjoying first-time fatherhood?'

'It's everything I hoped it would be and more – Kestrel really is my best ever production,' he jokes, ever the showman. And he even has the nerve to add, 'Of course, Consuela's a big help, isn't she, Jazz? I don't know what we'd do without her.'

You mean you don't know what you'd do without a sexy Spanish fox to massage your pathetic male ego, you prick. I wonder what she sees in him – well actually it's obvious (remember when Mrs Merton asked Debbie McGee, 'So, Debbie, what first attracted you to the millionaire Paul Daniels?').

I'm relieved when the interview is over and I can head for home. Raoul and Shelley left ages ago, they probably couldn't wait to rip each other's clothes off. At least I've got Toby's party tonight. Jasmine takes an overwrought Kestrel upstairs to bed, and Stevo shows me to the door. 'Thanks for being so patient with us, Ruby. You *will* let us know when the magazine's out, won't you? I could even give it a plug on my show.'

'Of course I will – and thank *you*, Stevo, I know it's been a long day for everybody.'

As the smug bastard opens the front door to let me out, I can't resist delivering a parting shot: 'Oh, one word of advice, Stevo – I'd switch that baby monitor off when you're not using it. You'll save a fortune in batteries.'

# ELEVEN: SAM

I've tried on at least six different outfits and none of them looks right. I'm trying to replicate the effortless boho chic of Jade Jagger, say, or the Appleton sisters, but right now I look like Ivana Trump on a bad day. This hairdo is far too bouffant and this clingy blue satin dress screams 'tart!' I knew it was a mistake when I bought it in the Monsoon sale. I should have known better – I mean my *mother* shops at Monsoon. I would never have stepped over the threshold if it weren't for the lure of those straw sun hats in the window, and even *they* proved to be a big disappointment. After another two changes, I finally settle on loose, centre-parted hair with a faux orange gerbera hair grip, a simple black slip dress with lace trim, jazzed up with a couple of beaded bracelets, and my Bertie leather thong sandals.

I've arranged to meet Amy and the dreadful Toby in a pub in Hackney. I've booked myself a cab because I'm not keen to wander round east London after dark – don't believe those people who tell you that Hackney is the new Clapham, it's still got a long way to go. When I arrive at the King's Arms with my carrier bag of New World wines, I can't see the others anywhere. This place is a bit spit-and-sawdust and not Toby's usual sort of hangout at all. After I've bought myself a vodka-tonic, walked right round the lounge bar *and* the public bar and then back to the lounge bar again, I finally spot them tucked away in a corner next to the gents'. The smell of stale piss wafts through the open door as a heavily tattooed customer goes to relieve himself.

'So this is where you two are hiding. Hi darling,' I say, giving Amy a kiss on the cheek. 'You look wonderful as usual . . . it really suits you with your hair up like that.'

'Do you think so? Toby says it makes my face look fat.'

'Toby has been spending too much time round stick-thin models. He's forgotten what *real* women look like, haven't you, Tobe?' He hates it when I call him that. 'Nice local by the way – d'you know, they don't even sell Red Bull here.'

'It's not really my local at all. I mean I hardly ever come here, it's just that it's right round the corner from my loft,' he says defensively. 'Don't worry, Ruby, we'll be moving on as soon as the others have arrived. Amy tells me you're on the pull tonight.'

'Well, I wouldn't quite put it like that but yes, I am footloose and fancy free at the moment.'

'Jamie's coming – are you sure you two couldn't make it work?' says Amy.

'Absolutely no fucking way, Amy. I told you that New Year's Eve thing was a mistake.'

'What happened on New Year's Eve then?' says Toby, a lecherous smile playing around his lips. 'Get lucky did you?'

That man really is obnoxious. I'm going to have to get very, very drunk if I'm to survive the evening without smacking him.

By ten-thirty, quite a crowd of partygoers has gathered in the pub and Toby suggests we make tracks to his flat, sorry *loft*. It's pretty much as I imagined it – lots of blank white walls and stainless steel, very cold, very industrial. By twelve-thirty the place is heaving and I'm feeling pretty pissed, having consumed one bottle of Chardonnay, two Margaritas and a Pernod and black (I was sixteen last time I drank that). It's then that I spot Jamie standing on his own on the other side of the open-plan living room. In a moment of misguided drunken sentimentality, I decide that, despite my earlier assurances to Amy, maybe he *is* worth a second viewing. I have to squeeze through several groups of people to get to him.

'Hey Jaymeee, long time no see,' I say, slurring my words ever so slightly.

'Ruby! Great to see you.'

I step forward and give him a kiss on the cheek, not an air kiss, but a proper smacker. 'We must arrange to meet up for a drink one of these days. It's been too long. How are things at *Viva*?'

'Really good actually, especially since I've been promoted to Ad Director.'

Jamie works in the advertising department of a monthly health and fitness title, which is where I first met him when I was doing work experience in the editorial department, six years ago. I'm just about to offer my congratulations, when a snooty-looking blonde appears from nowhere and puts one hand territorially on Jamie's shoulder and gives me that 'And who might you be, bitch?' look.

'Oh, you haven't met my girlfriend have you, Ruby? This is Celeste. Celeste, this is Ruby – she's the one I told you about, you know, she works at *Wow!*'

'Hi there!' I say, trying desperately to inject a note of spontaneous enthusiasm into my voice. I can't believe it. Jamie has a girlfriend. I really missed my chance there. Hang on, what am I talking about? It would never work, and anyway he's a crap snogger. And what does he mean – 'she's the one I told you about'? I can just imagine it – 'She's the one who leapt on me at Simon and Katie's New Year party. I only gave in 'cause I felt sorry for her and now she won't leave me alone.'

Celeste and I engage in four minutes of excruciating small talk. I ask if she's in advertising too (no, she's a hairdresser), she compliments me on my Titian mane ('Is that Clairol?' she asks. No it fucking well isn't). Then I pretend to spot an old, old friend on the other side of the room and make my escape. Well at least now I can rule out Jamie as my stalker, unless he's playing a particularly cunning game of hard to get. No, I don't think so – when I look back over my shoulder, I see that he's all over Celeste like a rash. In fact I'm so busy looking behind me, that I forget to look where I'm going, and I walk slap-bang into some poor guy. He's carrying a plastic pint glass of lager, which splits on impact and splurts its contents down the front of his blue linen shirt.

'Omigod, I am so sorry. Let me get you a tea towel from the kitchen.'

'No really, it's okay. It was an accident and anyway, I was feeling a bit warm, that's cooled me off nicely.'

'Well at least let me get you another beer.'

'I tell you what, let's both go to the kitchen and get a drink.'

'Sounds good to me. I'm Ruby by the way – Toby's girlfriend's best friend.' I figure I owe the man a few minutes of casual conversation.

'Ruby . . . is that because of your hair?'

'That's what people always assume, but actually I owe my name to a song, "Ruby Tuesday". My mum and dad met at the Stones' concert in Hyde Park.'

'The one where Mick Jagger released the three thousand butterflies in memory of Brian Jones?'

I'm impressed – he even knows the number of butterflies. 'The very same. My mum was crying because Brian was her favourite Stone and my dad went over to comfort her, or so the story goes. I think they were both off their heads to be honest.'

'That's pretty cool. I'm Sam, and I'd shake your hand only it's a bit sticky.'

'I promise to look where I'm going next time . . . So how do you know Toby then?'

'He's a friend of a friend of mine – I think they were at school together. I barely know him, to be honest.'

That augurs well and now that we're in the kitchen, where it's a bit brighter, I can see that Sam's rather attractive. He's got mid-brown hair with gold flecks and it's longish, down to his collar, and grey eyes and fair skin, like mine, with a light smattering of freckles. And he's got this great dimple, right in the middle of his chin. When we've collected our drinks – I'm sticking to tonic water until I sober up a bit – we manage to negotiate a space on Toby's brushed aluminium staircase and slip into easy conversation. Whenever you get talking to someone at a *meeja* party, one of the first questions people ask is what field you're in. Then you can say, 'Oh really, you're at *Vogue* . . . you must know Bibi in features,' or, 'You work in the Arista press office . . . why, I was at Momo with Zak only last night.' I decide to get this spiel out of the way early on in the conversation.

'Amy and I – Amy being Toby's girlfriend – met at journalism college. She's at *Teen Scene* now and I'm a writer on *Wow!* magazine, you know, *Britain's best-selling celebrity weekly.*'

At this point most people get all excited and ask me if I've ever met their favourite celebrity, be it Madonna or Brad or Leonardo. Sam, however, is refreshingly unimpressed.

'I'm not much of a showbiz buff, I'm afraid. I hate soaps, don't read the gossip columns, never buy *News of the World*. In fact, I've only just discovered that Liz Hurley and Hugh Grant have split up. I can't see the point of celebrities, they're overpaid, over-rated, over-exposed, they just make ordinary people feel inadequate.'

How very refreshing. 'I couldn't agree more. You wouldn't believe the amount we pay so-called *stars* for access to their home, or their baby or their wedding. It's a sick business. So what game are you in then?'

'I'm a gardener.'

'Oh, right. So you dig people's flowerbeds and mow their lawns and stuff?'

'Yeah, something like that.'

'That sounds fun. It must be nice working in the outdoors.'

'It's brilliant, I wouldn't swap it for a nine-to-five office job, not if you paid me a million pounds.'

'Well it's good you feel so passionately about your work. I must admit mine's beginning to lose its lustre after two years.'

'But you must get to go to loads of great parties.'

'Frankly I couldn't care less if I never set foot inside Sugar Reef or Home House ever again.'

'I've never even heard of those places. I don't go into

the West End much, my raving days are well and truly over. I think I must've entered boring middle-age-dom, because these days I like walking and fishing and going to friends' houses for dinner.'

'That doesn't sound boring at all.'

And I mean it. It's rare in my line of work to meet someone as down-to-earth and unaffected as Sam. I like the fact that he's a gardener, that he does something so physical, so literally hands-on. Actually, it's quite sexy really – all that *big rough hands*, doing-it-in-the-potting-shed sort of stuff, very Lady Chatterley. Normally, ten minutes is about my limit for small talk at a party, but there's something very charismatic about Sam, a kind of unselfconscious intensity, that stops me making my excuses and moving on to someone else. He's just incredibly easy to talk to and for once, I'm not the one asking all the questions. As the conversation progresses, it turns out that we have a surprising amount in common. We're both Virgo (although at 31, he's three years older than me), both have an 'SE' postcode, both have a fondness for fondue and Lemon Puffs and the work of Oliver Postgate (he's the proud owner of a limited edition Clangers boxed set). *And* he plays bongos in an easy listening band, so we even have a shared interest in Andy Williams.

I'm so engrossed in conversation with Sam that I don't notice the party start to thin out. In fact, it's only when Amy walks past us on the stairs and announces that she's going to bed that I look at my watch and discover that it's four-fifteen in the morning. I feel rather proud of myself for having stayed up so late. I tell Sam I ought to be making tracks and he says his mate Jim is driving back to Camberwell and do I want a lift?

Fifteen minutes later and Sam and I are in the back of Jim's Mazda, speeding our way to south London while drum 'n' bass blares out of the speakers, making conversation practically impossible. We're just emerging from the Rotherhithe Tunnel when Sam turns to me and asks if I fancy meeting up for a drink sometime. In fact he has to ask me twice because the music's so loud. I've really enjoyed tonight, so I tell him, sure, that would be nice. We're just trying to find a mutual window in our respective diaries when I remember the two Arsenal tickets that Lee Jackson gave me as a thank you for the *at home* (he and CoCo just *lurrved* the eight-page spread – thankfully, news of the engagement didn't leak out beforehand). I *had* been planning to take Raoul, who is no longer in the frame obviously, but I still wanted to go all the same – I mean, Lee had arranged a VIP box, so there'd be free booze and everything.

'I know this is short notice, but I don't suppose you want to see Arsenal v. Chelsea at Highbury this Sunday, do you? I've got a couple of freebies.'

'Well I'm a Liverpool supporter really – have been ever since my Nan gave me a pair of Kevin Keegan slippers when I was nine – but yeah, that would be really cool.'

'Okay, that's a date then. Give me your number and I'll give you a bell tomorrow to arrange the details.'

By this time we're outside my flat, so he scribbles his number down quickly on the back of a travelcard.

'I'll speak to you tomorrow then.'

'Yeah. I'll look forward to it. And Ruby . . . it was really nice talking to you tonight.'

'You too.'

He leans over in the back seat of the car and gives me a light kiss on the very corner of my mouth.

'Until Sunday, then.'

Roll on Sunday.


Sam is attempting to explain the offside rule to me; I'm nodding, but between you and me, I still don't get it. This is my first real-life football match and I have to say that, despite my ignorance, I'm really enjoying it. The stadium is so much bigger and cleaner than I imagined and this must surely be the only form of public entertainment where there's no queue for the ladies. The refreshments – champagne and dainty little sandwiches – are excellent, but then we are getting the VIP treatment. I doubt I'd be having so much fun stuck down there in the stands, scalding my mouth on a meat pie and drinking lukewarm Bovril out of a styrofoam cup. Sam seems to be enjoying himself too and, unlike a lot of men, he doesn't feel the need to provide a running commentary throughout the game. Take Simon, for example: we'll be in the pub on a Sunday afternoon and he'll pretend not to be watching the match on the big screen over your shoulder, but then suddenly he'll shout, 'Box it, box it . . . you fucking wanker! A four-year-old could've scored from there.' It's extremely irritating.

At half time, Sam nips to the gents. I flick through the programme, which entertains me for all of three minutes, and then I notice the big dot-matrix scoreboard at the end of the pitch, which is currently displaying a selection of heart-warming birthday messages and wedding anniversary congratulations. What a brilliant idea – ten-year-old Sean must be thrilled his parents have been so thoughtful, he'll be able to tell all his friends at school on Monday. Suddenly, a huge sick wave engulfs me. It's nothing to do with the volume of champagne I've drunk, but the words that are currently exhibited on the board for the entire 38,500 capacity crowd to see:

    Precious Ruby, Will you be mine forever?
        All my love, a Secret Admirer.

It's only up there for a matter of seconds, but I'm sure that's what it said. How the fuck could he possibly know I'd be here today? Is there a possibility that Alan Kramer and Lee Jackson somehow know each other? I seriously doubt it, they don't move in the same circles at all. It must be another Ruby, but those familiar words *precious* and *Secret Admirer* . . . No, I must have got it wrong. It's a sunny day and maybe it's just a trick of the light, a reflection on the board. Yes, that must be it, I saw the word *Ruby* and somehow conjured up the *precious* bit.

And as for *Secret Admirer*, well that is a pretty common nom-de-plume – her boyfriend was obviously too embarrassed to reveal his real name because his mates would probably have ripped the piss out of him.

I've succeeded in convincing myself that I imagined the whole thing when Sam returns – it's just as well he wasn't here five minutes ago to see the colour drain out of my face. The second half goes by surprisingly quickly and afterwards Sam suggests we go for a drink. There hasn't been much opportunity for talking during the game, so it'll be nice to get better acquainted somewhere a bit quieter. We head down to Islington, where there's a million designer watering holes to choose from, and make ourselves comfortable in a little Mexican bar just off Upper Street. There isn't a single lull in the conversation as we talk about our friends and our homes and our ambitions. Sam really listens to what I'm saying and he's retained loads of information from our first conversation, which I find immensely flattering. I decide to find out a bit more about his work, and make the rather embarrassing discovery that far from being a common-or-garden gardener, as I had assumed, he is in fact a leading light in Greenwich Council's Parks and Gardens department. A university-trained horticulturist, he heads a twelve-strong team, responsible for landscaping and maintaining the borough's recreational spaces, including the famous Royal Park.

'You know, you should come to Greenwich Park one day soon. I can show you round, we've got some great displays at the moment and the rose garden will be in bloom soon.'

'Yeah, I'd really like that, Sam. I'm absolutely crap with plants. Every houseplant I've ever owned has died within four months. I don't know what I'm doing wrong because I always follow the instructions on the little label: *keep away from direct sunlight, feed regularly* . . . I even talk to the damn things. I suppose you've always had green fingers.'

'My mum loves to embarrass me by telling this story about how when I was six, all I wanted for Christmas was a packet of mustard and cress seeds. *Dear Santa*, I wrote in my letter. *Please bring me some mustard and cress seeds so I can grow my own sandwiches*. I didn't want an Action Man or a Chopper bike, I just wanted those seeds and I became obsessed with the idea of creating something from scratch. I must've been a right little control freak. Anyway, Santa brought me the seeds, ten packets of them, and I grew them in margarine tubs on the kitchen windowsill. I can still remember how excited I felt at my first sight of those little green shoots poking through the damp kitchen roll . . . I practically wet myself. It's still the same for me now, except I've got more bladder control these days. You know, when you've spent hours designing a floral display, and you've dug the bed, and planted the bulbs and fed and nurtured them and watched them grow from tiny green shoots to big colourful, dazzling blooms, you get such a sense of satisfaction. It's kind of like watching your children grow up and feeling really proud of them because they've turned out so well. And then if you discover that someone's dog or ball has damaged them, you feel quite hurt. I've been on my knees, cradling crushed flowers before now, like I can somehow bring them back to life; it's stupid really.'

'No, it's not. It's beautiful. You don't know how lucky you are to have such a creative job.'

'Well your job's pretty creative too. You start with a blank computer screen, then you play your dictaphone and in a few hours you've created this fascinating snapshot of somebody's life.'

'Except, unfortunately, the writing part is only a tiny fraction of my work. It's the chasing of agents and negotiating of contracts that takes the time, and there's something so tawdry about haggling over how much someone's baby, or house, or wedding is worth. I'm a broker really, not a journalist. A lot of celebs get copy approval anyway, so they change what you've written. I sometimes feel like saying to them, "Tell you what . . . *you* write the story the way you want it and I'll just add the punctuation."'

Sam lets out a big belly laugh. 'Sounds like you're in the wrong business, Ruby.'

'Well I do wonder sometimes.'

The barman's calling time. It doesn't feel like we've been here for four hours, the evening's just flown by. We gather our coats and walk the ten minutes to Angel tube station in companionable silence. It's not because we haven't got anything to say to each other, it's almost as if we both know this is the start of something, but neither of us quite knows how to say it, or indeed if it's best left unspoken. I've never felt this way about any man after just one date – in fact, I don't think I've ever felt this way about any man, full stop. I certainly didn't feel this way about Raoul, who now seems terribly shallow and insipid in comparison to this deep, strong, thoughtful man. Oh, and I got a good look at his hands – his nails are surprisingly clean and neat and he has these long tapering fingers, life-giving fingers that I wanted to reach out and kiss, back there in that noisy, smoky bar.

We catch the crowded southbound Northern line – Sam's going all the way to Oval, but I need to change a few stops earlier at Bank. I *could* ask Sam if he wants to come back to mine for a 'coffee', but I've had such a lovely time I don't want to spoil it by rushing things. And anyway, I don't think Sam is a rushing kind of man. When we've passed Moorgate I start saying my goodbyes and I'm uncharacteristically coy about it.

'Thanks Sam, I had a brilliant time today. Maybe we can meet up next week sometime?'

'That would be great. Listen, are you sure you'll be okay getting home on your own?'

'I'll be fine, honestly. There's a cab office right opposite the station.'

'Well if you're sure . . . Here, write down your phone number and I'll give you a call in the next couple of days.' He rummages in his pocket for a chewing gum wrapper and a Bic Biro.

## WOW!

By the time I've written down the eight digits, we're pulling into Bank. As I get up, Sam rises to his feet too, grabs my elbow, pulls me gently towards him and kisses me on the lips – no tongue tango or anything, just a soft, warm, sincere kiss. The train doors slide open and I'm carried out on a wave of people. As I make my way down the escalator to the DLR, I've got the most enormous smile on my face.

# TWELVE: DIVA

Today is a big day for me. I've been granted an audience with Ciara Powell, one of the hottest singing stars on both sides of the Atlantic. The 33-year-old r 'n' b diva flew into London the day before yesterday for this weekend's concert at the Albert Hall, the only UK date in her whirlwind world tour. This interview took three months to set up and was only secured after seventeen phone conversations, two meetings between her people and our people, a written guarantee of copy approval and the small matter of $30,000.

Ciara's is a real rags-to-riches story. Born in Brooklyn, New York, she was brought up by her Hispanic mother after her cab driver dad cleared off when she was a baby. As a teenager, she often played truant from school, where she was regularly bullied on account of her severe dyslexia (only diagnosed in adulthood). She went into care at the age of fourteen after her mum was jailed for persistent shoplifting, and by the time she was eighteen and living in Brooklyn's infamous Projects, she looked set for a life of drudgery and petty crime. Her only saving grace was a powerful singing voice – gravelly but incredibly soulful (like 'cream on sandpaper', as a critic once described it). Ciara's life changed forever two days after she turned eighteen when, standing on a subway platform, waiting for her train and singing Aretha Franklin's 'You Make Me Feel Like A Natural Woman', a record company executive chanced to walk by. In true Eliza Doolittle fashion, he signed her on the spot, set her up in an apartment, groomed her, gave her singing lessons and a choreographer – and a year later she had her first number one single. Since then, she's had five platinum albums and earned two Grammys plus a Palme d'Or for her one and only film role, playing a prostitute in a Tarantino flick. As for her personal life, she's married and divorced a Calvin Klein model (he got the Montana ranch and $10 million, as stipulated in the pre-nuptial agreement), embarked on a well-publicized fling with her personal trainer, which ended in tears when he sold his sordid story to the *National Enquirer*, and is now dating gangsta rapper Kool Def.

I've already been told I can't ask about her romantic life, so I guess I'll have to concentrate on her shopping habits, her fitness regime, her charity work and her musical inspirations. Hopefully *Wow!*'s readers will just look at the pretty pictures and not concentrate too hard on the words. Speaking of pictures, the shoot is scheduled to take place tomorrow, thank God, so I won't have to contend with the army of stylists and hairdressers and make-up artists that will inevitably be involved. We submitted a shortlist of three possible photographers (none of whom charges less than 5k for a day's work) and Ciara agreed to Tony Darcey, a veteran Cockney snapper who's been around since Bailey was in short trousers, but is still regarded with great affection by the New York set.

At one-fifty-two p.m. precisely, I enter the Lanesborough Hotel in Knightsbridge, a favourite A-list hangout which aims to capture *the gracious style and warm hospitality of an early 19th-century residence,* according to the promotional literature. It's certainly swanky – the £4,000-a-night Royal Suite, where Ciara is currently ensconced, has three bedrooms, a drawing room, dining room and kitchen, 24-hour security, dedicated personal butler and use of a chauffeured limousine. My interview is scheduled for two p.m. and as soon as I walk into reception I spot my contact, Albert Hall PR Sally McAlister, straight off. She's the petite thirtysomething brunette with the clipboard and the harried expression who's gabbling away into her mobile.

'. . . but she's demanding we re-carpet the dressing room in white shagpile . . . I told her we don't have the time or the budget and she threw a vase at my head, it missed me by inches . . .' I hear her say as I draw near. She looks up with a start and cuts short her phone conversation.

'Ah Ruby. How wonderful to meet you,' she says,

extending a slender hand that's shaking only slightly – otherwise she's doing a remarkable job of appearing calm when it's obvious that the shit has hit the fan bigtime. Ciara has earned a reputation as something of a diva and I've no doubt she's been running this poor woman ragged. It's rumoured that her Radio City dressing room had to be completely remodelled for the Millennium Eve concert. She insisted on an all-white decor – a white roll-top bath, white toilet rolls, white clary sage-scented candles of a four-inch diameter (they help align her yin with her yang, or some such nonsense).

'Everything okay?' I ask her.

'Yes, yes, couldn't be better.' She's so convincing I almost believe her. 'Ciara's on top form and looking forward to the interview. I'll take you up there now.'

We take the lift to the top floor, which has been totally booked out by Ciara's entourage of twenty-four. According to Sally, this includes three assistants, two stylists, a hairdresser, manicurist, masseur, shaman, holistic dentist, personal trainer and ambience co-ordinator (he moves the furniture round and lights a few joss sticks). She's already given the hotel's personal butler his marching orders, Sally tells me, as she finds it too upsetting to have a strange face around, poor pet.

When we step out into the hallway, the first thing I see is two massive unsmiling bodyguards, dressed in co-ordinating black Adidas tracksuits and baseball caps. They're both wearing those walkie-talkie headsets with the little microphone in front of their mouth and when they see us one of them says – and I kid you not – 'The eagle has landed. Do I have authorization to proceed?' The answer is obviously in the affirmative because the ape – his neck is about as thick as my waist – lumbers over to us and says, 'Welcome ladies. Miss Powell is ready for you. Please be kind enough to follow me.' He leads us to Ciara's suite, where a stunning-looking black girl, about my own age, greets us at the door with a big smile.

'Welcome. I'm Tonisha, Ciara's PA. Won't you come through to the drawing room?'

At this point, Sally makes her excuses and heads back for the relative security of reception – I don't blame her, she's obviously desperate to avoid another confrontation with Ciara.

'I hope you don't mind, but we *will* need to search your bag,' says Tonisha as I make myself comfortable in a reproduction chair.

This is highly unusual, even for a star of Ciara's calibre. Cher's people didn't ask to search my bag, nor did Claudia Schiffer's or Scary Spice's. I'd like to know what she thinks I'm capable of. I think her music's crap, it's true – but that doesn't make me a would-be assassin.

'No problem,' I chirrup in my smiley *Wow!* voice, mentally going over the contents of my Russell & Bromley tote and praying that there are no inadequately wrapped pieces of chewed gum or stray panty-liners floating in its depths.

# WOW!

Tonisha disappears through a connecting door and returns with another tracksuit-wearing bodyguard, only this one has a black bandanna round his head instead of a baseball cap. Without a word, he walks over to the coffee table where my bag is sitting, unzips it and proceeds to examine each and every item inside. He uncaps my moisture-rich lipstick (what's he expecting to find – a phial of cyanide?), flicks open my silver-plated Marlboro Lights promotional lighter (nicked from a gameshow hostess), and even opens the battery cache on my dictaphone (I suppose it *could* have been programmed to self-destruct, *Mission Impossible*-style). I'm on pins during the entire inspection, even though I know full well I'm not packing anything that could possibly qualify as an offensive weapon.

When the ordeal is over, the bodyguard slinks back to his lair and Tonisha offers me a drink. I plump for a cup of Earl Grey – I figure it's best to make myself appear as quintessentially English as possible, because the American stars love that stuff. I've lost count of the times I've been complimented on my 'cute' accent and my English Rose complexion. When Tonisha comes back with my drink (it's black with a slice of lemon, which is *not* how I take it, but I won't kick up a fuss), she tells me that Ciara is about to make an appearance. I quickly grab my dictaphone and my list of questions from my bag and put them on the table in front of me. Then I stand up and smooth my hair back with the flat of my hands, like I'm about to meet the Queen. The connecting door opens and in walks La Diva. I'm pretty impressed, I must say. She's not a tall woman – about five foot four I'd say – but she's got great presence. Her long, dark, chemically straight-ened hair is pulled back into a high ponytail and she doesn't appear to be wearing too much make-up – just a touch of mascara and a slick of gloss – and she's dressed casually in DKNY jog pants and sweatshirt. She's not drop-dead gorgeous, but she does possess a certain trans-lucent beauty – at least she would if she wasn't scowling. Trotting behind her is a Shar-Pei – you know those funny little dogs with great, disgusting folds of skin. Surely she can't have brought it from the States, so what on earth is it doing here?

'Hi Ciara, I'm Ruby Lake, it's great to meet you,' I say, as she swooshes past me, totally ignoring my greeting and my outstretched hand and takes a seat on a plush red armchair directly opposite me. The dog settles around her ankles and she rubs the loose skin at its neck with her stars-and-stripes nail extensions.

'Right, you've got forty-five minutes, starting now,' she says, checking her Rolex. 'No relationship questions, no autograph requests, no mention of my parents – clear?'

'Er, yes, I understand. Is it okay to switch on my dictaphone?'

She gives me the faintest nod and then screams at the top of her lungs, 'Toneeesha!'

The PA comes scurrying into the room like a frightened rabbit.

'Where's my recorder? I thought I told you to have it ready on the table,' Ciara snaps.

'I'm so sorry, Miss Powell. I took it to my room to change the batteries, I must have left it there. I'll go and get it now.'

'Stupid girl! I don't pay you to be useless. I want you back here with that machine in thirty seconds or you're fired.'

She sits in stony silence until Tonisha returns with the dictaphone twenty-nine seconds later and places it on the table in front of her mistress. 'Shall I set it to Record?'

'No, I want you to stick it up your ass.'

I feel a wave of sympathy for poor Tonisha. I wonder if Ciara's normally this abusive, or if she's just having a particularly bad day.

'I record all my interviews because I'm sick of being misquoted,' explains Ciara. 'You print one word out of context and my lawyers will have you in court so fast your feet won't touch the ground.'

Right that's that sorted. I was going to begin the interview by asking Ciara if she had a pleasant flight from New York, but frankly, I hope she hit turbulence and anyway I'm working against the clock, so there's no time to waste on pleasantries.

'So how does it feel to be back in London for the first time in over a year?'

'Oh I just love London, the shopping here is so fantastic. They opened up Selfridges especially early this morning, just for me. I was like a kid in a candy store!'

Ciara clearly has no problem performing in an interview. She's a totally different person now the tape's running. 'So what did you buy?'

'That's private.'

'Oh, okay. Um, is it true that when you go shopping in New York, you take a Winnebago with you, so you can freshen up and so on?'

'That story is pure fiction, dreamed up by the tabloids. I would never get a Winnebago through the New York traffic. I take a stretch limo, white of course.'

'Yes, I hear you have quite a passion for the colour white. Did you really spend $12,000 having your Radio City dressing room remodelled?'

'I made a few minor adjustments – I don't know the total cost, Tonisha deals with that kind of thing. But every year I give thousands of dollars away to charities – in fact I recently donated one of my Valentino gowns to Elton's Aids foundation, you know. I'd only worn it once.'

When we've done the charity thing, we move to Ciara's fitness regime, which consists of *Spinning* (cycling very fast on a stationary bike), *Reggaecise* (working out to Bob Marley), and *Boot Camp* class (I dread to think). And, just when I think we're building up some sort of rapport, Ciara decides to exercise her lungs again.

'Toneeesha!'

After two nano-seconds, there's no response, so Ciara jumps up, walks across the room and yanks open the connecting door. The Shar-Pei follows obediently and I notice that there's a dark brown turd congealing on the carpet where it was sitting.

'Where *is* that girl?' she screeches into the room on the other side of the drawing room. Her face looks really ugly when she screws it up like that.

'She's gone to see the concierge about changing your black limo to a white one,' comes the reply from assistant number two.

'I want some food,' says the diva like a petulant child, 'and I want it now.'

'I'll be happy to arrange that for you, Ciara.'

'And don't call me Ciara, only my friends and my manager call me Ciara, you should know that by now.'

'I'm so sorry, Miss Powell, it won't happen again. Now what shall I have room service bring you?'

'I want two onion bagels, cut in half, with the dough scooped out so there's just the crust left. And two ounces of Atlantic prawns, all of a similar size – it upsets me when I see great big ones in the same dish with little baby ones – and a spoon of low-fat mayo on the side. And I want a hunk of watermelon with the seeds removed, but still attached to the rind. And I want Evian water – it must be Evian, they've only got Perrier in the minibar – with a twist of lime.'

'I'll order it right away, Miss Powell.'

Ciara returns to her chair – she appears not to notice the turd by her foot – without bothering to ask me if I want anything from room service, it was too much to expect I guess. I sincerely hope she's going to deduct this five-minute conversation from my time allowance. A quick glance at my watch reveals I have only twenty-three minutes left, so I decide to try a tougher line of questioning or this interview will be exceptionally ano-dyne, even by *Wow!* standards.

'Is it true that you refused to present a trophy to Jennifer Lopez at the MTV awards because you didn't want people to make unfavourable comparisons?'

'What do you mean by "unfavourable comparisons"?'

'Well, certain unkind people might for example say that Jennifer is younger or prettier or even more talented than you.'

'That's utterly ridiculous. I pulled out of MTV because of a serious throat infection. I was laid-up in bed for two weeks – just ask my publicist.'

'So there's no ill feeling between yourself and Jennifer?'

'Absolutely not. Jen is a dear, sweet, darling girl who I'm sure will go a long long way. In fact, I would like you to put on record that I wish her continued success with her fantastic singing career. Obviously there will always be those who say she should stick to the acting, but I'm not one of those. Definitely not.'

'Fair enough. Now perhaps you can attest to the veracity or otherwise of this story in today's *Sun* news-paper, which claims you were refused entry to the women-only Sanctuary health spa yesterday because you insisted on having four male bodyguards accompany you.' I rummage in my bag and pull out the offending publication. 'It says here: "When Powell was politely refused admittance, she threw a temper tantrum and bellowed at the top of her voice: *Don't you idiots know who I am?*" What's your reaction to that story – true or false?'

'You wanna know my reaction? This is my reaction,' she says, snatching the newspaper out of my hands and ripping it in half.

I'm starting to enjoy this, now that it's become a battle of wills. 'Okay . . . is it true that you operate a stringent set of rules for your housekeeping staff, rules which are known as "Ciara's Commandments"?'

The diva's eyes widen and she leans forward in her chair. 'You can't honestly believe that story? I mean if this set of rules exists, then what exactly *are* they?'

I deliberately don't reply, at least not right away.

'See, you can't tell me that, can you?' She folds her arms and looks at me triumphantly.

I look down at my notes. 'Er, let's see . . . Rule number one: maids must check departing guests' suitcases to make sure they haven't made off with any "souvenirs". Rule number two: every item of your clothing, including underwear, must be dry cleaned. Rule number three: no member of staff is to look you directly in the eye. Rule number four . . .'

She interrupts just as I'm getting to the good stuff. 'You journalists think you're so clever, don't you, always trying to catch me out? Well you can't prove a god-damned thing!'

'Yes, but we both know number six exists, don't we? I

mean I've seen it with my own eyes. Let's see . . . Rule number six: no member of staff to address you by your first name.'

I stare her right in the eye, daring her to deny it. For ten seconds or more, she stares right back, nostrils flaring like a stallion on heat. 'Next question,' she suddenly snarls. But before I can put the next allegation to her, there's a timid knock at the door, and in walks assistant number two, carrying a silver tray of food. As soon as she plonks it down on the table in front of Ciara, the diva throws a massive hissy fit.

'I said WATER melon, you idiot – this is HONEY-DEW!' And then she picks up the melon segment and hurls it across the room. The assistant and I watch as the melon hits one of the framed pictures on the wall, knocking it out of alignment and splattering sticky juice everywhere.

'I'm sorry, Miss Powell, I asked room service for watermelon, I did, honestly . . .'

'I-AM-SO-SICK-OF-DEALING-WITH-INCOMPETENTS. GET-OUT-OF-MY-SIGHT-BEFORE-I-DO-SOMETHING-WE'LL-BOTH-REGRET.'

The assistant goes scuttling off quick smart, and it's just me and the diva, together, alone. She's breathing very heavily with a hand on her chest, as if she's having palpitations or something, and the little Shar-Pei is quite excited too, it's running round in circles, chasing his tail like a Tasmanian devil.

'You've no idea how difficult it is to get good staff

these days,' she says. 'I must've hired and fired a dozen assistants in the past year. Tonisha's the only decent one – she's been with me for two years now.'

'Would you say that you're a demanding employer?' I ask boldly.

'Not especially. I think I treat my staff very considerately.'

She must be having a laugh. 'But it's not very considerate to shout at people and throw things at them, is it?'

I can tell I've pushed her to the limit with this one. Her eyes narrow into slits and she pinches in her mouth so it looks like the Shar-Pei's arsehole.

'This interview is now terminated,' she barks, as she gets up, snatches her dictaphone from the table and walks towards the main door that leads out into the corridor, the Shar-Pei trotting loyally behind her. There are now two turds on the floor where it was sitting, I thought the smell was getting worse.

'But I've still got seven minutes left,' I say to her departing back.

The door slams shut behind her with a loud, final bang, so I guess that's my cue to leave. I'm just packing up when Tonisha comes in.

'Did you get everything you need?' she says, all bright and breezy.

'She diddled me out of seven minutes – the magazine's lawyer will probably want to re-negotiate the fee, you know.' I'm not letting her get away with short-changing me.

'Tell him to get in touch with Ciara's agent – I'm sure they can come to some agreement. I'm afraid Ciara's still feeling a little fragile after her flight, so sorry if she was a little tetchy with you. She's gone for a walk round Hyde Park with her bodyguards to clear her head.'

'Tetchy? She's a complete bitch. I don't know how you lot put up with her.'

Tonisha looks down at her feet embarrassedly and I hope I haven't offended her.

'Well, I look on it as good experience. If I can put up with *her*, I can put up with any celebrity. I'll probably move on next year. I'd like to work for an actress – I've heard from friends of mine that they're generally less difficult.'

'I dunno about that. If you ask me, most celebrities are prima donnas – they're so used to being pampered and fussed over, they start to expect it from everyone they meet, not just their employees.'

'Maybe you're right, maybe I should get out of this business altogether.'

'Well, you seem like a really efficient person to me and I wish you luck, whatever you end up doing. Oh, and by the way, there's two dog turds on the floor over there . . . where *did* that dog come from, surely Ciara didn't bring it over from the States?'

'Oh Ciara loves dogs – she's got three Shar-Peis back home. We always hire one to keep her company whatever country we're in, although they're not always easy to get hold of. We got little Boo-Boo from a local breeder, he's really taken to Ciara, follows her everywhere. Don't print this, will you, but at night he even sleeps in her bed.'

How perfectly disgusting. I wonder if he shits in the bed too? I pick up my bag and walk towards the door, and then a very wicked thought flashes through my head.

'Er, Tonisha, would it be okay if I used the loo quickly? I'm absolutely bursting after that Earl Grey, tea always goes straight through me.'

'Ciara doesn't normally let anyone else use her personal facilities . . .'

'Oh go on, I'll be ever so quick.'

'Well, you've had a tough day, so I guess it'll be okay just this once.'

'You're an angel, Tonisha. I'll tell you what – just to show how grateful I am, I'll even flush those dog turds down the pan for you.'

'Oh no, that really won't be necessary.'

But I need those turds – and before Tonisha can stop me, I pick up a big wodge of tissues from the gold-plated dispenser on the coffee table and scoop the poops (luckily they've already started to harden, which makes it easier to get a purchase on them).

'Well okay, now that you've got them . . . the bathroom's just through here.'

Tonisha directs me through the connecting door, into the master bedroom with its king-size four-poster, and into the en-suite. I lock the door behind me and put the turds on top of the cistern for safekeeping. There's only one toothbrush on the shelf above the sink – a gold-plated electric jobbie – which must be Ciara's. I pick it up, flick up the lid of the khazi, and proceed to rub the toothbrush head underneath the rim for about thirty seconds, which should be enough time for plenty of germs to adhere. Next, I rifle through the huge collection of cosmetics on the shelf until I find a nice Lancome moisturizing fluid. I unscrew the lid, work up a good gob of saliva in my mouth and then spit the foamy slime right down the neck of the bottle. My aim's not brilliant, so half of it ends up on my hands, but a fair bit went in, so I'm satisfied. I screw the lid back on and give the bottle a good shake before returning it to the shelf.

Just one thing left to do now . . . I pick up the turds in their tissue parcel and look around the bathroom for inspiration. I find it in the form of a pair of white towelling slippers, lying on the floor next to the bath. Each has the word *Diva* embroidered across the toe in gold thread, so Ciara must have brought them with her – naturally she wouldn't want to wear anything as beastly as hotel slippers. I pick up the left foot and let the two dog turds fall inside, then I give the slipper a shake, so the shit falls right down into the toe-piece. Perfect! Ciara obviously prefers animals to humans so hopefully Boo-Boo won't be reprimanded too severely for his little 'misdemeanour'. I flush the toilet, wash my hands and make my way back to the drawing room where Tonisha is waiting.

'Thanks Tonisha. I feel so much better for that,' I say, flashing her a big grateful smile. 'I'll see myself out.'

# THIRTEEN: EASY LISTENING

Amy and Jo look bloody amazing. Amy's waist is tinier than usual in a black satin corset, which she's teamed with a frothy net skirt. Her corkscrew curls are crowned with a diamante tiara and a black feather boa adds the finishing touch to her 1950s studio starlet style. Jo has gone for the Audrey Hepburn look in a sleeveless sheath of coffee-coloured satin with a high square neckline and armpit-length black gloves. Lashings of black liquid eyeliner and false eyelashes complete her gamine glamour. As for me, I'm Diana Dors (before she got fat) – finger-waved hair clipped to one side, black pencil skirt with thigh-length split, tight white shirt knotted at the waist and open at the neck to reveal push-up boobs, and high-heeled patent leather mules.

Tonight is easy listening night at the Regency Ballrooms, a splendid Grade II listed dancehall in Lambeth. The girls and I have been to the monthly event a few times in the past, but tonight is extra special because

Sam's band, Kempinski, is playing. I must admit to feeling a little nervous as we give our names to the Monroe lookie-likie with the guest list. Don't get me wrong . . . Sam and I are getting on like a house on fire. We've been on several brilliant dates since the football – dinner at his place, a trip to the cinema, that promised walk in Greenwich Park (the floral displays were truly magnificent) – but this is the first time my friends have met him and I'm desperate for them all to get on. It will be the final seal of approval on a relationship that I'm certain is destined for great things.

'What time is the band on?' asks Amy, as we queue for our dry martinis at the bar.

'Around eleven-thirty.'

'I can't wait to see what he looks like,' says Jo, fitting a Consulate into her tortoiseshell cigarette holder. 'Are any of the other guys in the band single?'

'Why, are you hoping for some action tonight?'

'I should bloody well hope so, considering all the time and effort I spent getting ready.'

'Well I think we all look drop dead gorgeous,' says Amy. 'Any man would be a fool to turn us down.'

We carry our drinks to one of the little booths at the edge of the dance floor. The red velvet seating is rather stained and the gilded woodwork is a little chipped, but it still feels amazingly grand. It's only early, but there's quite a crowd here already, all dressed in their easy listening finery. DJ Warren Ramon – the snake-hipped, ponytailed, gipsy-esque 'King of Easy' – spins Sergio Mendes and there's a mass exodus onto the dance floor.

'Have you told Sam about the Secret Admirer?' asks Jo.

'God no, I don't want him to think I'm some sort of freak magnet, and anyway, the SA's been pretty quiet of late. With any luck he's given up on me.'

'You really like Sam, don't you, Ruby?' says Amy, who has been treated to a blow-by-blow account of each and every one of our dates thus far.

'Yeah, I really do . . . you know, Ames, I think he could even be The One.'

She does a stagy gasp and puts a hand to her mouth in mock horror. I should explain at this point that I'm known as the Ice Princess among my friends. I've had my fair share of boyfriends over the years, but I have to say I've never got really excited about any of them, even the ones I went out with for years. I've never been tempted to move in with a man, never been able to tolerate any of them for more than a couple of days at a time. In fact, I've usually been tearing my hair out at the end of a weekend break in the Lake District. I'd actually reached the stage where I thought I could never cohabit. I'd just get married and then we'd live in separate houses on opposite sides of the park, like Woody Allen and Mia Farrow. But there is something shockingly different about my relationship with Sam. I can't get enough of him. I'm never irritated by the frequency of his phone calls and I have yet to invent a fake appointment at the gym or the hairdresser's to get out of meeting him. He and I could talk for hours at a stretch, with no need for a wine bar hubbub, or mutual friends to help the conversation along. He is, in short, everything I've ever wanted in a man. He showers me with compliments, but in a genuinely appreciative way, rather than a slavish 'I-think-you're-so-fucking-wonderful' way. He's attentive but not a doormat and always remembers my friends' names and who is doing what to whom, even though he hasn't actually met any of them yet.

'When will we get to meet the wondrous creature?' asks Jo, chasing the olive round her glass with one finger.

'I said I'd meet him by the stage when they've finished their set. God, I hope they're not crap.'

I must admit I *am* a bit worried I might find the whole experience a little toe-curling. I mean I know the real-life Sam is a really cool guy, but his easy listening alter ego could be a different kettle of fish altogether. What if he's really cheesy, slapping on those bongos, legs akimbo in tight lee-sure slacks, tongue in the corner of his mouth, half a bitter shandy at the side of the stage? What if he keeps hitting duff notes or the band is booed off stage? I am being unusually pessimistic, even by my own 'always look on the black side' standards, but I'm not really a miserable bitch, it's just a kind of self-defence mechanism. I've managed to avoid disappointment on numerous occasions by always imagining the worst possible case scenario.

## WOW!

'Well we're about to find out,' says Amy, as a Bryl-creemed compere in a cream lounge suit and purple cummerbund bounds onto the stage.

'Ladies and gentlemen, for your listening pleasure, may I present Kem-pin-ski!' he says, as the red velvet curtains are lifted to reveal the six-piece combo.

Well at least Sam *looks* all right. He's wearing ice blue Farahs with a particularly lurid Hawaiian shirt, but he carries it well.

By the end of the band's twenty-minute set, I'm their Number One Fan. They were bloody brilliant and the whole place was grooving away to their selection of Burt Bacharach and Tony Hatch covers, peppered with original material. And Sam exuded a kind of powerful, sexy confidence that I actually found rather arousing. 'See that ... that's my boyfriend,' I wanted to announce to my fellow Easies. Afterwards Amy and Jo head for the bar while I hover round the stage like a groupie until Sam appears.

'You were great!' I say, flinging my arms round his neck and pressing my nose into that soft spot just behind his ear. 'My friends are dying to meet you, they're over here . . .'

I take him by the hand and lead him across the dance floor to our booth where Amy and Jo are waiting. They both compliment him – Amy on his bongo playing and Jo on his Hawaiian shirt. In a little while, Sam's band-mates join us and everybody's chatting to everybody else and the drink is flowing. The keyboard player lights a surreptitious spliff under the table and when it comes my way I take several deep lungfuls and enjoy the caress of its smoky fingers on my brain. 'Fancy a spin round the dance floor, gorgeous?' says Sam, as the mellow sound of Herbie Mann fills the ballroom.

'Why not?' I say, and we take to the floor. Sam certainly knows some fancy moves and we twirl and tango our way through six tracks on the trot until I'm quite breathless. Jo and Amy meanwhile are getting down with Larry the drummer and Daniel the lead guitarist respectively. Isn't it great when your friends get on, not only with your boyfriend, but also with your boyfriend's friends?

All too soon, the lights come on and it's time to drag ourselves home. As I'm queuing to retrieve my coat from the cloakroom, I catch Amy snogging Daniel. Result!

'Shall we share a cab home?' says Sam as everyone's saying their goodbyes in the street. 'I think we're the only ones going south of the river.'

'Sure,' I say. Then, after a two-beat pause, I add, 'Actually, how do you fancy coming home with me?'

As I was getting ready earlier, I'd thought that this could possibly be – in actual fact, would most probably be – The Night. With this in mind I had made careful preparations: my legs, underarms and bikini line are now freshly Immac-ed, my entire surface area has been coated in Molton Brown firming body lotion, and underneath this clingy outfit I am sporting a cream-coloured Oscar de la Renta lace G-string and matching plunge bra. Not that I'm taking anything for granted – in fact, I'm actually holding my breath while I wait for his response. Please God, I'll never eat another Marks & Spencer's Swiss Mountain Bar in one go as long as I live if you'll just make him say 'yes'.

'I can't think of anything else I'd rather do right now,' says Sam, as he enfolds me in his arms and starts kissing my earlobes with his soft warm lips.

Sam is one great shag, and I mean that most sincerely. As soon I'd closed the front door behind us and slipped the deadbolt, he was a man on a mission ... nibbling, nuzzling, stroking, sucking, we staggered into the bedroom, tugging off each other's clothes as we went. By the time we hit the mattress, we were both completely naked – except for my G-string, which Sam removed with his teeth (a cliché, I know, but a very enjoyable cliché). And when we finally fell apart, some four hours later, both of us damp, sticky and very very satisfied, I went to sleep with Sam's body curled around me spoon-style. Amazingly, when I woke up, about half an hour ago, we were still in the same position. This is a highly significant development for me because normally I absolutely positively cannot get to sleep unless there's a good six-inch gap between my bedmate and me. But this, this is such bliss that I've been lying in the same position, very still so as not to wake Sam, just so I can feel his skin on mine. I risk craning my neck backwards to look at his sleeping face. There's a little constellation of freckles on his right shoulder; I wish I could kiss them. What the hell, I *will* kiss them. I wriggle out of his embrace and start to plant small kisses on the soft skin of his shoulder. He stirs slightly and says the word, 'Ruby', which is a good sign – he knows where he is then.

'Morning Sam,' I say, kissing him on the lips. His eyelids flicker open and a lazy smile forms on his lips.

'Can I get you anything . . . orange juice, toasted teacake, Frosties?'

'There's only one thing I want right now – and it's right here,' he says, drawing me down on top of him.

Forty-five minutes later, and we've worked up quite an appetite. I slip on a T-shirt and knickers and go to the kitchen for supplies. We feed each other mouthfuls of teacake, in between kisses, and I feel so loved up it's untrue. Finally, I drag myself out of bed and head for the shower. 'Make yourself at home,' I say as I disappear into the bathroom. 'Watch TV, put a CD on, I won't be long.'

Standing under the power shower, working up a lather with a bodymop and a bar of Dove, I'm vaguely aware of the sound of the front door opening and shutting a couple of times. For one awful moment, it crosses my mind that Sam might be doing a runner, but I don't believe he'd do that to me after the night *we* just had. When I emerge from the bathroom, buffed, moisturized, perfumed and wearing a touch of concealer and two coats of mascara, Sam has vacated the bed. I slip on my denim skirt and a lilac T-shirt and go through to the lounge where I see Sam sitting on the sofa. In front of him, on the coffee table, are three cardboard cake boxes, stacked one on top of the other.

'Special delivery,' he says, gesturing at the boxes.

'What on earth are they?'

'I've no idea. Your entry phone buzzed when you were in the shower and it was some guy in a van saying you were expecting these, so I signed his delivery docket and brought them in for you.'

'How strange, I haven't ordered anything . . . not unless it's that delivery from Ann Summers,' I joke lamely.

When I reach the coffee table, I see that each of the boxes has a gold logo printed on the side:

Goldberg's of Hampstead

Master Baker &
Confectioner of Distinction

'What the . . .' My voice tails off as I open the lid of the top box.

'What is it?' asks Sam.

My mouth is opening and closing like a stranded fish, but no sound is coming out, so Sam gets up and peers into the box.

'It's a wedding cake.'

It is indeed – the top tier of a wedding cake, to be precise, complete with miniature bride and groom. Any notion that Goldberg's of Hampstead might just have delivered to the wrong address goes out of the window as soon as I see that little naked bride, who is clearly supposed to be a fondant replica of my good self ... except my stomach isn't concave and my hair isn't quite that long. I don't recognize the groom at all – medium height, medium build, short mid-brown hair, no distinguishing features to speak of except for that ivy leaf over his todger. He could be anyone, but it doesn't take a genius to work out that he's supposed to symbolize the Secret Admirer. I move the box to the floor, so that I can open the second one. It's another layer of cake, only this one's larger. Like the first tier, it's heart-shaped and covered in white icing doves and a kind of trailing green ivy effect – most unusual for a wedding cake, although it seems to ring a dim and distant bell at the back of my mind. I don't bother with box number three, I can guess its contents.

Sam is sitting there in what is presumably a stunned silence. What on earth must he be thinking? How am I going to explain to him that this is the handiwork of a madman?

'Look, Ruby, I'd better get going,' he says, standing up abruptly. 'I promised Jim I'd help him change the spark plugs on his car. He doesn't know the first thing about motors.'

'Sam, don't rush off. I know this must look seriously odd, but I can explain.'

'Let me guess ... you're getting married this afternoon, only you forgot to mention it.' His voice has developed a horrid icy edge.

'No, you don't understand, I didn't order this. There's this guy, he's got a thing about me, this is his way of trying to win me over.'

'This gets worse ... you mean your ex-boyfriend sent this to you? I really think you should finish your previous relationship before you embark on a new one. I'll see you around.'

He goes to the bedroom to retrieve his jumper from the floor, where it landed after I'd ripped it off last night. For a few seconds, I stand frozen to the spot. Then instinct kicks in and I go running out to the hall, where he's already fumbling with the lock on the front door.

'Don't go, Sam, please just hear me out.' I'm surprised to feel tears pricking the back of my eyes. I can't stand the thought of some nutter sabotaging my one chance of true happiness. God knows, I've waited long enough to find my Mr Right. Sam pauses, the door half open, and my lip must be wobbling big style, because he gives a huge sigh and wraps his arms around me. I bury my head in the rough wool of his jumper and I start crying, big, ugly sobs that seem to bypass my throat and come straight from my chest.

'It's okay, Ruby,' he says gently, stroking my hair with

one hand. 'Let's go and sit down and you can tell me all about it.'

In between noisy sniffs, I tell him about the now-obsolete *preciousruby.com* and the chocolates (I leave out the digitized message at the Arsenal game because it sounds too flaky). I relay Amy's theory that Alan Kramer is the man behind it all and give Sam an edited account of my two encounters with him.

'So you think this Secret Admirer – whoever he is – sent you the wedding cake?'

'I'm absolutely sure of it,' I say, reaching for a man-size tissue so I can blow my snotty nose. It must look really red and revolting, and I know my eyes really swell up when I blub.

'I wish you'd told me about this guy sooner. I hate to think of you shouldering all this worry on your own.'

'I thought it would put you off me, and anyway, I assumed he'd just go away eventually.'

'Well he sounds like a pretty persistent type to me. So, just to recap, you haven't got a hard copy of *precious-ruby.com*, and you didn't keep the *Congratulations!* card with his handwriting on.'

'Yeah. I know that was a bit stupid now, but I really wasn't too worried at the time. I just thought it was some *Wow!* reader. But maybe I should be worried – this cake thing . . . well, it's the work of a seriously deranged individual.'

'You need to do two things: one, ring Goldberg's and get as much information as you can out of them – tell them the truth, that you're being stalked and you need all the details they can supply. Then if it all points to Kramer, we can work out what to do next.'

'Good idea . . . the phone number's there on the cake box. What's the second thing?'

'You need to call the police and get everything you've told me down in a statement.'

'Don't you think that's a bit over the top? He hasn't actually threatened me or anything.'

'Ruby, it doesn't matter. Stalking is a criminal offence – they passed some law or other a few years back, I remember reading about it after Jill Dando was murdered. You'll be able to get an injunction against him or a restraining order or something. The man knows your home address, which means you're at risk . . . you've got to report it. There's no time like the present, so why don't you ring Goldberg's now? I'll stay with you for moral support.'

'I thought your mate's car needed fixing.'

'He'll just have to wait . . . this is more important.'

Despite my reluctance to involve the police, I'm pleased that Sam has such deep concerns for my safety. Sometimes I get tired of being the tough single female, always having to be in control, always having to sort problems out on my own. Sam suggests we compile a list of questions before I ring Goldberg's, just so I don't leave anything out.

- Did the client come into the shop or order by phone?
- If he came in, what did he look like?

- What name and address did he give?
- Did he pay by cash, cheque or credit card?

Sam reads the shop's phone number from the cake box and I make the call. A female voice answers on the third ring and when I explain I am in receipt of a wedding cake I didn't order, she advises me to speak to Felicity Goldberg, the shop's proprietor. When I finally get through to her, after waiting on hold for an age, I explain my case as clearly and simply as I can: that I have been receiving unsolicited gifts from a lunatic and that she may be able to provide vital information that will help me uncover his identity. I get quite excited when she tells me that the Secret Admirer actually came into the shop.

'Yes, I recall the gentleman very clearly,' she says. 'He was most charming and I felt quite sorry for him when he told me his fiancée was very ill . . . He implied, you know, that she didn't have long to live.' I feel physically sick when she tells me this.

'When I heard that, I made his order a priority, rushed it through in four weeks, put him ahead of other clients, very prominent theatre people actually. He paid me a little bit extra, but even so . . . I can't believe he was a fraud, he seemed so, so . . . terribly nice.'

'I'm sure he was very convincing, Ms Goldberg. As you will appreciate, I'm keen to find out as much as possible about this man – he's been making quite a nuisance of himself – in fact, I'm thinking of reporting him to the police. I'd be most grateful for any information you can give me.'

'I acted with the best intentions,' she says, clearly embarrassed at being an unwitting pawn in some sicko's game. 'I really don't want to get involved, I can't afford to attract any negative publicity, I have a lot of celebrity clients, you know.'

'I just need the answers to some very straightforward questions, Ms Goldberg. Please help me, you're the only one who can provide any sort of clue to his identity.'

Reluctantly she agrees, and I plod through my list of questions, taking notes as I go. When we're done, I thank her profusely and she says she hopes she's been of some help. I hang up and turn to Sam, who is holding up the little fondant me and shaking his head.

'So what could she tell you?'

'Her physical description was pretty detailed: early to mid-thirties, average height and build, quite good-looking with an olive complexion, short, sandy hair, rather tousled in appearance, thick glasses with rectangular frames, a few days' worth of stubble and a well-spoken voice with no noticeable accent.'

'Does that sound like Kramer?'

'It's a fair match, except he doesn't wear glasses and his hair isn't sandy, it's mid-brown, but he could've been in disguise – Goldberg said the stubble looked darker than the hair, so maybe he was wearing a wig. He told her his name was Domcot, Mr Domcot, no christian name. It doesn't ring any bells with me, so I assume it was a false name.'

'Domcot, Domcot, Domcot . . . dotcom!' says Sam triumphantly.

'Pardon?'

'Domcot is a poorly disguised anagram of dotcom – as in *preciousruby.com*. He obviously didn't spend too much time dreaming that one up.'

'Hey, well done Sherlock! Not that that helps us much. Apparently he didn't give an address either. He paid cash, the whole lot upfront . . . four hundred and fifty big ones, can you believe it? So there's no way of tracing him through a cheque or credit card.'

'He obviously thinks you're worth it.'

'He asked for the cake to be delivered to the bride, i.e. me, and he told Goldberg that I'd left the design completely up to him. Apparently, he gave a very precise description of his requirements – even produced a whole load of magazine clippings showing the kind of things he wanted . . .' Suddenly the penny drops. 'Goddamn it, I knew that cake looked familiar!'

I go charging over to the kitchen and grab a Sabatier knife, the biggest one I've got, a great big meat cleaver.

'What on earth are you doing, Ruby?'

'Just testing out a little theory.'

I march to the coffee table, fling open the lid of the smallest cake box and plunge the knife in, decapitating the miniature groom as I do so. I gouge out a section of the cake and pop a piece into my mouth. 'Carrot cake

. . . that figures.' I move on to the second box. 'Vanilla sponge. Mmmm, it's lovely and moist.'

'Ruby, you're acting very strangely.'

'Just hang on one second and all will be revealed.'

Finally, box number three gives up its secret. 'Traditional fruit . . . now I've sussed his little game.'

'I can't wait to hear your explanation.'

'Celebrity weddings.'

'Sorry?'

'Well we know the Secret Admirer is a big fan of *Wow!*, don't we? He reads my articles, cuts out photos of me to stick on other women's bodies. Well this cake he has so lovingly designed for me is an amalgam, a compilation if you will, of three very famous people's wedding cakes: David Seaman – he had three heart-shaped tiers; Scary Spice – her cake was plastered in white icing doves and topped with naked sugar replicas of the real bride and groom; Posh 'n' Becks – one tier of carrot cake, one vanilla sponge and one fruit, all decorated in green fondant ivy leaves. I rest my case.'

# FOURTEEN: SECRET ADMIRER

The Secret Admirer loves to shop for lingerie. He's not one of those men who shuffle self-consciously around the underwear sections of anonymous department stores, inspecting gaudy items that their wife or girlfriend will never wear in a million years, making hasty purchases without even checking the size label, that the colour will suit, that the fabric and trimmings are pretty but comfortable. No, lingerie shopping is a veritable pleasure for *this* man, an experience to be planned and savoured. *He* knows his demi bra from his balconette, the pros and cons of satin versus stretch lace, the crucial differences between a waspie and a basque. Yes, when it comes to ladies' flimsies, he is definitely something of a connoisseur.

The venue for today's shopping expedition is Agent Provocateur, a splendid designer underwear emporium in Soho frequented, he has heard, by supermodels, no less. On entering its chinoiserie boudoir interior, he stands for a moment, enjoying the assault on his senses – soft piped music seduces his eardrums as he views the rack upon rack of taffeta panties, gossamer negligees and chantilly lace suspender belts which beg to be filled with pliant flesh.

He browses happily for a good fifteen minutes, examining the garments quite boldly, rubbing the various fabrics between forefinger and thumb and sometimes even touching them surreptitiously to his cheek. That sheer quarter-cup bra in red tulle is probably too risqué, as is the boned fuchsia corset with back lacing. No, what he wants is something alluring but not tarty, pretty but not girlie, something that will make her feel good when she wears it underneath a slinky designer frock at one of her fancy schmancy celebrity parties.

He catches the eye of one of the minxy assistants in her high heels, seamed stockings and fitted Vivienne Westwood uniform ... a terribly clever gimmick, far preferable to being served by one of those broad-in-the-beam chain store frauleins in a pleated skirt and half-moon glasses.

'Do you need any help with your selection?' she asks pertly.

'Yes please. I would appreciate a female opinion, I'm buying for a very special woman you see and I want to get it absolutely right.'

He divulges his requirements and she guides him to a collection of gorgeous items, quite plain, no excess lace or decoration, but sexy all the same. 'Our *Diva* range was inspired by classical sculpture,' she tells him.

He can see exactly what she means, the clean fitted lines would make any woman look like a goddess (not that his precious girl needs any assistance at all in that department). And *Diva* – how utterly appropriate. He had loved Ruby's interview with Ciara Powell, which he had read over and over again. What a fantastically flamboyant woman La Powell had sounded, a real star in the traditional mould. It was quite clear that she and his precious girl had got on like a house on fire.

'Very nice indeed . . . in fact that could just be what I'm looking for. What fabric is this?'

'Duchesse satin – and as you can see the range comes in three colour ways.'

His eye is immediately drawn to the pale pink, but with Ruby's colouring, she would doubtless prefer the black. 'I'll take the bra, V-front briefs and suspender belt, all in black,' he says.

'And madam's size?'

'She's 34C and a size 10–12. I'd like also to buy another item, something a little, how shall I put it, frivolous.'

'Ah, well in that case allow me to show you our accessories range.' He trots obediently across the store behind her.

'What about a pair of our fully fashioned nylon stockings with classic back seam?'

An involuntary shudder goes through him. What does she take him for? Seamed stockings indeed, he has a little more imagination than that. It must be this wig he's wearing, makes him look like a creep. His distaste is obvious and she hurriedly moves on to another item.

'No? Well how about one of our *Oils of Love*? They're terribly popular with our female customers.'

He'd like nothing better than to grease up his palms and rub them over Ruby's silken flesh, but a gift like that just isn't appropriate at this early stage of their relationship.

'I know, I've got just the thing!' she exclaims, tottering over to a display at the back of the boutique. 'Classic Hollywood-style satin mules with marabou trim. What woman could resist them?'

He takes the proffered shoe and positions it on the upturned palm of his right hand. Yes, they are quite exquisite – glamorous yet fun – just the ticket. She'll look like a proper little Jayne Mansfield in these.

'These would be perfect . . . there's just one problem. I don't know her shoe size. I'd say her feet were medium, neither large nor small, a five or a five and a half perhaps.'

'Well you can always return them if they don't fit. And of course, being a mule, the sizing isn't quite as crucial as with a regular shoe. Take me, I'm a four normally, but in an open-toed shoe I can get away with a four *or* a three.'

She's certainly a good saleswoman, give her her due, and those mules really are quite delicious.

'Very well, you've convinced me. I'll take a pair of size fives, in the black. And can you gift wrap everything?'

'It would be my pleasure. Now, if you'll just follow me to the till.'

Soon, he's walking out of the shop with a large flat box and a smaller shoebox, each trimmed with a silky black ribbon. He'd love to see her face when she opens his gift. Designer lingerie doesn't come cheap but he enjoys treating her. Admittedly, he did have to think long and hard before deciding to make this particular purchase. His beloved has been a naughty girl you see. He paid her a visit the other week and surprise, surprise, she was out. It was a Saturday night so he supposed it was only to be expected. He'd parked in his usual spot, only intending to wait till midnight, but somehow he ended up falling asleep in his car, lulled to sleep by the radio. Two and a half hours later, he had been woken by the throb of a black cab's diesel engine. With an emotion approaching horror, he had watched his beloved emerge from the cab, accompanied by a strange man in a terribly garish shirt. As she struggled to open the door – clearly hindered by the effects of the alcohol she'd doubtless consumed in great quantity – the man had placed his arms around her waist and nuzzled his face into that lustrous mane of hair. She'd turned to him, laughing, and wrapped her arms around him. That romantic scene had cut him to the quick and when he saw them sharing a passionate kiss, he'd actually been forced to look away. By the time he'd looked up again, they'd gone inside and all he saw was the closing door. He'd half considered walking round to the river path to peer through Ruby's windows, but he really didn't have the stomach for it. He could well imagine the torrid scene that was being played out within those four walls.

# WOW!

By the following day, he had rallied, however. Ruby was too much of a career woman to want to settle down just yet. No, she was simply playing the field. And anyway, no man would ever be able to give her the love, security and support that he could offer in abundance. She'd be a fool to turn him down. But that doesn't mean he is going to rush things. No, he is like the fabled tortoise – 'slow and steady wins the race' – and each step in his strategy of seduction has so far been planned quite painstakingly: *preciousruby.com* had been his introduction, his calling card, if you will, and he'd paid a considerable sum for the services of a freelance web designer; the *Congratulations!* card and chocolates a sign that he admired her ambition and considered her writing a talent worthy of recognition; the digital message at Highbury proved he wasn't afraid to declare his feelings in public; the wedding cake symbolized his honourable intentions; and now the lingerie, a truly sensuous gift that will demonstrate his thoughtfulness and good taste. By wooing her in this truly imaginative way, she will soon be putty in his hands. Then and only then, will he reveal his true identity.

# FIFTEEN: RENDEZVOUS

This morning, just as I'm getting ready for work, a red post office van pulls up outside the flat. Seconds later, the entry phone buzzes and when I go to the door, the postman proffers a large package, wrapped incredibly neatly in plain brown paper with a printed address label. I am immediately suspicious.

'Is this registered post?' I demand. 'Do you have a record of the sender's name and address?'

'Sorry love,' he replies, clearly taken aback by my aggressive line of questioning. 'It's just regular first class, it's too big to fit in the postie's bag that's all.'

I carry the package into the living room and tear off the outer wrapping. Two boxes come tumbling out – one is a large flat box, the other a smallish shoebox and both are bound with a black ribbon. When I see the Agent Provocateur logo emblazoned across both of them, I practically retch. I suppose it was only a matter of time before the SA (or Sad Arsehole, as Sam has christened him) presented me with underwear. There's no card, no note, nothing to say who sent the package, but I know it's the work of the SA. Half of me wants to chuck the boxes in the bin unopened, but the other half is over-whelmed with curiosity. The curious half wins and I slide the ribbon off the big box and tentatively lift the lid. Nestling in folds of tissue paper is a black satin knicker and bra set and coordinating suspender belt. They're quite tasteful actually – I might have chosen them myself – but even so, the sheer intimacy of the gift makes me feel strangely violated. I picture the SA going into the store and rifling through piles of stuff before alighting on those particular items – the perv probably got a hard on imagining how my breasts would look spilling over the top of that bra, how the satin knickers would fit my bum snugly. Yuck, now I do feel like vomiting. The really creepy thing is that he got my sizes exactly right, as I discover when I examine the labels. I don't see how a magazine reader could deduce that from a mere photo-graph of me. No, this is definitely the work of someone who has seen me in the flesh . . . Even so, it's pretty good guesswork, especially for a man. I mean, to get the cup size and everything. I brace myself for the second box, holding my breath as I pull off the lid and tip the tissue-wrapped contents onto the sofa. A pair of black mara-bou-trimmed mules, how odd. I wonder what thoughts were going through his sick brain when he picked those; maybe he's one of those foot fetishists . . . I'm relieved to discover that they're a size too small – he doesn't know me *that* well then. Retrieving the brown paper wrapping from the floor, I squint at the 'W1' postcode. I rack my brain to think of any possible connection, however tenuous . . . Snappers, the photo lab that *Wow!* uses, is based in Soho, but I can count on one hand the number of times I've been in there; surely not often enough for one of those lanky, Mambo-clad youths to develop a crush on me. Kramer of course would have plenty of opportunity to post a package in central London. Come to think of it, I'm sure his agent's office is just off Great Marlborough Street. Let's face it though, the Secret Admirer could be anyone in possession of a Zones 1&2 Travelcard.

By coincidence, today is the very day I have arranged to call in at Rotherhithe police station en route to work to make a statement about my alleged stalker, so I'll be able to take the undies with me as evidence. Before setting off, I give Sam a quick call to tell him about the SA's latest offering.

'This is getting out of hand, Ruby,' he says, his voice heavy with concern. 'I want you to promise to be extra careful from now on. Don't answer your front door without checking the caller's identity and even then you've still got to be wary. Look at that postman, for example – for all you know, *he* could've been the Sad Arsehole.'

'Well he had a uniform and his post office van was parked on the street behind him so I think he was kosher,' I say a little too flippantly.

'But you see what I'm saying, don't you? This man is obsessed with you and he'll probably do anything he can to get near you. Just be on your guard that's all. I couldn't bear it if anything happened to you.'

That last sentence sends a warm tingle through me. Sam cares about me, he *really* cares about me. And I feel exactly the same, in fact I'd go as far as to say, I'm falling in love with him, except I haven't told him that, not yet. 'Well I'm going to the police station this morning, so I'll take the underwear in to show them.'

'You do that – and don't forget to bring Kramer's name into the picture, maybe they could warn him off or something. I wish I could come with you, but I can't get out of this wretched meeting with the Blackheath Society. I'll call you later to find out how you got on.'

In the event, the police weren't much help. A very nice female officer took down some details, looked at my underwear, and said that basically there was nothing she could do. In theory, she explained, a restraining order *could* be granted under the 1997 Protection from Harassment Act. But apparently, sending a couple of gifts in the post doesn't constitute harassment, although WPC Wilkes did agree that the wedding cake verged on the macabre. As for *preciousruby.com*, well I've no evidence the site ever existed, not that Wilkes appeared to disbelieve me, or maybe she's just a good actress. She told me that cyber-stalking is now a recognized crime and that people have been jailed before now for sending 'threatening and abusive' emails, not that there was anything especially threatening or abusive about *preciousruby.com*. When I tentatively suggested that the police might like to pay a visit to Alan Kramer, just to suss him out, she said absolutely, definitely, no way, not. There wasn't a shred of evidence to connect him with the gifts, she said, and of course she's right. She simply told me to get in touch if the SA made any threatening advances to me and that was that really. Sam couldn't believe it when I spoke to him on the phone, back at the office. He got all indignant and macho, bless him. He's made me promise to call him any time day or night if I hear the slightest suspicious noise in the flat, or feel scared in any way. I was half hoping he'd suggest moving in, just temporarily you understand, to protect me, but it didn't come. I don't blame him, it's still early days in our relationship – four weeks, two days and eight hours to be exact.

Most of my working day is taken up with Operation Jedi. Weddings are always very time-consuming projects. You wouldn't believe the things I have to do in the name of showbiz. Technically, the magazine doesn't get involved in the organization of the wedding itself, but couples often rely on us to pull a few strings. I once spent an entire week trying to negotiate three hundred bottles of heavily discounted champagne for a satellite TV host and his weather girl wife. You can imagine their reaction when I told them the best I could do was a hundred bottles at 50 per cent of cost price. I mean, the bride-to-be actually wept down the phone. You'd think I'd told her the groom had run off with another woman. Another time, I had a panicky phone call from a track athlete's fiancée three days before the wedding to say that the tablecloths for the reception had been delivered and they didn't match the napkins. I don't know what she wanted me to do about it – get out my Singer and run up 150 new ones I expect.

As you can imagine, Jedi is proving to be a particularly demanding job. I've had to organize the design and printing of the laminate security passes, book the accommodation for all Special K's men (the editorial team will be staying at Kellaway Castle itself but the security men have to make do with a local bed and breakfast) and even compile a shortlist of wedding gifts for Eva to choose from. In the end, she plumped for his 'n' hers Prada weekend bags (on expenses of course, so it's all tax deductible).

Yesterday, I did a phone interview with wedding co-ordinator Hugh Willoughby-Smith, during which I discovered that the theme of the wedding is 'Greek Gods' – apparently Niamh has been obsessed with ancient Greece since visiting Knossos on a modelling assignment in Crete three years ago. All the guests have been asked to wear white, gold or a combination of the two. A themed wedding is practically compulsory for any celebrity worth her salt (and in my experience, it *is* the women who decide these things).

Unfortunately, the date and venue of Joe and Niamh's wedding have already been leaked, as predicted. I suppose it was inevitable, once the two hundred invitations went out. All but one of the tabloids went to town on the story and I know the manager at Kellaway Castle was besieged by reporters, wanting to know what was on the wedding menu, and had any overnight bookings been taken under the names Schiffer, Spielberg or Paltrow? Not that any of these celebs have been invited, it's just guesswork on the part of the newspapers. And even if they were coming, I doubt they'd book under their own names anyway. I love those fake names celebrities give. Johnny Depp, for example, reportedly uses the soubriquet 'Mr Donkey Penis'. Anyway, the long and short of it is every tabloid reporter and paparazzo is going to bust a gut to gain access to that wedding, whether it be in person or with the aid of a long lens or a hidden microphone. And anyone who does manage to sneak a photograph will be able to name his or her price.

But thankfully security is Special K's responsibility, not mine. Actually I'm feeling rather pleased with myself because I've just secured an interview with Donatella Versace, who has agreed to meet me for a brief chat on the wedding day itself – which is great news, because the readers can hear about the wedding dress from the horse's mouth so to speak. Checking through the rest of my emails, I'm pleased to hear from Amy that she and Daniel enjoyed an illicit date last night – illicit because she's still seeing Toby, but hopefully she'll give him the elbow before too long. She adds that 'Sam's really nice . . . you two are just perfect for each other,' which is the first time I've heard her say that about any of my boyfriends. There's a message from Simon too. I haven't heard from him in ages and it sounds pretty intriguing:

> How do you fancy meeting up for a quick drink after work tonight? An associate of mine really wants to meet you and believe me, it'll be well worth your while. We'll be in All Bar One in Covent Garden from 7 p.m.
> Si xx

I hesitate for a second because Simon has got some pretty dodgy mates. God knows, I've had a close encounter or two in the past. But I'm seriously in need of a drink after the day I've had, so I hit Reply and type:

> Okay . . . but he'd better be good looking.

Just my little joke, I haven't looked at another man since I met Sam, honest.

When I arrive at All Bar One, nearly an hour late, Simon and friend are sitting at a table by the window. Simon introduces his mate as 'Nick Porter . . . he's a reporter for *News on Sunday*.' What a sleazy job that must be – *News on Sunday* specializes in catching footballers with their keks off and soap stars snorting coke in nightclub toilets

– but Nick seems quite respectable on a first impression: reasonably good suit, short well-cut hair, expensive after-shave. I wonder why he wants to meet me.

'How do you two know each other then?' I say as Simon pours me a glass of champagne from the bottle on the table.

'We're both in the publishers' five-a-side football league,' explains Nick. 'Simon's team thrashed us last week. We're out of the tournament now.'

'Really . . . I've always thought Simon had two left feet. Of course I'm only basing this on his dancing ability, I've never seen him play football.'

'Thanks Ruby,' says Simon indignantly. 'For your information, I've been our team's highest goal scorer this season.'

We chat a bit more about Simon's footballing prowess and then the conversation moves on to footballers I have interviewed, at least that's where Simon steers the conversation.

'Ruby interviewed Lee Jackson the other week. His house was hideous, the man has got no taste whatsoever, except when it comes to women, of course.'

The two of them share a mutual smirk. They're prob-ably remembering those huge billboards featuring CoCo Fernandez lying on her back in a meadow wearing nothing but a translucent bra and a smile. I go to help myself to more champagne, but the bottle's empty, so I get my purse out of my bag and stand up, intending to go to the bar.

'No that's okay, Ruby, I'll get this one,' says Nick smoothly, waving aside my protests.

When he's gone, I ask Simon, 'What's all this in aid of then? Why is Nick so keen to meet me and what did you mean by it being "worth my while"? I'm quite happy to sit here drinking champagne with you all night, but I think you've got something up your sleeve so how about you come clean.'

'I'm just acting as a middleman. I think Nick should be the one to explain. He'll be back in a minute.'

'You're such a tricky sod, Simon. What have you two been cooking up?'

Nick returns with a bottle of champagne – the stakes have obviously been raised because it's Laurent Perrier this time, not the house stuff.

'I think you should put Ruby out of her misery, Nick. She's starting to imagine all kinds of things. Now I've done the introductions I'm going to leave you two to it. I'm meeting Katie outside Armani in half an hour.'

'Oh right, I'll call you tomorrow, Simon – let you know I'm still alive,' I say, with a mock grimace.

'You're in perfectly safe hands,' he says.

We kiss each other goodbye and off he goes. I look at Nick expectantly. He clears his throat and I think I detect a slight trace of nerves. What on earth is he going to say?

'I'll put my cards on the table, Ruby, no messing about. Now I don't want you to be offended by what I'm about to suggest. It's a business proposition, plain and simple.'

'I'm all ears.'

'Well, the thing is everyone in the media knows that Wow! has the exclusive on the Lucas–Connolly wedding and Simon tells me you're one of the main players.'

I make a mental note to bollock Simon next time I see him. He knows full well he's supposed to keep every work-related thing I tell him under wraps, not that I've told him much about this particular project, it's so sensitive, simply that I'll be heading the reporting team.

'Go on.'

'You obviously know how keen Wow!'s rivals would be to get some information ahead of publication – you saw it all with Maisie and Christian's wedding after all.'

'You mean how keen *your* newspaper would be to get some information.' I think I'm beginning to get the picture.

'Yes, and we'd pay a considerable sum of money to obtain such information.'

'Let me guess, *you* want *me* to get one of your photographers past our security, so he can take loads of pictures with his long lens and ruin our exclusive. I don't think so.'

'Not quite, Ruby. Pictures are too much to expect from you, it's words we're after. Would you consider "sharing" some information with us? We'd need it on the eighteenth itself, so that we could run it in Sunday's paper.'

'What do you take me for? I'm no Judas – and anyway, it's more than my job's worth. If I got found out, I'd be out on my ear and no reputable magazine or newspaper would touch me with a bargepole.'

'Oh, but you wouldn't be found out, Ruby. No one would suspect you, one of the longest-serving, most highly trusted members of the *Wow!* team. No, they'd think it was a waiter or one of the front-of-house staff at Kellaway. This deal would be strictly between you and me, no one else will ever know.'

'But it's so, so, underhand. I don't think I could live with myself afterwards . . . what kind of information would you be looking for exactly?'

'Really straightforward stuff. We wouldn't expect you to give the whole game away, we just want a paragraph or two – a description of the bride's dress, details of the groom's speech, what's on the menu at the reception, all fairly innocuous. It won't spoil *Wow!*'s exclusive, in fact it'll probably just whet people's appetites for more.'

'I really don't think so, Nick.'

'We're one of the most generous tabloids in the business . . .'

'How generous?'

'Let's see . . . how does two grand sound?'

'Two thousand pounds – you're having a laugh, aren't you?'

'Okay, make it three grand, and I guarantee, no one at the newspaper will ever know you were the informant.'

'And you'll be hailed as *News on Sunday*'s conquering hero I suppose.'

'Well, it certainly won't do my career any harm,' he

admits, clearing his throat and self-consciously adjusting the knot on his tie.

'And what might Simon's introduction fee be – twenty per cent? Don't tell me he brought us together out of some macho footballing loyalty.'

'Well, I said I'd see him right. But don't keep me in suspense. What's your answer?'

'I'm sorry, Nick. I'm just not interested.'

'Five grand and that's my final offer.'

'And "no" is *my* final answer. Now if you'll excuse me, I think I'll go home. It's been a long day. Thanks for the champagne.'

As I get up to leave, he presses his card into my hand.

'It was nice meeting you, Ruby. And if you change your mind, give me a call.'

'I'm not *going* to change my mind, Nick. But it was nice meeting you too. Maybe I'll come and watch you guys play football one of these days. I love seeing grown men make fools of themselves.'

# SIXTEEN: SECRET ADMIRER

The Secret Admirer is no animal lover, not by a long stretch. Puppies are cute but they inevitably grow into great lolloping creatures that shed hair on the soft furnishings and shit on the stairs when you aren't looking, but at least you can take them for walks. Cats, on the other hand, are totally pointless. Budgies and parrots would drive him to distraction with their endless chattering and whistling, and the current vogue for reptiles and snakes is totally beyond his comprehension – who wants to spend their Saturday afternoons shopping for dried insects and frozen mice? But fish . . . now there is an animal he can really relate to: easy to maintain and cheap to feed, endlessly entertaining, particularly the more exotic species with their cartoon-like features and vivid markings. And they're reputed to be therapeutic too. What could be more soothing than a well-stocked aquarium filled with gently drifting fish? No wonder they are such a popular choice for dentists' surgeries.

According to the free paper that is pushed through the Secret Admirer's letterbox once a week, Aquacadabra offers 'an unrivalled selection of tropical fish, a full range of aquatic accessories, free friendly advice and tank installation'. The reality is somewhat disappointing. The atmosphere in the cramped shop is unpleasantly muggy and on the slimy concrete floor, bags of bottom gravel are piled dangerously high next to barrels of long-handled fishing nets. He spends a good ten minutes browsing the dimly lit tanks that line the walls before any help comes forth in the shape of a paunchy middle-aged man who is sporting a grubby V-necked pullover with nothing underneath (a definite fashion no-no, as far as the Secret Admirer is concerned) and smells off-puttingly of digestive biscuits.

'May I be of assistance?' the man asks obsequiously, smoothing back his greasy hair with one hand. The Secret Admirer suppresses a shudder and outlines his requirements – a comprehensive free-standing beginner's aquarium to delight his beloved, something to lift her spirits at the end of an exhausting day at the office. The man smirks knowingly and leads him off towards the back of the shop, where a selection of empty tanks is stacked on the floor. Using his foot, he points out a vast glass oblong, sitting atop a vile melamine stand. 'How about this beauty? It comes with a fitted canopy and this rather eye-catching stand. Look, there's even a handy cupboard underneath – ideal for all your paraphernalia,' he says, pulling a plastic handle to reveal a small storage area.

'I was looking for something more low-key actually, more, how can I put it ... classic,' says the Secret Admirer, pleased with his tactful choice of adjective.

A wounded look crosses the man's face, but he forces a smile and gestures towards a more modest tank.

'Perhaps this is what you're looking for ... available in ten-, twenty- or thirty-gallon sizes. The cover is plain black plastic and it comes with a black metal stand, very classy, very discreet.'

He makes it sound like a sex aid, thinks the Secret Admirer, smiling to himself ... now there's a thought. 'Yes, that's much more like it,' he says, visualizing the tank in Ruby's lounge, standing against the wall opposite the long low bookcase, so it was the first thing you'd see when you walked in. It would complement the room but not dominate it.

He settles on the twenty-gallon tank and then strides off to scrutinize the fish in their watery prison. Mr Aquacadabra follows on his heels. The Secret Admirer has already earmarked some species and now he points out a particularly magnificent specimen – an elegant black creature with disproportionately long fins, swimming boredly in solitary confinement.

'I'd like a couple of these,' he says, squatting by the tank and peering at the prize catch through his Specsavers glasses.

'Oh no, you don't want to do that, not with the males,' says the man, positively oozing with smugness at his superior knowledge. 'That's a *Betta splendens* – or Siamese Fighting Fish to you – originally bred by the Thais for combat. Put two in a small tank and they'll fight to the death.'

'But the females are okay?' asks the Secret Admirer, who, used to being in charge, hates the fact that he has to kowtow to this dolt.

'Yep, the girls can be kept together, no problem.'

'Then I'll take two of them.'

Mr Aquacadabra produces a small dog-eared notebook from his trouser pocket, pulls a stubby pencil from behind his ear and makes a note of the fish.

'May I suggest you invest in some tetras?' he says, drawing the Secret Admirer's attention towards a large tank filled with small, darting fish. 'They're cheap, hardy and very alert, they'll bring a sense of movement to your aquarium. They're schooling fish, which don't thrive when kept alone, so you'll need half a dozen or so.'

'I like those ones with the phosphorescent blue marking. What are they called?'

'Neons, and very popular they are too. Your lady friend will get hours of enjoyment out of those.'

'I'll have ten,' says the Secret Admirer.

'Very good, sir, excellent choice.'

Before long, Mr Aquacadabra has a list of twenty or so fish listed in his little notebook. The Secret Admirer is thrilled with one particular specimen: the Black Ruby

Barb, no less, with her red snout and black belly and fins – how splendidly appropriate is that?

'That's a nice little community we've put together . . . She's obviously a very special lady,' says Mr Aquacadabra. 'Have you been together long?'

This oily, smelly man is really beginning to get on the Secret Admirer's nerves. He hates shop assistants who don't know their place. He came in here to make a purchase, nothing more nothing less, and now this idiot is prying into his personal affairs.

'I like to keep my private life private,' he snaps, fixing his interrogator with an icy stare. Mr Aquacadabra looks away quickly. He's been in the fish game twenty-odd years and he's seen all kinds come through the doors and regards himself as a good judge of character. This one's a queer fellow and no mistake – he can tell by those cold unfeeling eyes and that fake tash that's coming loose on one side. He often views people in terms of their fishy counterparts and this one puts him in mind of a piranha. Pity the poor girl who's going out with him.

'No offence intended,' he says hastily. 'We'll get you kitted out with some accessories then, shall we?' He leads the way across the shop floor. 'You'll need a heater, filter and pump, a bag of bottom gravel, some plants – we're running a special offer on water lobelias – and maybe a piece of bogwood or two . . .'

As he drones on, the Secret Admirer switches off, letting the words wash over him. His precious girl will be beside herself when she receives this gift. 'Swim to me, my little Black Ruby,' he whispers, almost under his breath.

'Pardon?' says Mr Aquacadabra, turning round abruptly.

'Just talking to myself,' says the Secret Admirer.

Definitely a freak, Mr Aquacadabra thinks to himself. The sooner he gets shot of this one, the better.

# SEVENTEEN: SEE HOW THEY RUN

Catford Greyhound Stadium is not one of my regular haunts. In fact I've always tried to give SE6 a wide berth. Sam, however, has an uncanny knack for persuading me to do things I wouldn't ordinarily consider in a month of Sundays – that's one of the things I love about him. Hence tonight's double date of doggie delight . . . perhaps I should rephrase that: Sam, Amy, Daniel and I are spending the evening at the dogs. It's a bit chilly outside in the concrete stands, so we're watching from the relative comfort of the viewing gallery, whose huge glass window affords an excellent view of the canine contestants.

With their arched bodies and pointy snouts, I've always regarded greyhounds as rather ugly, freakish creatures – but then I've never seen them in context. Here on the race track, going hell for leather after that little toy rabbit, they're poetry in fucking motion. I never knew there was so much muscle and sinew buried in those super-skinny bodies. I've already won a fiver on Little

Miss Strange and I've just put a quid on Megastar (the name makes him an obvious choice) in the fifth race. And I'm not the only one on a winning streak – good old Daniel is doing an impressive job of courting Amy; I can't remember the last time I saw her so animated with a man. At this rate, Toby should be history pretty soon.

'You two seem to be getting on very well together,' I remark, when the boys have disappeared to the bar in a lull between races.

'Yeah, I'm quite surprised actually,' Amy says, pulling on one of her long corkscrew curls. 'I never thought I'd have anything in common with an accountant. I've always found personal finance so incredibly dull. Here I am, fast approaching the big three-oh and I've only just got round to organizing a pension. Daniel would be horrified if he knew.'

'But Daniel's hardly your stereotypical accountant, is he?' I point out. 'I mean he plays the guitar, uses recreational drugs and wouldn't be seen dead with a ballpoint pen clipped to his breast pocket.'

'True,' she says, nodding. 'He's invited me to his parents' place in the Lake District next weekend, but I don't know if I should go. I promised Toby I'd help him decorate his bedroom. He's got this ridiculous idea about covering the walls in poo-coloured hessian and mirror tiles . . . the man's a slave to *Elle Deco*. I've told him it's going to look hideous but he doesn't seem to have much faith in my opinion, particularly when it comes to matters of interior design.'

'Never mind Toby and his artistic sensibilities,' I say crossly. 'Invent an excuse . . . tell him you've been asked to do a *Teen Scene* "on-location" interview at short notice – "Britney Spears Larges It in the Lakes", I can see it now. Or better still, give him the elbow. You really shouldn't keep both of them on the go, Amy, it's not fair. You wouldn't like it if Toby was seeing someone else behind your back, would you?' I rarely criticize Amy because she's my best friend after all, but in this instance, I really think she needs to make up her mind – and fast.

'You're totally right of course but I want to keep my options open, just until I'm sure this thing with Daniel's got some kind of future,' she says in a vague and unconvincing attempt at self-justification. 'And anyway, I haven't shagged him yet, so I haven't technically been unfaithful. I have to say it's taking every ounce of will-power I've got – have you checked the man's glutes? Pert just isn't the word. I'll make a decision soon, I promise. But enough about me . . . How's it going with you and Sam?'

'Fantastic, fabulous, wonderful. What more can I say? The man's a total dreamboat. I get a tingle down my spine every time I hear his voice on the phone. God, listen to me! I should be writing for Mills & Boon, never mind *Wow!* magazine.'

'You're so lucky, Ruby, you've really got it sorted – perfect flat, perfect job, perfect man . . .' Amy says, a tad wistfully.

'I think you're forgetting a certain Secret Admirer,

aren't you? I know it's only a few stupid presents, when it could be so much worse, but he's always there at the back of my mind, casting a shadow over everything I do. I got another one of his wretched gifts yesterday.'

'So what was it this time? Don't tell me . . . a Neil Cunningham wedding dress?'

'Don't even joke about it, Ames. Actually it was even weirder than that – a massive aquarium and a shit load of tropical fish delivered to my door by a geezer from some pet shop in north London, who had instructions to install the damn thing in my living room. Apparently a Mr Domcot went into the store earlier in the week and handpicked the lot – tank, stand, pump, filter and all these bloody fish. Said it was a present for his girlfriend.'

'That man is such a sicko . . . What on earth have you done with it?'

'Well at first I told the delivery guy he could take the whole lot straight back to the shop. But then I had an even better idea. Do you remember that charity ball at the Dorchester I covered for *Wow!* a couple of months ago, the one to raise money for a respite centre for kids with leukaemia?'

'Yeah, vaguely.'

'Well Brian, the guy who organized it all, was really grateful. He phoned me after the spread appeared in the mag and said the charity had had a flurry of donations as a result. The respite centre opens its doors next week and I figured that a tropical fish tank would really bring a smile to those kids' faces. So I told the delivery guy to wait, called up Brian on his mobile and asked him if he could use the aquarium. I told a little white lie and said it belonged to a friend who was moving overseas. He was over the moon, couldn't thank me enough, said it would be perfect for the centre's reception area. The delivery guy was a bit peeved at having to drive all the way to Bromley, but I slipped him a fiver and he soon grudgingly agreed.'

'You clever bugger, what a brilliant idea. At least someone is benefiting from the Secret Admirer's sick game. You know I'm absolutely convinced it's Kramer, Ruby. Who else would have that kind of money to fritter away?'

'The jury's still out on that one. I phoned the pet shop and had a very interesting conversation with the owner. He remembers serving Domcot, said he was a real cold fish, if you'll pardon the pun. The description he gave was almost identical to the one that cake shop woman gave me, except this time he wore a fake moustache – the guy knew it was fake because it was peeling away from one side of his lip!'

'There you are then! It must be Kramer because he obviously doesn't want to be recognized.'

'Not necessarily . . . I mean authors are fairly anonymous creatures. Look at James Herbert – he's ten times more famous than Alan Kramer, but most people don't have a clue what he looks like. I'm sure Kramer can go on a simple shopping trip without being recognized. Maybe this guy just gets off on dressing up. Whoever he is, he paid in cash and didn't leave any contact details, so the trail goes cold.'

'Have you told the police? Didn't they tell you to get in touch if you received any more gifts?'

'I spoke to WPC Wilkes on the phone and she said she'd make a note of it on the file. She says that unless his behaviour is threatening or abusive, there's not much they can do. I'm sure she thinks it's some ex-boyfriend of mine who can't let go. I tried to bring Kramer's name into the picture again, but there's no way they're going to haul him in for an interview, not without proof.'

'How's Sam taking it? It must be really weird for him, knowing that another man is totally besotted with *his* girlfriend.'

'He's been brilliant, really supportive, but it's enough to test any man's patience. I don't know that *I* would be so understanding if the roles were reversed.' Over Amy's shoulder, I see Sam and Daniel making their way towards us, carrying four bottles of Becks, so I swiftly change the subject. I'm sure Sam can do with a break from the SA, just for one day. We are supposed to be enjoying ourselves after all.

'How's work going, Ruby?' asks Daniel when he's taken his seat opposite me. 'Interviewed anyone good recently?'

'Oh the usual motley crew. I'm trying to get an interview with Catherine Carney at the moment – you know the teenage film actress who's just checked herself into the Priory.'

'Oh yeah, I read something in the *Sun*, she took an overdose didn't she?'

'A cry for help. If you want my opinion, it's a classic case of too much too young. I sent a nice bouquet of Paula Pryke flowers as soon as the story broke. The Editor authorized me to spend up to eighty quid, which is unheard of *largesse* – normally it's fifty quids' worth, max. But we're desperate for the story – Cathy Carney *is* the new Kate Winslet after all. I know it's ambulance chasing, but if we don't get in there first, someone else is bound to.'

'Ruby interviewed Ciara Powell a couple of weeks ago,' says Sam, taking a swig of beer.

'Ciara Powell? I'm impressed,' says Daniel. 'What was she like? I've heard she's a bit of a witch.'

'A *bit* – the woman's a fucking monster. She holds court in this massive hotel suite, surrounded by all these pumped-up bodyguards and browbeaten personal assistants and she treats everyone around her like they're not fit to lick the shit off her shoes. I had a real job making my piece sound positive and upbeat. That's one of the things I hate about working for *Wow!* – you can't tell it like it really is, you always have to wrap every story in cotton wool and sprinkle it with fairy dust.'

'You know I'm always amazed that people like that get to be so famous in the first place,' says Amy. 'Ciara Powell must have one hell of a publicist.'

'Oh, but Ruby got her revenge,' says Sam. 'Go on, tell them what you did.'

I relate the story, sparing no detail. The others are totally agog.

'Ruby, I can't believe you did that,' squeals Amy. 'Imagine her face when she put those slippers on, eughh!' She pinches the end of her nose and pulls a face.

'That's my girl!' says Sam proudly. 'I told you she had balls, Dan.'

'Yeah and you weren't joking. Let's have a toast . . . to Ruby, the avenging angel!' The four of us clink beer bottles and Sam squeezes my knee under the table.

'Hey, why don't you and I go for a wander round the stadium?' I say to Sam, pulling him to his feet. I have an ulterior motive in mind: I want to give Amy and Daniel some time alone, enough time for Daniel to work his magic and convince Amy she'd be better off with him.

'Do you think those two will ever get it together?' Sam asks me as we stroll arm in arm around the track's perimeter fence. 'Daniel's a pretty patient guy and I know he really likes Amy, but I'm not sure how much longer he'll tolerate her relationship with Toby. He doesn't want to share her any more, he wants her all to himself, which is perfectly understandable.'

'So you do believe in monogamy then?' I say, grateful for this opportunity to probe Sam's own level of commitment.

'God, that's a serious question. Of course I do . . . I mean, I played the field a fair bit in my youth and I think I probably upset a few women along the way, which isn't something I'm particularly proud of. But around my mid-twenties I started to understand the female species – and myself – a whole lot better. I discovered that it's much more satisfying to work at building a really strong relationship with one person than trying to develop superficial relationships with several people at once. And I think that if you're lucky enough to meet somebody you really care about, somebody who can always lift you when you're feeling upset or depressed, and somebody that you really fancy like mad, then you should grab them with both hands and not do anything to jeopardize that relationship. Because people like that don't come along too often in a lifetime.'

That is so beautiful. I don't say this out loud, of course, because it'll probably sound really facetious, but it's what I'm thinking.

'How about you?' he asks. 'Ever done an Amy and had two blokes on the go at the same time?'

'Not really . . . the beginning of one relationship has sometimes overlapped with the dying throes of another, but I've never practised full-scale deception. I wouldn't have the energy, to be honest. One man is more than enough for me.'

'And what about marriage? Is that an institution you believe in?'

This conversation is getting really heavy. I don't want to sound like I'm desperate to bag a man, but on the other hand I don't want to appear glib, so I head for the safe middle ground.

'Well you know, if the right man came along . . . but

I'd have to be really really sure I was doing the right thing. I mean I wouldn't get married unless I thought we'd be together for ever.'

'Actually my mum and dad have always been a great source of inspiration to me,' says Sam. 'They're still madly in love, even after thirty-five years of marriage. As a kid it always used to surprise me when I went round to my mates' houses and their parents were arguing or not speaking to each other or their mum was on her own because their dad had pissed off years ago. Not my mum and dad . . . in fact it's embarrassing being around them sometimes, they're like a pair of teenagers, kissing and holding hands. But that's how I'd like to be with my wife when I'm that age, still totally loved up.'

I think I've died and gone to heaven. The man's obviously been reading the How To Be A Brilliant Boyfriend Handbook . . . read it, he wrote the fucking thing!

'Anyway, shall we get back to the others, see if wedding bells are in the air yet?' jokes Sam.

'Okay, but there's something I want to tell you before we go back in. But first you've got to promise not to breathe a word of it to anyone – I haven't told another soul, not even Amy.'

'Scouts' honour, my lips are sealed.'

I describe my encounter with Nick Porter and his attempt to recruit me as a wedding spy. Sam is incredulous at the amount of money on the table.

'You mean he offered you five thousand pounds just for a bit of stuff about the dress and the speech and the food? I had no idea celebrity journalism was such a cut-throat business. What did you say?'

'I turned it down. It's not worth the risk. And anyway, it's a really mean thing to do, betray the magazine like that. Not that a few paragraphs from me would seriously undermine *Wow!*'s exclusive, in fact Nick was probably right when he said it would only encourage people to buy the magazine so they could drool over the glossy, fifty-two-page coverage. I just wouldn't feel comfortable about it, that's all.'

'Weren't you tempted just a little bit?'

'If I'm being honest, yes I was. But five grand is pretty tight, you know – it's peanuts compared to what a photographer would get for a snatched shot of Niamh in her wedding dress or a picture of the happy couple kissing. What would you have done in my position?'

'It's difficult to say. My knowledge of industrial espionage is fairly limited. We get the odd bulb theft from Greenwich Park, but that's about it. I would probably have done the same as you. I suppose five grand isn't much when you think of all the sleepless nights you'd endure, worrying about being found out.'

That makes me feel a bit better. I must admit, Nick's offer has been preying on my mind. I'm not having second thoughts exactly, I've just been fantasizing about how I'd spend the money. I can picture Sam and me relaxing on Richard Branson's Necker Island . . .

By the time we rejoin the others, the six dogs in the fifth race are being paraded in front of the spectators. I note that my dog, Megastar, is evacuating his bowels fulsomely onto the turf. I take this as a good sign – at least he'll be carrying less weight. My faith in him turns out to be sadly misplaced, however, when he romps home second to last.

'Bad luck, darling,' says Sam, who fared only slightly better – his dog came in third to last. I tear my betting slip in two and toss it disgustedly into the ashtray.

'Bloody celebrities,' I mutter to no one in particular.

# EIGHTEEN: PARTY ANIMALS

I've been to some flash parties in my time, but this promises to be one of the more memorable. Tonight, part-time novelist and full-time daddy's girl Layla Squires is celebrating her engagement to one of London town's hottest male models and it's all being recorded for posterity by moi. And if she's anything like her father – heavy metal hellraiser Davey Squires, drummer with the legendary Prowess – she knows how to have a good time. Back in the 1970s, 'Crazy' Davey drove cars into swimming pools, tossed drum kits out of hotel windows, and threw parties where the women were naked and the drugs were lined up on the coffee table like candies. Given this party's potential for debauchery, I'm rather surprised Layla agreed to give us access – even more surprising she actually approached the magazine in person to negotiate the deal. I guess the 15k fee will be a welcome boost to her rapidly emptying trust fund. Thing is, celebs know they're in safe hands with *Wow!* – we're interested only in good, clean fun, so generally we turn a blind eye to the vomit and the bulging eyeballs and the shagging in the stairwells. And like most of our party hosts, Layla has stipulated a cut-off point of one a.m., which signals the time that the reportage ends and the serious partying begins. No guest is going to really hang loose until the reporter and photographer have split.

The bash is being held at Sheridan House, a private members' club in the heart of Mayfair. The nineteenth-century townhouse was recently renovated to the most luxurious standard by one of England's most talented interior designers; there are Art-Deco bathrooms, great sweeping Georgian staircases and dramatic Gothic bedrooms, where weary club members can find a premium-rate four-poster for the night. More importantly, the Manhattan-born head barman mixes the meanest pisco sour in town . . . No wonder club memberships are so highly prized.

Layla's guest list is pretty comprehensive – a respectable handful of A-listers (including a supermodel and a Rolling Stone), a score or so of Bs (the main attractions being a couple of premier division footballers and a teenage pop diva) and a swarm of Cs (the inevitable ex-Radio One DJ plus lots of COFPs, that's Children of Famous Parents). When the list was emailed to me yesterday, I was extremely perturbed to see Alan Kramer's name included, although it's not that surprising, considering that he and Layla share a publisher. Sam told me to ignore him – I can tell he's upset at the thought of another man sniffing around me. But actually, Kramer's attendance may be a blessing in disguise. It'll give me a chance to suss him out, see how he acts around me, maybe even gather some evidence.

Tonight is also a big night for Charley, his chance to prove himself. He's been T. K. Stead's regular assistant for the best part of two years and has also worked ad hoc for several other photographers, including Raoul of course. He's wanted to set up on his own for ages and has done the odd job on the side – small-time stuff for one of the news agencies, hanging out outside Leicester Square film premieres, that kind of thing. Angela took T.K. out for lunch the other day and he managed to persuade her to take a look at Charley's portfolio, which was very nice of him. Good, reliable assistants are hard to find, but T.K. is obviously keen to see his protégé progress. Anyway, Angela liked Charley's work and has decided to test his mettle with a party shoot. Parties are pretty straightforward, photographically speaking, and Charley's only going to be shooting on 35mm tonight, which means he doesn't need a tripod or lights or any equipment other than his camera and flash. I just hope he proves to be a fast worker. I want to be home by one-thirty at the latest as I have an appointment with a certain horticulturist, who is currently watching my TV and eating my home-cooked aubergine parmigiana and apple flapjack crumble (well, he'll need all the energy he can muster when I get my hands on him, I don't care how late it is).

Charley and I have arranged to meet at the venue at ten p.m. When he arrives, I'm sitting at the bar drinking a Virgin Mary, having made my presence known to the hostess, who seems to be off her face already and keeps dabbing at her nose in a very compulsive fashion.

'I hardly recognized you!' I say, admiring Charley's cream-coloured riding breeches and short, red, military-style jacket trimmed with gold brocade.

'And look at you; eat your heart out Helena Bonham Carter!'

I, you see, am modelling an Angels and Bermans flower-sprigged Empire-line dress and my hair has been teased into ringlets and loosely tied back. Oh, I forgot to mention – it's fancy dress; *Pride and Prejudice* to be precise. Layla harbours literary aspirations, although her own poorly received first novel, a tale of sex 'n' drugs set in the supposedly glamorous world of international hair-dressing, was hardly Booker material, and relied heavily on the strength of her family name for sales.

There's only a handful of guests here at the moment, so Charley and I decide to familiarize ourselves with the layout of Sheridan House. We haven't worked together since Mustique, and I must admit I still feel a slight hostility towards him after that whole Mariah business. As far as I know, he's still seeing Emma, so whether he cooled it with the make-up artist once he got back home, or whether he's still got both of them on the go, I really don't know – and frankly I don't want to know. I'm going to avoid the whole subject of Charley's tangled love life tonight.

'This place isn't half bad,' he says, running a finger along the hand-painted wallpaper in one of the comfortable lounges, with its William Morris-print sofas and stuffed moose head mounted on the wall above the fireplace.

'Memberships are like gold dust and it's not just a question of having the necessary dosh – new members have to be proposed by three existing members,' I tell him. 'And apparently anyone can have their membership revoked at a moment's notice – discourtesy to staff and vandalism are among the punishable offences.'

'But being an obnoxious tosspot with more money than sense and no useful purpose in life is fine I suppose,' laughs Charley.

'Yeah, there'll be a few of those here tonight.'

We stick our heads into the dance arena, a high-ceilinged, wooden-floored room, where the DJ is warming up his decks. His face is familiar, but I can't remember his name – he's one of those Ministry guys I think . . . bet his services don't come cheap. Next door is an ambient chill-out area, where the lights are low and psychedelic images are being projected onto the white walls. This place will be littered with semi-comatose Trustafarians before the night's over, mark my words.

By eleven-thirty, the place is packed. Charley's doing pretty well – he just managed to persuade the supermodel to pose – and I'm at his side, helping him accost celebs and taking down all the captions. After a little while, he offers to go to the bar to get us a well-earned drink. I nip to the ladies', and very nice they are too, lots of scents and sprays and hand lotions and a nice lady to hand you a linen towel, what an awful job that must be. I'm just walking past the foot of the staircase when I spot him, standing by a towering arrangement of tropical fruit, chatting to a middle-aged woman in a poke bonnet. It's hard to tell which Austen character he's supposed to be, but in his black morning suit and black top hat, trimmed with a black silk band, he resembles a nineteenth-century funeral director. Trust a horror writer to be so bloody morbid. I think about marching up to him, catching him by surprise, just to see what his reaction will be – maybe he already knows I'm here tonight, I don't know. But while I'm thinking about it, Charley appears with two glasses of champagne and I miss my opportunity. I've tried to keep my stalker to myself as much as possible – only Sam and a few of my closest friends know, I haven't told anyone at work and I'm certainly not going to bear my soul to Charley, not when I know he's so patently untrustworthy.

'Come on, Charley, let's get some shots of Layla and Gaz together,' I say when we've drained our glasses.

'Is Gaz the fiancé then?'

'Yeah and he is *bee-yoo-tiful*. He fronted the last Hugo Boss campaign and modelled for Ozwald Boateng at Fashion Week – he and Layla met at the after-party and they've been inseparable ever since. I need to chat them up a bit anyway, 'cause when they name the day, I want the wedding exclusive.'

'Always thinking one step ahead, aren't you, Ruby? I can see why T.K. thinks you're such hot shit.'

'He does?'

'Oh yeah. He'd rather work with you than any of the other writers at *Wow!* Says you're always very professional.'

This is praise indeed, coming as it does from one of magazine land's most sought-after photographers. I'll have to be extra nice to him next time we work together.

We find Layla and Gaz feeding each other finger food on a sofa by one of the huge stone fireplaces.

'Hi guys, is it okay if we get a few shots of you together, nothing too formal, just carry on as you were.'

'Yeah, that's cool,' says Layla, picking up a miniature sausage, split and filled with mashed potato, and popping it into her amour's full-lipped mouth.

Charley fires away, as they eat and kiss and laugh, both of them loving the camera. She, like me, is wearing an Empire-line dress, only hers fits better than mine because it's made to measure and she's accessorized it really well with a midnight-blue velvet choker and matching drawstring bag. Gaz looks exceedingly dapper in a grey silk ruffled shirt and long brocade coat. That said, it doesn't look very Jane Austen to me, but then he is a model so it's hardly surprising he hasn't followed the brief.

'Hey, you wanna get a shot of this,' says Layla, grabbing Gaz's left arm and pushing up the sleeve of his period costume to reveal a fresh tattoo, unpleasantly crusted at the edges, on his upper arm, just below the shoulder.

'It was his engagement present to me. Isn't he adorable?' She pulls him towards her and gives him a big wet kiss on the mush.

The tattoo is a red heart with a little wavy banner across the centre. Etched in dark blue letters through the middle of the banner is the name *LAYLA*.

'That is sooo cool. I guess that means you're gonna be together forever, huh Gaz?' I gush. 'Charley, get a nice close-up of that tattoo, will you? And what was Layla's engagement present to you, Gaz?'

'She got me this 18-carat yellow gold bracelet from Asprey,' he says, looking like the cat that got the cream. Personally I think wrist jewellery on men looks terribly effeminate, it doesn't matter how good-looking they are.

'Have you got an engagement ring?' I ask Layla, who seems to have drawn the short straw in the present-giving stakes.

'We're going to choose it next week, once the cheque from *Wow!* has cleared.'

Talk about doing things in the wrong order. Shall I mention that she needs to submit an invoice before a cheque can be issued? Nah, let her find out for herself.

Charley and I thank them and move on to seek out the

bride-to-be's infamous father and his wife of the past twenty-eight years, former Bunny Girl Josie Squires. I expected Davey to be elbow deep in his own vomit and Josie to be dancing on the bar with the Rolling Stone by now, so imagine my disappointment when we find them sitting quietly at the bar. They haven't even made much effort with their fancy dress, talk about party poopers. Davey's obviously a changed man since he went into property development four years ago after Prowess finally split up – they were never the same after lead guitarist, 'Kinky' Ken McGuire, died while in the throes of a particularly adventurous bondage session.

'Don't think of it as losing a daughter, more as gaining a son-in-law,' I say to Davey, as Charley lines up his shot.

'Don't I know it . . . this party's costing me an arm and a leg.'

Josie shoots him a warning look, forcing him to add, somewhat reluctantly, 'But of course when it comes to the wedding there'll be no expense spared for my little girl.'

We move to the dance floor and Charley insists on taking a couple of 'action' shots on a slow shutter speed. I tell him he's wasting his time. Angela likes nice, crisp, posed, smiley shots. I know she won't use Charley's arty-farty nonsense so I leave him to it and go in search of somebody who can tell me about the canapés. I'm just looking for the kitchen when I feel a hand on my shoulder. I spin round, expecting to see Charley, but instead I come face to face with Alan Kramer. His topper's gone but it's left an unpleasant red band around the top of his forehead.

'Hi Ruby, long time no see,' he says, smiling nervously.

'Alan.' Fuck, my mind's gone blank. Just breathe deeply, Ruby, try to act natural. 'How are you?'

'Oh fine thanks. I've been pretty busy this past week. *Leather Devil* is about to be published in paperback, so I've being doing that interview thing. It's only served to remind me how much I hate talking about myself, but it's a necessary evil I suppose.'

'Right. Yeah . . . great party isn't it?'

'Fantastic. I must admit I was quite surprised when I heard Layla had got engaged. I've known her for a while now and she's always struck me as such a free spirit, I didn't imagine she'd settle down so young. She's only twenty-two or twenty-three, isn't she?'

'Actually she's twenty-five.' Stop wasting time with small talk, Ruby, and get digging; you *are* a journalist for goodness sakes.

'Oh, well, I guess that's not so young after all. Did Gaz show you his tattoo? It's quite a work of art.'

'Yeah. I thought it was pretty cool. I mean he must be so in love with her, to go through all that pain. It's a real sign of his commitment.' Now you're just rambling.

'Do you think so? I must admit I hadn't really thought of it that way,' he says, frowning slightly.

'Oh definitely. I mean, that tattoo's permanent, he wouldn't have done it if he didn't think she was the

228

woman he was going to spend the rest of his life with. All the celebrities celebrate their love by self-mutilating. Look at Angelina Jolie. She had Billy Bob Thornton's name tattooed on her arm before the world even knew he'd split with Laura Dern. And Jonathan Ross had his wife's name tattooed on his arm in scrabble letters for Valentine's Day . . .' You don't half know some useless information, girl.

'But look at poor old Johnny Depp,' he interrupts. 'He had Winona Forever stamped on his bicep and then they split up.'

'I guess . . . but I still think it's kinda romantic.' Stop waffling and find out if he's still got the hots for you.

'Is there a, er, lady in your life at the moment, Alan?'

'No one special. Actually, Ruby, I wanted to apologize again for my behaviour at my birthday party. It really was unforgivable. I'd had a few drinks and well . . . you're a very beautiful woman. And then sending you those flowers . . . highly unimaginative of me. I'm not surprised you didn't call.'

'Well you know, I just didn't want to get involved.' Tell him how you *really* feel. Say it: I wouldn't go out with you if you were the last man on earth and by the way, can you stop sending me your freaky gifts.

'So why don't I take you to dinner, somewhere really nice – how about The Ivy, you journos love that place, don't you? It's Tony Parsons' favourite restaurant, you know. I remember reading that in an interview somewhere.'

Hmmm. The Ivy, Tony Parsons ... it all sounds frighteningly familiar, in fact he's practically regurgitated my SA's entire *preciousruby.com* CV, or could it just be coincidence? The Ivy after all is London's most famous media hangout. Should I confront him? Ask him outright if he's the SA? I can't. What if I've got it all wrong, it would be so embarrassing. All of a sudden, I've had enough. Had enough of talking to Alan Kramer, had enough of this wretched party, had enough of wondering who the SA is. All I want to do is go home to Sam's strong, sinewy arms, to security.

I see Charley emerge from the dance arena. 'Charley, Charley.'

Several heads turn as I bellow across the room. Thankfully, Charley's is one of them and he starts walking towards me. Kramer is still standing there, looking somewhat bemused, and I don't bother offering any sort of explanation, nor do I bother responding to his dinner invitation.

'Come on, Charley, it's time we were going.'

'But it's only twelve-thirty, why don't we hang out a while longer?'

'But my *boyfriend* is waiting for me at home. He's very protective, you know. He'll call the police if I'm not back soon.' This is said purely for Kramer's benefit.

'I didn't know you were seeing someone, Ruby. Didn't take you long to get over Raoul then.'

'Shut up, Charley. Let's go.'

'Okay, okay ... hang on a minute, you're Alan

Kramer aren't you? I've just finished *Poison Ivy*, brilliant book. Nice to meet you, mate. Hey Ruby, how about a picture of you with Alan for the magazine?'

'I'm going, Charley, you can do what you like.' I march off and as I'm handing in my cloakroom ticket, Charley materializes.

'Why did you go running off like that? You didn't even say goodbye to Alan Kramer. I didn't know he was a friend of yours.'

'He's not a friend of mine, Charley. In fact, there's every possibility he's a sick freak who gets his jollies from harassing women. Now if you're ready, let's blow this joint. I've had enough of these crazy people.'

# NINETEEN: SECRET ADMIRER

This isn't a decision the Secret Admirer has taken lightly. Not a bit of it. He has deliberated long and hard before making the appointment and now that he is here, quite literally on the threshold, he has absolutely no second thoughts, no last-minute nerves. This is, quite simply, the best gift he can possibly bestow on his precious Ruby. Actually, he thinks, it is more of a tribute than a gift – the ultimate act of worship, a sign of his true and everlasting commitment. If she doesn't respond to this, then he has surely lost her forever . . . a prospect he scarcely dares contemplate.

He pushes open the heavy wooden door and is immediately greeted by a young female receptionist. She's a pretty girl, despite a multitude of facial piercings, including both eyebrows, tongue and lower lip. She shows him to a waiting area and presents him with a thick portfolio of artwork, which includes photographs of satisfied customers showing off their new acquisitions.

With its bohemian population, Camden had seemed the ideal place to come for such an undertaking and he had been pleasantly surprised by the choice of establishments in the north London *Yellow Pages*. After circling those claiming to be *Health Authority Registered* (he wasn't sure what that meant, but it sounded reassuring), he had then picked out the biggest and most impressive display advertisement. And now that he's here, he is reassured by the sterile surrounds and the high quality of the artwork he is viewing. The portfolio is conveniently divided into subject categories and he quickly finds the section he is looking for. The number of variations on this single simple theme is quite astounding, but one stands out above all the rest. Yes, this will fit the bill very nicely.

After a brief wait, he is ushered into the artist's studio, a brightly lit room that is as clean as any dentist's surgery he has visited. The artist – a muscular fortysomething with a goatee beard – is displaying his own quite spectacular array of body ornamentation. The Secret Admirer explains his requirements and refers to the specific item in the portfolio, before describing his own unique addition. The man gestures towards a laminated sign displayed on the wall:

```
A tattoo is forever.
(But love doesn't always last.)
```

The Secret Admirer appreciates this display of concern, but will nevertheless not be put off. He watches as the

Claudia Pattison

artist dons a fresh pair of latex gloves and takes a few
minutes to explain the sterilization process: he is com-
forted by the thought that all reusable materials have
been subjected to 270 degrees Fahrenheit. The necessary
tools are then assembled – inks, disposable ink cups and
needles, Vaseline, and of course the tattoo machine which
will deliver ink into his skin, approximately one-eighth of
an inch deep, much like an electric sewing needle. The
Secret Admirer is instructed to straddle the treatment
chair before the artist shaves the relevant area of skin and
disinfects it with green antiseptic soap.

A buzzing noise like a dentist's drill signals the start of
the procedure and he braces himself as the skin above his
left shoulder blade is punctured at up to two thousand
times a minute. He has been advised that areas located
close to bones hurt more than fleshier regions, like the
chest or upper arm, but the pain is not as bad as he
anticipated. It's like a moderate dose of pins and needles
or the feeling of being continuously snapped with a
rubber band.

As a creative artist himself, the Secret Admirer appreciates the skill of the tattooist. He knows that if the ink is
placed too deeply into the skin, the subject's own body
fluids will cause the outline to spread and lose definition
– too shallow and the colours will fade or even disappear.
Once the shape's outline has been completed, the artist
cleans the area with antiseptic soap and water. He then
adds shading and colour. The finished tattoo is then
cleaned again and the artist applies gentle pressure with a

disposable towel to remove any blood and plasma excretions.

The procedure complete, he is able to view the artist's handiwork with the aid of two carefully positioned mirrors and he is exceedingly pleased with the result. His fresh adornment is then covered with a dressing that must be kept in place for at least six hours. He won't be tempted to peek – after all, he has the rest of his life to look at it. The artist tells him that once the tattoo is exposed, he must not itch or pick at any scabs that might form, and he must keep it clean and covered with a thin layer of antiseptic cream until it heals in approximately ten days' time. He must not swim or sunbathe and he should take care to wear old, soft clothes that have been washed often enough to have the excess dye removed. Why, it's like looking after a new pet, he thinks to himself.

Travelling home in a black cab, the Secret Admirer feels quite triumphant. Doubtless, the artist would explain that his disposition results from the endorphins released by his body in response to the stimulation from the tattooing needles. But he knows this is much more than a chemical reaction. He is closing in on his prey and when she sees this, his final gift to her, she will surely surrender.

# TWENTY: SWEETHEART

Tonight is a special night because it's the last time I'll see Sam for four whole days, as tomorrow I fly to Ireland. When I was single, I didn't mind being away from home so much, but it's different now that I've got Sam. All my friends are so envious that I'm attending 'the showbiz wedding of the year', they think I've got the best job on earth, but right now I'd happily swap places with a nine-to-five Miss Selfridge shop assistant. I'm sick of describing bridal bouquets and tablecloth fabric and tears of emotion. And it's not as if I'll actually get to enjoy myself, quite the opposite in fact. Weddings are the most gruelling jobs of all. You spend the entire day on tenterhooks, worrying in case you miss a word of the best man's speech or wondering how you're going to extract a nice quote from that notoriously grumpy sitcom star. And there's a knock-on effect too – whenever I attend friends' weddings, they're always so horribly apologetic: 'We would have loved our little bridesmaids to be dressed as woodland flower fairies, like Posh Spice's, but we had to make do with off-the-peg Laura Ashley,' or 'I know you're used to vintage Moet, but I'm afraid our budget only ran to Asti Spumante.'

I have to tell them to stop being so ridiculous and reassure them that I'm having a million times more fun at their wedding, however low-key, than I ever do at any showbiz bash. No, if I never do another celebrity wedding again, it'll be too soon.

Sam and I have arranged to meet at a tapas bar on the South Bank straight after work and I've just spent the last half-hour getting ready in the ladies'. I've retrieved the kitten heels from my desk drawer, serum-ed my hair, and reapplied my make-up (I even bothered to remove the original layer first). I'm not especially pleased with the end result and this harsh fluorescent lighting does me no favours, but hopefully I'll look more alluring by candlelight. When I get back to my desk, Julie, Eva's secretary, hands me a smallish red envelope, the kind you'd get with a birthday card, with my name and job title typed on a sticky label glued to the front.

'It's just been delivered by courier,' she tells me. 'If it's an after-party invitation and you're not going, can I have it?'

'Sure,' I tell her. Julie's only twenty-two and still has the energy to party all night, so she gets all my leftover invitations, which is about 90 per cent of them. I've been to enough of those sort of do's to last me a lifetime, so I never go just for fun. I'm already running late, so I stuff the envelope into my bag, shut down my iMac and head for the DLR. Canary Wharf is a notoriously busy stop and I never get a seat if I leave during rush hour, which means I have to spend the fifteen-minute journey to Bank pressed up against an overweight suit snaffling a particularly pungent BLT. It's only when I've switched to the relative comfort of the Waterloo and City line that I get a chance to check out my couriered envelope. I tear it open and pull out the contents. It's a Polaroid photograph and for a second, I'm not exactly sure what I'm looking at. Then I realize that it's a picture of someone's shoulder blade and just above that hairless shoulder blade is a tattoo, a very cleverly executed tattoo of a fat red heart – a fat red heart borne by two feathery wings, one on either side. And written on the heart, inside a flowing banner in scrolled letters is my name: Ruby. My heart starts pounding in my chest like it's about to fly out of my body and even though I never suffer from claustrophobia, I suddenly feel hot and panicky. The fucking shitbag has gone too far this time. How dare he adorn a part of his body with *my* name. That tattoo looks real enough, so real it's still got fresh scabs round the edge, just like Gaz's had, and it's scratched indelibly on a real, human shoulder blade. I know there are some clever things you can do with PhotoShop, but this is a simple Polaroid and impossible to doctor. I can't believe anyone would be this obsessed, what a stupid, irrational, lunatic thing to do. Suddenly, I realize that my hand, holding the photograph, is shaking. I can't believe this bastard is really getting to me. For the first time, I feel scared, really scared. If he's mad enough to mutilate his own body in this way, what's to stop him hurting me? At least now I know for certain that Kramer is the SA – and he obviously wants me to know it's him.

As soon as I emerge from Waterloo underground station, I pull out my mobile and call the courier firm whose name and number are stamped on the back of the envelope . . . maybe, just maybe, he left some incriminating details.

'Er, we've got a Mr Domcot as the contact name, no address or phone number. He dropped the package off at our offices in person,' the receptionist tells me.

'What did he look like – was he about five foot eleven with short dark hair?' I bark down the phone.

'Keep yer knickers on, love. I wouldn't know, I've only just started my shift. Kim would've been on duty, 'cept she's gone on holiday now, won't be back till Friday week.'

Great. Not that it matters really. I know it's Kramer.

When I get to El Chicano, Sam's waiting for me at the horseshoe-shaped bar. He looks utterly delicious in his work outfit of torn jeans, fleece jacket and Rockport boots.

'Hi sweetheart,' he says, pulling me between his legs for a big bear hug. 'Good day at work?'

'Oh, you know, same as usual. I'll be glad when this wretched wedding's over. It's really doing my head in. If

I get another phone call from Niamh's manicurist asking if I'll give her a credit in the wedding feature . . .'

'Here, have a drink,' says Sam, handing me a San Miguel that he purchased in anticipation of my arrival. I love it when a man does that.

'Listen Sam, there's been a development on the SA front, a *big* development . . . do you want the good news or the bad news?'

'Er, let's think . . . the good news.'

'The good news is, I know for sure that Kramer is the Secret Admirer.'

'You're kidding! How can you be certain?'

'You're supposed to say: "And the bad news?"'

'And the bad news . . .'

'And the bad news is, the gimp has had my name tattooed on his back.'

'Sorry, I don't think I heard you right. Run that by me again.'

I pull the Polaroid out of my bag and thrust the evidence under his nose.

'That man is seriously sick. I can't believe he's done this. Are you sure it's not one of those tattoo transfer things?' says Sam, who is patently struggling to keep the timbre of his voice normal, as opposed to agitated.

'Well it could be – but look at those scabs, they look real enough to me.'

'And there was no note, no explanation?'

'Nothing . . . same as always. I called the courier

company, but they were no help. Kramer used the name Domcot again.'

'So how come you're so sure it's him?'

'You know I told you about bumping into Kramer at Layla Squires' engagement party?'

'Yeah. I can't believe that geek asked you to have dinner with him.'

'Anyway, what I didn't tell you – because it didn't seem relevant at the time – was that Layla's fiancé Gaz has had a heart with her name inside it tattooed on his arm as an engagement present.'

'Just like yours you mean?'

'Well not exactly, his heart was bigger and it didn't have wings. But the interesting thing is that later on, when I was talking to Kramer, he made a point of asking me if I'd seen Gaz's tattoo. I said I had and that I thought it was really cool because it showed he really loved her, that he thought they'd be together forever, that it was the ultimate sign of commitment.'

'You said all that. I thought it was a short conversation.'

'Well I was nervous, on edge, I was rambling a bit. It was just something to say really. But he's obviously taken it to heart, if you'll forgive the pun, and misguidedly believes that now he has this tattoo I'll fall for him.'

'Did the photographer take a picture of the tattoo?'

'Yes, a nice close-up.'

'So how do you know it's not a besotted *Wow!* reader who's seen the tattoo in the magazine and copied it?'

'The feature hasn't appeared in the magazine, nor is it ever likely to. Layla and Gaz split up a couple of days after the party.'

'Talk about the fickle world of showbiz . . . what happened?'

'He did the dirty with a lapdancer and she kissed and told to *News on Sunday*. Layla, quite understandably, gave him his marching orders. I had her on the phone in tears, although I think she was more upset about losing her fee than losing Gaz. We had to pull the story and Eva was practically spitting blood.'

'And now Gaz is stuck with that tattoo . . . what a chump.'

'So, as you can see, the finger's pointing firmly in Kramer's direction.'

We notice a couple leaving one of the corner tables, so we go over and bag the spot. We select a handful of dishes from the menu – chorizo sausage, *patatas bravas*, stuffed aubergine, chickpeas in garlic and deep fried plantain (sorry, my years at *Wow!* compel me to name each and every dish) – and a bottle of Rioja. Then the conversation returns to Kramer.

'So what do we do now – go to the police again?' asks Sam.

I love the 'we' bit. A lot of men would be frightened off by a nutter who's just had their girlfriend's name tattooed on his back, but not Sam. He's with me all the way.

'I still don't think they'd act, not even with this Polaroid. As far as they're concerned, the evidence is still only circumstantial. I can't really see them beating on his door, demanding to see his naked back – and even if they did see the tattoo in situ, as it were, he's hardly committed an offence, has he? Besides which, there's nothing to link him to the cake or the website or the underwear or the aquarium. No, I need to think of a way to warn Kramer off, to let him know I'm not going to stand for it any more. Got any bright ideas?'

As the night wears on and we get progressively drunker, Sam comes up with increasingly impractical suggestions.

'Let's start sending him little gifts in the post, see how *he* likes being hassled . . . dead rats, dog faeces, human vomit.'

'Nice idea, but I don't know his address.'

'But you know his phone number. I could ring him up, put on my deepest, butchest voice and threaten to send round the heavy mob unless he leaves you alone.'

'That's a possibility, but surely we can think of something more humiliating.'

'I've got it! Why don't we take out a full-page ad in a Sunday newspaper, that reads in big fuck-off letters: *Alan Kramer is a pervert*? That would stop him in his tracks and just think how his book sales would drop off.'

'Yeah, except we'd probably get sued for libel and we don't have a spare twenty grand to spend.'

'Does it really cost that much?'

''Fraid so. Hang on a minute though . . . there's more than one way to skin a cat.'

'Such as . . .'

'Just hold on, I'm thinking.' I take a big slug of Rioja, and let the idea take shape in my head. It's quite a bold move, but it might just work.

'What if I submit a little item to *News on Sunday*'s *Exposed* column? A waspish little dig at Kramer which would embarrass him into stopping. He's sure to see it – all the celebs read *News on Sunday*, it reminds them there's a reason for their existence.'

'Sorry, you've lost me. I haven't read *News on Sunday* since I worked on a building site during my university holidays. What's the *Exposed* column?'

'It's absolutely the best thing about that rag. It's a kind of who's doing what to whom gossip column. Except none of the celebs is actually named, for example:

'Guess which teenage soap actress threw a wobbler when she was refused entry to Sheridan House at the weekend? "Don't you know who I am?" shrieked the raven-headed one. "Yes madam," said the doorman calmly. "And you still can't come in."'

'So which actress was it then?'

'No one. I just made it up off the top of my head. But you get the picture.'

'Okay, so you write a piece about this horror writer who's stalking a celebrity journalist and he'll read it and get scared you'll start naming names unless he stops harassing you.'

'Something like that. Whaddaya think?'

'Can't you just do something similar for *Wow!*? It would be a lot simpler.'

'Eva wouldn't touch it – we don't do those sort of spiky stories, everything's happy-shiny-smiley in the world of *Wow!* Anyway, no one at the mag knows about the Secret Admirer. I've only told you, Simon, Amy and Jo.'

'So how are you going to persuade the newspaper to run the story?'

'I'll speak to my new best friend, Nick Porter. I'm sure he'll be grateful for my tip-off.'

'Do you really think it'll work?' asks Sam, pushing aside the tapas dishes to take my hand in his.

'I certainly think it's our best shot. Kramer can't afford any negative publicity – what celebrity can? And who knows? Maybe I could supply *News on Sunday* with gossipy titbits on a regular basis – I'm sure they'd love to hear about the antics of Stevo Hollis and his nanny, for example, and that kind of stuff wouldn't compromise my work for *Wow!*'

Yes, the more I think about the idea, the more I'm convinced it will work. And if it doesn't . . . well we'll just have to resort to Plan B, Sam's threatening phone call. I had promised myself I'd make tracks by ten-thirty as I've got a ridiculously early start tomorrow. But I'm having such a brilliant time with Sam I don't manage to tear myself away till gone eleven. Every time we meet, I just have to congratulate myself on bagging such a wonderful man. It seems doubly weird given that we met by accident. If I hadn't bumped into him at that party, our paths might never have crossed. It's too awful to contemplate. I wish I could spend tonight with him, but it would be too cruel to inflict my five a.m. check-in time on him. As we walk towards the underground together, he puts his arm around me and kisses the top of my head.

'You're really something special, you know that, Ruby?' he says. 'Anyone else would have gone to pieces over this whole stalker thing but you . . . you just put your thinking hat on and work out the best way to tackle it. I really admire you for that.'

'Yeah, but I don't mind admitting that underneath this calm exterior lies a shit-scared woman. What if he comes after me, Sam, breaks into the flat when I'm asleep?'

'Well I can spend the night at your place any time you want. It would be no problem for me to get to work from Rotherhithe . . . only if you want me to of course, I don't want to crowd you or anything.'

'I think it's a brilliant idea,' I say, grinning from ear to ear. 'I'm so glad I've got you and I'm not handling this thing on my own; you've no idea how good it feels.'

'Don't worry, Ruby, we'll run the Sad Arsehole to ground one way or another,' he says, stepping off the kerb into the street to hail a black cab for me.

# WOW!

It's suddenly immensely important that I tell Sam exactly how I feel about him before I go away. In the past, I've waited for boyfriends to put their cards on the table before *I* commit myself, but Sam's different, Sam's *very* different. I've only got about ten seconds because the cab's pulling over, so I grab his hand and look him right in the eye. 'Listen Sam, I'm not entirely sure how *you* feel about *me*, but I just want you to know that I'm falling for you bigtime; in fact I think I ell-oh-vee-eee you, well actually I don't *think* I ell-oh-vee-eee you, I know I do.'

There's a moment's pause, when I wonder if I might have said the wrong thing. And then he stops walking, turns towards me and pulls me close. He's half a foot taller than I am, so my face is pressed into his collarbone and his mouth is in my hair.

'What's with all the phonetics then?' he says softly into my ear, making the hairs on my lobe tingle. 'Why don't you tell me properly?'

I laugh, embarrassed at my failure to say what I mean. I take a deep breath and it comes out in a rush. 'IloveyouSam.'

'And I love you too, Ruby Tuesday,' he says. 'And I really mean that from the bottom of my heart.'

I turn my face towards his and we lock lips for what seems like the longest time. What he's just said is such a turn-on, I could shag him right here in the street, I mean it, my whole pelvic region is tingling with desire. However, my sense of decorum gets the better of me and I have to content myself with some serious frottage. I hate to imagine what those passers-by must think of us, getting it on in the middle of the street, but I'm too loved up to care. Finally, I peel myself away from him.

'I sooo don't want to go home now and I sooo don't want to go to Ireland tomorrow,' I say, as I climb into the cab.

'Now you look after yourself, don't forget to double lock your door tonight and try to enjoy the wedding.'

'Fat chance. I'll call you every day, just to let you know how depressed I am. I'll get in touch with Nick Porter too, I want him to run that story as soon as possible.'

We give each other a final embrace before Sam slams the car door shut. As the cab pulls away, I wave to him from the window and mouth the words, 'I love you', and I keep looking back at him till he's a tiny speck in the distance.

# TWENTY-ONE: THE GROUNDWORK

We walk through the arrivals hall at Shannon Airport: me, Eva and Ali, three ball-busting *Charlie's Angels* on an extra special secret mission. Despite all the hard work and long hours that celebrity weddings entail, you do get a certain buzz just before it all kicks off. I think it's the knowledge that so many other people – journalists, photographers and fans – would love to be in our shoes right now.

We spent the entire flight scrutinizing our fellow passengers, looking for the telltale bulge of a concealed Nikon or the furtive look of a veteran gatecrasher. After all her years on the nationals, Eva knows most of the hardcore paparazzi by sight and she hasn't spotted any of them yet. They're probably already here, trying to get the locals on side and figuring out a way to breach our security, speaking of which, Special K has arranged to meet us by the tourist information booth, which I've just spotted by the sliding doors. I lead the others towards it and as we get nearer I see Keith inside, trying to be inconspicuous by spinning the carousel of brochures while frowning slightly in the manner of a genuine tourist. He takes his job ever so seriously, you know, in fact he's probably wearing a bulletproof vest under that lemon Pringle jumper.

'Hey sir, here we are, all present and correct and reporting for duty,' I say, with a cheeky little salute.

'Good afternoon, ladies. I hope you had a pleasant flight,' he says, failing to respond to my verbal jousting.

'Fine thanks, Keith. Have you spotted any paps coming through today?' asks Eva, getting straight down to business.

'There were a couple on the last flight, *Express* boys I think. We've got about fifteen of them already down at the castle and we've had a couple of choppers flying overhead, trying to get aerial shots, not that there's anything much to see at the moment, just the marquees going up. I've got a car waiting outside; we'll be there in twenty minutes and you can see for yourselves.'

Keith leads us to his vehicle, a three-year-old Volvo, the colour of an under-ripe tomato. 'It's the best the hire-company could offer,' he says apologetically as he loads our luggage and the office laptop into the boot. We pile inside and Keith's flat-nosed colleague sitting behind the wheel hastily stubs out his Rothmans. I recognize him from another job, but I can't remember if it's Terry the Ant (he can lift three times his own body weight, apparently) or Mad Dave. All Keith's muscle men have nicknames, I think it's a throwback to their army days – lots of them served in Bosnia and/or the Falklands. A couple of them are slightly dubious characters and when they're not poncing round in DJs at celebrity parties and weddings, I've no doubt they're involved in the more physical side of the job – nightclub bouncing, debt-collecting, knee-capping . . . no, I'm only joking about that last one, really.

En route to Kellaway, Eva inquires about Joe and Niamh's arrival yesterday afternoon. I saw the footage on the six o'clock news and boy was it a scrum, with flashbulbs going off and questions being yelled. 'What's the dress like, Niamh?' 'Will you promise to "obey"?' 'Is Joe's first wife coming to the wedding?' With their matching Gucci sunglasses and heads firmly down, the couple didn't give a single quote, the little beauties – well, it's in their contract after all. I have to say their personal bodyguards did a great job of keeping the press at arm's length, poor Keith must've been green with envy – *and* Joe and Niamh's guys had better suits.

'Oh, it wasn't as bad as it looked on TV. We got them into the 4 × 4 pretty quickly,' says Keith, smiling smugly. 'Of course we were tailed all the way to Kellaway, but once we arrived at the gates they had to give up the chase. Joe and Niamh are staying in the Turret suite, we've put up blackouts at the windows, so there's no chance of anyone getting a picture and the couple have been given strict instructions not to set foot outside the main building. My men are managing to hold all the paps at bay at the gates, so I think we're gonna be okay. Now, I'd better issue you with your laminates. It doesn't matter who you are you've got to wear this at all times once you're inside the castle grounds.'

He rummages in the glove box and pulls out three security passes on stainless steel neck chains, one for each of us. Mine says 'R. Lake, *Wow!* magazine' and next to it is the little passport photo I gave Keith last week. Our art department designed the logo, under my supervision – an intricately entwined *J* and *N* – which should deter would-be interlopers from attempting to make reproductions. As we approach Kellaway's north entrance, I see a cluster of people standing just outside the wrought-iron gates, probably around thirty in total. The majority are media, with their cameras and booms – even the BBC have turned out – but there's also a handful of ordinary folk, local people and fans who are hoping to catch a glimpse of the happy couple. They'll be lucky. I feel like telling them to go home now, instead of standing out here with their Thermos flasks and waterproof jackets. I spy a one-man tent erected on the grass verge behind the main throng – not even Christian and Maisie inspired this kind of dedication.

Two of Keith's men are positioned just inside the gates and they wave us straight through. A barrage of flash-bulbs is fired through the car windows – surely these photographers don't think anyone remotely important would be seen dead in an orange Volvo? We travel up the winding drive to the castle itself, and while Keith unloads our luggage, we check in at reception. It's all go here: a team of florists carrying armfuls of heavily scented white lilies mince past us, narrowly missing a man in chef's whites who bursts out of a side door, clutching a packet of cigarettes and screaming to an unseen colleague: 'If the Jersey Royals don't arrive by four, we're doomed!' And by the way, he's talking spuds, not wedding guests.

We have an hour or so to chill out in our rooms, and when room service has brought me a smoked salmon sandwich on rye and a pot of tea, I sit by the window, watching a helicopter swooping back and forth across the castle estate. Tomorrow we'll have our own craft occupying the air space, and keeping the others at bay. Keith will be in constant radio contact with the pilot, so he can give him specific instructions during the 'danger' times – when the couple leave the castle to go into the marquee, for example. This gives our pilot advance warning so that he can commandeer the appropriate airspace, thereby blocking out other helicopters.

I decide to use this small window of free time to call Nick Porter, as it could be the last opportunity I get for a while. And the sooner I present my idea to him, the sooner it will appear in the newspaper and the sooner Alan Kramer will be out of my life. I retrieve Nick's business card from the flap in the leather cover of my Filofax and pump out the digits on my mobile.

'Nick Porter, Newsdesk.'

'Hi Nick. It's Ruby, Ruby Lake from *Wow!* magazine, Simon's friend.'

'Ruby! Good to hear from you. I was beginning to think you'd never call. I bet you're at Kellaway now, aren't you? Don't tell me you've changed your mind at the eleventh hour?'

'Er, not exactly. I am at Kellaway, but I'm not calling about the wedding, it's something completely unrelated actually.'

'Oh, I see. What can I do for you then?' he says, sounding quite crestfallen.

'I've got a little story you might be interested in, something for the *Exposed* column, it's quite a nice one, I could even write the copy for you.'

'Okay, run it by me.'

'Right, well it's something that's actually happening to me right now, but I wouldn't want my name mentioned or anything . . .'

'I don't want to rush you, Ruby, but I really haven't got long. I'm due in conference in ten minutes.'

He's trying to be polite, but I can tell he's harassed. I wouldn't be surprised if the conference is about the wedding spoiler they're planning for Sunday's edition. They might not have beautiful posed shots and words straight from the horse's mouth, but they'll definitely try and cobble something together. Maybe they'll dig up one of Joe's old girlfriends and ask her what he's like in bed or something.

'Sorry, Nick, I know you're busy, so I'll get straight to

the point. Basically, I interviewed Alan Kramer a little while back and now he's stalking me. He keeps sending me all these gifts – he built a website for me and that was followed by chocolates, underwear, an aquarium full of fish, even a three-tier wedding cake, complete with my fondant doppelgänger on top.'

'Alan who?'

'Alan Kramer, you know, the horror writer . . . *Plague of Zombies, Killer Babes.*'

Silence.

'He was on *Through the Keyhole* a couple of months ago . . . I don't know about you, but I thought the Herman Munster novelty toilet brush was a dead giveaway.'

'I think I know who you mean, but to be honest, I don't think he's a big enough name for us.'

'But it's such a great story: a celebrity – a C-list celebrity, granted – stalking a member of the public. Kind of tantalizingly subversive, don't you think?'

'But strictly speaking he's not actually stalking you, is he? He's just coming on a bit strong. Okay, so the wedding cake's a bit weird, but there's nothing particularly offensive about chocolates or underwear. He's just trying to woo you the old-fashioned way. Now, if you went out with him, got between the sheets and he turned out to be really kinky in a ghoulish kind of way – wore fangs in bed, only wanted to ravish you during a full moon – now that *would* be a story.'

It's obvious that Nick is having a laugh at my expense.

In fact, he's actually chuckling out loud now. For the first time since I devised my fiendish editorial mantrap, it occurs to me that Nick Porter might not want to play ball. I mean why should he? My Kramer story is hardly scoop of the century and it isn't as if I'm going to be naming names. But I'm not beaten yet; I still have my ace card . . .

'How about this then? The guy has had this tattoo done on his back, it's a heart and it's got my name on it – he sent me a photograph of it and everything.'

'I'm sorry, Ruby. Tattoo or not, this Kramer story really isn't suitable for *Exposed*. Do keep in touch though – I'm sure you get to hear loads of juicy stories that are far too racy for *Wow!*'

Now I'm really desperate. 'I wouldn't want paying or anything. I just want to get him off my back, fire a warning shot across his bows. I could write the copy right now and fax it to you.'

'I'd like to help you out, Ruby, honestly I would, but it's just not us.'

He pauses for a second and then the whole tone of his voice changes from bright and businesslike to mellifluous charm.

'On the other hand, it *could* be us if you changed your mind about contributing to our wedding feature.'

The slimy little scumbag, I should have known he'd try and pull this one.

'Nick, you know my feelings about that.'

'Come on, Ruby, just a few details. Forget the dress, I

256

know that's a big deal to *Wow!* Just give us the names of a few celebrity guests, the menu, a bit of crap about the table decorations, and a few nuggets from the groom's speech. That's all. We'll run your Kramer story – maybe not this Sunday, but certainly next – and I'll give you a grand into the bargain.'

I'm going to hate myself in the morning, but I'm going to do it anyway. 'Forget the table decorations and the cash and you've got a deal.'

'What, you don't want paying?'

'It'll make me feel better about committing such a heinous act. It would be bad enough if they found out, but if they discovered I got paid for it as well . . .'

'I'm telling you, Ruby, I can guarantee anonymity. This is strictly between you and me. So have we got a deal then?'

'Deal. When do you need the info?'

'As soon as you can get it to me. Call me on my home number tomorrow evening.'

I take down his number and arrange to call him by eight p.m. at the latest.

'Until tomorrow then. And Ruby . . .'

'What?'

'It's been nice doing business with you.'

I hit *end call* without bothering to reply. I hope I've made the right decision. It should be okay, those few pieces of information could easily have been supplied by any one of the guests or waiting staff. It'll be worth it to get rid of Kramer, but I still feel shitty. Suddenly the room phone trills into life and I practically have a heart attack, I'm so on edge. It's Eva and I half expect her to tell me she's heard every word of my illicit conversation, but she's only asking me and Ali to meet her in reception. I take a few deep breaths to calm myself, pick up my notebook and go down the hallway to Ali's room.

First port of call is the dining marquee, a mammoth structure, something akin to a Big Top, situated to the rear of the castle, beside the lake. Inside, Hugh is hard at work organizing a posse of construction workers, who are struggling to erect two huge Corinthian columns on either side of a raised stage at the far end.

'Good afternoon, Hugh. I hope we haven't arrived at a bad time,' says Eva when it's quite clear that we have.

'Oh hello there,' he says with a nervous smile – *and* his right eye has developed a slight twitch, so he must be really up against it. 'We're just having a few tiny problems with the decorations for the bridal alcove. The thrones were delivered ten minutes ago and they're covered with velour and not the crushed velvet we requested.' He gestures towards a scruffy youth who is on his knees stretching gold velvet over the seat of a huge gilt chair. 'And the hand is being repaired outside in the garden. It got slightly damaged in transit, but I don't think anyone will notice by the time our plasterer has finished with it.'

'Did you say "hand"?' says Ali. This is her first celebrity wedding (I'm not counting the Bucks Fizz girl), so she has yet to learn that absolutely anything goes when you've got megabucks to spend.

'Yes, the couple are going to be sitting on their thrones in the palm of a big plaster hand,' explains Hugh. 'It's a kind of "in the lap of the Gods" idea – rather fun, don't you think?'

Actually, I find the idea quite abhorrent. Who wants to feel like a Lilliputian on their Big Day? But like the sycophant I am, I throw back my head and laugh in a very theatrical way. 'That's quite brilliant, Hugh!'

We exchange a bit more chit-chat about Hugh's imaginative design concepts and then I excuse myself, so that I can go for a wander around the four-thousand-square-foot marquee, notebook in hand. It's quite bare at the moment – the tables and chairs won't be in position until tomorrow morning – but it still looks pretty impressive with its white and gold colour theme. It's got windows, real glass Georgian-style windows, draped with heavy gold velvet curtains and swathes of white muslin. A plush, yellow-gold carpet is being tacked into place on the floor and the tarpaulin walls have been covered in metres of pleated ivory taffeta. Dotted throughout the room are three quarter-size gold plaster-of-Paris figurines from Greek mythology: I manage to identify Eros (natch) with his bow and arrow, Poseidon brandishing his trident, and judging by his winged sandals, that must be Hermes, messenger of the Gods. At the back of the room, scaffolders are erecting a 12ft-high mezzanine to accommodate

the 18-piece orchestra, which will be playing a selection
of pop music medleys during the reception (I hear they
do a terrific version of 'Karma Chameleon').

There are literally hundreds of contractors working on
this wedding and Louie Bresler has made each and every
one sign a contract, which bars them from talking about
the event to the media. Information has leaked out
already: yesterday's *Mirror* ran a two-paragraph story
about the water screen, a 30ft-high sheet of water, gushing into an artificial pond, filled with green lily pads and
ornamental frogs. It's positioned just behind the bridal
alcove and during the reception, a loop of the 1963
adventure classic, *Jason and the Argonauts*, will be projected directly onto the water.

In a little side annexe, shielded from the main marquee
by heavy gold velvet curtains, a five-strong team is hard
at work making the table decorations. These consist of
olive branches, twisted into a wreath around a golden
dish bearing white church candles of assorted size, inter-
spersed with clumps of genuine Irish moss, white roses
and bunches of gold-sprayed grapes – a bit of a fire
hazard I would've thought, but I'm sure Hugh has thoroughly investigated their combustibility.

Back at the bridal alcove, Eva and Hugh are engaged
in a heated discussion, while the giant hand is being
manoeuvred into place behind them. The noise of the
lawnmowers outside drowns out most of their conversation, but I catch odd words and phrases, like 'lovebirds', 'rotor blades' and 'guests splattered in blood', and

I deduce that Hugh's concern is that *Wow!*'s helicopter will cut short the flight of the one hundred specially trained lovebirds he's planning to release at the drinks reception. I leave them to thrash it out and go through to the second marquee, attached to the first by a short walkway and lined with shoulder-height columns of white plaster. An artist is busy daubing the columns with a special paint effect to make them look like archaeological artefacts. On cross-examination, she tells me that by tomorrow, these columns will be swathed in trails of green ivy and topped by Grecian-style urns filled with white arum lilies – rather a funereal choice of flower in my opinion, but what do I know?

When I reach marquee number two, my jaw drops to the floor. I thought nothing could beat the sumptuous Bedouin splendour of Christian and Maisie's disco tent, but this one is in a class of its own. Hugh has surpassed himself by creating an amphitheatre-style arena, with graduated tiers rising up to about half the marquee's height from a circular dance floor. Two girls are scattering gold and ivory velvet cushions randomly over the steps and one is kind enough to divulge that the tassels on the cushions are made of real silk. 'Real silk tassels,' I write slavishly in my notebook – a seemingly insignificant detail to most people, but it will be lapped up by the *Wow!* reader. A wide deck has been built on the top level of the amphitheatre, where sound engineers are messing around with wires and mike stands. This must be where the sixties' soul band will be positioned. It's rumoured that Harry Connick Jr, one of the invited guests, may give an impromptu performance, but I can't confirm or deny at this stage, even Hugh doesn't know. The bar area is situated to the rear of the marquee on a kind of open-fronted balcony, which also doubles as a viewing gallery from where guests will be able to watch the firework finale. The walls of the balcony are covered with midnight-blue silk, studded with luminous stars.

By the time I've finished my grand tour, it's four-thirty, which means I should be getting back to my room to do the final preparations before my interview with Joe and Niamh. I stop off at the castle kitchens en route, where Eva sent Ali to interview the catering staff. I find her standing very close to a taut-buttocked young chef who's demonstrating his skill in making the spun sugar baskets which will house the lemon chiffon mousse and redcurrant coulis dessert.

'How's it going, Al?'

'I've got loads of great stuff, Ruby. I know the ingredients of every single canapé at the champagne reception, and I've even managed to get hold of one of these,' she says, producing a thick white card with scalloped edges, picked out in gold. It's the table menu, which is almost always reproduced in the magazine, so that *Wow!* readers can marvel at the quality of the stationery and the excellence of the calligraphy.

'I'll look after that,' I say, swiping it out of Ali's hand and sliding it into my shoulder bag. I'll need it when I'm talking to Nick later on. 'Carry on as you were. I'm going back to my room 'cause I'm meeting Joe and Niamh in half an hour.'

'Okay. Good luck with the interview. I think I'll just hang out here a while longer, see what else I can get.'

'Yeah, you do that. I'll catch up with you at dinner.'

Back in my room, I go over the questions I've spent the last two days preparing. I'll only get one chance at this, so it's vital I ask the right questions in the right order and don't make any glaring omissions. I've got a lot of ground to cover: their blossoming romance, Niamh's pregnancy and their thoughts on parenthood, plus all the nitty-gritty about the bridesmaids' dresses, the choice of best man and, very importantly, the wedding rings (designer, carat, number of diamonds, inscription). I check and double-check my Sony: Are the new batteries inserted? Yes. Do I have a brand new D90, plus a back-up cassette in the unlikely event that they ramble on beyond my allotted hour and a half? Yes. Is the pause button set to *off*? Yes. I once did an entire interview with the pause button on, which meant the bloody tape heads didn't move an inch, even though I'd pressed *record*. The celebrity in question – an American talkshow host – had flown back to LA by the time I discovered my error the following afternoon, so there was no chance of trying to beg another interview. I'd briefly considered writing up the thing from memory, but as the celeb in question is notoriously litigious, I decided that was too risky. I hadn't been at *Wow!* long, and after three days of absolutely shitting myself, I eventually told Eva my handbag had been stolen in a pub, with the dictaphone and cassette inside. I think she believed me.

At five minutes to five, my room phone rings.

'Hi there, Ruby. Are you ready for our interview?'

'Ready as I'll ever be, Louie. How are Joe and Niamh? I expect they're still jet-lagged, aren't they?'

'Actually, they're both on pretty good form, considering. They absolutely cannot wait for tomorrow. I've known Joe for ten years now and I've never seen him so excited. I think you'll find them a charming couple, Ruby, I really do.'

We arrange to meet in the castle's morning room, where I'm delighted to discover that Louie has forked out for afternoon tea. The interview goes off without a hitch. Despite their megastar status, Joe and Niamh both come across as really nice, sincere people. They spend the entire interview holding hands and, though I'm reluctant to admit it, I find this strangely touching. I think my own burgeoning love affair has softened me, made me less cynical. Niamh's pregnancy was entirely unplanned – she'd had a nasty bout of diarrhoea after eating oysters, rendering her contraceptive pill ineffective (rather more information than I wanted). However, it's apparent that they can't wait to be parents, even though Joe will be an OAP by the time the kid's at Uni.

Despite the 17-year age gap between them, I'd say this was definitely a love match. But then I thought that about Christian and Maisie – and their marriage lasted only eight months. I'll never forget the pre-wedding interview, which took place a week or so before the Big Day at London's fashionably minimalist Hempel hotel. They couldn't keep their hands off each other, and I swear you could've powered the Glastonbury sound stage with the electricity coursing between them. I was really surprised when I read they were joining the long list of stars who have fallen victim to what the tabloids call 'the curse of *Wow!*'. It doesn't seem to put people off though. As long as we're prepared to pay big bucks for the chance to record the nuptials for posterity, there will always be celebrities happy to pose in our glossy pages, even if it means their marriage will eventually end up in the divorce courts.

Just before I leave Joe and Niamh, I have a flash of sheer genius. Remembering the wedding menu that's still in my bag, I ask if they'd mind signing it for me – as a personal memento, I explain, me being such a big fan and all. (I can always grab another menu for the magazine from one of the tables tomorrow.) The interview had gone so well – I didn't mention Joe's short-lived first marriage to go-go dancer-turned-soap star Lola Dukes once – they were more than happy to oblige. Give it a couple of months, and I reckon that signed menu will be worth a tidy sum at an internet auction, that's if they're still together of course.

# TWENTY-TWO: THE BIG DAY

Keith and his twenty-strong team have just swept the castle grounds, the two marquees and the various rooms inside the main building that will house the wedding party. Here's what they found:

- One tabloid reporter masquerading as a groundsman in wellies and leather apron – Big Dave (that *was* him driving the Volvo) got suspicious when he noticed the man attempting to water the rose bushes with an empty watering can.
- One freelance paparazzo in the back of a baker's van, concealed under a mound of poppyseed twists. Photographer and baker were both ejected and Hugh has sworn the bun boy will never work for him again.
- Two micro-listening devices in the Great Hall, where the wedding ceremony will take place. They were hidden, rather cunningly, in the ceiling smoke detectors, but you've got to get up pretty early in the morning to catch Special K out.

# WOW!

It's now just four hours before the first of the two hundred guests starts to arrive and everyone is working flat out. Eva has taken Louie to our makeshift photo lab, which has been set up in a disused storage cupboard in the castle cellars. She's introducing him to Jason, our processor, who will turn David O'Connor's film into transparencies for the couple to approve tomorrow morning. Having got up at six-thirty this morning to type up my interview with Joe and Niamh on the laptop, I'm now holed up in the dining marquee with Ali. Above our heads, two gigantic crystal chandeliers are being hoisted into position, while Hugh's workers dress the twenty circular dining tables, which are draped with cream-coloured Irish calico, overlaid with gold organza. Each guest's place is marked with a traditional 'favour' – in this case, it's a gold velvet drawstring bag with a cream cardboard luggage label attached. Each label is inscribed in copperplate with the guest's name and inside the bags are Tiffany keyrings for the male guests and compacts for the ladies.

'Those gifts are so showy. Why couldn't they just have had a macaroon biscuit in Cellophane or a net of sugared almonds like everyone else?' says Ali. 'They must've cost an absolute mint.'

'I expect they'll have got a decent discount. These upmarket jewellers know a good PR opportunity when they see one,' I say with my usual cynicism.

We pause to watch a guy push a gargantuan black wheelie bin through to the disco marquee, followed by another guy carrying a huge ball of mesh netting.

'That bin will be full of rose petals,' I say to Ali. 'Hugh told me they're rigging up a net on the roof of the marquee, and after the band's played the final number, they'll cut the net and a million white rose petals will rain down on the guests.'

'Now that's pretty cool,' says Ali, who is new to the game and therefore easily impressed.

Eva comes striding into the marquee and from the look on her face it's clear that all is not well. She barges past one of the men who's holding a rope that's attached to one of the chandeliers, while a second man on a scaffolding tower secures it to the roof of the marquee. Man number one stumbles and almost loses his grip on the rope, the chandelier sways precariously and for a second I think it's going to come crashing down on the head of man number two, but luckily number one manages to regain his balance. Eva carries on walking towards us, without so much as a backward glance, never mind an apology, while behind her back the man with the rope mouths the words, 'Stupid bitch.'

'What's up, Eva?'

'It's Donatella. She's not coming,' she says in clipped tones.

'You're kidding. Louie told us she was a definite, and I spoke to her office two weeks ago. Her PA said she was fine for a ten-minute interview during the champagne reception.'

'She's gone down with flu and isn't fit to travel apparently, so her assistant's coming in her place. The assistant knows everything about the dress, so we'll be okay from that point of view. It's just that it would've been great to have pictures of Donatella with the couple.'

'Yeah, she always looks so glamorous. Oh well, I'll just have to get the gen from the assistant.' I'm not quite as put-out as Eva, who is literally wringing her hands at the injustice of it all.

'And remember, Ruby, we need a good 250-word description of that gown, so make sure you get every last detail – petticoat, shoes, right down to what colour knickers she's wearing.'

'Will do. Any sign of David O'Connor yet?'

'He's just arrived . . . three hours late. I knew we should've booked him a flight for yesterday, but the silly sod insisted on doing that Jodie Kidd cover for *Tatler*. You two had better go and introduce yourselves and then you should start getting ready.'

Eva hares off in search of a florist so she can beg a rose buttonhole to go with her white Armani trouser suit. I hate dress codes, they make choosing an outfit so difficult, and white and gold are my two least favourite colours, they make my skin look ashy. Ali, with her dark brown hair and sunbed tan, will look stunning, on the other hand. *Wow!* staffers don't get a clothes allowance, worse luck, so I haven't bought anything special. I just hope I won't look too out of place in my Karen Millen sale ensemble.

We find David O'Connor and his three assistants in reception, surrounded by a mass of equipment. In fact I've never seen so much camera stuff in one place before.

The man himself is in his early thirties and quite geeky-looking in a Woody Allen kind of way, with bushy sideburns and big, dark-framed glasses.

'Hello David, I'm Ruby, senior writer at *Wow!*, and this is my colleague Ali,' I say breezily.

'Hi there, nice to meet you both. I'm running a little behind schedule. The flight was delayed and then Hertz didn't have a car big enough to carry all the gear. Anyway, I'm here now, and raring to go.'

He seems mighty relaxed for a man who is about to be entrusted with the biggest showbiz event of the millennium. I just hope he's worth his fifteen-grand fee.

'Just so you know, I'm going to be writing the body copy and Ali's going to shadow you so she can do the picture captions.'

'That sounds cool. This is my first wedding, so I wasn't sure how you lot worked. What time does the ceremony start?'

'Three p.m. – but you'll need to set up a good hour ahead, before all the guests arrive.' Doesn't this guy know anything?

'Shit! I'd better get myself organized. I'll see you in the Great Hall around two-ish then.'

'Righty-ho . . . and you do know it's a white-and-gold dress code, don't you?'

'Oh yes, I'm all sorted on that front.'

When I see David dressed in his finery, a couple of hours later, he looks like a poor man's Engelbert Humperdinck, circa 1978. He's wearing possibly the most hideous white tux I've ever seen, or maybe it's just his own idea of retro-cool. The double-breasted jacket and slightly-too-short trousers with gold military stripe are teamed with a white ruched dinner shirt and gold dickey bow. Like I told you, dress codes are a nightmare. That said, the guests have managed rather well. Since I've been sitting here in the oak-panelled Great Hall, I've spotted several immaculately turned-out famous stars (Christy Turlington, John Rocha, Keifer Sutherland) and it's still only two-thirty.

At two-forty-five, the groom makes his entrance, cutting a dash in his cream-coloured Versace suit and gold waistcoat, embossed with a design of tea roses. I'm glad he didn't plump for one of those ghastly frock coats, so beloved of soccer grooms. Accompanying Joe is his brother and best man, Tom Lucas, star of his own eponymous CBS sitcom, which has just been snapped up by Channel 4. The pair take their seats in the front row, and Joe turns round to chat to his father, veteran actor and three-time Oscar nominee Leo Lucas (he finally won one of the coveted gold statuettes in 1981 for his role as a deranged hotelier in cult thriller, *Vacancy*). Next to Leo sits his dripping-in-diamonds wife, Candice, who gave up her career as a Norman Rockwell model to raise her sons. I like her ostrich-feather hat, but that facelift's so tight, it's a wonder she can still move her lips.

In the interview, Niamh told me she wasn't planning to keep her husband-to-be waiting and at one minute past three, a flautist, seated in the minstrel's gallery, strikes up Pachelbel's *Canon and Gigue*. The door at the rear of the hall is flung open, and in walks Niamh, on the arm of her builder's merchant father, who's looking terribly red in the face. Maybe he had a quick tipple for Dutch courage; these all-star weddings can be terribly nerve-wracking for non-famous family members.

There's an audible gasp from the congregation as father and daughter make their way up the aisle towards the waiting registrar. I jot down a few notes on the dress; Donatella's assistant will be able to fill me in on the details later on. The on-the-shoulder gown is made of ivory satin and consists of a fitted bodice with cowl neckline that gives way to a clingy straight skirt, through which Niamh's small pregnancy bump is just visible. She wears no veil and her long brown hair is piled on top of her head and dressed with miniature yellow rosebuds and she carries a simple posy of white double tulips and berried ivy. Behind her, four grown-up bridesmaids (all fellow models) wear elegant knee-length sheath dresses of oyster-coloured satin and matching elbow-length gloves. Each girl carries a single Casablanca lily, dressed with a wide ivory ribbon, and wears the Tiffany diamond cross that Joe and Niamh presented to them this morning.

The civil ceremony is brief and to the point and thankfully, the noise of helicopters whirring overhead doesn't prove too intrusive. Vows and rings are exchanged, a few tears are shed and fifteen minutes later, Mr and Mrs Joe Lucas walk back down the aisle to the anthemic 'There's No Business Like Showbusiness', blasted rather vulgarly through loudspeakers.

David has been taking pictures throughout the ceremony and now he and his assistants hastily pack up their gear and follow the happy couple through to the Richmond Gallery, where they have agreed to pose for photographs while their guests enjoy a champagne and canapés reception. Ali goes with him, so she can gather some anecdotes for the captions, quite a skilful job when you've got three lines of 12-point to fill: 'The stunning bride wiped away a tear of happiness as she and her proud groom posed for their first photograph as man and wife' is one I've used on many occasions. She doesn't even need to shed the tear, just rubbing her eye is justification enough.

Next door, Eva and I are mingling with the guests in the Gainsborough Room, an elegant, high-ceilinged drawing room, dressed with towering flower arrangements of white roses, fuchsias and gold-sprayed ferns. White-gloved waiters in nehru jackets serve Veuve Clicquot or elderflower cordial with raspberries and a selection of canapés. As I recall from Ali's notes, they include Thai chicken skewers with cashew dipping sauce (let's hope none of the guests has a nut allergy), miniature goat's cheese and sun-dried tomato tartlets, and grilled basil chicken with a rich damson chutney. Eva's role today is mainly ambassadorial, so she makes a beeline for Christy Turlington (I really can't see her agreeing to an *at home* in her Martha's Vineyard beach house, or wherever it is she lives, although Eva can be very persuasive). Meanwhile, I grab a few words with the registrar, who is visibly awe-struck at being in such illustrious company. Naturally, he was only too delighted to accept the couple's invitation to join them for a drink; in fact he's even been joined by his wife who must've been hiding in a broom cupboard up to now, because her name certainly wasn't on the guest list.

'I don't see it as a marriage of two celebrities, but of a couple who are very much in love,' he gushes, then thrusts an order of service under my nose and says, 'Do you think you could get them to autograph this?' No, I bloody well can't – apart from anything else, it would devalue my own signed menu.

At this point Donatella Versace's assistant, a tall stick insect of a girl in a fitted gold bustier, makes herself known to me. She's spared me the ordeal of yet another interview by helpfully typing out the details of Niamh's dress on a sheet of A4. They include the number of fittings required (five), the fabric (Clerici duchesse satin), the hidden details (a tiny blue silk bow sewn on the inside hem for luck). I thank her profusely and wish Donatella a speedy recovery.

After twenty minutes or so, Ali emerges from the Richmond Gallery and asks for my help in rounding up the bride and groom's nearest and dearest. This is always a tricky time. We really only want bridesmaids, best man, parents and siblings (and just the attractive ones at that), but inevitably, little Auntie Dolly with her lopsided hat and the hem of her petticoat hanging out beneath the bottom of her dress (the same one she wore to Uncle Jack's funeral) wants to get in on the action. You've got to be incredibly tactful when you say *no*; in fact I can't usually bring myself to say it at all, so I'll say something like, 'It's just immediate family at the moment ... I'll come and find you later when we're doing aunts and uncles', and hope she's too busy sucking raspberry seeds out from under her plate to realize that the photographer's packed up and she's missed her chance.

Another twenty minutes and it's time to gather the celebrity guests. It's not uncommon for a famous guest to shy away from the camera. Maybe they're worried about stealing the limelight from the happy couple or maybe they think an appearance in *Wow!* will damage their career. Luckily, this bunch is pretty amenable; lots of them are American so they probably figure the magazine will never be seen in the States. They aren't to know that Eva's already negotiated second rights with *People* magazine.

David proves to be a quick worker – I just hope he got all the right guest combinations (still, there's always PhotoShop) – and finishes a whole five minutes before our one-hour timeslot is up. There's just time for the bride and groom to make a brief appearance at their own drinks reception before the mass lovebird release outside. In the light of Hugh's concerns, Eva contacted the RSPCA, who advised that the lovebirds were intelligent enough to avoid any carnage. However, Keith was worried that a powerful telephoto lens, trained over the castle wall, might capture any activity in the grounds, so guests are forced to remain indoors for the event, watching the birds with their noses pressed up against the Gainsborough Room's French windows.

Once the lovebirds have made good their escape, the guests are invited to make their way to the dining marquee, a ten-yard dash from the French windows. The route is lined with security holding huge golfing umbrellas to thwart any lensmen. Following tradition, the bride and groom are the last to take their seats, and as Kellaway's resident master of ceremonies – clad in a tailor-made gold morning suit, paid for by the couple – announces their entrance, the marquee is filled with noisy cheers and whoops. Joe and Niamh take their places on the golden thrones in the palm of the big plaster hand (Hugh's people did a terrific repair job . . . you hardly notice that missing little finger). Their table for two is strewn with white rose petals and half a dozen or so stubby gold candles, while behind them, the gushing water screen depicts Jason's epic voyage, much to the obvious delight of the assembled guests. A serving wench dressed in a flowing white toga climbs the five steps leading to the bridal alcove and places a coronet of laurel leaves on each of their heads. This act – the 'crowning of the deities' as Hugh described it to me earlier – brings them a huge round of applause and a standing ovation from their guests.

'Who the fuck do those two think they are?' whispers Ali in my ear.

A little harsh I feel, particularly when they've had the decency to lay places for the entire *Wow!* team, which means I don't have to spend the meal pressed up against the side of the marquee, trying to look inconspicuous while the other guests chomp on the delicious fare. That said, David's three assistants, Ali and me have been assigned to what is clearly the plebs' table. Situated right at the back of the room, just below the orchestra's mezzanine, we're sitting with Joe's accountant, Niamh's gynaecologist and her childhood nanny. Eva and David have fared rather better: not only is their table a good five metres closer to the bridal alcove, it also includes Louie Bresler and a minor Australian soap star.

'Hey, where are our favours? I was looking forward to owning something from Tiffany,' says Ali, looking disparagingly at the simple white place card that marks her place.

The girl's good, but she's got a lot to learn. 'Just be grateful you're getting fed,' I reprimand her. At the last marquee wedding I covered, I had to dash across the road to the nearest pub for eight bags of pork scratchings or the photographer and I would've fainted with hunger.

A team of waitresses clad in white togas and flat gold sandals with cute little wings at the ankles move in to serve the starter (prawn and lobster timbale with a balsamic dressing, in case you're interested). As the orchestra strikes up its first number (Robbie Williams' 'Angels') I try and coax some usable anecdotes from the bonafide wedding guests on our table. The accountant and the gynaecologist are sticking rigidly to their Hippocratic Oath, but the nanny is more forthcoming, particularly after a few glasses of Merlot. Apparently, Niamh was a bed wetter until the age of seven, but somehow I don't think that little gem will get past the copy approval procedure. The starter is followed by roast rack of lamb with seasonal vegetables – the Jersey Royals obviously arrived in the nick of time – and port wine *jus* (it's just a posh word for gravy); while for the non-meat eaters, it's vegetable filo parcel (isn't it always?). Dessert is lemon mousse in those fantastic spun-sugar baskets, and then it's time for the speeches. This is where my work really begins and I flip open my notebook to a new page. I haven't drunk a drop of alcohol all afternoon, just so I can keep a clear head for this moment.

First up is Niamh's father who gives a predictably rambling, ill-thought-out speech and the combination of alcohol and his thick Irish accent mean I can barely make out what he's saying at times. Unsurprisingly, his joke about Joe being old enough to be his big brother barely raises a titter.

Then it's the turn of the best man, Tom Lucas, who begins by describing how Joe and Niamh met. 'Joe was absolutely besotted with Niamh from the moment he saw her on the cover of British *Vogue*,' he reveals. 'And when he learned she was coming to Beverly Hills on a modelling assignment, he had his PA invite her to a dinner party at his home . . . except when she arrived, she discovered that no one else had been invited!' It's a well-worn story, in fact I'm sure it even appeared on some official press release issued by Lucas's people – but it still gets a big laugh.

Finally it's over to the groom himself – and what a performance he gives. 'I used to think I had everything a man could want . . . a fantastic career, great friends, fast cars, a Lear jet,' he says, using all the skills of projection that Lee Strasberg taught him. 'But then I met Niamh, and she made me realize I was missing one crucial element . . . the love of a good woman. She made me the happiest man in the world when she agreed to be my wife. And when she told me she was expecting our child, I experienced a joy, the intensity of which I have never known . . .' etc etc etc. And if that wasn't toe-curling enough, the groom has a dramatic finale up his sleeve. Reaching into the swathes of white silk that line the walls of the bridal alcove, he pulls out a microphone that's obviously been carefully pre-positioned. Taking Niamh's hand, he serenades his new bride with that Nat King Cole song, the one that goes, 'When I fall in love, it will be forever . . .' All very touching I'm sure, but rather an ironic choice of song, don't you think? After all, he's already fallen in love at least once before – to go-go dancer-turned-soap star Lola Dukes – and that wasn't forever, was it? There isn't a dry eye in the house by the time he's finished, except for mine of course.

After the umpteenth Veuve Clicquot toast, the final ritual act of the evening is the cutting of the cake. One of David's assistants scuttles over to help his master position the tripod in front of the towering, five-tier creation (one fruit, one chocolate sponge, one ginger, one lemon buttercream, one coffee and walnut), smothered in American-style white frosting. Each tier is supported by a circle of gold ceramic Grecian figures, their outstretched arms bearing the weight of the layer above. The entire confection is studded with white icing rosebuds and topped with two fondant figures of the bride and groom in their wedding garb. Niamh's miniature alter ego even has a little pregnancy bulge.

I check my watch – seven-forty-five and time I called Nick Porter. Coffee, petits fours and wedding cake are being served and then the guests will move through to the second marquee, so now is a good time to escape.

'Ali, I'm just nipping back to my room for another notebook, I've filled this one up already. Keep an eye on David and when you see him go through to the disco tent, go with him, okay?'

'Will do,' mumbles Ali through a mouthful of cake.

Back in my room, I dial Nick's number on my mobile again – I don't want to use the hotel phone and risk Eva seeing the number when she signs our itemized bill. He answers on the second ring.

'It's me, Ruby. I've got the information, but I'm gonna have to be quick.'

'Good girl, go ahead, I'm listening to every word.'

I recite the information: the names of three prominent celebrity attendees (spitefully omitting Christy Turlington), the menu and the highlights of Joe's speech.

'You mean he actually sang to her! What a fantastic anecdote, the readers will love that. Was he a good singer? That's one hell of a tune to carry.'

'Oh, you know, pretty good, those old-school actors were trained to do everything, sing, dance, walk on their hands. Okay Nick, that's your lot. I really gotta go now.'

'Wait a second, Ruby . . . You know if you're prepared to give us a little more information – a description of the groom's outfit, say, and maybe some details from the party, who's dancing with whom, that sort of thing – we'd really make it worth your while.'

'Absolutely no chance. We made a deal and I'm sticking to it – and remember, no mention of my involvement whatsoever, not even to your colleagues at the paper. If this comes out, my career at the magazine is over. I'll call you in the week to discuss my Kramer story. Goodbye Nick.'

I kill the call, then I dial Sam's number. I need a dose of normality . . . and fast.

'Hi darling, it's me.'

'Ruby, how's it going?'

'Oh you know, as well as can be expected . . . just the party to get through now. I just wanted to call and say "hi" . . . I miss you.'

'I miss you too, Ruby Tuesday.'

'I've done a deal with Nick Porter over Kramer.'

'The newspaper guy . . . you mean he's agreed to run a story?'

'Well, under certain conditions. I can't talk now, but I'll tell you all about it when I get back. I'll be back in London tomorrow afternoon, but we'll be going straight to the office to check the proofs, so I'll see you Sunday, shall I?'

'I'm counting the hours.'

'I love you.'

'And I love you.'

I wish I was with Sam right now, so I didn't have to face those two hundred dreadful people and churn out all those thousands of words of anodyne copy. But, in the words of the song, the show must go on, so I steel myself and get back out there.

The dining tent is empty, save for a couple of elderly relatives who obviously don't appreciate the decibel level in the disco tent. Oh, and there's an incredibly drunk member of an Irish boyband crashed out in the corner, lying under the watchful eye of a four-foot-high Dionysus, how appropriate. I'd better not name any names . . . I'm not sure whether he's past the legal age of consent.

In the amphitheatre, everyone's getting down to sixties' soul provided by the six-piece band, Cafe Crème, positioned on their lofty perch. There's no sign of Harry Connick Jr, in fact, come to think of it, I haven't seen him all day. *Quelle disappointment* . . . Harry's gorgeous. I catch sight of Ali in the middle of the dance floor bopping away to 'Knock on Wood' with Leo Lucas, who looks as if he's about to have a heart attack. I climb to the fourth tier of the amphitheatre and after much hissing and gesticulating I finally draw Ali's attention. She leans forward to shout something in Leo's ear and makes her way over to me.

'I'm having such a great time . . . Joe's dad may be a living legend but he is *sooo* down to earth. He's promised to take me sailing on his yacht,' she gushes. And if she believes that, she'll believe anything.

'Ali, what the hell do you think you're playing at? You're not here to enjoy yourself, you're here to work. Now did you get the *first dance* stuff?'

'The what?'

'The bride and groom's first dance – did you get the name of the song?'

'Oh, it was that Celine Dion thing, that awful whiny theme from *Titanic*.'

'You're slurring your words, Ali. How much have you had to drink?'

'Only a coupla glasses of champagne. I'm not *pished* . . . honest.'

'Where's Eva? You better pray she didn't see you on that dance floor.'

'Dunno, she was talking to Louie last time I saw her.'

'And where's David? You're supposed to be doing his picture captions, remember.'

'Oh yeah, I started doing them and then we lost each other.'

'I've just seen him, he's up there, taking shots of the

band. Now get your notebook and get up there with him and don't leave his side till he puts his lens cap on.'

'Yes boss,' says Ali petulantly and stomps off to the top of the amphitheatre.

After much searching, I eventually find Eva in the bar area, deep in conversation with Louie. I hang around, nursing a passion fruit cocktail, till I catch her eye.

'Everything okay, Ruby?' she asks. 'Louie and I were just running through the approval procedure one more time. You'll be able to have the copy done by eleven a.m. tomorrow, won't you?'

'Yeah, I'm only planning on grabbing a few hours' sleep, so that should be fine. Ali's doing picture captions with David and I thought I'd just get a few more quotes from the guests.'

'Fine. I'd better keep Louie sweet so I'll see you later. Keep up the good work and keep a close eye on Ali. From where I'm standing, it looks like she's enjoying herself far too much!'

I spend the next two and a half hours wandering from famous guest to famous guest trying to beg, borrow or steal a quote to liven up the feature. I don't know why I bother, they all say the same thing. I mean, if you were at a wedding and someone asked you, 'Are you having a good time?' or 'What do you think of the bride's dress?' You'd say, 'Fantastic!' or 'Lovely!' or 'Super!' wouldn't you? So as the evening draws to a close, I've got a notebook full of gushing adjectives and not much else.

# WOW!

I can't tell you how relieved I am when Cafe Crème's frontman announces the band is about to play the last song of the night, and everyone rushes onto the dance floor to shake a tail feather to Al Green's 'Let's Stay Together'. Joe and Niamh look really happy as they float around the dance floor locked in each other's arms. The song ends, the net is cut, the rose petals come raining down on the guests, who emit a collective, 'Aaah!' Then everybody crowds onto the balcony for the twelve-thousand-pound firework display. As the first bars of Tchaikovsky's *1812 Overture* (predictably predictable) rise out from the 18-piece orchestra, which has re-positioned itself on the lawn outside, I see the first mini-explosion light up the night sky. My work is done now and all I can think of is Sam and sleep – Sam because I miss him so much and sleep because I've got to get up at five a.m. to write this wretched copy.

I am absolutely shattered. It's just gone seven and already I've churned out two thousand words of vintage wedding copy. In the words of the brochure, Kellaway may be *Ireland's most sumptuous country retreat ... offering guests the ultimate in luxury, peace and privacy*, but right now, I'd gladly swap the canopied king-size bed and the Jo Malone bath oils for a simple desk and chair. I've been forced to work on the bed, hunched over the laptop, and my neck and shoulders are killing me. If Sam were here, he'd soon see me right with a good pummelling from those powerful hands of his. But I mustn't let my mind wander, I've still got another couple of thousand words to go.

I managed to write almost half the copy before the wedding itself. Last week's telephone interview with Hugh netted me eighteen hundred words, he gives a great interview, old Hugh. He said that planning Joe and Niamh's Big Day had been 'an utter joy' and that he felt 'privileged' to have spent time with such a 'deeply charismatic' couple. Meanwhile, my chat with the couple themselves yielded a nice fifteen-hundred-word Q & A. It would've been longer, only Louie took me to one side during the drinks reception and politely but firmly requested that I leave out the stuff about their new beach house in Malibu. He's worried it'll leave them open to burglars and bothersome fans.

Ali was supposed to be here ten minutes ago to take over the writing. I can't imagine she'd be much use, given the state she was in last night; the reception must've passed in a blur. The last time I saw her, she was snogging the double bass player from the orchestra. I'm starving hungry, so I dial room service and order Earl Grey, orange juice and a couple of croissants. While I'm waiting for it to arrive, I read over what I've written so far. I'm not sure if I've included enough adjectives. Let's see: *beautiful, exquisite, gorgeous, dazzling, stunning, stylish, lavish, sumptuous, dramatic* . . . no, looks like they're all there. I wonder what's happening at *News on Sunday* right now. The editor probably pissed his pants when Nick submitted his own, second-hand wedding copy. My contribution may seem pretty meagre, but the Sunday market is highly competitive and any story about the Lucas–Connolly nuptials, however small, is sure to give them the edge.

At around eight-thirty, I'm just agonizing over whether to describe the giant plaster hand as *spectacular* or *magnificent* (*ludicrous* is what I really want to say – I wonder if the subs would notice if I slipped it in?) when the phone rings. It's Eva, calling to check up on me.

'How's the copy shaping up, Ruby?'

'I'm right on track. I'm aiming for completion around ten-ish, which will give you plenty of time to read it before we get approval from Louie and co.'

'Splendid. Is Ali pulling her weight?'

'Er, I haven't seen Ali this morning. I expect she's in her room collating her notes.'

'But I gave her precise instructions to meet you at seven to take over on the laptop. You mean you've been working on your own since five?'

'Oh, it's fine, Eva. I concentrate better on my own anyway.'

'It is absolutely *not* fine. You carry on writing, I'll get her out of bed. She'll be with you in twenty minutes.'

I start to protest, but Eva has already put the phone down. Shit, I hope I haven't got Ali into trouble. I dial her room extension so I can warn her that the boss is on the warpath. I let it ring for ages, but she doesn't pick up. She's gonna have one hell of a hangover when she finally regains consciousness.

A few minutes later I'm rudely jerked out of my creative reverie by a commotion in the corridor outside. As I open my door and peer in the direction of the noise, I'm just in time to see a bare-torsoed man in black suit trousers fleeing through the fire doors, pulling a huge upright instrument case on wheels behind him. Suddenly, the door to Ali's room is yanked open and Eva comes striding out with a bow in her hand. 'And you can take your bloody fiddling somewhere else!' she screams, throwing the bow after him. He's so frightened, he doesn't even stop to retrieve it. It doesn't take a genius to work out what's happened. Ali spent the night making beautiful music with the double bass player. Hardly the crime of the century, I know, but we *are* here to work. This wedding is the biggest thing that's ever happened to the magazine and we really need all hands to be on deck. Ali has done some great work for *Wow!* in the past and won a lot of respect, mine included, but she has just made two Grade-A fuck-ups. The first was shagging Nigel Kennedy there (violin, double bass, they're practically the same thing); the second was getting caught red-handed.

I retreat to my room and write a couple more paragraphs, waiting for the inevitable knock at the door. When it comes, I call out, 'It's open,' and in comes Ali. She looks really rough: her hair's all over the place and last night's mascara is smeared over the tops of her cheeks.

'Have you got an aspirin, Ruby? My head's throbbing.'

I toss her the packet of Anadin from my washbag and watch her fumbling to push out two tablets from the blister pack.

'Is that orange going spare?' she says, spying the half-glass of juice lying next to the remnants of my Continental breakfast on the bedside table. Without waiting for an answer, she pops the aspirin, picks up the glass and drains it in one giant gulp.

'I suppose you heard the shit hit the fan out there.'

'Well I saw some half-naked man scurrying out of your room while Eva did her angry mother routine.'

'The bitch just came barging into my room, she didn't knock or anything. I must've forgotten to lock the door last night, I guess I had other things on my mind. Emile and I got the fright of our lives, and the worst of it is she sent him packing so quickly, I didn't get his phone number. Do you think Hugh will have it?'

'Hell-oh. Ali, I'd be more worried about losing my job if I were you.'

'Eva wouldn't do that, would she? Mind you, I got a right bollocking. She said I was thoughtless, selfish, and a bad ambassador for the magazine. A bit strong, don't you think? I mean I haven't been that out of order, I just overslept.'

'Ali, you've just left me to write the entire bloody epic on my own. You were due here, ooh let's see . . .' I make a big show of examining my wristwatch '. . . two hours ago.'

'I know and I'm really sorry, Ruby. I just had too much to drink last night and one thing led to another. Anyway, I'm here now, so what can I do to help?'

She doesn't sound nearly contrite enough.

'We're doing the approvals at eleven, so I suggest you get your notebook and haul your arse over to the photo lab. David will be there by now, editing the shots, so you can start matching names to faces. That way if you're left with any blanks to fill, you can run them past Joe and Niamh. Oh, and don't forget to wash your face before you meet them. You look a right state.'

'Will do. I'll see you in the lab later then.'

I just hope she's got all those captions. It's fatal to rely on the happy couple to help you out because they won't necessarily know the names of all their mates' arm candy. If Ali's got a single '. . . and friend' in those photos, Eva probably will give her the chop. That said, doing captions is no easy task. The celebrities, of course, are readily identifiable, it's the ordinary folk that give you grief. You haven't got time to write down a lengthy physical description, so I find the best method is to take down details of the individual's hair and main item of clothing. So I might write something like this: *Keifer Sutherland and Lauren Weinberger (long blonde, burgundy bias-cut)*. You've got to be careful though. I remember the time I took down the name of an exceptionally unattractive wedding guest and I wrote: *Lesley Papadopoulos (grey rats' tails, too-tight pinafore)*, which would've been fine, except she insisted on checking I'd spelled her name right. Before I could stop her, she'd grabbed my notebook out of my hand. When she read my less-than-flattering descriptive notes, she gave me the filthiest look before stalking off in a huff.

At a quarter to ten I finally finish the copy. I've done a pretty good job, though I do say so myself. Approval shouldn't be a problem, there's nothing in the text that anyone could possibly take offence to – although I did describe the groom's mother as 'curvaceous in Calvin Klein' but maybe I should change that to *shapely* (what I actually mean, of course, is *fat*). Oh what the hell, there's nothing wrong with *curvaceous*, so *curvaceous* she will stay. I pop the disk out of the laptop and take it down to Kellaway's office, where the general manager has kindly agreed to let me use his facilities to print out my copy. When that's done, I track down Eva in the breakfast room, where she's enjoying caffe latte and grapefruit segments with Louie. However intimate they are (and they do look pretty intimate) I know that she'll want to read the copy in private, before handing it over to him, so I arrange to meet her in the lab in half an hour.

'And Ruby, don't let that copy or the disk out of your sight,' she instructs me. 'Our rivals would kill for that information. Go straight to the lab and don't talk to anyone you don't recognize.'

'Yes Eva.' Christ, you'd think I'd never done this before.

I'm pleased to see Ali slaving over a hot lightbox when I get there. Jason has done a fantastic job, working through the night. David's assistants were feeding him film throughout the course of the wedding, and he had it all processed into colour transparencies by six a.m., in plenty of time for David's eight a.m. edit. I'm dying to see the pictures. I must admit I'm a little sceptical about David's capabilities as a wedding photographer, it's so different to the studio work he's been used to. His pictures need to reflect the whole gamut of wedding emotion: laughter, tears, revelry, romance – pretty tough, especially for a first-timer.

'How did you find it last night?' I ask him. 'Hard work, huh?'

'You can say that again,' he says, pushing his glasses back up his nose. 'But I really enjoyed it. Niamh and Joe were wonderful hosts and I met so many interesting people.'

I would've really enjoyed it too, if I was getting 15k for a day's work – and he'll make a mint on syndication too. But I mustn't let it eat me up.

'And Ali, have you managed to identify all these interesting people?'

'Um, most of them. There's a couple I don't recognize at all, but I guess we can just leave those ones out.'

It doesn't quite work like that, but I'm not about to lecture Ali. I'll leave that to Eva.

'Is it okay if I take a look at some of the shots?' I ask David. Some photographers are so precious about their work, they won't let you near them until the editor's had a look-see.

'Sure, the wedding ceremony and drinks reception shots are right here,' he says, pointing to a second light-box, crammed with transparencies. 'I'm pretty pleased with them.'

I take the eyeglass he's proffering and spend a good fifteen minutes examining the pictures.

'Like them?' asks David when I finally lift my head up.

'They are absolutely bloody brilliant. You should change your speciality, mate. Forget shooting super-models, you'd earn a fortune as a wedding photographer.'

'Well I'm glad you approve,' he says, laughing. 'That was definitely my first and last wedding. Supermodels are an awful lot easier to control than people's relatives.'

When Eva comes in, she goes straight for the lightbox. My words can wait because the real story of the wedding will be told through the pictures. People read magazines like *Wow!* and *Yeah!* in a very unique way. They don't look at the contents page, don't thumb through the mag until they find an article they like and then stop and read it from beginning to end. No, the celebrity junkie starts by taking the cover firmly between forefinger and thumb and then flicks the pages over one by one, quite briskly, bam bam bam, right to the end, just to get that short, sharp visual fix. Then they go back to the beginning and turn the pages over, more slowly this time, stopping at particular photos – the ones that show make-up caked on the face of an unsuspecting celebrity in a ridiculously close close-up or a really nasty wallpaper border in someone's front room. Viewing of the magazine is frequently done in groups of twos or threes, or as many heads as you can get round a coffee table. As the pages are turned by the pack leader, each individual will jab their finger at an eye-catching page, thereby halting the flicking process for a couple of minutes. It's only on the third, and probably final inspection, that the 'reader' actually reads anything and even then, I seriously doubt that anybody takes in every word.

'David, these are just fantastic,' purrs Eva. 'You've really caught the mood of the party very well, and these shots of Niamh and her bridesmaids are just adorable. I'm very happy, very happy indeed.'

Good, so now that we're all happy, can we just get on and read my copy? I'm on pins here. I wave the pages at Eva and she takes them outside to read in the peace and quiet of the sprawling castle gardens. When she returns twenty minutes later she has a big smile on her face, so I know I've delivered.

'Well done, that's great work, especially considering you did it all on your own.' She shoots a poisonous look in Ali's direction, except Ali's face is still glued to the lightbox, so she misses it completely. 'I don't suppose you've any more details about the dress.'

'No, I put down every single cough and spit. There's really nothing more to say.'

'I suppose you're right. It would've been nice to have a quote from Donatella,' she says wistfully.

'Yeah, well it can't be helped. There's plenty of information here, and I'm sure we'll be seeing replica dresses in every high street bridal outlet before the summer's out.'

We have only to obtain Joe and Niamh's personal approval now and then we're home free. They finally make an appearance at eleven-forty-five, three-quarters of an hour later than the agreed deadline. We're buoyed up, though, and it was their wedding night after all, so we forgive them. Joe looks his usual craggily handsome self in golfing plaids and baseball cap – Kellaway's 18-hole course is said to be one of the best in southern Ireland – while Niamh, sporting a gauzy Betsey Johnson number, radiates a luminescent beauty. Yes, they really have got it all, that couple. We wait with bated breath while they examine the transparencies, and as Louie takes them through each one, two piles start to emerge: *approved* and *rejected*. David's edit has already knocked out the pictures where people's eyes are closed or they look really pissed or the shot is slightly out of focus. Joe and Niamh's edit is rather more idiosyncratic.

'My father's face looks flushed in this one,' says Niamh in her soft Irish lilt, pushing the shot towards the reject pile.

Yeah, well he should've stayed off the booze, at least until the ceremony was over.

'I don't think Tom would appreciate me letting this

grace the pages of a national magazine,' says Joe, chuckling to himself as he examines a transparency.

'Oh I really like that shot,' I say peering over the lightbox. 'Tom and his wife look so lovey-dovey snuggled up in the back row of the amphitheatre.'

'Yeah, 'cept his wife's back home in LA. This little cutie is his personal assistant,' Joe explains.

'Right, gotcha. That one's definitely a no-no then.' Everyone in the lab titters politely at Tom's expense, but it's his wife I feel sorry for.

By the time they've waded through all the pictures, about 50 per cent have been rejected. It sounds like a lot, but it's only average; we'll still have plenty to fill our fifty-two pages. Then it's time for my copy to be scrutinized. Joe, Niamh and Louie go off into a huddle and Louie reads the words out loud to them. I can see them nodding and even smiling at times, which is a good sign, and when Louie reports back, I'm delighted to hear that the changes are minimal. Joe wants to be described as 'handsome and distinguished' (as opposed to just 'distinguished') in his wedding regalia and Niamh wants me to add that her own parents are celebrating their ruby anniversary later this year. Don't ask me why. I guess she wants readers to know that fidelity runs in the family. We all shake hands with each other, and Joe and Niamh go off to enjoy married life. Tomorrow they leave for a three-week turtle-watching honeymoon in the Galapagos, lucky things.

Wonder if I'll ever get to go on honeymoon. I used to

think I'd never get married, but just recently I've caught myself fantasizing about my own Big Day – the kind of dress I'd wear, the sort of music I'd choose, who I'd ask to be chief bridesmaid. One thing's for sure, I'd make sure I did it in real style, none of this more-money-than-taste rubbish.

# TWENTY-THREE: GOOD NEWS, BAD NEWS

I'm nestling in a bed of bagel crumbs, savouring the most delicious Sunday morning lie-in. God knows I need it . . . those three days in Ireland totally wiped me out. We flew back late yesterday afternoon, with a two-man security escort to protect our precious cargo of photographs, which were stashed in an unassuming A3 Jiffy envelope. When we landed at City airport, Ali handed over her sheaf of caption notes (I gave them the once over during the flight and she'd done a surprisingly thorough job) and took herself off home. For me, however, the job wasn't quite over. Eva and I caught a cab straight to the office, where a team of subs and designers were waiting on tenterhooks for our arrival. They worked through the night to pull the fifty-two pages together in time for the seven a.m. deadline, watched over by the two security guards, who didn't let those transparencies out of their sight, not until they were locked away in the office safe. There wasn't much for me to do really, but I hung around till midnight, just in case the subs had any queries about my copy. Afterwards, I went home to unwind with a glass of Harvey's Bristol Cream (left over from a Christmas trifle – it was the only alcohol I could find) and a large spliff. Do you know, when I went to slide open the living-room sash – I hate the smell of stale smoke in the morning – I noticed that the window was closed, but not actually locked. I'm normally scrupulous about checking my home security when I go away, but I guess it just slipped my mind this time. I'm lucky I wasn't burgled, being on the ground floor and all.

I've got the whole of today and tomorrow off work and I'm planning to spend most of it with Sam. I missed him so much when I was away; it was almost a physical ache, a feeling that half of me was somewhere else. He's coming round for lunch and then, as it's such a nice day, we plan to go for a nice long walk by the river. Speaking of lunch, I'd better nip to the shops at some point. I'm not doing anything fancy – I've passed the stage of feeling that I have to impress Sam with my culinary ability – just a cold pasta salad and my signature lime and ginger cheesecake. I'll pick up a *News on Sunday* while I'm out, so I can see how they've handled the story.

I haul myself out of bed and head for the shower. Just as I've pulled off my nightie and pushed my hair into a transparent shower cap (I have to protect my hair from moisture at all costs), the phone rings. I trot naked into the lounge, hoping that those voile curtains are at least semi-opaque, and pick up the handset, fully expecting to hear Sam's voice.

'Have you seen the newspaper?'

It's not Sam, it's Eva, and she doesn't sound happy. I think I can guess what's put a bee in her bonnet. And is it my imagination or does her tone sound faintly accusatory? I'd better play dumb.

'Oh, morning Eva. I haven't seen any papers this morning, I've just got up actually.'

'Allow me to read the front-page splash to you.'

I hear a rustle of paper and my heart sinks as she reads out loud, 'World exclusive: Fairy-tale castle wedding for Joe and Niamh. See pages four and five.'

Christ, a front-page lead. And how on earth did they manage to stretch a bit of crap about a lemon mousse and a soppy song over three pages? 'I don't believe it . . . how could they? Keith didn't report any security breaches. The castle estate was totally sealed,' I blabber, trying to sound suitably stunned.

'I've absolutely no idea, but believe me, I intend to get to the bottom of this,' says Eva menacingly.

'Maybe one of the catering staff was responsible, or that scruffy guy reupholstering the thrones. There was something very shifty about him.' Best to question the integrity of the hired help as early as possible, sow the seeds of doubt and so on.

'Who knows? The pictures are pretty poor quality so

hopefully it won't impact on the magazine sales too much. It's still bloody annoying though.'

'Did you say *pictures*?'

'Oh yes, they've got pictures all right, three of them – and not just arrivals photos, snatched through car windows, but shots from inside the marquee. If it turns out to be one of Joe and Niamh's guests, I swear I'll slash their fee by ten per cent. I'm sorry to disturb you on a Sunday like this, Ruby, I just thought you'd like to know.'

'Absolutely, I've got to see this for myself. I'll go and buy a copy now.'

'I'll see you on Tuesday then. And Ruby, thanks for all your hard work over the past few days. It's been much appreciated.'

Eva's gratitude makes me squirm . . . if only she knew the truth. I skip the shower, tear off the shower cap, pull on a pair of jogging bottoms and a rather creased sweatshirt – I'll go bra-less just this once – and head for the newsagent's on the main road. When I get there, I see a big pile of *News on Sundays* sitting on the bottom shelf – and there's no wedding photo in sight. In fact I have to turn to page seven to see their half-page story, rather unimaginatively headlined: *Wedding Menu Secrets*. I could have done better than that myself. I scan the copy quickly, noting Nick Porter's by-line at the top. It's practically a verbatim account of what I told him on the phone, padded out with a bit of background stuff about how the couple met and the history of Kellaway. Rather uninspiring frankly. What on earth was Eva talking about? I decide to buy the paper anyway and have a good read-through at home just in case I've missed something. As I turn towards the man behind the till, my eye is caught by the front page of *Sunday World*, an even more down-market rival. There's only two copies left and they both look pretty well thumbed, but then that's hardly surprising – they have, after all, got a world wedding exclusive. So this is what Eva was referring to. My guilty conscience naturally assumed she was talking about *News on Sunday*. I pay for both papers and jog home as fast as my unsupported breasts will allow.

As soon as I get in, I spread the copy of *Sunday World* out on the breakfast bar. There on the front page is a blurred shot of Joe and Niamh sitting on their thrones in the palm of the plaster hand. How the fuck did they get that picture? Joe is standing up with a microphone in one hand and the other arm outstretched, so he must be singing to her. Fortunately, Niamh is sitting down so most of her dress is masked by the organza tablecloth, but you can still see the cowl neckline and you can just about make out the miniature rosebuds in her hair. For *Wow!* the wedding gown is the Holy Grail as far as weddings are concerned, and a full-length shot of the bride in all her finery would be the ultimate prize as far as a rival publication is concerned. That's if the bride is a celebrity in her own right, of course. A shot of a non-famous bride doesn't rate nearly so highly. Page four boasts another equally blurred shot, presumably taken during the speeches, showing Leo Lucas chomping on a big fat Cohiba and raising his half-empty champagne flute. My eyes instantly flit to the caption, but no, it looks like they missed an opportunity there: *The legendary Leo Lucas celebrates his son's second marriage with a champagne toast*. They obviously forgot that Leo's been a member of Alcoholics Anonymous for the past twelve years. In interviews, he always swears he hasn't touched a drop since his wife agreed to drop the battery charges. Still, if you can't have a drink at your own son's wedding . . .

The final picture, on page five, is downright cruel and shows the wasted under-age boyband member passed out on the floor of the marquee. *Man Power's Liam stays out well past his bedtime*, reads the caption. His manager's going to love that. Man Power only just withstood a drugs scandal a couple of months ago, closely followed by the departure of the original frontman to pursue a solo career, so I wouldn't be surprised if Liam's little transgression will prove to be the proverbial straw that broke the camel's back.

The newspaper did well to get those pictures, there's no doubt about it; in fact Special K must be flagellating himself at this very moment. I wonder if the paper had a plant in there, a bribed wedding guest, say, or if the photographs are the work of a lone maverick who got lucky and then called up the newspaper yesterday to score what was probably a five-figure deal. Having thoroughly digested the pictures, I settle down to read the copy.

> These are the pictures they said we'd never get, but here they are, the first photographs of Joe Lucas and his stunning new bride Niamh Connolly. *Wow!* magazine is said to have paid in excess of £1 million for exclusive coverage of the 'It' couple's lavish Irish wedding, and spent tens of thousands on stringent security measures. It appeared to be Mission Impossible, but *Sunday World* rose to the challenge . . .

This self-congratulatory tone is typical of the tabs – they love to put one over on us.

> Held in a monster marquee, the no-expense-spared wedding reception was OTT, even by celebrity standards. The theme of the wedding was ancient Greece, with waitresses clad in skimpy togas and gold statues of Greek gods decorating the reception marquee. Guests, who had been asked to follow a strict white-and-gold dress code, feasted on a three-course meal of prawn and lobster timbale, roast rack of lamb and lemon mousse, while the happy couple held court on a raised stage, sitting in a giant plaster hand. It must've been the hand of a mutant, however, as it only had four fingers.

Poor Hugh will be sobbing into his cornflakes when he reads that bit about the hand and Chef'll be pissed that there's no mention of the spun sugar baskets; he spent hours on those. The groom, meanwhile, isn't going to be happy about this reference to his first wife:

'When I fall in love, it will be forever,' Joe promised his new wife, as he serenaded her with the Nat King Cole classic. Except someone forgot to tell him he'd already spoken these words once before – to wife number one, soap actress and former stripper Lola Dukes. Not surprisingly, Lola wasn't invited to the wedding – word is, she's enjoying a sunshine break in the Bahamas with her personal trainer on the multi-million dollar proceeds of her divorce settlement. No doubt Joe's lawyers have learned their lesson and drawn up a pre-nuptial agreement this time round.

Phew, now I can see why Eva's knickers were in such a twist. It could have been worse though – these pictures really are grainy and at least they don't have anything about the dress or the wedding ceremony or the amphitheatre. And most importantly, the story has really taken the heat off me. Eva's not going to be worried about *News on Sunday*'s scrappy four paragraphs of copy in comparison. Poor Nick; his editor won't be best pleased. He'd better not renege on his promise to run my Kramer story though.

My reunion with Sam was everything I hoped it would be and more. As soon as he set foot in the door, we clasped each other in a massive hug and stood there for at least five minutes, gently swaying and inhaling each other's scent. These four days apart have felt like a lifetime.

'You feel so good,' he says running his strong hands up and down the length of my body. 'You'll have to go away more often.'

'Cheeky! I might have to withhold sexual privileges for that comment.' I am joking of course. It's all I can do to stop myself ripping his clothes off right here and now. 'And by the way, there's nothing for lunch either.'

'No sex and no lunch. What on earth am I doing here?'

I explain that I've been far too busy reading the papers to go shopping and offer to take him instead to my local pub, The Bear, which has a nice beer garden and a proper wine list. Over our roast loin of pork, I fill Sam in about my deal with Nick Porter and the photos that appeared in *Sunday World*.

'So two different newspapers both ran stories about the wedding, except the other paper had photographs too . . . how does that affect you?'

'Well it couldn't be better actually. Eva didn't even mention the *News on Sunday* story – and she's bound to have seen it, she gets all the Sundays. Her only concern is to find out who leaked those pictures to the other mob.'

'I can't believe the way Nick Porter held you to ransom over that Kramer thing. Do you think he'll stick to your agreement now that he's been trumped by that other paper?'

'He'd bloody better. He promised it could run in next

week's edition. I just hope Kramer reads it. And if *he* doesn't, one of his mates or better still, his agent, is bound to point it out to him. Being branded a stalker certainly won't do his career – or his social life – any good.'

We don't mention Kramer again after that and our two-day break passes in a wonderful fug of loveliness. Sam has booked Monday off work so he can spend it with me, even though he's right in the middle of a project to redevelop Greenwich Park's herb garden. We did lots of eating, drinking and shagging and by Monday lunchtime I'm practically on the verge of asking him to move in. I don't of course because I'm too chicken and because, after all, we've known each other less than two months.

In the event, I'm glad I didn't pop the question because when we're sitting in bed on Monday night, enjoying a post-coital spliff, Sam drops the bombshell. The conversation begins innocuously enough.

'You know I mentioned that one of my work colleagues spent last summer in Italy, working in the botanical gardens at San Liberato? It was a job swap thing – their head gardener came to work for us in Greenwich.'

'Oh yes, that place near Rome . . . something to do with a church, wasn't it?'

'That's right. San Liberato is a medieval church, set in the midst of this beautiful landscape overlooking Lake Bracciano, just a few miles north of Rome. There's a stretch of parkland, containing dozens of beautiful and really quite valuable trees – Canadian maples, Montezuma pines, camphors, lyriodendra, American Black Walnuts. And beside it is a whole cluster of lush gardens, filled with antique roses and magnolia and galtonias, with fountains and stone walls . . . real Secret Garden stuff.'

'It sounds absolutely idyllic.'

'Rob, my mate at work, said it was the most tranquil place he's ever visited. Apparently some count and his wife created the gardens in the late 1960s under the guidance of a quite well-known English landscape artist. Rob reckons it's just like stepping into a beautiful watercolour painting.'

'Is it a regular arrangement then, this job swap? What a wonderful idea, I'd love to swap places with a journalist in LA or Paris.' I'm chattering away but the stupid thing is I have no idea what's coming.

'Kind of – but this year it's slightly different. The head gardener at San Liberato can't spare any of his guys to come over to London, but he's invited one of the Greenwich horticulturists to go over there semi-permanently . . . they need some help with the rose gardens, you see.'

'Okaaay,' I say, as the penny begins to drop.

'The thing is, Ruby, back in February, before I'd even met you, I applied to be transferred to San Liberato. I didn't think I'd stand a chance – there's quite a strict pecking order at work and there are two horticulturists in my department who've been there much longer than me. But one of them has a young family, so he can't just up sticks and go, so the other guy, Tony, jumped at the opportunity. Only thing is, his father's just had a heart attack and he doesn't want to leave London. I'm next in line so they offered it to me. I heard on Friday while you were in Ireland.'

There is a long silence as I try and work out exactly what it is he's saying to me. I think he's saying he's leaving me, only he wants my permission to go.

'What does "semi-permanently" mean exactly?'

'Well I'd go over there for a three-month trial period and if it all works out, I'd stay there indefinitely. And if it doesn't work out, then Greenwich Council give me my old job back.'

'I see. And when does this sabbatical start?'

'Quite soon actually . . . the second week in June, to be precise.'

Fucking hell, that's less than three weeks away. 'So you've said you'll go then?'

'I haven't said one way or another. I've got to let them know tomorrow. It's certainly a fantastic opportunity.'

'Oh yes, you can't afford to miss out on it.'

'So you think I should go?' He's looking at me very seriously, like he's really interested in my opinion.

'Definitely, without a shadow of a doubt. You'd kick yourself if you forfeited it to someone else. It's a once-in-a-lifetime experience.' Maybe I'm going a bit over the top, but I'm determined not to show weakness. If he wants to go, I'll bloody well let him go. I'm certainly not going to do that please-don't-leave-me shit. I'm a big girl now, I can cope with a little rejection. And it's only Italy, not the moon. I can always fly out there for long weekends, that's if he wants me to.

'Promise me you'll come and visit. There's a little cottage that comes with the job. As I recall, Rob said it was a "rustic but charming two up, two down, smothered in crimson bougainvillaea".'

'Absolutely, you won't be able to keep me away. Is Rob considering a career move by any chance, because with those powers of description, I could get him a job at *Wow!*, no problem.'

Sam laughs and so do I, but it's a hollow laugh. I know full well that long-distance relationships rarely, if ever, last. I tried it once with a beautiful firm-bodied Greek I met on holiday in Kefalonia. I was only 19 and I thought it was true love. Dmitri and I tried to make it work and took turns visiting each other as often as we could afford to. At the time, I was an undergraduate in Manchester and during his visits Dmitri would wait outside my lecture theatre like a well-trained puppy. In the evenings we drank watery lager out of flabby plastic glasses in the union bar and then it was back to the halls of residence to copulate noisily on my hard single bed. My visits to Kefalonia were slightly more exotic and I have fond memories of drinking *raki* in the garden of his parents' white-walled, marble-floored villa and making love on the beach under the night sky. After four months the relationship foundered under the strain of being so far apart and the varied distractions of our respective homes. For me, it was the lure of the

Manchester club scene and its attendant pleasures, both sexual and narcotic; for Dmitri, a waiter in his family's restaurant, it was the weekly influx of fresh girl tourists. I still think of him with great affection, although at the time I didn't appreciate his attempts to persuade me to have sex 'Greek-style'. I never did find out exactly what that entailed, but I always fancied it was something to do with yoghurt.

When I return to work on Tuesday morning, rather heavy-hearted in the wake of Sam's shock announcement, there's a strange, subdued atmosphere in the office. Normally everyone's on a high for a good few days after a big wedding – particularly a corker like this – and we're all desperate to get our hands on a finished copy of the magazine, to see the fruits of our labour. The print run for this issue is a massive two million copies, nearly four times the normal amount, and I know Eva's hoping we'll sell at least three-quarters of them. But today is different. Everyone's sitting quietly at their desk and no one makes eye contact with me when I walk in, half an hour late (Sam and I slipped in a quick one this morning before he left for work).

I've no sooner sat at my desk when the Doughboy slithers over, hands in his pockets, so that the too-high waistband of his trousers is stretched even more tightly than usual across his slack gut.

'Nice holiday, Ruby?' he asks, shuffling through the unopened pile of post on my desk, like he thinks some of his stuff may have landed there by mistake. I hate it when people do that.

'It wasn't a holiday, Adrian. It was a day off in lieu for working my arse off on the wedding.'

'Oh yes, well that's what I meant.'

'So what's been happening here then? Why all the glum faces?'

'You mean you haven't heard . . .?'

He leaves the question hanging there instead of telling me exactly what it is that I haven't heard. I expect it makes him feel all big and important, like a kid in the school playground – I know something you don't know, *ner ner ner ner ner* . . . 'Haven't heard what, Adrian?' I say boredly.

'There's been quite an inquisition . . .'

I'm not going to give him the satisfaction of a second prompting question, so I just ignore him and start opening my post. Of course he can't hold it in for more than two seconds.

'. . . about the photos in *Sunday World*.'

'Yeah, bit of a bummer, those pictures. Still, Eva doesn't seem to think it'll affect our sales too much.'

'And you know who's been implicated, don't you?'

'No Adrian, but I expect you're just about to tell me.'

'Ali.' He virtually spits the word out, like it tastes ugly in his mouth. 'I knew that girl was no good.'

'Ali . . . don't be ridiculous. What on earth has Ali got to do with it?'

'Plenty. She was caught *in flagrante* with that double bass player, wasn't she?'

Only in your foetid imagination, Adrian. 'Not quite. Eva didn't exactly catch them at it hammer and tongs. She found him in Ali's bedroom the morning after the wedding. But Ali's private life has got absolutely nothing to do with anyone on this magazine.' Least of all you, you sad little man. I bet you're really getting off on this, aren't you?

'It does when she's fornicating with the man responsible for leaking those photographs.'

'Adrian, why don't you just come right out and say what you want to say, instead of beating round the bush?'

'Okay, but I'm warning you, it doesn't look at all good for your little friend Ali . . . One of Eva's friends from the *Daily Mail* is sleeping with the deputy picture editor at *Sunday World* and according to him, the person who took those photographs – and earned himself a cool twenty thousand pounds – was none other than Emile Marceau, Ali's musical shag.'

He sounds triumphant, like he's just sussed Fermat's Last Theorem or something. 'I fail to see how what you've just told me implicates Ali in any way, shape or form and I don't think you should be expounding your far-fetched theories to all and sundry when she's not here to defend herself. Where is Ali this morning anyway?' I say, noticing her empty desk for the first time.

'Eva's suspended her, pending further investigation,'

says Adrian smugly. 'Like I said, she's the number-one suspect.'

And then, having played his trump card, he wanders off again, to crawl back under his stone. I review the information. The double bass player ... that figures because if you look at the pictures they do appear to have been taken from a height. Once the band members were ensconced on their mezzanine I doubt if anyone, not even the security guards, paid them much attention. Taking a few pictures with a miniature camera wouldn't have been difficult. Hang on though, Special K's men frisked all the staff working on the night – waitresses, band members, even the guy in charge of the lovebirds. In fact, they did more than frisk the orchestra, they searched every instrument case, suit pocket, trouser leg. I remember watching them do it and thinking it was a bit excessive. God, that Emile really struck it lucky – once with the photographs and once with Ali, in fact she was probably his celebratory shag. Speaking of which, poor Ali. Suspended. Maybe I'll give her a call at home this evening. I won't do it now, with the whole office listening.

I spend the morning flicking through papers and magazines looking for potential victims. The wedding has absorbed so much of my time in the past few weeks, I don't have any other projects on the go at the moment. I note with some satisfaction that Jasmine Leigh has chucked her husband out of the house, although there's no mention of a third party – or, to quote Stevo's agent, 'the couple are undergoing a trial separation'. Trial separation my arse, that relationship's as dead as a dodo. Good thing we got that *at home* feature in the magazine a couple of weeks ago, or it would have been totally useless.

Just before lunchtime, Eva makes her first appearance of the day. I wait until she's had a chance to go through her emails and catch up with her secretary before I approach her. 'Hi Eva. Only another three days before the magazine hits the streets. Angela showed me the wedding proofs this morning – they look even better than I imagined. When will we see finished copies?'

'Not till Friday morning. I'll give you a shout when they come in. I reckon those magazines are going to walk off the shelves, you know.'

'So you don't think the *Sunday World* story will affect us too much?'

'Well I was a bit worried at first, but actually I think it might work in our favour. People who wouldn't normally dream of reading *Wow!* have seen that stuff in the paper and it's whetted their appetites – they'll want to check out our coverage to see if the wedding really was as over-the-top as it looks in those few snatched snapshots. There's been tons of media interest since Sunday. I've had three interview requests already, two print and one TV – they want to talk about how we clinched the deal and what it was like being a guest at the wedding of the millennium. Julie's even taken inquiries from the States – apparently CBS are interested in setting up a live satellite link. Speaking of which, I'd better book a facial . . .'

'Adrian tells me that you've traced the source of the leak,' I interrupt, not the slightest bit interested in the minutiae of Eva's beauty regimen.

'That's right. Emile Marceau, the orchestra's double bass player. I've already spoken to Hugh and Louie. Hugh has now struck the orchestra permanently off his playlist. Half their bookings used to come via him, so you can imagine how pissed off their agent was – put it this way, Marceau will never play with them again. Louie meanwhile has been scrutinizing Marceau's contract of employment – he's probably got grounds to sue, but I don't think he'll want to get the agency involved in expensive and protracted litigation.'

'So where does Ali figure in all this?'

'Presumably Adrian has told you that I've suspended her?'

'Yeah. It seems a bit harsh. Sleeping with the guy doesn't make her an accessory to the crime. I mean there's no concrete evidence connecting her to the leak is there?'

'Actually, Ruby, there is. Evidence from her own lips.'

'What are you saying . . . that she admitted it?'

'Yes. But I haven't announced it to the rest of the staff yet, not even Adrian knows all the ins and outs. I was going to wait until the planning meeting tomorrow morning, so I'd be grateful if you'd keep it to yourself until then.'

I still can't believe Ali could possibly be involved, but I'm interested to hear Eva's explanation. 'Absolutely. My lips are sealed. So what's the story then?'

'Well . . .' she begins, clasping her hands together rather theatrically. 'They played a two-hander. Marceau, up on that mezzanine, was in a prime position to take photos. With his double bass, he was the only musician standing up, so he had a perfect view over the rest of the band's heads and none of them would've noticed him snapping away because he was standing right at the back of the mezzanine. His state-of-the-art mini-camera was clipped to his shirt, directly behind his tie. A trigger switch positioned in his jacket pocket activated the shutter. So when he wanted to take a shot, all he had to do was pull his tie to one side, slip a hand in his pocket and squeeze the trigger. It was easy.' She pauses to take a breath . . .

'As soon as I learned that Marceau was the culprit, I knew there had to be someone else involved. He took the pictures, sure, but who provided the words? He wasn't in a position to gather all that information. Even more crucially, how did he manage to sneak a camera in? All the musicians and their instruments were thoroughly checked by Keith's men and pronounced clean. That's what got me thinking . . . Who on earth could have transported a camera into that marquee? Security had swept the entire place for suspicious devices just half an hour before the first guests sat down. The only people who weren't searched before they entered the marquee were the guests themselves and the *Wow!* team. I didn't think David O'Connor would jeopardize his worldwide copyright by passing a camera to a rival photographer. It could've been one of his assistants, I suppose, or indeed any one of the guests, but I decided to begin my investigations closer to home.'

'Bloody hell, Eva . . . Angela Lansbury's got nothing on you,' I say, somewhat stunned by Eva's well-rehearsed summation. And judging by the look of pure triumph on her face, I'd say she's enjoying every rotten minute of this.

'*You* had yesterday off,' she continues. 'Or else you, like everyone else, would've been under suspicion, I'm afraid.'

She sees me gulp and I can feel myself flushing too. I don't know what's making me feel more awkward: the fact that Eva thinks I would do something like that or the fact that I actually did do something like that.

'Please don't be offended, Ruby. I would've been utterly shocked if you had been involved, but I had to consider everyone. Obviously Ali was the number one suspect, given that I caught her in bed with Marceau, so yesterday morning I called her into my office and confronted her. I'm afraid I called her bluff rather, pretended I already knew she was involved. Rather a clever tactic I thought, I saw something similar once on *The Bill*. Of course Ali denied it at first, but she's an awful liar. It only took fifteen minutes to break her. She was in a terrible state, weeping and wailing, claiming she needed the money to pay off her student loan. She even offered to give me back her fifty per cent cut of the 20k blood money.'

'But she didn't know Emile before the night of the wedding,' I say in Ali's defence, unable to believe that she could really have been so calculating. 'When she came into my room the next morning, she was moaning about how she hadn't managed to get his phone number before you gave him his marching orders. I remember her asking if I thought Hugh would have it.'

'All an act I'm afraid, Ruby. Emile and Ali have known each other for almost a month and it was Ali who made the initial approach to *Sunday World*'s news editor, Bill Whately. She's got more balls than I gave her credit for. He, of course, signed her up straight away to provide the words. Thankfully, she's not nearly as good a journalist as you or she would've done a better job with her copy – and I don't expect that drinking as much alcohol as she did on the night did much for her powers of observation. But Whately knew Ali would never be able to take photographs herself on the day, being in such a high-profile position. So, having managed to obtain a list of the contractors working the wedding, he set about recruiting a willing accomplice. Enter Marceau. He and Ali had several meetings with the *Sunday World* people to discuss strategy and so on and it seems that somewhere along the way a relationship blossomed – he's a good-looking boy I must admit. A couple of days before the wedding, the newspaper furnished Ali with the camera. She carried it into the reception tent and passed it to Marceau in the staff toilets at an appointed time. So you see it was quite simple really. Her only error was not being able to control her libido. If I hadn't found them in bed together, I would never have made the connection. I know you two got on well together, but if I were you, I wouldn't have any contact with her from now on. She's bad news,' says Eva, laying a comforting hand on my arm. 'Her letter of dismissal is already in the post. She won't of course be getting a reference from me, but she can count herself lucky I haven't decided to take this any further.'

Well I'll be damned. Little inexperienced Ali – a spy. No wonder she seemed so lacklustre on the day. She was probably too busy scribbling notes for *Sunday World* to bother about putting in any effort on *Wow!*'s behalf. How could she betray us all like that? Mind you . . . I'm a fine one to talk.

# TWENTY-FOUR: D-DAY

You've all heard the one about the celebrity stalker – but a stalker celebrity? **Exposed** has it on good authority that a certain best-selling author is stalking a female journalist of our acquaintance. The man in question, a horror writer who shares something in common with a Hoffman–Streep movie double act, has been plying the poor journalist with a string of unwanted gifts. First he builds a website in her honour, then he tries to woo her with chocolates, underwear, a tropical aquarium and even a custom-made wedding cake, would you believe? His latest bizarre display of affection is to have her name tattooed on his back – creepy or what? If he continues to make a nuisance of himself, this little story might just turn into a great big story and then our stalker friend will wish he'd never started.

There it is in black and white. Page eleven, far left-hand column, story number five, sandwiched between the MTV presenter's secret abortion and the England footballer who's playing away from home. Every word just as I wrote it, not a single comma or full stop changed.

'Bravo!' says Sam, when's he's finished reading over my shoulder. 'If that doesn't put the wind up him I don't know what will.'

We're sitting in a greasy spoon a stone's throw from my flat, a copy of *News on Sunday* spread out in front of us on the yellow Formica table. As I'm reading my story for the seventh time, the waitress arrives with a fried breakfast in each hand. She waits impatiently, nostrils flaring, while we fold away the paper, before she lets the plates clatter noisily onto the table (she's just blown her chance of a tip). Egg, bacon, sausage, tomatoes, mushrooms, beans and a fried slice. I can't remember the last time I indulged in a full English. I never ate like this before I met Sam, no wonder I'm putting on weight. This skirt certainly feels much more snug round the hips than it ever used to. Forget music, I guess food must be the food of love.

Even though he doesn't know much about the machinations of the national press and the whims of celebrities, Sam was totally behind my decision to expose Kramer in print. He even sat with me on Thursday night, feeding me Normandy cider and Pringles, as I slaved for two hours on a laptop, filched from the office for the night.

It's funny, I can knock out a thousand-word *at home* in about two hours, but it took me the same length of time to compose just one paragraph for the newspaper. Writing in an unfamiliar house style was much harder than I'd anticipated, even though Nick Porter had given me some guidance. But I'm pretty pleased with the end result and hopefully I've managed to strike the right playful-but-threatening note. I deliberately didn't give any clues to my own identity because I don't want anyone at work putting two and two together and making a connection between me and the newspaper – that might set them thinking about the source of last week's Lucas–Connolly wedding story. Kramer must've been interviewed by dozens of female journalists in recent months, what with the hardback publication of *Killer Babes* and the paperback of *Leather Devil*, so I don't think my name will instantly spring to mind.

Not all of my friends support my current offensive, although they were unanimously horrified when I showed them the tattoo Polaroid. Sensible Jo thinks I should go back to the police and demand they take immediate action. Hothead Amy, on the other hand, favours a more public shaming.

'I told you it was that rat Kramer,' she raged down the phone. 'Never mind writing a piddling little story in some poxy little column. Let's have a demonstration outside his publisher's office, demanding they dump him. We could print leaflets and make banners and everything.'

'I appreciate your enthusiasm, Ames, but I think I'll try my way first and if it doesn't work, then I'll think about rallying the troops.'

Simon's pretty impartial really, but then it's hard to know what he's thinking at the best of times. He's the only one who knows my Kramer revenge story is half of a reciprocal deal – the fewer people who know about the other half the better.

'I can't believe you didn't take the money,' he said when we met up for pizza after work last week. 'Nick's authorized to go up to ten grand per story, you know.'

'It's a bit late to tell me that now,' I told him. 'But anyway, I'm happy with the deal I got, thank you very much. And remember – no mouthing off about it to anyone.'

I am stupidly grateful that Nick Porter kept his end of the bargain. He was mighty pissed off that *Sunday World* had scooped him – I didn't of course let on that one of my colleagues was responsible – but thankfully, he made no attempt to wriggle out of our agreement.

'Do you think I should ring Ali, see what she's planning to do now that Eva has given her the chop?' I ask Sam.

'I'd wait a while, if I were you, just till the dust settles on this Kramer business,' he says, reaching across the table to wipe away a smear of runny egg from my chin with his thumb. 'How did the rest of your colleagues react to the news of Ali's double-dealing, by the way?'

'Everyone was totally shocked, apart from the Dough-boy of course. He went around telling everyone that he knew Ali was trouble from the moment he laid eyes on her. That man is so offensive. He's just jealous that Eva thought she was good enough to cover the wedding in the first place.'

'Speaking of which, how's the wedding issue doing?'

'It only went on sale yesterday, so we won't get the mid-week predictions till Wednesday. Eva has promised to throw a staff party if we manage to hit the 1.5 million mark, so we're all keeping our fingers crossed. I think everyone in that office needs to let off a bit of steam – and no one more than me.'

'Well hopefully Kramer's out of your life for good now . . . I don't want to be worrying about you when I'm in Italy.'

I'm sure you'll forget all about me once you set foot in those magical gardens and no doubt there'll be a gorgeous, tanned, raven-haired Italian honey on hand to provide ample distraction. I'm afraid I can't help imagining the worst. It's in my nature and God knows I've witnessed enough break-ups in my time. So many celebrities have sworn undying love to each other down my dictaphone, only to split up mere months later. I've almost come round to thinking that it's not normal for two people to spend forty- or fifty-odd years of their lives together. Having said that, I can well imagine growing old and wrinkly with Sam. For the first time since I was a

kid, I feel like I've got permanent back-up – he's the
Tubbs to my Crockett, the Cagney to my Lacey, the
Starsky to my Hutch. And it's a wonderful feeling.

'You better had come and visit me at San Liberato,'
says Sam. 'I feel pretty bad about leaving you . . . maybe
I could try and postpone the trip, just till I'm sure
Kramer's not going to rear his ugly head again.'

'Don't be ridiculous,' I say, smiling bravely. 'Anyway,
you know what they say . . . absence makes the heart
grow fonder and all that.'

'Well I'll certainly miss you like mad,' he says, reaching
for my hand across the table – a gesture that threatens to
trick my lower lip into wobbling. Using my free hand, I
pick up my mug and take a big gulp of tea to mask my
emotions. It's sod's law, isn't it? You find the bloody man
of your dreams and then he pisses off. I don't blame Sam
though – it's a once-in-a-lifetime opportunity after all. I
just wish it was happening during some other girl's
lifetime and not mine. Actually, I've been thinking a lot
about my own lifestyle lately. I have a comfortable home
and a nice car and a good job, but sometimes that's just
not enough. What *would* be enough? I don't honestly
know. I just want to try something different, be somewhere different – and preferably as far away from the
fame game as possible.

I'm feeling rather pleased with myself because I've managed to pull the *Guardian Media* section from the pile of
papers on Julie's desk before anyone else can hijack it. At

9.05 on a Monday morning, there are only a couple of other people in the office, so I don't even need to read it covertly. Maybe I should switch to consumer journalism, like Jo. At least there's a point to what she does, at least it's helping people in some small way. What I do, on the other hand, is totally meaningless and only serves to perpetuate the myth that celebrities are super humans. They might be extremely rich and extremely famous, but apart from that they're just regular people who happen to have struck lucky. And in many cases it's more about being persistent or having the right look or being in the right place at the right time than possessing any great talent. People always ask, 'Don't you get nervous and tongue-tied when you're interviewing the stars?' There is a secret to it, and the secret is very simple. All you have to remember is to talk to them like they're normal people and you'll get a normal conversation back. Soon you'll forget that you're talking to the hottest soap actress or footballer of the moment or, more likely, the former star of what was once Britain's biggest-selling boyband, speaking from the luxurious surrounds of his very own surf shack in Torquay (oh how the mighty are fallen). Or maybe I should get out of journalism altogether. Just as I'm considering the pros and cons of running my own deli (in New York preferably), my phone rings.

'Hello, *Wow!* magazine, Ruby speaking.'

'You're there, thank God. I've been trying to get you on your mobile all morning,' says an anxious-sounding male voice.

'Sorry, it needs recharging. Er, who is this?'

'It's Nick Porter and we've got trouble.'

'Fuck it! I've been rumbled, haven't I? Has Eva been in touch? What have you told her? I was such an idiot to think I'd get away with it.' Stay calm Ruby and for God's sake keep your voice down. Lucie on the subs' desk has pricked up her ears and is looking over. 'Bloody PRs,' I mouth at her, putting my hand over the mouthpiece and rolling my eyes. As soon as she turns back to her page proofs, I hiss down the receiver.

'Go on, Nick, tell me the worst.'

'It's not the wedding stuff, it's your Kramer story . . .'

'What do you mean? Don't tell me your editor didn't like it, I followed your brief to the letter.'

'Ruby, if you'll just shut up for a second I'll be able to explain,' he says through gritted teeth.

'Sorry, Nick, go on,' I say. I'm so relieved that my cover hasn't been blown that at first I don't take in what he's saying and I have to ask him to repeat it more slowly.

'I said that Kramer is threatening to launch defamation proceedings against the newspaper for "substantial damages" – it could run into tens or even hundreds of thousands of pounds.'

'But that's totally ridiculous. I didn't libel him, I just told the truth.'

'The Editor had Kramer's agent on the phone at seven-thirty this morning. Apparently her client categorically denies sending any female journalist any sort of gift whatsoever, other than the occasional "thanks for a great interview" bouquet.'

I've had a few dealings with Kramer's agent in the past and she's a mercenary bitch. Adrienne Waterford, a 36-year-old Benenden alumna, isn't bigtime, but she's ruthlessly ambitious. Formerly a plain literary agent, she recently took on a couple of It girls in an attempt to diversify. She tried to milk *Wow!* for 15k for the story of Amber Morley-Moscrop's drug rehabilitation and got very sniffy when I told her we wouldn't even do it for zilch (Amber is overweight and over-exposed). I'm not surprised Adrienne's threatening legal action – it'll get her name in the papers if nothing else.

'That woman's got a nerve. Her "client" has been hounding me for weeks, *you* know that don't you, Nick?'

'Well I only know what you've told me, and that's another thing . . . I got a bollocking from my editor for not keeping proper notes. He asked to see the transcript of my interview with the source and of course I couldn't produce it. He'd fire me if he knew I'd let you write the whole damn thing, *Exposed* is supposed to be written by staffers.'

'Does your editor know about my involvement in the wedding story?'

'No. He doesn't even know you're the subject of the Kramer story. He did ask which *female journalist* Kramer was supposed to be stalking and I was vague, just said you were a friend of a friend who worked for a women's weekly.'

'Good, thanks Nick . . . now tell me, how can Kramer claim the newspaper has libelled him when he wasn't even named in the piece?'

'Defamation law only requires the plaintiff to be readily identifiable from a story. And I think he can justifiably claim that the reference to *the Hoffman–Streep movie double act* does just that.'

I can't believe this. First of all Kramer makes my life a misery with his sodding gifts and now that I've exposed him for the perv he is, he wants to sue. 'So where do we go from here, Nick?'

'Well the Editor has no intention of getting involved in a lawsuit – the outcome is far too unpredictable, even if the paper uses the defence of justification – which leaves us with two options. The first one is to brazen it out. The Ed recognizes a good story when he sees one and he thinks that if we really go to town on this story then Kramer will back down. All this defamation stuff is probably just posturing on his agent's behalf. She's got to be seen to be making a fuss, or his career – and her percentage – will suffer. So, the Ed wants me to persuade the source – that's you by the way – to do a nice interview about *My Stalker Hell at the Hands of Mr Horror* and he'll run it as a centre spread next weekend. We'll need some pictures of course – how about you with a wedding cake? It doesn't matter if you've already eaten it, we can mock up another one, no problem.'

'I suppose he wants me wearing the bra and suspenders too?'

'He didn't mention it, but actually that's not a bad idea. You'd be paid a few grand for your trouble, you know.'

'I was joking, Nick. There's absolutely no fucking way I'm doing it. I've already jeopardized my career with that wedding story and now you want me to humiliate myself publicly in the pages of your tatty rag.'

'Come on, Ruby, you want Kramer off your back, don't you? And you did threaten to turn the *little story* into a *great big story* if he didn't leave you alone.'

'That was just a figure of speech; I am absolutely *not* exposing my private life to a million *News on Sunday* readers. What's option number two?'

'Option number two is for the newspaper to publish a full apology and retraction. That's probably all Adrienne wants anyway.'

'But Nick, he can't be allowed to get away with it scot-free.'

'Well if you won't play ball, Ruby, that's the only alternative I'm afraid.'

It's a fucking Catch-22, that's what it is. I hate to admit defeat, but it looks like I don't have a choice. 'You can run the apology quite small, can't you? Just a few sentences at the end of a column on a left-hand page.'

'It's in the hands of the lawyers now. You really won't reconsider doing *My Stalker Hell* . . .'

This man is so goddamn persistent. The office is starting to fill up now and I've got to end this call. 'No Nick, I'm sorry. I've really got to go now; I'd say "keep in touch", but I think you'd agree that our liaison hasn't been terribly successful.'

'You can say that again. I'll probably be demoted to court reporting after this little balls-up,' he says unpleasantly.

Honestly, there's no pleasing some people. I say a curt goodbye and hang up. I spend the rest of the day silently fuming. When Julie's dishing out the afternoon post, she asks me if I'm okay. I tell her it's PMT, which is half true, because I certainly feel like killing someone. I can't believe how Alan Kramer can just throw his weight around like that. I want to ring him up and scream down the phone at him. But that wouldn't be wise right now, with the threat of legal proceedings looming.

By five o'clock I'm wound up tight as a spring and in desperate need of a drink, so I call Amy and persuade her to meet me in Covent Garden after work. Arriving at the basement wine bar, I waste no time in purchasing a bottle of house white, before hovering expectantly beside two yapping women who look ready to vacate their table, but then spend an absolute age gathering up their coats, mobiles, briefcases, etc., before finally making a move. By the time Amy arrives, a mere five minutes later, I've downed a glass and a half of a rather dodgy Muscat and have bummed a stress-relieving cigarette off some city boy sitting at the next table.

'I'm afraid I've started without you,' I say, gesturing at the wine bottle with the tip of my Camel Light.

'One of those days, was it?'

'You can say that again.' I pour Amy a glass of wine and proceed to tell her about the latest horrific development in the Kramer saga. She is suitably outraged.

'The-lying-egotistical-manipulative-little-fuckhead!'

'My feeling exactly. It just goes to show how much power a little bit of fame – even C-list-fucking-writer-fame – wields in the media these days.'

'So what are you going to do now?'

'What *can* I do? The newspaper will print the apology, Kramer and his bitch-agent will be happy and I'm supposed to climb back into my box like a good girl.'

'Aren't you worried he'll come after you?'

'I doubt it. He can't afford to make any kind of contact with me now that this is out in the open, or he'll just add weight to my claims of harassment. No, I'm pretty sure I've seen the last of that man. I just wish I felt a bit more triumphant about it.'

'Well the best thing you can do now is try and forget about him. Maybe you should book yourself a nice long holiday, really get away from it all.'

'Actually I'm thinking about getting away from it all on a more permanent basis,' I tell her. 'I might even chuck in my job at the magazine, have a complete change of career.'

'Shit Ruby, this is a bit sudden, isn't it? I knew you were getting pissed off with all the weekend working you have to do at *Wow!*, but I didn't think it was that bad.'

'It's not just the long hours, it's the sheer monotony . . . same questions, same answers, same interior decorators – just different people. And London's starting to get me down too. I crave green spaces, efficient public transport, reasonably priced accommodation.'

'But what about Emma Hope slingbacks and St Tropez fake tan and 24-hour Tescos?'

'Have you ever actually been to Tesco at three in the morning, Amy?'

'No . . . but it's comforting to know I have round-the-clock access to filo pastry should the need arise,' she says, pouring the last of the wine into our glasses. 'Have you talked this over with Sam at all?'

'What's the point? In two weeks' time he's leaving me. It's going to be awful . . . I just can't imagine him not being there. I'll never meet another man like him.' At this point I get a bit teary, although I suspect it's largely alcohol-induced.

Amy shifts her chair closer to mine and puts an arm around my shoulders. 'Well there is one glaringly obvious solution to all your dilemmas, isn't there?'

'What's that then?' I say, rummaging in my coat pocket for a tissue, but all I can find is a slightly soiled Pret A Manger serviette.

'Go to Italy with Sam.'

'But he hasn't asked me,' I whine.

'Well why don't you ask him then?'

'Are you out of your mind? What are you suggesting? That I reveal my soft underbelly, tell him I can't live without him, beg him to take me with him?'

'Er, yes.'

'But he should be the one to suggest it, it is his gig after all. There's absolutely no way I could set myself up for rejection like that. Imagine if he said no, I'd be gutted, not to mention hideously embarrassed.'

'But why would he say no? You're in love with each other, aren't you?'

'Yeah, but a lot of blokes say "I love you" because they want to get your knickers off – or because *you've* said it first and they feel they have to reciprocate, even when they've already got one eye on the escape hatch.'

'You old cynic . . . you know full well that Sam doesn't fall into either of those categories. You're just chicken.'

'I reckon you're right, Amy. Even in the unlikely event that he did ask me to go with him, it would still be a massive wrench, leaving my home and my friends like that. And imagine the culture shock. It's not as if I'm moving to another city . . . this San Liberato place is right out in the sticks. And there's no guarantee things would even work out with Sam. He might dump me once he gets an eyeful of all those olive-skinned Italian babes. And then I'd be stuck out there on my own.'

'You know something, Ruby . . . you're my best friend and I think the world of you. But I do wish you'd start looking on the bright side for once, instead of always imagining the worst,' says Amy, picking her purse up from the table. 'Now I'm going to get another bottle of wine in and when I get back I want you to list out loud all the positive points about going to Italy with Sam – and I think you'll find that the pros far outweigh the cons.'

When I get home, around eleven, I'm so fuelled with good intentions after Amy's pep talk – as well as Dutch courage from all the wine I've drunk – that I decide to phone Ali. I've been putting it off for days, but despite Eva's advice, I can't just cut her out of my life. After all, we were friends and I think she could probably do with a little support right now. Hopefully she won't have gone to bed yet.

'Ruby, what a surprise. I rather thought I'd been cast out in the cold. None of my other erstwhile colleagues has bothered getting in touch, so I assumed Eva had issued a directive,' she says bitterly.

'Not at all,' I say, bending the truth ever so slightly. 'I'm sorry I haven't called sooner but I felt a bit awkward, to be honest.'

'I don't blame you. I know I let everyone at the magazine down, including myself. I just wish I could turn back the clock but I can't, so now I've got to live with the consequences, i.e. unemployment.'

'You'll get another job eventually, Ali,' I say, although I don't think she'll find it easy without references. 'I'll keep my eye out for you, maybe my friend Amy knows of an opening at *Teen Scene*.'

'That would be great . . . if you don't mind me asking, why are you being so nice to me, Ruby?'

Of course the real reason for my generosity of spirit is

the fact that I feel guilty that I too gave into temptation and betrayed the magazine – not for money and not on the scale of Ali's little deception, but a betrayal nonetheless. Obviously, I'm not about to admit this, so I feed her some anodyne line. 'Oh I dunno. I figure everyone's allowed to make at least one mistake in their life.'

'Well I really appreciate you getting in touch. I've felt like such an outcast. I haven't been able to face my friends, knowing that I'll have to tell them I've been sacked . . . I haven't even got Emile any more.'

'What happened? Eva gave me the impression you two were love's young dream.'

'We were – until he lost his job with the orchestra. He loved his job, that double bass is his life. He may be ten grand richer, but now that his name's been posted on some sort of unofficial musicians' blacklist, no decent band will go near him.'

'But that's hardly your fault, is it?'

'Apparently it is because if I hadn't approached the newspaper with the story in the first place, then he would never have got involved and he'd still be the double bass king of the party circuit. We had a terrible row last weekend and he dumped me, told me he never wanted to set eyes on me again.' Much to my horror, Ali starts blubbing down the line.

'Well I'm sorry to hear that, but if that's his attitude, then you're probably better off without him.'

'I guess,' she sniffs. 'But it doesn't stop it hurting any less.'

'Why did you do it, Ali? I know you weren't very well paid at the magazine, but you were really going places. You know what really sticks in my craw? The fact that *you* made the approach to *Sunday World*, the way you planned the whole thing.'

'I know, it's awful. But what can I say? I needed the money – I've still got two years' worth of student loan to pay off – and as soon as Eva asked me to help cover the wedding, I thought I'd found the answer. The newspaper promised me I wouldn't get found out and I probably would've got away with it if I hadn't got the horn on the night of the wedding and dragged Emile to bed. He told me it was a bad idea, that we shouldn't risk being seen together, but to put it bluntly, I was gagging for it . . . champagne has that effect on me. I was shitting myself when Eva hauled me into her office that Monday morning. Have you ever seen that woman when she's *really* angry? I'm telling you, Ruby, the Incredible Hulk's got nothing on her. She said she knew I was involved and even though I thought she was probably calling my bluff, the guilt must've been written all over my face. I 'fessed up pretty quickly . . .' The rest of Ali's tale is lost in a fresh bout of sobbing and I struggle for some words of comfort.

'You did a really stupid thing, Ali, but it's not worth sacrificing our friendship over it. How about we put the whole thing behind us?'

'You've got yourself a deal,' she says in a hiccuping voice. 'I won't let you down again, Ruby, I promise.'

## WOW!

We chat a bit more and I give Ali the URLs of a couple of journalistic job websites, which I myself have been scanning of late, and by the time I put down the phone I think I've managed to cheer her up a bit. I'm glad we're friends again. I just won't mention it to Eva, that's all.

# TWENTY-FIVE: STRESS-BUSTING

Sam thinks I need to get away from it all, to lose myself in a basic and undemanding pursuit. I thought he was going to suggest a spot of light weeding in some municipal park, but he tells me he has a less taxing activity in mind. Our destination is Deal, a small coastal town in Kent, an hour or so's drive from London. My knowledge of Deal is limited to the fact that it was once the home of reclusive *Carry On* star Charles Hawtrey (I do wish I could stop relating every experience to one celebrity or another). Seeing as Sam's only vehicle is a rather elderly pushbike which conveys him to and from work every day, I'm providing the transport. First port of call is Sam's flatshare in Camberwell, where we need to pick up what he describes as 'equipment'. I am ushered into the kitchen, where Sam's mate Jim is inexpertly making scrambled eggs on toast for last night's pull: a tiny, blonde birdlike thing in knickers and an outsize grey marl T-shirt, presumably borrowed from Jim. Sam, meanwhile, goes off to load the 'equipment' into the back of my Golf. I don't know what it is exactly as he has insisted on keeping the precise purpose of our trip a secret, but he asked me where the catch was for putting down the back seats, so his 'equipment' is obviously sizeable. Maybe he's packing buckets and spades and an enormous picnic hamper with ham and egg pie and foie gras and home-made coleslaw or perhaps he's a closet treasure-hunter and he's taking me metal detecting on the beach. I've always fancied stumbling across an Anglo-Saxon cross or a crock of gold doubloons, and only a fool would declare it to the authorities as a treasure trove.

After ten minutes of being forced to listen to the agonizing small talk of a man and woman who clearly have nothing in common, except perhaps a shared interest in drum 'n' bass and a penchant for casual sex, I am finally rescued by Sam. Once outside, he refuses to allow me even the tiniest peek at the 'equipment', which is concealed by a mustard candlewick bedspread.

I do appreciate Sam going to all this trouble to organ ize an outing for me, but I really don't think anything will take my mind off Kramer. It's two weeks since *News on Sunday* ran my *Exposed* story and one week since they were forced to publish a grovelling three-paragraph *erratum*, apologizing for: *any distress or embarrassment caused to Mr Kramer*. What about my bloody distress and embarrassment? I've been a nervous wreck for months, worrying what kind of hideous offering he's going to bestow upon me next. Sam keeps telling me to chill out because at least I've achieved my objective, and it's true that I haven't heard a peep from the SA since receiving the tattoo Polaroid. But even so, my blood's still boiling at the injustice of it all. What's more, it's made me even more determined to instigate some changes and swap my frantic lifestyle for something more restful. Amy's right – going to Italy with Sam would be the perfect solution, but I never did broach the subject with him. Don't get me wrong, I would absolutely love to go – when I added them all up, the pros outweighed the cons by about six to one. It's just that Sam has to be the one to do the asking. I really need that demonstration of his commitment before I can ditch my old life. But I don't think it's going to happen at this late stage – not when he flies out next Friday – and I've kind of resigned myself to it now.

'Come on then, give me a clue,' I urge Sam as we motor down the A20, sucking on one of the sherbet lemons that he has thoughtfully provided.

'Let me just say that I'm about to introduce you to the most relaxing pastime known to man – or woman,' says Sam with a sly little smile.

'What . . . we're going to shag on a shingle beach in full view of the locals?'

'Maybe afterwards – but no, that's not the main event. Just be patient, Ruby. Believe me, by the end of today, Kramer will be a distant memory.'

When we arrive in Deal, it's practically lunchtime and

after parking the car on a little dirt road, close to the beach, Sam leads me to a seafront pub. He's obviously visited it before as he tells me what's on the menu before we've even crossed the threshold. This being the first Sunday in June, it's pretty crowded with an assortment of village locals and day-trippers but we manage to find a couple of seats beside a party of elderly ramblers tucking into seafood platter and chips. On Sam's recommendation, I'm joining him in a ploughman's – Cheddar for him, Stilton for me. When he returns from ordering the food at the bar, he's carrying two Cokes and six takeaway lagers.

'It's obviously thirsty work then, this *activity* you're planning.'

'They're not all for us,' Sam explains enigmatically.

'Are we expecting company then?'

'You'll see soon enough.'

Pub ploughman's are often disappointing affairs in my experience, but when ours arrive they're quite exceptional: hunks of fresh bread, crusty on the outside, doughy in the middle, generous wedges of creamy cheese and all the salad trimmings, including a mound of deliciously spicy chutney. By the time we've finished eating, I'm feeling pretty relaxed already. In fact, I could quite happily sit in this pub all afternoon. But Sam is a man on a mission and forty-five minutes later we're back at the car to collect the 'equipment'. At last, all will be revealed. I open the boot and Sam pulls away the candlewick bedspread with a great flourish to reveal . . . a battered fishing rod and a shallow Tupperware box that I sincerely hope does not contain a pile of writhing maggots.

'Fishing . . . I've seen enough bloody fish to last me a lifetime. I thought this trip was supposed to take my mind *off* Kramer, not bring it all flooding back,' I say petulantly.

'Chill out, girl, you'll love it, trust me,' says Sam, handing me the Tupperware and picking up the rod and the lagers. 'I've been fishing here since I was a kid. My mates and I used to spend whole days dangling our lines over the edge of the pier. We never caught much, mind you, but we always had a brilliant time.'

I find that hard to believe. Personally, I've never seen the fun in fishing. Look at those BBC2 angling programmes. They spend all day squatting on a tiny stool on a damp riverbank, doing nothing but gaze at the water and swat away horseflies. And what for? So they can take home a few measly sprats or maybe a pesticide-fed trout if they're really lucky. No, this is definitely not my idea of a good time. But Sam has gone to a lot of trouble on my behalf, so to back out now would be churlish.

We head off in the direction of a sturdy Victorian pier, which stretches across the gritty sand and into the grey English Channel. It's not the kind of pier with amusement arcades and stalls selling whelks and ring doughnuts, five for a pound. This pier is very basic – there's some kind of caff at the end and toilets and a wooden booth with an elderly man standing at the entrance. Despite the heat of the day, the man is wearing a thick pullover, and a greasy-looking peaked cap is pulled down over his leathery face.

'Afternoon, Stanley,' says Sam.

'Afternoon, son,' replies the man, before adding tersely: 'Pound-a-line.'

Sam hands over two pound coins and Stanley shambles back to his booth.

'Stanley's the pier-master,' explains Sam. 'He's been doing the job for donkey's. He hated me when I was a kid because I once got my fishing hook caught in his jumper. I was casting off and I didn't realize he was standing right behind me. By the time we'd untangled the hook there was a great big hole in his jumper. It took him a good six years to forgive me.'

'Not exactly Mr Personality, is he?'

'No, but he's part of the pier, old Stanley, it wouldn't be the same without him,' he says, far too generously in my opinion.

As we make our way along the promontory, I see that seven or eight other saddos have already set up camp with their rods and tackle at various intervals and a couple of them nod a greeting as we walk past. Sam nods back, I just scowl. Sam selects a spot, six feet away from the nearest fisherman. There's clearly a certain etiquette about this sport, if you can call it that, and every participant has commandeered his own bubble of personal space. We dump the gear and Sam rests on his haunches and starts to fiddle with his tackle, while I stand there feeling, and no doubt looking, like a spare part. After a couple of minutes, two youths, aged about 13 or 14, come swaggering over.

'Need any bait, mate?' says the bigger of the two, all cocky and full of himself in his Adidas track pants and Hilfiger T-shirt.

'What have you got?' asks Sam.

'Lug worms and fish heads,' says the kid, gesturing towards the Asda carrier bag his friend is carrying.

Yuck. Rancid fish guts on a full stomach. No thank you.

'How much for the lug worms?'

'A fiver a handful.'

'That's taking the piss. How about some beers instead?' Sam says, waving two cans of Stella under their noses.

'Three cans and I'll throw in a coupla fish heads,' says the little Del Boy.

'Done.'

The smaller urchin transfers a visceral mass from his Asda bag into a second smaller bag that he pulls from his trouser pocket and Sam hands over the cans.

'Should you be encouraging underage drinking?' I ask him when they've sloped off to bother someone else.

'It's better than being ripped off – five quid indeed. You can dig worms up on the beach for free, except I didn't think you'd fancy that.'

'Too right,' I say, forcing myself not to recoil in horror

as Sam reaches into the bag and pulls out a monstrous red worm that seems to be oozing a yellowish goo. He snags the struggling creature onto the barbed hook at the end of his line and then opens the Tupperware box to reveal an assortment of hooks and weights, plus a small plastic reel with nylon fishing line wound around it.

'This hand line is for you,' he says, returning to the bag to retrieve a second vile invertebrate.

'For me? But I don't know the first thing about fishing. I'm quite happy to sit here watching you.'

My protests are in vain, however. Sam forces the bait onto the silver hook dangling from the loose end of the hand line and gives it to me.

'Now what do I do?' I say, holding the reel at arm's length so that the cone-shaped weight at the end of the line swings like a pendulum.

'Just drop the end off the edge of the pier, reel in the slack, then hold the line just here, like this . . . then when you've got a bite, you'll feel it go tight.'

I follow his instructions, but I really think this is a pointless waste of time. We could be going for a gentle walk along the beach or hunting down a teashop for a pot of English Breakfast and a nice strawberry sundae. Sam casts his own line over the iron railings and into the murky water below, then we sit down on the hard boards of the pier and crack open a couple of beers. I'm only going to drink half a can because I'm driving. I wonder if I should go back to the car for the bedspread – I don't want to get fish slime on my Armani jeans, this is only the second time I've worn them. Maybe not, I don't want Sam to think I'm a wimp.

'See how relaxing it is?' says Sam, patting my leg affectionately.

'Hmmm,' I mumble, smiling through gritted teeth.

It's certainly good to feel the sea air in my lungs instead of the polluted grime of London, but my arse has gone to sleep and we've been sitting here for fifteen minutes without so much as a nibble.

'How long do you normally have to wait before you catch something?'

'Oh it varies – hours sometimes.'

Great. Absolutely bloody fucking marvellous. Anything would be better than this. I've a pile of washing at home that needs doing. But then, as if by magic, I suddenly feel a small tug at the end of my line, which is lying slackly in my hands. I'm not at all prepared for it and the plastic reel almost slips out of my grasp.

'Omigod, I think I've got something,' I say in disbelief.

Sam looks over at the twitching line and holds it between forefinger and thumb to test the tension. 'You could be right. Give the line a good sharp yank. It'll make sure the hook's really embedded in the fish's mouth.'

I do as I'm told and then Sam tells me to reel the line in slowly. As it emerges from the sea, I see a small silvery fish snared on the end, its tail flicking from side to side.

'It's a codling, well done,' says Sam, examining the fish as it thrashes on the deck of the pier.

I positively glow with pride as he plants a congratulatory kiss on my cheek. I feel ridiculously pleased with myself, having only ever encountered raw cod at the fish counter at Sainsbury's.

'It's quite a small one. Shall we throw it back?' says Sam.

'Throw it back? I've waited twenty-eight years for this. I'm buggered if I'm letting it go,' I say indignantly. 'I want this fish for my dinner, fried in garlic butter and served with herb mash and steamed broccoli, thank you very much.'

'Okay – so are you going to put it out of its misery or shall I?'

'You'd better do the first one, then you can show me how it's done.' It'll give him a chance to show his macho side.

Sam grasps the fish, removes the hook from its gaping mouth with surprising delicacy and then bangs its head sharply on the wooden struts of the pier. It stops moving instantly. Now I feel guilty . . . but what the hell, I caught my first fish!

Three hours pass remarkably quickly and, despite myself, I discover that I really rather enjoy fishing. There's something terribly peaceful about sitting there in companionable silence, feeling the sea current tugging gently on the line. I suddenly realize that for the first time in absolutely ages I feel totally and utterly stress-free. Life at *Wow!* is always so frenetic – rushing about from interview to interview, battling to meet deadlines, working round the clock to produce a magazine whose sales go towards lining someone else's pocket. The wedding issue sold a respectable 1.3 million copies, by the way, and even though we didn't quite reach our target, Eva has promised to lay on a party anyway. Yes, I could definitely adjust to a slower pace of life. I wouldn't miss the cut and thrust of the media world or London nightlife or the Northern Line in rush hour, not for a nanosecond.

By the end of the day, I am thrilled to have caught three fish – although I threw one back because it was only a tiny whitebait – and Sam, despite his years of practice, has caught just one.

'Beginner's luck,' he says with a smile, watching me gloat over my catch.

'I reckon I'm a natural,' I retort.

Driving back to London, I feel so happy and relaxed, it's hard to imagine that in a few days' time I'll be saying goodbye to Sam at the airport . . . although he hasn't actually invited me to see him off yet. Maybe he'd prefer it if I stayed away. There I go again – Ruby, the eternal pessimist. I must take Amy's advice – think positive thoughts, try and look on the bright side once in a while.

'Thanks for a great day, Sam,' I say, glancing across at him in the passenger seat. 'I never knew I liked fishing until today and you were right about it being the ultimate relaxant.'

'Good, now I know what to get for your birthday – a fishing rod.'

'But my birthday's in September and you'll be in Italy.'

'Well then, you'll just have to come and collect it in person.'

'You're such a lucky bastard getting the chance to go away like that. I can't tell you how many times I've felt like throwing in the towel at work and just pissing off somewhere hot and quiet. I've even been thinking about giving up journalism altogether.'

'Seriously?' asks Sam, a frown creasing his wind-burned forehead. 'I always had the impression you loved your job. You sound so enthusiastic when you talk about it.'

'Do I really? I suppose it is exciting sometimes, but it's draining too. If I have to eat another piece of designer wedding cake I think I'll top myself. Oh let's stop talking about work, it's only going to spoil our lovely day.'

'Hang on though, Ruby. If it makes you stressed, you should do something else. What would you do if you weren't a journalist?'

'I dunno. My only skills are shorthand, typing and arse licking.'

'Come on, don't sell yourself short. There are loads of things you could do.'

'Such as?'

'Such as re-train as a lawyer, or a diving instructor or set up your own business. I can see it now: *Ruby Tuesday's Teashop: Fondant Fancies Our Speciality*.'

'Don't think I'd be much cop as a lawyer – I was on the verge of being sued a couple of weeks ago remember. And I couldn't possibly run a teashop – I'd eat all the profits. But I quite like the diving instructor idea. Just think, I could qualify in England, and then work abroad . . . Bali, Mauritius, the Maldives.'

'Yeah, but if it came down to it, you wouldn't really want to give up your lovely flat and all your friends and your shopping trips to Selfridges.'

'Yes I would, in an instant . . . if the right opportunity came along.'

'You really surprise me. I always thought you seemed so suited to your city-girl lifestyle.'

'Well that just goes to show you don't know me half as well as you think you do, Mr Smarty Pants.'

'I suppose you're right. I only met you a couple of months ago, we've still got a lot to learn about each other I guess.'

'And I'm looking forward to exploring every little nook and cranny of you,' I say, tucking a loose shank of hair behind my ear and smirking lewdly. This time next week he'll be out of my life, so I'd better make the most of him while I can.

Back in Camberwell, we unload the fishing gear and I carry our three precious fishes into the kitchen. Jim is DJ-ing at some bar in Brixton tonight – presumably his latest consort is in tow as her Wonderbra is dangling from the corner of the bathroom radiator – so we've got the place to ourselves. Sam cleans the fish under a running tap and then slices each one down the belly, scooping out the guts with his hand, before topping and tailing them and slicing off the fins. It's fascinating to watch – his movements are so quick and confident. Sadly, Sam's fridge fails to yield the hoped-for potatoes and broccoli, so I prepare a pseudo-Greek salad with tomatoes, cucumber and green olives, substituting chive 'n' onion cottage cheese for feta. While I rummage in the cupboards for plates and cutlery, Sam flash fries the fish with butter, garlic and coriander and soon a delicious herby aroma fills the kitchen. The cod, when it's served, tastes divine, so much fresher and more flavoursome than bland supermarket fish.

'Sam, you're a genius,' I say, mopping up the fish juices with a slice of granary bread.

'We aim to please.'

My offer to wash up is brushed aside and Sam suggests we repair to the balcony with cups of coffee to catch the last dying rays of sunshine. Even though he doesn't have a garden, he's made the most of his little balcony, with beautiful terracotta pots of gardenias and heady jasmine. There's even a shallow trough of tomato plants trained on bamboo poles and heavy with pale orange fruits.

'Are you really serious about wanting to work abroad?' says Sam, as we sit, side by side, in white-painted wrought iron chairs, looking out into the leafy street below.

'Totally. This isn't an overnight decision – I've given it a lot of thought.'

'So why haven't you said anything before now?'

'Well, I didn't want to bother you. I know you've got a lot on your mind at the moment, tying up all those

loose ends at work before you go to Italy, saying goodbye
to all your friends—'

'Ruby,' says Sam suddenly, interrupting me mid-sen-
tence. 'Why don't you come with me?'

'Pardon?'

'Hand in your notice at the magazine and come with
me to Italy. I've already got rent-free accommodation and
I'm sure you could find some sort of work out there.'

'Oh no, I wasn't angling for an invite, that's not what
I meant at all.'

'I know you weren't – but I want you to come anyway.
I wouldn't be asking you otherwise. I would've asked
sooner but I didn't think you'd be interested. It means
you giving up a lot, after all, and I know it's short notice.'

'Do you really mean it, Sam . . . I mean, *really really*
mean it?' My heart is going like the clappers and my
palms suddenly feel all moist. Please let him say yes, God,
and I'll never say another unkind word about a celebrity
ever again.

'Absolutely, Ruby Tuesday,' he says, reaching over the
arm of his chair to take my hand in his.

'When do you leave? It's next Friday, isn't it? God, I'd
never be able to get myself together in time . . . I wonder
if I could find a tenant for the flat . . . My Italian's not up
to much you know . . .'

Suddenly Sam clamps his hand over my mouth.
'Ruby,' he says. 'Stop procrastinating and just say *yes*.'

'Yes,' I say, pulling his hand away and kissing the tips

of his fingers, while sudden tears prick the back of my eyelids. 'Or should that be *si, mi amore?*'

In the office on Monday morning, I'm on pins waiting to see Eva. Sam and I were up most of the night, talking and making plans for our new life together (in between shags, that is). Much as I'd love to drop everything straight away and fly out with Sam on Friday, it's simply not practical, so we've agreed that I'll follow him out at the end of the month. There's a million and one things to organize before I go – finding a letting agent for the flat, putting my stuff into storage and, most importantly, handing in my notice at *Wow!*, which is today's mission. Julie has booked me in for an eleven-thirty with Eva and my resignation letter is signed and sealed.

I am supposed to be waxing lyrical about the 50th birthday celebrations of an eighties' sitcom actor and former Nescafé star, but try as I might I can't summon up any enthusiasm for the job. Maybe I'll just write it as a total piss-take, although I wouldn't be surprised if nobody even noticed. Just think . . . a few more weeks and I'll never have to write the word 'lovely' again, or make painful small talk with a footballer's wife, or pretend to be a lover of small fluffy dogs. What absolute bloody bliss. This time next month I'll be kicking my heels in the Mediterranean sunshine. I'm deep in fantasy land, imagining myself wafting around an Italian rose garden in a décolleté dress made of some impossibly gauzy fabric, when the Doughboy comes sneaking up behind me.

'There's no time for day dreaming, Ruby,' he snaps, slapping down a new A3 flatplan on the desk in front of me. 'The subs are crying out for that story.'

'Yeah, yeah, yeah. No need to get your effing Y-fronts in a twist,' I mutter, just loud enough for him to hear. He shoots me a look of pure contempt and goes off to make someone else's life a misery.

Finally the time for my meeting rolls around and Julie summons me to the Editor's office. Eva is smiling as I walk through the door. She obviously hasn't got a clue what all this is about, she probably thinks I'm angling for a pay rise.

'What can I do for you, Ruby?' she asks, gesturing at a leatherette chair.

Sitting down, I push the white envelope containing my resignation letter across the desk towards her. 'I'd like to hand in my notice,' I say. Then I lean back in my chair and wait for her reaction.

She frowns and tilts her head slightly, as if to say, 'Are you having me on?' before speaking in an earnest tone.

'Are you serious about this, Ruby? Have you really thought it through?'

'Deadly serious,' I say, keeping a poker face. 'It's not a decision I've taken lightly.'

'But I thought you were happy here.'

'I used to be. But just lately the glossy pages of *Wow!*

have lost some of their lustre. I don't feel, er, creatively fulfilled any more and I think it's time to move on.'

'Is it *Yeah!* magazine? Have they made an approach?' she says in a sharp voice. 'I'm sure we can match whatever they're offering . . .'

'Don't worry, Eva, I haven't been head hunted. It's much simpler than that. My boyfriend has got a job in Italy and I've decided to go with him.'

'Oh I see,' she says, her face softening. 'Money wouldn't have been a problem, but I can't compete with true love.' Strange – I would never have had Eva down as the romantic type. I wonder if Louie Bresler has got anything to do with her new-found sensitivity. 'Well don't make any rash decisions right now. I'd be prepared to hold your job open for, say, three months . . . just in case things don't work out for you in Italy.'

'That's very kind of you, but I want to make a clean break, get out of journalism altogether, at least for the time being.'

'Well I shall be terribly sorry to see you go, all the staff will. Everyone here thinks very highly of you and rightly so. You've done some great work this year – the Jessie Reynolds exclusive, your mouthwatering coverage of Joe Lucas's wedding, the way you persuaded the Philadelphia cheese girl's agent not to sue when we pulled out of her wedding at the eleventh hour . . . If ever you need a reference, just let me know.'

As soon as I've escaped Eva's clutches, I call Sam to

let him know I've done the deed. He has some good news for me too.

'I've just spoken to Giovanni, the head honcho at San Liberato. He's absolutely fine about you coming and he's looking forward to meeting us both. Apparently the cottage is plenty big enough for two, although he did warn me it's not exactly luxurious.'

'Who cares? It's going to be the most fantastic adventure and I can't wait to get out there,' I tell him. 'I just wish I was flying out with you on Friday, but I've promised Eva I'll work till the end of the month to give her a chance to recruit my replacement.'

'It's going to be awfully lonely in that cottage by myself. I'll be counting the days till you get there, not to mention dreaming of your luscious breasts and pert bum.'

'Down boy!' I say, giggling.

Someone else patently finds my conversation amusing. Spinning round in my chair I come face to face with my sniggering features editor, who is leaning against the photocopier, plainly eavesdropping. Quickly, I finish up my call and then turn back to Adrian.

'Can I help you?' I ask him peremptorily.

'When you've quite finished whispering sweet nothings to your latest love interest, perhaps you could spare me five minutes of your precious time to tell me which features you're going to be writing for the next issue, as shown on the new flatplan I've just distributed,' he says nastily, jabbing a finger at the wretched sheet of A3 on my desk.

# WOW!

At last – a chance to tell this disagreeable man what I really think of him. Taking a deep breath, I let rip.

'You really are an irritating, talentless, smug little shit, Adrian,' I say without a trace of irony. 'Why don't you take your stupid flatplan and shove it up your fat arse? Or better still . . . let *me* have the pleasure.'

# TWENTY-SIX: SECRET ADMIRER

The Secret Admirer is beside himself. One minute every-thing had been going perfectly to plan and then, literally overnight, his world had fallen apart at the seams. Sitting on the soft leather recliner in the office of his four-bedroom townhouse-with-garden in Highgate Village, he mulls the situation over. This is his very favourite place to relax and cogitate; only here, surrounded by all the tools of his trade, does he feel truly at peace. In front of him on the mahogany desk lies his highly prized album of photographs – some originals, some clipped from the pages of *Wow!* Turning the pages, he thinks regretfully of what might have been, but now that dream has been brutally shattered by the object of his affection herself. He pulls out his favourite picture of all, the stolen snap of his bikini-ed love sunning herself on a beach in Mustique. He traces the soft curves of her body with his index finger, touches the finger to his mouth, then presses it to the lips in the photo. 'Goodnight, precious Ruby,' he whispers, before carefully returning her to the protective plastic sheath.

The end had begun four days earlier, a Thursday. Squatting beside the privet hedge at Galleon Place, some time between ten-thirty and eleven p.m., the Secret Admirer had witnessed a strange and distressing scene. His sweet girl was packing – not for a weekend break or some exotic business trip, but a mammoth journey, judging by the great piles of clothes, underwear and hair accoutrements that were heaped on the bed. He had watched with mounting agitation as she carefully arranged each item in two gigantic suitcases: skirts and trousers rolled, socks pushed into the toes of shoes, Velcro rollers wedged into corners. When the suitcases were packed, zipped and belted, she had gone to the kitchen and pulled a roll of black bin bags from a drawer. Opening the doors of her food cupboard, she proceeded to clear out each and every item: jars, packets, boxes, her collection of herbs and spices, even non-perishable tins were all scooped into the bag. Afterwards she had emptied the fridge and freezer, given them a quick wipe with a damp cloth and switched them off at the mains, not forgetting to sensibly spread several tea towels on the floor around the appliances to absorb the melting frost.

The lights in the apartment finally went off just after midnight and the Secret Admirer had seriously considered returning to his car to keep watch till morning, just in case she was planning a dawn escape. But what was the point? He was hardly going to confront her and swear undying love, or drag her into his car, kicking and screaming, and hold her captive till she pledged her troth. Given fair warning, he might have considered either one of these options, but this was too short notice. The Secret Admirer was a meticulous creature and knew the importance of careful planning and attention to detail. And anyway, he had an early start in the morning, a breakfast meeting to discuss a lucrative project with an important new client.

The Secret Admirer didn't sleep at all well that night. His dreams were full of Ruby: Ruby hurling a wedding cake in the face of Botticelli's Venus; Ruby in the *Diva* underwear, dancing in front of some faceless suitor. He had woken at five a.m. drenched in sweat and had been forced to take refuge in satellite TV. Friday had been hellish and his distraction and tiredness had left him totally unable to concentrate on his work, an unusual and discomfiting experience – he was always so focused. In fact he had been so abrupt and unenthusiastic with the important client that he probably wouldn't get that fat commission, not that he cared less right now.

As soon as darkness fell, the Secret Admirer had returned to his beloved's riverside home to find her parking space vacated and the apartment quiet and empty. Checking he was unobserved, he had pressed his nose to the living-room window and was horrified to see all her personal possessions – books, CDs, the framed industrial photographs – now removed. His precious girl had deserted him, but why?

He had fretted all weekend, spent hours speculating on the reasons for Ruby's sudden disappearance. First thing this morning, in sheer desperation, he had called her place of employment. Dialling her direct line, he'd been greeted by the over-perky voice of a secretary, who had informed him that: 'Ruby no longer works for *Wow!*' Confused and bereft, he had slammed down the phone without even discovering the reason for her sudden departure. 'I'm not at liberty to divulge that information,' the stupid secretary had insisted. Perhaps, he theorized, it was somehow linked to the item in that foul publication, *News on Sunday*. He'd been taken aback – well, stunned actually – by the little one-paragraph story that detailed the actions of the man who was pursuing the 'female journalist of our acquaintance'. The 'stalker' bit had cut him to the quick, he'd always thought of himself simply as an ardent admirer. And how could the gifts possibly be 'unwanted' when he'd put so much thought into each and every one? The story was doubtless written by some jealous tabloid hack who probably wanted Ruby for himself. Those people never told it like it really was, they always had to add some lurid spin – *and* there was no mention of his public declaration at the Arsenal game. *That* hadn't been easy to arrange at short notice, he'd had to call in a special favour. The published apology had come one week later. He'd been expecting it, it was the only fitting course of action. After all, he would do the same in Kramer's position, wouldn't he?

At first he'd been puzzled as to why she thought Kramer was her man, but then he remembered the Wolfman's birthday party and his clumsy pass on the dance floor. No wonder she wanted that oaf warned off; of course it would be quite a different story if she knew the real identity of her secret admirer. He, after all, was something of a catch – an affluent, good-looking, successful man who was going places. In fact he was fast becoming something of a celebrity in his chosen profession. It was scarcely surprising he'd had more than his fair share of casual encounters over the years – beautiful women, rich women, even famous women . . . all mere palliative agents, of course.

On his desk, the cordless phone starts ringing. Is there no escape from these wretched people? Still, he'd better answer it, he needs a constant supply of work to fund his comfortable lifestyle.

'Yes,' he says into the receiver, a touch irritably.

'Could I speak to T.K. Stead please?' asks a hesitant voice.

'This is T.K. speaking.'

'Oh T.K., I thought I had the wrong number there. It's Angela at *Wow!*'

'Angela, great to hear from you. Sorry if I sounded abrupt, I was just checking over some transparencies,' he says, forcing a friendlier note into his voice. *Wow!* was a nice little earner for him and it wouldn't do to piss off the art director.

'I was wondering if you were free to do a shoot on Thursday week. It's a nice *at home* with Arsenal foot-baller Lee Jackson and his new girlfriend, Kim Fraser,' says Angela. 'You won't have heard of her, she's a nobody, works behind the beauty counter at John Lewis.'

'Yeah, that should be fine; Thursday's completely clear in the diary. I did Jackson at home for you a few months ago, you know, different girlfriend mind you.'

'That's right, CoCo Fernandez. They broke off their engagement soon after the shoot. He caught her in bed with another woman.'

'Another *woman*?'

'I know, weird isn't it? According to the gossip columns, Lee asked if he could watch and CoCo threw him out. Anyway, now he's with this Kim girl and he's just splurged £1.5 mill on a new love nest in Epping. She's a bit nervous about featuring in the magazine, being new to the fame game and all, so I'm going to come along to the shoot just to gee her along if that's okay with you?'

'That's fine, Angela, it'll be nice to see you again – and if you're really lucky, I'll even take you out for a drink afterwards,' he jokes. Angela's a nice girl, easy to deal with and not bad-looking either, and if he keeps her sweet, she'll continue throwing work his way . . . no doubt she's wetting her knickers at the thought of a semi-date with him.

'I'll hold you to that, T.K.,' she says flirtatiously, before reeling off the details for the shoot – time, location, writer's name. Just as she's saying goodbye, T.K. has a sudden flash of inspiration.

'One more thing before you go, Angela . . . What's happened to Ruby Lake? I used to enjoy working with her, but someone told me she'd left *Wow!* – bit sudden wasn't it?'

'Tell me about it! We couldn't believe it when Ruby announced she was chucking in the best bloody job in the business to follow some bloke to Italy. Eva said she would've made a great editor one day, but no . . . it seems she would rather live in a gardener's cottage in the middle of nowhere.'

'Italy . . . how long for?' His voice is calm, but in his chest, a giant hand is slowly squeezing his heart.

'Indefinitely – she's cut all her ties with the magazine. Eva said she could take three months' leave and her job would still be waiting for her, but Ruby wasn't having any of it.'

He can't believe what he's hearing. How much worse could it possibly be?

'So who's the lucky man then?' he asks, stumbling over the words as his breath catches in his throat.

'I never met the guy but I believe he's some sort of gardener for the council. They've only been seeing each other for a couple of months, but it's obviously true love. I took Ruby out for a farewell drink last week and she was dead excited about the whole thing. I've never seen her like that before, she was so, so . . . radiant, that's the only word to describe it.'

By the time he puts down the phone, T.K. is incandescent. After everything he's done for her, she's left him for another man, the ungrateful girl. In a sudden fit of anger, he brings his clenched fist crashing down on the desk, sending six rolls of film flying. Seeing the photo album spread out on the desk only enrages him further. Picking it up, he systematically rips each plastic sheath free of its moorings and watches as each memento of his precious girl flutters to the wooden floor. He'd love to get his hands on that pretty neck right now, so he could wring the life out of it. After all the time and trouble he put into wooing her, the little bitch has thrown it all back in his face, betrayed him in the worst way imaginable – and with a gardener, of all people. What could this pathetic manual worker possibly have that he didn't? And to think, now he's going to have to have this wretched tattoo removed or altered – and that won't be cheap. He would never have acted so rashly, had he not truly believed she would one day be his.

His mind flashes back to the first time he met Ruby, at a christening party in Clapham for the offspring of a celebrity hairdresser. He had given her a lift home that day and as she had climbed out of his convertible Mercedes, her skirt had ridden up, not especially high, but just enough to give him a glimpse of smooth white thigh. That, believe it or not, had been the trigger – not the motive, but the springboard. Slowly but surely his obsession had grown until she seemed to consume his every waking thought. He really believed he had met his match in Ruby. She had a pretty face and a good body, but more than that, he had been captivated by her cool professionalism, the confident way she handled even the most difficult or reluctant celebrity, the unselfconscious way she tossed those auburn locks out of her face. She was a feisty girl, who knew her own mind and was reliant on no one, not like those insipid, fawning women he usually bedded. God, how excited he used to be when Angela commissioned him for one of Ruby's jobs. He'd lived for those 'hello' and 'goodbye' kisses when she arrived at and departed from a shoot. And she had seemed to like him too – why her behaviour at that Lee Jackson engagement shoot had been positively coquettish. And see how she had turned to him for comfort and support when the uncouth Kramer had manhandled her at the London Dungeon. No, he hadn't misread the signs, he was sure of it.

T.K. had been quite amused by her brief flirtation with his erstwhile assistant Charley, a move clearly intended to make him jealous. Luckily the boy was smart enough not to take it any further, he knew which side his bread was buttered. Later on, of course, Charley had proved a useful informant, feeding him all the gossip about Ruby's short-lived fling with Raoul and putting a name to the photographer he'd seen in the Mustique photos on top of her fridge. Actually, he had Charley to thank for this blasted tattoo. Keen to learn how his young protégé had fared at Layla Squires' engagement party, T.K. had held a debriefing session with Charley: had he captured all the main players, had he provided the magazine with the right mix of serious and fun shots, etc, etc? In the course of this little chat, Charley had alluded to the needlecraft on the arm of Gaz whatshisface. More significantly, he talked about how very admiring Ruby had been. And T.K., impetuous, naive thing that he was, had been enchanted by the idea of a tattoo as the ultimate, ever-lasting gift of love, the final tribute to his chosen one before he stepped out of the shadows. But Charley had said nothing of this gardener chap. If T.K. had known of a serious rival, he would have revealed himself to Ruby sooner, forced her to submit to his not inconsiderable charms.

Not that this new relationship could possibly succeed – a career girl like that, dropping everything to live in some foreign backwater . . . he'd give it a month tops. And if she thought he was going to be here, waiting to pick up the pieces when it all went wrong, she had another think coming. She'd had her chance and she blew it. Why there were girls who would give their right eye for a date with T.K. Stead, photographer to the stars; in fact, he was going to put his mind to it right away. And if he ever laid eyes on Ms Ruby Lake, *B.A. dip journ*, again . . . Well, she had better watch out, that's all.

# EPILOGUE: 28 OCTOBER

I can't believe how well I've adjusted to my new rustic lifestyle. The gardener's cottage turned out to be pretty basic – the bougainvillea is utterly gorgeous, but the simple wooden furniture, lack of central heating and unreliable hot water supply took a little getting used to. Still, Sam and I have made it feel like home with framed photographs, vases of fresh flowers, lots of vanilla-scented candles and a couple of handwoven rugs that I picked up for next to nothing in the local market. Since being here, I've come to realize just how material-istic my old life was, and I can't tell you how good it feels to be free of all that shit. And of course it's wonderful to be rid of the spectre of the Secret Admirer at last. I really needed to get away from Kramer physi-cally as well as mentally so that I could stop being Mrs Angry of Rotherhithe and put that whole upsetting busi-ness behind me once and for all. Now that I'm thousands of miles away, he's just an unpleasant memory lodged at the back of my mind and one that's growing fainter by the day.

I'm still unsure about my next career move and fortunately, there's no pressure to make an immediate decision. The rental on my flat, plus the money I got for my VW, more than covers my cost of living out here, but I don't like to be idle, so I do a bit of voluntary work in the church, just a few hours a week – cleaning and helping arrange the flowers.

Sam and I will be staying here permanently as it turns out. Giovanni, San Liberato's head gardener, is most impressed with Sam's 'vision' and 'commitment' and he sailed through his three-month trial period.

There *has* been one other development . . . a very significant development actually. You see, Sam and I got married yesterday. There was no pomp, no schmaltz, no theme, no dress code, no lovebirds, no fireworks, no thrones. It was all terribly simple and of course we had a stunning ready-made venue right on our doorstep. I wore an ivory strapless gown of raw silk, run up by a little seamstress I found in Rome, and carried a hand-tied posy of antique roses that Sam had cut from the botanical gardens. The reception was a buffet meal in a pavilion overlooking Lake Bracciano (assorted crostini, wild salmon stuffed with herbs, strawberries and marscapone cream), followed by dancing into the small hours (easy listening – what else?).

The medieval church and gardens looked quite beautiful/stunning/exquisite in the soft autumn sunshine but they were totally outshone by my darling groom. He didn't present me with an Asprey's ring, didn't serenade me with Nat King Cole, hasn't whisked me off on an exotic honeymoon; he was just Sam – and I love him with all my heart.

The proposal came totally out of the blue. There we were, sitting on the shores of Lake Bracciano one Sunday afternoon in late summer, doing a spot of fishing, when Sam just dropped to his knees and popped the question. I, soppy sod that I am, immediately burst into tears and so the 'yes' came out in a strangulated sort of way. But all the same, it was terribly romantic. You'd think that all the celebrity break-ups I witnessed during my time at *Wow!* would have been enough to put me off marriage for life, but I know that in Sam I've finally found my soulmate. We've known each other only six months, but we both wanted to get married as quickly as possible and our friends at San Liberato pulled out all the stops to help us organize everything.

You know, the only thing I miss about my old lifestyle is my friends. There's no telephone in the cottage, but at least once a week I head off to an internet café in Athens to email the entire gang and pick up the messages they've sent me. Sam and I were desperate to get all our family and friends together for the wedding and, much to our delight, fifty-odd people flew out to Italy to share what was, undoubtedly, the happiest day of my life. Amy and Daniel couldn't keep their hands off each other (she finally saw sense and dumped Toby). Good old Jo (still looking for the man of her dreams) turned down a TV appearance to fly to Italy. And Simon was the life and soul of the evening reception, which was pretty surprising, seeing as Katie called off their engagement three weeks ago. Ali politely declined the invitation, saying she couldn't face Eva, not even after all these months. I don't blame her. She's promised to come and visit me soon and tell me all about her exciting new career in telesales.

I invited only a couple of people from *Wow!* – Eva, of course, who was accompanied by her fiancé, Louie Bresler (*their* wedding will be a lavish affair, take it from me) and art director Angela (we share a special bond, having started at the magazine on the very same day). You'll never guess who her '. . . *and guest*' turned out to be – only bloody T.K. Stead. Apparently they got together soon after I left England. She's really landed on her feet there. Not only is T.K. minted, he's also a really nice guy, despite being a bit in love with himself.

My only regret about the Big Day is that it went far too quickly, and before we knew it, Sam and I were saying goodbye to the final drunken guests. Angela and T.K. were the last ones to leave – the poor girl was so pissed she could barely form the word 'goodbye'. Her photographer beau, on the other hand, was his usual gentlemanly self and after I'd pressed my lips to his cheek, he put his hands on my waist and thanked me for an 'absolutely unforgettable' day. Just as I was about to pull away, he suddenly drew me back towards him and put his mouth to my ear.

'Goodnight precious Ruby,' he said in a sibilant whisper.

It's a common enough term of endearment, but it still sent a shiver up my spine.